STAKEOUT

Midnight.

From the cassette player the familiar, breathy voice filled the car with mocking, loathsome words of betrayal, triggering an overpowering sensation of hate and jealous rage. *The conniving bitch had gone too far. Much too far. There was only one appropriate punishment. A punishment no beautiful woman could live with.*

He stared at the house across the street through a screen of black. Visible beyond the bay window, in the ghostly blue glow of the television, she sat curled up on the end of the sofa, the telephone to her ear, her shiny dark hair falling over the receiver and across one side of her face. Her flawless beauty was apparent even from this distance.

The voice on the cassette droned on, though he no longer heard the words. He watched the woman on the phone, his gloved fingers caressing the polished steel of the straight razor.

He smiled. Beneath the dark nylon stocking the grin felt tight, strangely numb. He pulled the black cap down over his flattened ears. With hands as steady as those of a surgeon, he grasped the straight razor and reached for the door handle.

WIVES, LIES AND DOUBLE LIVES

MISTRESSES ($4.50, 17-109)
By Trevor Meldal-Johnsen
Kept women. Pampered females who have everything: designer clothes, jewels, furs, lavish homes. They are the beautiful mistresses of powerful, wealthy men. A mistress is a man's escape from the real world, always at his beck and call. There is only one cardinal rule: *do not fall in love.* Meet three mistresses who live in the fast lane of passion and money, and who know that one wrong move can cost them everything.

ROYAL POINCIANA ($4.50, 17-179)
By Thea Coy Douglass
By day she was Mrs. Madeline Memory, head housekeeper at the fabulous Royal Poinciana. Dressed in black, she was a respectable widow and the picture of virtue. By night she the French speaking "Madame Memphis", dressed in silks and sipping champagne with con man Harrison St. John Loring. She never intended the game to turn into true love . . .

WIVES AND MISTRESSES ($4.95, 17-120)
By Suzanne Morris
Four extraordinary women are locked within the bitterness of a century old rivalry between two prominent Texas families. These heroines struggle against lies and deceptions to unlock the mysteries of the past and free themselves from the dark secrets that threaten to destroy both families.

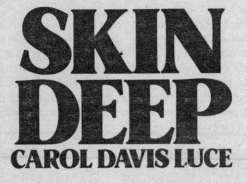

SKIN DEEP

CAROL DAVIS LUCE

PINNACLE BOOKS
WINDSOR PUBLISHING CORP.

I wish to thank doctors Gary Pomeranz, Harry Huneycutt, and Eugene Le May for medical advice and lab demonstrations.

Special thanks go to these friends: Patti and Michael Specchio for their continued support; Priscilla Walden for her west coast public relations; The Farrells, Schmanskis and Martinezs; my reader, amateur therapist, and alter ego, Katina Schafer, for all those things; and, again, to my husband Robert for being there.

There is no excellent beauty that hath not some strangeness in the proportion.

— Francis Bacon

Prologue

San Francisco 1970

The cheers and applause still echoed in her ears. White dots from the bright, popping flashcubes danced before her eyes. Her jaw ached from smiling for the cameras. Her legs, weak from hours on her feet in high heels, began to cramp. But it was worth it. Every minute of it. She was flying high.

Corinne Odett hugged the long-stemmed roses and breathed in their sweet fragrance. She touched the crown on her head. It was hers. Really hers. The crown, the money, the prizes of a car, a wardrobe, even a screen test at a Hollywood movie studio; but most important of all, the title. Miss *Classic.* The chic, sophisticated woman of San Francisco. A woman whose beauty equaled the beauty of the city's stunning landscape and imperial position.

She looked around. The changing room of the auditorium was finally empty of people. The four runners-up, Regina, Amelia, Tammy, and Donna, had left on the heels of the news media for the Coronation Ball upstairs in the hotel. Corinne waited, pacing nervously.

The pay phone on the wall rang. She snatched it off the hook, said a terse hello.

The voice she hoped to hear tentatively spoke her name.

"Jack? Oh Jack, I'm so glad you called. I was afraid you wouldn't, that you —" Corinne's chaperon poked her head in the door and tapped her watch. Corinne cupped a hand over

9

the receiver and said to her, "Mrs. Myer, would you please go up and tell them I'll be right there?"

The chaperon nodded, backed out, closing the door.

"I did it, Jack," Corinne said into the receiver. "*I really did it.* I still can't believe it. You should've heard them. The applause, the cheers. I'll remember it always. It was . . . God, it was fantastic! Me, Corinne Odett, Miss Classic. If only you could've been here." Before he could respond, she rushed on, breathless, "I know, I know, Jack, and I understand now, I really do. I was awful, wasn't I? Selfish and bratty—an absolute bitch. I'm so glad you're not mad at me. Jack . . ." she said with a slight tremor in her voice, "will you escort me to the ball?"

His answer was a simple yes.

"I'll wait for you in the changing room. Jack, please hurry."

After hanging up, Corinne paced, keyed up, restless. Finally, after several minutes, she forced herself to sit at the long vanity. Alone now, the quiet began to feel heavy—oppressive. As she waited, she studied her image. She glanced sideways to see her mirrored reflection multiplied and refracted smaller and smaller as it lined up into infinity. She breathed deeply. Her own beauty, the magnitude of it, never failed to surprise her. A product of poor, uneducated, austere parents, she had learned early in life that her looks were special. Regal, even. The *San Francisco Chronicle* had likened her to Grace Kelly. With her gift of beauty, she was told, she would go far. Far indeed.

But without Jack, it meant nothing. Jack . . .

She was drawn out of her reverie by a soft tapping at the door.

"It's open," she called out.

Another tap.

With a sigh, still gazing at herself in the mirror, Corinne rose. She straightened the crown, then crossed the room and pulled open the door. The hallway was dark and empty.

"Mrs. Myer? Jack?" Corinne said, stepping across the threshold. "Anybody there?"

10

She detected a movement to her left. A flash of dark clothing, a glint of sparkling glass, and then something wet and warm splashed against her face.

She gasped, stunned.

A stinging sensation spread across her face and ripped into her throat, constricting her vocal cords. She breathed in sharply as delicate sinuses exploded in pain. The skin over the left side of her face seemed to shrink, to pull tight, to throb. It was sheer torture to breathe. She held her breath. Her heart pumped wildly.

No, oh dear God, no.

NOOO!

In anguish and disbelief, shock dulling the pain, Corinne clutched at the crown. Holding it to her head, she whirled around and, with faltering steps, rushed to the vanity.

She glared into the mirror and from somewhere deep in her body came a low moan filled with utter despair.

The image before her wore her gown and banner. She saw the rhinestone crown, glittering defiantly, atop a cascade of sun-streaked curls. One green eye was as bright as cut glass. But the other eye . . . the face . . . the throat . . .

Through a flashfire of agony, with a devastating sense of wretchedness and sorrow, Miss Classic 1970, in that split second before the instinctive act of self-preservation took over, realized that the world was no longer hers.

The Finalists
One

Torture, mutilation, and, finally, blessedly, death, would make up his long-awaited game plan of sweet revenge.

"Oh, Christ, give me a break," John Davie said in exasperation. He pressed *escape* on the computer keyboard and, watching the screen clear, wished that he, along with his stagnating brain, could slip away as readily as the text on the monitor. Sitting up straight, he pulled his damp shirt over his head and tossed it aside. San Francisco sweltered in a mid-June heat wave, but it wasn't the weather that had him swearing. Sinking into a creative pause — he refused to call it writer's block — he was now further distracted by the voices in the front of the apartment house.

He rose from his desk, walked to the window, and looked out. Two women stood talking on the sidewalk by a tan station wagon.

Watching them in quiet contemplation, he sensed something oddly familiar about the older of the two. He'd seen her before, he was sure of it. Where? When? It would come to him eventually, he thought, it always did.

He opened the window all the way, hoping for a breeze of some sort. None was forthcoming. With a sigh, he went back to his desk . . . to his computer . . . to the stalled novel

2

As Regina Van Raven climbed the brick steps of the two-story apartment house alongside her daughter, she heard the creak and clatter of a window sash rising to her right. She caught a glimpse of a man's naked back as he moved away from the window.

"It looks nice from the outside, Mom," seventeen-year-old Kristy said.

"Wilma wouldn't live in a place that wasn't nice," she answered blithely.

Regina felt the cotton blouse sticking to her back. They opened the outer door, walked into the entry, and pressed a button under Szabo-manager. A moment later they were buzzed through another door into a wide hall.

It was cool inside and smelled of wood polish and Pinesol. Before Regina could knock, the door to 1A opened and a pleasant-looking, heavyset woman in her late sixties came out. "Mrs. Van Raven, yes?"

Regina nodded. "Mrs. Szabo, this is my daughter Kristy."

The woman clasped her hands at her chest and said with a thick European accent, "Oh, the little one is such a beauty."

Kristy smiled modestly.

"Come, come, come," Mrs. Szabo said, leading the way to the staircase. "Second floor. Mrs. Axelrod, she say she'll move her furniture out in three days."

Mother and daughter hurried to keep up.

At the end of the hall, the landlady opened the door to 2B. Bright sunlight poured out into the dim hall. Regina stepped inside, taking in the clean, airy living room. 2B was in the front of the apartment house. Large windows wrapped the south and east corner, facing the distant bay. Under fringed area rugs, hardwood floors gleamed.

"We'll take it," Kristy exclaimed.

"Kristy! I'd like to see it first," Regina said evenly, trying

14

to keep the enthusiasm from her voice. "That is, if it's all right with you?"

Kristy shrugged, smiling sheepishly.

Regina strolled through the two-bedroom apartment, her excitement mounting. It was everything she had hoped it would be. And the price was right. Coming back into the living room, she heard her daughter talking to the landlady.

"Right now we live in this monstrous house in Berkeley," Kristy said. "My dad died six months ago, and I'll be leaving in September for college, Cal Poly, that's in San Luis Obispo, so she's gonna need a smaller place. When her friend, Wilma—y'know Wilma, the woman who lives here?—well, when she told her about this apartment coming up for grabs, well . . . jeeze—and it's so close to the station where she works. My mom's a co-producer at—"

"We'll take it," Regina quickly cut in. "If for no other reason than to spare Mrs. Szabo the entire family history."

"You love it," Kristy teased. "Admit it."

"I love it." But Regina had another reason for wanting out of the house in Berkeley, a reason that not even her daughter knew about.

Regina looked at her watch. 3:20. If she didn't get moving now, she'd be late for the taping of "City Gallery." Donna Lake depended on her to soothe the guests and smooth out any preshow hassles. "I can give you a deposit now, then come back after work and sign the lease," she said to the landlady, reaching for her checkbook.

3

Inside the studio at KSCO TV, under the bright lights of the set, Donna Lake felt her hair cling wetly to the back of her neck. Although her antiperspirant hadn't failed, her underarms itched maddeningly. She was dry, but miserable.

Her guest on "City Gallery" that afternoon was tattoo artist Mark Coontz, whose claim to fame was his urbane tattoo salon, just off Union Square, where, catering to the rich and

15

famous, he specialized in the permanent application of eye-liner, eyebrows, lip lining, strategically placed beauty marks and, naturally, the avant-garde, discreet tattoo.

Stork, the floor director, signaled Donna to wind it up.

"Fascinating subject, Mark. Unfortunately, we've run out of time." She turned to the camera. "Mark Coontz, proprietor of "The Mark of Beauty Shop—"

"Salon," he amended.

"—Mark of Beauty Salon. Next week our guest will be Crystal Downey, former beauty queen, top model, and most recently the author of the best selling beauty book, *Crystal Clear*. Until then, this is Donna Lake with "City Gallery.""

The lights blinked out. Before Donna could remove her mike and thank her guest, her husband swooped down on her, his handsome face like granite.

"Forget Crystal Downey," he said tightly.

Donna stood and quickly walked off the set. She knew all too well that expression, that tone. The last thing she wanted was a confrontation within earshot of the guests and crew. She stepped into a dark control room, waited for him to enter, then closed the door.

"What happened?" she asked.

"Crystal canceled, that's what happened. She was hot to trot when I talked to her. Then she talks to Regina and it's suddenly a no-go."

"Honey, Regina warned us she was a flake and couldn't be counted on."

He slapped his clipboard down on the counter. "Okay, so any suggestions?"

She looked at him, surprised. Nolan rarely asked her advice or opinion. In a quiet voice she said, "I'll check with Regina. She—"

"Regina, Regina," he cut in sharply. "Always Regina." He snatched up the clipboard and consulted it. "We'll go with the Classic finalists. Same premise. The five of you could easily fill the time slot."

"They're scheduled for next month. I just wrote to them two days ago."

16

"Call them. Have your precious Regina get her butt in gear."

"I'm sure we can get the runners-up, it's Corinne I have my doubts—"

"Corinne's a must."

"I don't want to push this—"

"Push it," he said abruptly. "Move in fast before she has a chance to think it over." His voice softened. "Sweetheart, you're wonderful at what you do. No one can touch you in the talent department. But, please, leave the decision making to me, okay? This is our chance to put some meat into the show. We have six days. Use everything you've got to convince her. And if she'll agree to come on alone, then dump the others." He strode across the room. At the door he stopped, looked at her, and smiled. "Great show today. You looked sensational." Then he was gone.

She turned, facing the large window which looked out onto the now dark set and stared at her reflection in the glass. She saw a pretty woman with windblown blond hair, wide-set blue eyes, and a full mouth with even, white teeth. Her smile, Nolan reminded her daily, was her best feature. In this light, gazing into the tinted glass, she could pass for the girl, twenty years ago, who was voted fourth runner-up in the Miss Classic Beauty Pageant.

She thought of the other finalists. Regina Van Raven was the show's co-producer and her best friend. Amelia Corde did volunteer work for PBS—Regina hinted she had a sapphire blue eye on Donna's job at KSCO. Tammy Kowalski, in the throes of marital problems, bounced in and out of their lives like a fishing bobber. And last, but certainly not least, Corinne. There had been no contact aside from that one encounter the day following the assault. Donna tried not to think about that. After two decades she still felt a wave of nausea whenever she thought of that brief visit at San Francisco General where Corinne, heavily sedated, moaning in pain, her swollen face a mass of . . .

It was still so difficult to think about it. But Corinne had recovered. And from a nurse at S. F. General, Donna learned she had undergone reconstructive surgery prior to her release three months later.

Yes, maybe it was time they all got together again.

4

Regina was at her desk sorting through the afternoon mail. She paused at the greeting-card-sized envelope addressed to her and felt an instant gripping sensation in her stomach. The familiar vertical handwriting seemed to jump out at her. It was from Garrick. Without opening it, she could guess its contents. A nostalgic card of sea shells, or ocean waves, or lovers walking hand in hand along a twilight beach, with a "miss you . . . thinking of you" type of greeting.

She picked up a pen and, across the face of the envelope, boldly scribbled "Return to sender," then dropped the envelope in the out-mail tray.

Eager to put Garrick out of her mind, she turned to a stack of office memos. The first one got her attention. She reread it, puzzled.

Still holding the memo, Regina walked around the partition to Donna's tiny cubicle. Standing in the doorway, she could see herself in the oval mirror on the opposite wall. Her dark brown hair, pulled into a clip at the nape of her neck, seemed dull and frizzy today. It was her habit to wear little or no makeup, and today, with the heat, humidity, and the rushing around, she felt washed out, unattractive. She quickly looked away.

"What's this, a joke?" Regina asked Donna, holding up the paper.

Donna smiled, leaned back in her chair, and motioned for Regina to come in. "No joke."

"The Classic Beauty Pageant," Regina said, reading. "Jeeze, Donna, that was fifteen years ago."

"Twenty."

"Lord."

18

"I know I should've consulted you first. After all, you are the coproducer, the talent coordinator, and the chief cook and bottle washer—but knowing you, you would've nixed it. There's one major change. We're aiming for next week's time slot. We've got to make some calls."

"You've already invited the others?"

Donna nodded. "Tammy. Amelia . . ."

"Corinne?" Regina asked.

Donna nodded again, this time solemnly.

"Why? Why in God's name—"

Donna held up a hand to silence her. "I know. I know. Let's just say I'm in a position to bring us together again—publicly—and I . . . I want to, that's all."

"What's the slant?" Regina asked.

"We have two options. If Corinne declines, we interview four local, former beauty contestants—"

Behind Regina a male voice said flatly, "But if Corinne agrees to come on the show and talk about the acid incident, we go for it."

Regina turned to face Nolan Lake. "And that's what you're really shooting for, isn't it?"

Nolan shrugged.

"Are we resorting to sensationalism?"

"That's the kind of business we're in," Nolan said. "It sells."

"I like to think 'City Gallery' is above that sort of thing."

"That's why it's Donna's show and not yours," Nolan said with a thin smile, failing to keep the sarcasm from his voice.

"Nolan, please," Donna said quietly.

Nolan perched on the edge of the desk and massaged the back of Donna's neck. "It's going to be a great show. Period."

Regina looked from his determined face to Donna's hopeful one. For Donna she would do it.

"I'll start making the calls," Regina said dryly, turning to leave.

Nolan blocked her way. "You were the first runner-up, Regina," he said. "Haven't you ever wondered what course your life would have taken if you had won the title instead of Corinne?"

Fixing him with a direct gaze, Regina said, "No." Then she moved around him and walked away.

5

Amelia Corde cautiously moved the key ring. Without picking up the gray snakeskin wallet she opened it flat and, with long, burgundy-lacquered fingernails, wriggled the thick sheath of bills out far enough to see the denominations. There were hundreds, then fifties, and on down to the fives. Matthew never carried ones in his wallet. He probably tossed them away, she thought with rancor. The man was frivolous with his cash—except where his wife was concerned.

She counted the money. Four hundred and eighty dollars. She slipped one of the three fifties from the stack, dropped it on the floor, then nudged it under the dresser with a stockinged toe.

A toilet flushed in the bathroom. Amelia quickly stuffed the rest of the money back into the wallet, closed it, then positioned the key ring exactly as it had been. She had just crossed to her vanity and snatched up the morning mail when Matthew Corde strolled into the room. Their eyes met briefly before he disappeared into the walk-in closet.

She forced herself to breathe normally as she sorted through the brochures and business-size envelopes. The one addressed to her from KSCO TV caught her eye. Too impatient to look for her sterling letter opener, Amelia slit it open with a thumbnail. She read the letter quickly, then reread it more slowly.

Donna Lake wanted her on the show. Well, she thought haughtily, it was about time. This was perfect. The interview could only enhance her prospective venture. The publicity was just what she needed.

She turned to the mirror, staring at her image critically. She smiled. Although she had recently passed the forty mark, little had changed about her. A few gray hairs,

20

plucked immediately when they appeared, several fine lines at the corners of her eyes, but essentially, she was still as slim and beautiful as the girl in the contest. Her shoulder-length black hair would need a touch-up. Perhaps she'd go with mahogany highlights this time.

Matthew came back into the room tying his necktie. At fifty-three, he was a thin man of average height with a perpetual grave expression. His eyes were prominent, giving him a bug-eyed countenance. The top of his head, bald except for a dozen long strands, was shiny and mottled with brown liver spots.

He looked up, saw his wife reading the mail. "Anything interesting?"

"Donna wants me as a guest on her show." She waved the letter.

He raised an eyebrow quizzically.

"The Classic Woman. The beauty contest. She's doing a follow-up show—two decades later. I was queen, remember?" When he failed to comment, she added, "All right, so I was queen by default. You know as well as I do that I should have won."

"That was a long time ago." He dropped his keys in his pants pocket and slipped the snakeskin wallet into the inner pocket of his dark blue suit jacket. With his back to her, he asked, "Do you suppose she ever suspected that you slept with one of the judges?"

"Really, Matthew," she said, admonishing.

"I'm only teasing, my darling," he said. "Go—have your hour of renown." He went to the door, then stopped. "I suppose you'll want a new dress for this momentous event?"

"Oh, darling, you're so perceptive."

Taking out his wallet, he carefully selected a credit card and, moving behind her, dropped it on the vanity top. "Don't get carried away. Leave the card and the receipt on my desk."

"Thank you, Matthew," she said sweetly, biting back the bitterness she felt at being treated like his mistress instead of his wife of eighteen years.

21

"Give my best to the illustrious Mrs. Lake," Matthew said. His hand came around her shoulder and reached inside her kimono to cup a breast.

Amelia's voice was tight. "It's inconceivable to me how that woman ever bagged her own TV show. She's a mousy little jellyfish — afraid of her own shadow. Her husband, naturally, is the driving force behind her success, and I don't wonder. She's incapable of an original thought."

"I found her to be a stimulating conversationalist and quite intelligent."

"When did you have this profound revelation?"

"When you placed her next to me at our dinner party for the mayor."

"Is that all you found her to be?"

"No. She's quite sensual as well."

Amelia glared at him in the mirror.

His hand came away. "No need to be jealous. She is nowhere near as sensual as you. Speaking of which, while you're shopping, pick out something frilly that will please me, humm?" He smiled, then turned and left the room.

After he had driven away, Amelia crossed to the dresser, retrieved the fifty, and went to the telephone on the nightstand. She dialed the number on the letterhead, then asked to speak to Donna Lake. As she waited, she thought of Fletcher, her young lover. In one hour she would be in his arms, his solid body pressed to hers. Fletcher adored her and would do anything to please her. Not that Matthew didn't adore and lust after her, but it wasn't quite the same.

She sighed, thinking that if Fletcher had only half of Matthew's money, he would without a doubt spend it on her freely, not make her grovel and steal. No matter; she and Fletcher together would make all the money they needed. In a month's time, if everything went well, she would be free of the Honorable Matthew Holstead Corde. The only thing she'd miss would be this magnificent house in Pacific Heights. Not a mansion by California standards, but a long ways from the rathole trailer she'd grown up in. Well, one occasionally had to compromise.

Soon she would be in the limelight again and, without a doubt, the fairest of them all. She thought about the others. Donna still looked okay, but in no way extraordinary. Regina seemed to have an aversion to maintaining what looks she had. And Tammy had let herself go all to hell since giving birth to the twins. Corinne couldn't possibly be a threat. Twenty years ago, Amelia remembered with a shudder, the woman had been rendered a monster, and no amount of plastic surgery could change that.

"Sweetie!" Amelia said cheerfully when Donna came on the line. "And how is San Francisco's numero uno celebrity?"

6

Tammy Kowalski opened the front door and quickly ushered her nine-year-old daughters into the house.

"Go in the living room and watch TV," she instructed the girls. "Don't get into anything. I don't want Daddy to know we were here."

"Why *are* we here?" Kerry asked.

"Never mind. Just stay out of trouble," Tammy said, pushing the girls toward the living room. "Watch TV and keep your hands off stuff."

Tammy beelined to her estranged husband's bedroom and, with a practiced hand, sorted through each drawer of his dresser and nightstands. She found nothing new since the last time she had been through his things.

At the unmade bed, she threw back the covers and bent over the mattress. Directly in the middle, on the mauve colored sheets, she saw a white, crusty stain. Then another. Semen? "Cunt," she whispered. She tossed the covers over the stain.

She moved into the bathroom where she rummaged through the vanity drawers, medicine cabinet, and laundry hamper. In the wastebasket she found the cardboard cylinder to a tampon. "Scuzzy bitch."

23

On the floor, on her knees, digging in the wastebasket, Tammy caught sight of her reflection in the full-length mirror. She turned slowly and stared intently at her pale blond image. The summer had just begun, yet her skin was already the color of golden toast. Her round, icy gray eyes were bright in contrast.

She stood, pivoting this way and that, delighting in the scrutiny of her body in the mirror. The aerobics instructor, at thirty-eight, in pink spandex pants and black midriff top, studied her tall, lean figure critically. Tammy cupped her new breasts. The incisions had healed and that tenderness and swelling was gone completely. She had a strong compulsion to see her firm breasts in Gary's mirror. She pulled at the elastic top, about to take it off, when the phone rang.

She flung open the bathroom door and shrieked, "Don't answer that!"

After six rings the answering machine clicked on. Gary's voice filled the room with a recorded greeting. After the beep a woman's voice, sounding cool and sophisticated despite the tinny speaker, said: "Hi, hon. Bad news. Can't make tonight. Have to fly to L.A. Call you tomorrow."

"Great vocabulary. Me Jane. You Tarzan. Fuckin' home-wrecking retard," Tammy muttered as she rummaged through the rolltop desk in the bedroom. She came across the payment books for the car and the house in Daly City that Gary had bought for her after the separation four months ago. He'd paid for the new boobs, too, although he didn't know it. He thought he could buy her off. Fat chance. She wasn't giving up that easily. She'd trade it all in to be with him again. To have his love. To share his bed.

"Mom, we're hungry." The girls, miniatures of their mother, stood in the doorway.

"Okay. Okay. I'm done here." She threw an arm around each girl and started down the hall. "Oops, hold it a sec." She shooed the girls out of the room and crossed to the nightstand where the answering machine sat. She rewound the tape, listened to several messages, and then, with a self-satisfied smile, she erased the last message—the one from

24

the "homewrecker."

In the living room, Tammy checked to make sure nothing was out of place. She sent the girls to the car as she locked up. Before joining them, she opened the mailbox, took out the mail, and sorted through it. There were a doctor bill, a couple of circulars, and a business envelope from KSCO TV. Tammy frowned. KSCO was where Donna worked. What would a TV station want with a dentist? Then she realized it wasn't Gary they wanted. The letter was addressed to Tamara Kowalski.

She tore it open, read it, and then whooped. Donna wanted to interview her on TV. Hot damn! She couldn't wait to tell Gary.

7

Corinne Odett took a long pull on the bottle of beer before slamming it back down on the Formica kitchen table. She picked up the two pieces of paper, the formal letter with the fancy embossed letterhead that she'd just torn in half, and carelessly matched the ragged edges together. She leaned forward to see better. At eleven in the morning, she was already well on her way to getting drunk.

She has her nerve, that "Little Miss All American Girl Next Door Pretty as a Picture Goody Two Shoes," Corinne thought bitterly. Twenty years ago Miss Fourth Runner-up wasn't good enough to be Corinne's lackey. When it came to beauty, there'd been no comparison between the two. Not one of the runners-up had been in the same league as Corinne Rayann Odett. Not one.

That was twenty years ago.

With a trembling hand, she rooted through an overflowing ashtray, looking for the longest butt. She carefully straightened it, put it to her lips, and, leaning over to the stove, lit it from the gas flame under the coffeepot. She heard sizzling and smelled the acrid odor of singed hair.

Sparks dropped unheeded onto her lap as she turned her

head to look out the window. She coughed, then winced at the sharp pain in her lungs. On the countertop in front of the window was a toaster. She could see her reflection in it. The greasy and dented chrome distorted her face. She moved her head slowly, studying the wavy image as her face shortened, then lengthened; her nose hooked down, long and pointed like a witch's, then pugged up, nostrils large and round like an ape's.

Corinne chuckled. The funny part was that her face looked better in the distorted metal than it did in a mirror. Corinne hadn't bothered to really look at herself in a long time, but in her mind's eye the true hideous image was cast forever. After two extremely painful operations by a plastic surgeon, the damaging effects of the acid had been altered little. She had lost the sight in her right eye. The angry, purple-and-white puckered skin on the one side of her face pulled her eye and mouth downward. The Phantom of the Opera had nothing on her.

Corinne heard a phlegmy cough from the tiny bedroom off the kitchen. Her father called her name.

Maybe she would accept Donna's *gracious* offer to appear on her show. It would serve the bitch right. She could sit with them, the four runners-up, swapping beauty and fashion tips and all that wonderful stuff glamorous women talk . . .

"Cory?" her father called out in a weak, hoarse voice.

Now that the old man's income had been cut off because of his bum health, maybe Donna would offer her a cohost position on the show. Everyone would benefit. Surely, people would tune in to see the marred beauty queen. The ratings would go up. And she'd have something to do, some place to go. God knows she didn't get out much these days.

"Corinne? I'm hungry, daughter. You gonna let your daddy starve?"

The checks from welfare were regular and she only had to tolerate those do-good social workers snooping through the house now and then. They never stayed long. It was too much of a hassle for them to avoid staring at her, so they did

26

a speedy check, then split.

"Corinne? Corinne? I know you're out there. I can smell cigarette smoke. I thought we was outta butts." He coughed. "Corinne, how 'bout some food? You know I gotta eat regular."

"Shut up, you stupid old man!" she screamed, and hurled the half bottle of beer at the opposite wall. "You'll get your goddamn food when I'm damn good and ready!"

Two

1

John Davie woke at 7:10 in the morning to the delightful sensation of someone expertly manipulating his penis. Lying on his side, he reached down and took hold of the slender hand caressing him. He felt warm breath on his back, then the light nip of teeth on his shoulder.

"It ain't fair," he said.

"What ain't?" Wilma, John's upstairs neighbor, whispered against his neck.

"That women get hornier with age. Men, on the other hand, only get limp and bald."

"You're not getting bald." She wrapped a leg around him. "And you're certainly not limp. Quite the contrary, my dear boy. And I'd appreciate it if you wouldn't mention age."

He chuckled deep in his throat. "So whose turn is it?"

"I believe it's mine."

"Ummm." John rolled over onto his back and closed his eyes.

Wilma took the cue without prompting. She straddled him, sighing as she fitted herself to him. She slowly moved up and down. "What a pity this will be our last time. I'm getting married."

John opened his eyes and looked at her incredulously. "Married? Who? When?"

"This afternoon. To Dr. Greenwood, the chief of surgery

at Bayview General. We're flying to Reno. I'd invite you to the wedding, but I might forget myself and take you on the honeymoon."

"Christ," he said. "Today? Getting married — *today*." Wilma nodded. "Well, hell . . ." He rose up and turned her over on her back. "In that case, you just relax and let me give the bride a proper send-off."

"You'll spoil me. Oh dear . . . ohh . . ."

An hour later, John, wet from the shower, stood in the bathroom doorway and watched Wilma dress. For a woman who was more than a decade older than he, she had a remarkable face and body. Not beautiful, but attractive, extremely attractive and very sensual. Wilma took care of herself. Exercise, nutrition, and a healthy outlook on life.

"I'm gonna miss you," he said. "I had no idea you were moving out."

"I gave your aunt notice last month. For a landlady, she's not very gossipy."

"She's too busy worrying about me."

"I think she's quite relieved that I'm going. I'm sure she suspects that you and I occasionally wind up sleeping on the wrong floor. She has a good Hungarian girl in mind for you."

John nodded, smiling.

"A virgin."

This time he made a face.

"When's the new novel coming out?" she asked.

"In the fall."

"I want an autographed copy. It'll be a best seller." Wilma stepped up to him, kissed him briefly. "Good luck with the one in progress, John Tyrone Davie."

"Good luck with the new husband, Assistant District Attorney Axelrod."

She started to walk away, then stopped and turned back. "Regina Van Raven, a friend of mine, will be taking over my lease. I think you'll like her. She's about your age. Widow."

John groaned. One matchmaker in this joint was enough. Then he remembered the woman in the front of the apartment house the day before. The one who was familiar, but as yet, unknown to him. "Wilma, does she have dark hair and drive a station wagon?"

"That's her. I see your feelers are already out and twitching." Wilma kissed his cheek, winked, then quickly went out the door.

2

Sitting at the antique claw-foot desk in the den of her four-bedroom house in Berkeley, Regina said good-bye and hung up the phone. She had just spoken to Tammy and was about to call the next on the list.

As she looked up Amelia's number, she stroked a hand over the scarred wood of the desk and felt a tugging in her stomach. This, her husband's favorite piece, had been sold along with the entire houseful of furniture. Leo Van Raven had had a passion for antiques. When she married him nineteen years ago, she had moved into his two-story Victorian house, and they had remained there. Rather, she and Kristy had. Leo had been placed in a nursing home the two years preceding his death.

Early in his career Leo had been a successful screenwriter in Hollywood. Disillusioned by the studio's cutthroat tactics, the pressure, and the long hours, he turned to free-lance writing. At the University of California at Berkeley, Regina met and fell in love with the charismatic guest speaker in her creative writing class. He was twenty-three years her senior and the brightest man she had ever known. Fourteen years later, Alzheimer's robbed him of his brilliant mind, and then, after reducing him to little more than an infant, it took his life.

At her elbow was Leo's last book, finished except for final editing and typing, which Regina had been working on in her spare time. She had promised the editor it would be on his desk by the end of the month.

The phone rang.

"Reggie?" a familiar male voice said.

Regina closed her eyes and gripped the receiver tightly.

"Reggie, I've got to see you."

"No, Garrick. How many times do I have to tell you no?"

"Damnit, Regina, he's dead. Face up to it. There's no reason now for us not to see each other."

"I'm going to hang up now. Please don't call me anymore." She heard his voice raised in anger as she replaced the receiver. She crossed her hands over her mouth and closed her eyes. Oh God, why wouldn't he leave her alone? It had been a mistake, one she would regret for a long time. Couldn't he see she wasn't interested. Didn't he know that the sight of him, the sound of his voice, brought back, in full force, a rush of guilt and shame?

Leo, oh, Leo, forgive me.

3

At Cossan's Boutique, in the heart of San Francisco's shopping district, Amelia Corde posed before the three-way mirror. The white peplum dress with its squared, padded shoulders, tapered sleeves, and taupe snakeskin belt was perfect. It fit as if designed for her.

Lydia, one of two proprietors of the boutique, poked her head in the door of the dressing room. "How we doing, Mrs. Corde? Oh, that's lovely. The moment I laid eyes on it I knew it was meant for you." Lydia smiled slyly. "Naturally, it's on sale."

"Naturally."

A few minutes later at the counter, Amelia handed Lydia Matthew's credit card. Although the dress was a sale item, the woman rang it up at the full retail price. She opened the register, counted out a number of hundred dollars bills, and handed them to Amelia. Amelia returned one of the hundreds to Lydia and stashed the remaining cash in her eyeglass case.

"Thank you for your patronage, Mrs. Corde," Lydia said,

pocketing the money.

"And thank you, Lydia. Wonderful doing business with you."

Amelia walked to a shoe store on Powell, where she bought a pair of taupe snakeskin pumps and the matching handbag. She resisted the urge to buy a second pair of pumps—Matthew's generosity had its limits. And thinking of Matthew, she crossed to Sutter, to the Victorian Boudoir, where she selected a sheer, lacy corset in black and peach. The sales transactions were handled the same as at the boutique. The proprietors of at least four other shops in town honored her system. And when these clothes had become dated, she would sell them to a store south of Market that handled pre-owned clothes of exceptional quality.

As she headed back to her car, Amelia mentally counted her financial take for the day. Fifty from Matthew's wallet, two hundred from Cossan's, seventy-five from the shoe store, and thirty from the Boudoir. Three hundred and fifty-five dollars in less than two hours. Not bad. And she didn't have to do a thing for it. Well, Matthew would want a return on his money. But if she closed her eyes tight and imagined it was Fletcher, she could breeze through it without too much repulsion.

Within twenty minutes of claiming her late-model Mercedes at the parking garage, Amelia was in the Marina district, knocking at the door of her lover's apartment.

4

To the blaring sound of a rock beat the last of the students filed out to the lockers and showers. Tammy Kowalski jumped down from the gym platform and pulled off her sweat-drenched headband. She had worked to her maximum, sparing no energy. She was the only aerobics instructor at the Fitness Center. In less than twenty minutes she'd have to do it again. Then one last time that evening. Hard, exhausting work, but it kept her sane.

Her goal was to lose a few more pounds before the television interview. She hadn't seen Regina, Amelia or Donna in months and they were all going to shit when they saw how great she looked. She could compete with any of them again.

Would Corinne be there, she wondered? Tammy got sick just thinking about her. All those years ago, right after that awful thing had happened to Corinne, she had gone to the hospital to visit her. What Tammy had seen that day would forever be, horribly, seared into her brain — she had stumbled out of the hospital room, with its sickening odor, on the verge of blacking out, to vomit violently in the hall.

Don't think about Corinne, she told herself. Think about a new beginning. The TV show. The timing couldn't have been better. A year ago she'd been fat and flabby. A dreary housewife with nothing to do but watch garbage TV. No wonder her husband had left her. Gary was a handsome, intelligent, professional man. A dentist needed a wife who was close to his equal socially and intellectually. And that was the reason she was getting her mind, as well as her body, in shape. She now watched TV shows that were informative, educational, and cultural — PBS, "20/20," Oprah — though much of it went over her head or bored her to distraction. She was also making an effort to read something besides true confession and romance novels. *People* magazine was okay because the articles were short.

When Gary left her, she had gone into shock. After the shock came the crying and pleading. For the first time her threats of suicide fell on deaf ears. And then there was the breakdown and those awful weeks at that nuthouse in the country. Her psychiatrist had assured her that after she had gone through the gamut of emotions, acceptance would eventually occur. Never, she thought, she could never accept life without Gary. *Never.*

The only thing that had kept her from going completely insane had been her desire to improve herself and get Gary back. The intense dedication kept her from dwelling on his absence. At four that afternoon she had an appointment

33

with her plastic surgeon for an estimate on a face-lift.

Wiping the sweat from her face and throat, she hurried to her locker, took a quarter from her purse, and went to the pay phone on the wall. She dialed the dental office, asked for Gary, gave the receptionist the name of his girlfriend, and while waiting, stretched her muscles.

"Mandy," Gary said, eagerly. "what the hell happened to you last night?"

"Gary, it's Tammy."

There was a pause. Then in a deadened tone, Gary said, "I was told Amanda was on the line."

"Someone made a mistake."

"What do you want, Tammy?"

"I wanted to share my good news with you. Donna Lake wants me as a guest on her show. Isn't that a kick?"

Silence.

"My best friend, Donna. Y'know, 'City Gallery'?"

"Yeah, sure."

"Guess you're wondering why she wants me on the show." She paused for his response. The only sound was the distant conversation of another party on a crossed phone line. "Gary?"

"I'm in the middle of a root canal. My assistant is signaling to me."

Tammy clenched her fist. "The girls have a birthday next weekend."

"Yes, I know. If it's all right with you I'd like to take them to Marine World for the day."

"Oh, I don't believe this, that's what I had in mind," she lied. "It's perfect. We could do it as a family thing. Nothing could make them happier."

"Tammy, look, I . . ." He cursed softly. "I don't think so. Not this time. I, uh, already invited Mandy. The girls know about it."

A painful knot formed in her stomach. She felt a rush of heat in her chest, hotter and heavier than the air in the sauna across the hall. He was going to introduce that bitch to her daughters. On their birthday. And they knew about it and were keeping it to themselves. How could that be?

No way. No. No. No.

"No," she said quietly.

"You can't stop us. I have my rights."

"Gary, no."

"You're only hurting the girls."

"Gary . . ." she said, tears welling in her eyes. "Please, no."

"Suit yourself. Tell the girls I love them and that I'm sorry we can't get together Sunday. And tell them why." There was a soft click before the dial tone came on.

Tammy carefully hung the receiver on the hook.

She stumbled the few feet to the sauna and entered. It was thick with steam, impossible to see into. Without the least concern as to whether she was alone or not, Tamara opened her mouth and screamed.

5

Donna looked up from basting the chicken to see her husband enter the kitchen. It was 6:00 P.M., and although it was still hot, Nolan looked crisp and cool and incredibly handsome. His necktie was straight, his dark hair in place, his shoes as shiny as though just polished; he rarely looked anything less than immaculate.

"Hello, darling," she said. "There's a mug in the freezer."

As he took a Heineken from the refrigerator, he stopped to look at a child's drawing on the metal door.

"Nigel did that," she said. "I thought it was quite good."

"Yes, I agree." He slipped the drawing out from under the magnet and laid it on top of the refrigerator — out of sight — then took a frosty beer stein from the freezer.

"Dinner will be ready whenever you are," Donna said. "Where would you like to eat tonight?"

"There's something of a breeze coming up. The terrace, I believe."

Donna smiled to herself. What Nolan called the terrace,

35

she and the boys called the deck. Nolan tended to elevate the status of everything. Chicken was "the bird." Chocolate pudding was "mousse." Even something as common as beer, became "lager."

The Lakes lived in Marin County, in prestigious Kentfield. Nolan wanted the boys enrolled in the Ross School District. The house was small, with only two bedrooms, but it was the best they could manage in that expensive neighborhood. Plans to add on and renovate were in the works. Donna, by choice, did all the cleaning, shopping, cooking, and laundry for her family of four.

A half hour later Donna, Nolan, and their sons, Nolan II, "Junior," nine, and Nigel, seven, freshly scrubbed and in clean clothes—a ritual Nolan had insisted on from the very beginning—sat down to dinner on the terrace. A slight breeze from the ocean pushed cooler air around them. Gulls screeched, dipping and soaring just yards away. As Nolan skillfully poured lager into a frosted, clear glass stein, Donna cut up the bird.

"Carol called this morning. She wanted to know if you had planned to see Amy on Father's Day."

Carol was Nolan's ex-wife, and Amy was his eleven-year-old daughter from that marriage. Amy had been born with a severe club foot. Early efforts to correct it had eliminated most of the crippling effects, but the girl would always walk with a noticeable limp.

"Call her back and tell her I may have to go out of town. Tell her—hell, tell her anything you like."

Donna looked away, uncomfortable. Shortly after Nolan graduated from San Francisco State with a B.A. in broadcasting, he divorced Carol. He rarely saw his daughter. If he chose to spend time with any children, it was with his bright, healthy sons, whom he favored. This nearly broke Donna's heart. His daughter was a sweet, lovable child. If only Amy hadn't been born a girl and *flawed*. Donna chided herself for even thinking such thoughts, but, may God forgive him, Nolan had this thing about . . . perfection.

Donna loved him. He was good to her, though he tended

36

to put her on a pedestal, to elevate her status, as he did with everything that was his. But she was nothing without him. When they had met, she was part of the production staff of KSCO, made local commercials, and acted in small theater productions. Nolan had taken a naive but eager bit-actress and had gotten her a talk show of her own. And she wouldn't always be just a local celebrity; her brilliant husband was determined to get the show on Cable or in syndication.

"We'll take the Chris-Craft out tomorrow," Nolan said, cutting the chicken neatly from the bones. "Anyone for waterskiing?"

"Great, Dad!" Junior said.

Nigel, looking up from his labored effort to carve his chicken, smiled and nodded.

"Amy would love to go out," Donna said, cautiously. "I know she can't waterski, but she enjoys boating."

Nolan fixed her with a cool stare before saying, "We'll see." But she, and everyone at the table, knew that the subject was closed.

Nolan took a sip of his Heineken. "Luv, that dress you wore on today's show was rather unflattering."

"But you approved of it at the taping."

"The camera added pounds, and with that horizontal pattern, it made you look — well, somewhat overweight. I wouldn't say anything if I didn't know how conscientious you are about your image." He reached over and positioned Nigel's knife correctly across his plate.

At the end of the meal Nolan asked, "So, how is the Miss Classic segment coming?"

"Affirmative from everyone expect Corinne. Reg will call her tonight."

"Perhaps you should call her yourself. Regina has no real stake in this and, I'm afraid, she can't always be trusted to do the job right. We *need* Corinne there." He rose, casually looked out over the landscape, then bent and kissed her forehead. "*You* call her, hum?" he said in an offhand tone before going into the house.

6

Corinne let the phone ring. On the seventh ring her father called out from the bedroom, "You trying to drive me nuts with that damn ringing! Answer!"

"Answer it yourself! I ain't your flunky," she shouted back as she picked up the receiver.

"Hello?" she said sweetly. Her voice was deep and rich, like the resonant and sexy tone one gets just before laryngitis sets in. It was one of the aftereffects of the acid fumes and a heavy cigarette habit.

"Corinne Odett?"

"Yes."

"Corinne, it's, uh, Donna Lake. I, uh —." The woman sounded unsure of herself, not at all like the cool, blond celebrity who dazzled thousands of San Franciscans with her wide, bright smile and glib tongue.

Corinne said in a melodious tone, "My, oh, my. How are you, Donna?"

"I'm fine. And you?"

After a long delay, Corinne finally broke the silence. "I couldn't be better."

"Oh, that's good to hear. Corinne . . ." Donna cleared her throat.

"You're calling about the upcoming show, correct? I have your letter right here in front of me. I'm sorry I didn't get right back to you, but I've only this morning returned from a trip abroad."

"Oh?"

"It was grim. I do believe I'm finished with traveling for awhile. In every airport — Athens, Rome, and even London — I worried myself sick about terrorists. We cruised, my fiancé and I, the Greek Islands, and even aboard ship I didn't feel safe. But you didn't call to hear about my boring excursions."

"Oh, no really, I'd love to hear about your trip."

Corinne lifted the beer bottle to her lips and drank, taking

38

long gulps. Pulling the bottle away, she wiped her mouth with the inside of her wrist. She lowered the receiver to her side then belched loudly. After taking another swallow of beer, she put the receiver back to her ear.

"Corinne?" Donna said. "Corinne, are you there?"

"So you want me on your show?"

"Yes. I'm afraid the taping has been moved up three weeks, so there's not much time to—"

"The others are coming?"

"Yes. Would you believe that the five of us still live right here after all these years."

"I moved to Beverly Hills for a couple of years. Did the sun goddess scene for awhile, but it was all so superficial. Couldn't wait to move back."

"Oh . . ."

"When's the taping?"

"Friday." Donna waited. "If that's too soon, we could possibly move it back. My husband—"

"You'd do that for me?"

"Well . . . yes. After all, you were the queen."

"The queen's reign was very brief."

A pause, then in a tone filled with compassion, Donna said, "Corinne, I can only imagine how devastating it must have been for you. I wish you would have let me do something, help in some way . . ."

Corinne paused before saying, "There was nothing you could do. But that was years ago. Everything's fine now. Thank God for plastic surgeons."

"Were they able to . . ."

"Beyond my wildest dreams." Corinne smiled, touched the network of scars on the side of her face. "I'll do it."

"Pardon?"

"The show. I'll do it."

Corinne's father went into a fit of coughing. From where she stood in the dining room, she could see the end of his bed and the impression of his foot under the covers. She plucked a porcelain figurine off the knickknack shelf beside her head and sent it flying. The figurine hit the mound of

39

covers, the old man cried out, cursed. The coughing stopped.

"You're willing to talk about . . . ?" Donna stammered.

"Isn't that why you want me on the show?" Corinne sensed how difficult this was for Donna and she was enjoying every minute of it.

"Yes," Donna answered softly.

Corinne reached for a pen and pad, "Where do I go and at what time?"

After hanging up, Corinne walked into the bathroom, took a Quaalude from the medicine cabinet, and swallowed it with the remaining beer.

So she was to be the star attraction again after all these years. How thrilling. What woman wouldn't be excited?

She closed the medicine cabinet halfway. Leaning forward, she pressed her face to the edge of the mirror so that only one half of her face showed—the unscarred half. She studied the image with a strange sense of dispassion. What she could see was not beautiful any longer; age and abuse had seen to that. But with makeup? With her hair fixed decently? Could anything possibly be salvaged from this . . . this monstrous insult?

She smiled. The smile brightened her face. She'd forgotten how lovely her smile was.

7

It was dusk. Regina turned on the small lamp on Leo's desk. The phone rang just as she was in the process of reaching for it to call Corinne, a task she could not embrace with relish or enthusiasm. She had yet another reprieve.

It was Donna.

"Reggie, you don't have to call Corinne, I've already done it."

"Nolan didn't trust me," Regina said flatly.

"Reg, that's not—." After a pause there was a drawn-out sigh. "Please don't take it personally. You know how he can

40

be sometimes."

How well she knew. So Nolan had again pulled the rug out from under her. The funny part, the really outrageously hilarious part, was that Nolan had less status and authority than either his wife or Regina. His was a token position, insisted upon by Nolan himself, and inadvertently achieved because of his marital status to Donna. For him, producer of "City Gallery" was little more than a title. Ten years ago, Nolan — as an assistant producer and on shaky ground at the station — had gotten Donna the job, married her, and had then proceeded to crawl up her back to perch dogmatically on her shoulders.

"Come on now, Reggie, he's not the chauvinist you make him out to be."

Regina bit her tongue to keep from saying what she really thought, and that was that all women, to Nolan, had a definite place in the business — at the bottom, without status or power. Except for Donna. But she was merely an extension of his ego. "So, how'd it go with Corinne?"

"I think she'll show," Donna said. "I'll tell you all about it tomorrow. Gotta go now, bye."

With a sense of disquiet, Regina slowly replaced the receiver.

The phone rang again. A woman asked for Kristy.

"Kristy's not in."

"Are you her mother?"

"Yes."

"Oh, Mrs. Van Raven, I'm so eager to meet you. My name is Marianne Nash. I'm Kristy's appointed chaperon for the Miss Golden Gate Model Search."

"Chaperon?"

"I'm afraid it's necessary since she's under eighteen. I can't tell you how delighted I am to have this opportunity to look after such a stunning child as your daughter."

"The Miss Golden Gate what?" Regina repeated in a dull tone.

"You know, of course, that she's a candidate in the contest?"

41

Silence.

"Mrs. Van Raven?"

"Oh Lord," Regina said under her breath. Her former disquiet doubled.

8

Slowly he cruised the tree-lined residential street. In the middle of the block he pulled to the curb across the street from the large, two-story Victorian house. The windows were dark except for one upstairs, where a soft light from a desk lamp glowed. Her late-model, tan station wagon sat in the driveway. Through the front window he saw her pacing. She came to the window and stood looking out, her fingers clasping and unclasping in a nervous, distracted way. He wondered if she could see him, and decided it was too dark. She moved away from the window.

He was about to drive away when he noticed the sign on the front lawn. Across the name of the real estate agency, he saw SOLD.

He pulled away, cursing. If she intended to leave the city, his plans would have to be altered.

Three

1

Midnight.

From the cassette player the familiar, breathy voice filled the car with mocking, loathsome words of betrayal, triggering an overpowering sensation of hate and jealous rage. *The conniving bitch had gone too far. Much too far. There was one appropriate punishment. A punishment no beautiful woman could live with.*

He stared at the house across the street through a screen of black. Visible beyond the bay window, in the ghostly blue glow of the television, she sat curled up on the end of the sofa, the telephone to her ear, her shiny dark hair falling over the receiver and across one side of her face. Her flawless beauty was apparent even from this distance.

The voice on the cassette droned on, though he no longer heard the words. He watched the woman on the phone, his gloved fingers caressing the polished steel of the straight razor.

He smiled. Beneath the dark nylon stocking the grin felt tight, strangely numb. He pulled the black knitted crew cap down over his flattened ears. With hands as steady as those of a surgeon, he grasped the straight razor and reached for the door handle.

Marilyn Keane tucked her feet under her and shifted the receiver to her other ear.

A branch snapped outside. She paused only briefly before resuming her conversation.

The slim, ivory-skinned, twenty-two-year-old, one of thirty candidates in the Golden Gate Model Search, ecstatic beyond words to have made the first cut, talked to her mother in nearby San Francisco.

Another branch snapped. She heard a faint screeching sound, like that of fingernails on a blackboard.

She shivered, drew her knees up to her chest, and divided her attention between the voice of her mother and the rustling sounds coming from somewhere at the back of the house. A dog or cat in the garbage, she told herself.

In the kitchen, the pair of finches began to set up a racket, thrashing about the cage, squeaking incessantly like children's squeeze toys.

Her pulse accelerated. Her mouth suddenly felt dry, tasted acrid.

"Sssh," Marilyn hissed into the mouthpiece.

"What is it, dear?"

"Mom," she whispered, "I think someone's trying to get in the house."

"What?"

Except for the television screen and the green glow of the dial plate on her trimline phone, the room was dark. She heard a rattling sound, then something crashed to the floor.

"Someone's in the house!" The shrill sound of her own voice frightened her.

"Marilyn, who's there?"

A finch flew through the kitchen doorway and circled the living room, frantically ricocheting off one wall and then another above her.

"Marilyn . . . !"

She gaped at the bird, her fingers gripping the phone, her heart pounding maniacally in her chest. She looked back at the doorway to see a dark figure coming toward her. Odd, she thought through a choking hysteria, there was no relief in the blackness rushing at her. The intruder was sheathed from head to toe in black. No, not everything was black, she realized dully, there *was* a relief in the inky void. Yes, something glittered. Something, long, catching a sliver of light from God knows where, flashed metallic.

She felt a light object drop onto her lap. With a shudder Marilyn pushed the other bird, now bloody and headless, away. She tried to scream and managed only a pathetic cry and the word "Momma."

In her ear she heard her name over and over.

The blade came down, slashing across one side of her face and then the other.

It was a mistake. It wasn't meant for her. She had too much to live for. Through the gushing roar of a panic pulse in her brain, she heard words spoken. Words she understood, yet could not relate to. Curses.

The blade came down again. *Not my face,* she thought with a sick horror. *Oh God, not my face.* Her hands came up to cover her face and she felt the blade cut into the soft flesh of her upper torso. She was dragged down to the floor, her jeans cut away, her legs forced apart.

Like a moth paying homage to the light, the tiny bird continued to flutter above her with a papery crunching sound as its delicate wings batted against hard, pitiless objects. She held tight to the receiver.

"Marilynmarilynmarilyn . . ."

As the blood gushed out, as she surrendered to the violation of her body, words from long ago came back to her: *A bird loose in the house forebodes ill will . . . forebodes death . . .*

Her last conscious thought was of the bird. She prayed it would rot in hell.

Four

Donna

At seven o'clock Saturday morning, Donna reached over to find Nolan's warm body close to hers in the king-size bed. She shifted over, nuzzling her head in the hollow of his shoulder, and began to rub his chest, running her fingers through the triangle of dark hair. His eyes were closed and his breathing was controlled; not the regular breathing of slumber. When he didn't speak or move away, she let her hand burrow under the covers and traverse downward to his groin. He was beginning to swell. He murmured softly, finally reaching up to caress her shoulder while she tenderly stroked him to a full erection. He turned over and, kissing her throat, cupping a breast, he pushed inside her. There was some resistance, she wasn't fully lubricated yet, but within moments he was gliding in and out with ease. She hoped he wouldn't hurry. There was no reason to rush. It was her birthday and they had all the time in the world.

She felt the lovely tingling and knew she would make it this time if there were no interruptions and if he'd just go slower. It had been so long. She couldn't remember the last time she had been sexually fulfilled. It wasn't Nolan's fault, it just took her so long. But this morning would be different, if only he could last a little longer.

Her breathing became shallow, heavy. Please, she said to herself, *please*. So close . . . almost there . . . almost . . .

He stopped abruptly. Nooo, not yet! She felt him stiffen, and knew that it was over for him. Then he was leaving her, and all erotic feelings seemed to evaporate with the void.

He patted her shoulder, smiling. "Happy Birthday, Luv." He rolled over and climbed from the bed.

A half hour later, Donna critically studied her face in the mirror. She was thirty-nine today. Did she look any older? Did she look like a woman who was on the last leg of her youth?

Completely devoid of makeup, she noticed fine lines around her eyes and mouth. When she smiled they deepened. Her skin had begun to look splotchy over the cheekbones. And was it her imagination, or did her eyes and mouth seem to get smaller with age? One day last week, as she and Nolan viewed the videotape, Nolan had said, "Try to watch how you hold your mouth when you're not talking, it looks pinched — see there," he said, pausing the play and nodding at the TV screen.

Now, looking in the mirror, Donna moved her lips; a smile, then repose. Before Nolan's remark she hadn't been conscious of that pinched look. Now it was with her all the time, everywhere. Standing in the check-out line at the grocery store, sitting in the bleachers at Junior's and Nigel's little league ball games, looking at merchandise at a craft fair, she found herself lifting the corners of her mouth to soften the line, wondering if she looked younger to those around her, or just plain simple-minded?

Lately she'd begun putting her makeup on upon arising, before having her first cup of coffee. Just that morning Nolan had asked her what she thought of cosmetic surgery. Sometimes, unfortunately, he could be so much like her father.

Reminding herself that her father was coming today to take the boys to a tennis tournament at his club, she abandoned the scrutiny of her face and hurried to get ready.

An hour later Donna sat on the shaded deck, drinking coffee. Nolan cooked breakfast and the boys served it. He made her a mimosa, and even poured a small amount of

47

champagne in Junior's and Nigel's glasses of orange juice.

After eating she opened her gifts. Junior's present was a bottle of Evening Jasmine bubble bath. Nolan presented her with a generous gift certificate for Neiman Marcus, and announced that he'd reserved a table — with a view of the bay — for four at Angelino's in Sausalito.

Nigel ran into the house and returned a moment later with a single pale pink geranium — the same color as the ones in the pot on the front porch — and a small tissue-paper package heavily laden with transparent tape.

"Did you wrap this yourself?" Donna asked with a tender smile.

He nodded.

She carefully unwrapped it. Inside was a stone with a high gloss appearance. On one side was a painted ladybug.

"It's just an everyday rock," Nigel said, "but I polished it with my rock polisher. Then I painted it."

"It's beautiful," she whispered, turning it over in her fingers. "I'll make it my good luck stone."

He seemed to beam. "Happy Birthday, Momma," he said blithely, throwing his arms around her and hugging tightly. "I love you."

Donna felt tears spring into her eyes. Nigel had a way of doing that to her. He was so sweet, so compassionate. Somehow his lovable nature made her feel a strange void.

Nolan unfolded the morning newspaper. "Donna, my shirts should be ready at the cleaners. Before you take any more in, call around and get some prices. I think they're screwing us."

"I could do them myself."

"We've been through that before. You have enough to do at the station." He poured coffee for her, then himself. "In fact, I wish you'd look into getting help around the house. Someone to come in once or twice a week to do the hard jobs. I don't want my wife having housemaid hands and knees."

"I'd rather do it myself. Really. I'll wear gloves."

"Amelia recommended a cleaning service. Why don't you

48

get the number from her."

Donna inhaled deeply, but said nothing. How could she find fault with a man who wanted her to have more leisure time? He pampered her, spoiled her, made her feel important. *If only Daddy* — her thoughts were interrupted by a deep baritone voice.

"Greetings," Stanley Cragg, Donna's father, called out as he stepped through the slider, his arms filled with gift-wrapped packages.

Nolan quickly stood, went to his father-in-law, and heartily shook his hand. "Good to see you, sir. Can you stay a bit? We have champagne for a mimosa."

"Not for me. You go right ahead though."

Donna felt a surge of elation. He had brought her birthday presents. Making an effort to hide her eagerness, she crossed to him and kissed his cheek. "Oh, Dad, you remembered." She touched the bow on the top package.

"How could I forget my grandsons. Sort of a belated Easter. Men," he said to Junior and Nigel, "come and see what your grandfather picked up for you in New York."

Donna dropped her hand, rubbed the palm along the side of her cotton slacks as she shifted uneasily from one foot to another.

The boys raced to their grandfather. The old man handed out the gifts and tousled their hair. "We'd better be going, men. We don't want to miss the first match. Open your presents in the car." He steered the boys ahead of him through the door. "I'll have them home before dark. Nolan, we'll have to have a game at my club soon."

"Any time, sir," Nolan replied cheerfully. "Just sing out."

"Oh, Dad," Donna said. "I hate to sound like a broken record, but don't forget brunch here on Father's Day."

A stricken look came over his face. "Good gracious, Donna, I'm sorry. I'd forgotten you'd made plans. Warren called and invited me to join him in a regatta in San Diego, and I accepted. I suppose I could . . ."

"No, no, that's okay, Dad."

"Next year, I promise." He waved and hurried through the

door.

Nolan gathered up the discarded wrapping paper and headed toward the trash can. Donna slowly sat back down. She sighed, then began to pick absently at her nail polish.

Warren again. This year she had asked her father well in advance and still her brother had won out. And she was certain her father remembered every one of Warren's birthdays.

When Donna was eight and her brother ten, their parents divorced. Every other Saturday he picked them up and took them to his ranch in the country for the weekend. Stanley and Warren engaged in fishing and hunting, all male activities, not suitable for young ladies, her father said. Donna spent her hours with her stepmother. She meticulously drew pictures, knitted slippers, or baked sweets for her father. When she presented her gifts, each one handmade with love, her father would carefully look them over — pointing out a flaw or two in the workmanship — before thanking her and setting the gifts aside and forgetting them.

In high school Donna excelled in all subjects. She tried out for the part of Nora in *A Doll's House* and got it. The night it played in the school auditorium, Warren broke his wrist playing basketball, and both of her parents — a captive audience — attended, instead, his debut in the hospital emergency room.

Warren graduated with honors and went on to Harvard. Two years later when she graduated, also with honors, the final blow was yet to come. Her father refused to pay her tuition to college, saying that attractive women enrolled for only one reason, to snare a suitable husband. His offer to her was a new car and a trip to Europe. She could take it or leave it.

She took it. Then she sold the car, banked the $5,000 vacation check, and enrolled at San Francisco State, where she majored in theater arts. She went to school by day and bussed tables at Tarantino's on the wharf at night.

A drama professor, aware of the Hollywood screen test, had encouraged her to enter the Miss Classic Pageant. Donna dreamed of winning the contest. If she accomplished something that her brother couldn't do, just maybe her father would love her as he did Warren.

She was thankful he hadn't shown up on the night of the crowning to see her fail so miserably. As fourth—and last—runner-up, Donna won $250 in cash and a year's supply of Ingenue cosmetics.

Five

Tammy

Tammy anxiously looked out the window of her new house on Strawberry Lane. She had told Brad 6:00 P.M. It was now 6:35. In less than two hours she would have to pick up the girls at the movie theater. That wouldn't give her and Brad much time.

She'd met Brad Segal at The Fitness Center the month before when he came to work there as a trainer. He had the body of an Atlas, but, she told herself ruefully, he could never measure up to Gary.

With a tooth-gnashing roar, a motorcycle pulled into the driveway. Her date, wearing faded Levis and a camouflage tank top under a denim vest, hopped off the bike. As he headed toward the front door, Tammy looked down at her aqua minisheath and pumps. She'd have to change clothes to match Brad's scruffy attire. She opened the door, ushered him inside, and greeted him warmly with a kiss, saying nothing of his lateness.

"Say, babe, would you mind if we stayed in tonight?" he asked. "Maybe call for a pizza or somethin'?"

Disappointment washed over her. In the four weeks they'd been seeing each other on a regular basis, he'd taken her out once — the first date. The rest of the time was spent at her house. "No, of course not," she said, smiling.

"I could sure use a Bud to wash the bugs outta my throat."

"Comin' up."

"Christ, it's hot in here." He walked to the sliding glass door that led to the patio and opened it. Before Tammy could shout a warning, Warrior, the Kowalskis' black Labrador, raced around the side of the house, barking like a mad dog, and became airborne. Brad slid the door shut just as the dog slammed against it.

"Jesus Christ, I keep forgetting about that fucking beast," Brad said.

"Sorry, sugar. He's really very friendly. He's just not used to you yet. Maybe if you—"

"Look, forget it, okay?" Brad said. "I don't like him. He don't like me. There's no law says we gotta be friends."

Brad flopped down on the La-z-boy recliner and, with the TV remote control, zipped through the channels until he found an English-dubbed Kung Fu movie.

Tammy ordered pizza. She made a green salad, set the table in the dining room with cloth napkins, candles, and a bottle of chianti. At least it would be romantic.

When the pizza came, Brad made no move to reach into his pocket. He had invited her out to dinner that night, but she would end up paying. Again. She kept the refrigerator stocked with his favorite brand of beer and snacks. She bought his chewing tobacco, which he spit in her good glasses. She lent him money when he was short, loans he seemed to forget.

Feeling a tension headache coming on, she clasped her hands together and said, "Salad and pizza's ready in the dining room."

"Here's fine." He patted the arm of the chair.

While he watched TV and devoured the pizza, she went to the bedroom, changed into her jeans and a halter top, then returned to sit on the floor in front of his chair, massaging his feet and thinking about Gary.

When the movie ended they went to bed. Although she had a blinding headache, it never crossed her mind to refuse. They undressed themselves. The slow, easy manner in which he shed his clothes made Tammy think of a strip-

53

tease. He stood motionless, looking down at her while she kissed and caressed his body, his muscles jumping, flexing beneath her fingers. With subtle prompting, he cupped her breasts, rubbing almost absently, while she brought him to full erection. Then standing, facing each other, he entered her. Suddenly he came alive, turned into a sex machine, his fingers teasing, his moans filling the room, his slick muscled body moving rhythmically, like choreographed moves in dance. At one point amid his sighs and controlled thrusts, she stole a peek at his face to find his eyes open and directed at the dresser mirror, watching his own performance. Minutes later, when he cried out in orgasm, she felt a measure of happiness.

He dressed silently, facing the mirror. Tammy sat cross-legged on the bed and marveled at his muscular form. The tight jeans hugged his buttocks and she was mesmerized by the circle of faded denim on his back pocket made by the canister of Copenhagen. He glanced up, caught her gaze in the mirror, and momentarily looked surprised, as if he'd forgotten there was someone else in the room.

"Do you think I have a nice body?" Tammy asked.

"Sure, you got a fine body. Especially for your age."

"Yours is fine too."

He grinned, winked. "Gotta go," he said.

"It's early."

"I'll call ya."

"When?"

"Tomorrow or the next day."

"Come for dinner on the weekend," she said. "I'll rent some Stallone movies."

"Yeah . . . sure. Sounds good."

"What night?"

"I'll call ya."

"I'm going to be on TV Friday," she said proudly. "Actually, it's taped on Friday and aired on Saturday."

Without comment he sat on the bed and laced up his boots.

"Maybe you could come over and watch it with me, huh?"

54

"Maybe." He squeezed her knee and rose. "See ya."

To his broad back as he walked down the hall, she called out, "Saturday at four."

He stopped, turned halfway to her, and said, "Hey, if I can't make it, don't get all bummed out, all right?"

"No, no, I won't," she said too quickly. "If you can't, you can't. I know how it is. It's just that . . . well, I told you how my husband was trying to get back with me. I thought if you were here, he might take the hint that I don't want to see him, and, y'know, stay away."

"Yeah," he said. "Yeah, well . . ." He turned and continued down the hall.

Before the sun had set completely he was gone.

Alone now, lying there, she thought he wasn't so bad. At least he smelled okay. And he wasn't rough or abusive. He could pay a little more attention to her body, though. She had worked damn hard to get it in shape. And what she couldn't build naturally, she bought. It wouldn't kill him to say something nice about it, without prompting from her, once in a while. A tear spilled out of the corner of her eye. She ignored it.

All she ever wanted was someone to notice her; someone to say something nice; someone to appreciate her efforts.

At the age of seventeen Tammy Blanco entered the 1970 Miss Classic contest. A current boyfriend had encouraged her to enter. The top prizes included a cashier's check for $1,000, a new wardrobe, a fur coat, a Hollywood screen test, and a Pontiac GTO. The boyfriend wanted the car. Her prize, as third runner-up, had been $500 and a Catalina sports wardrobe.

A barking dog brought her back to the present. It was Warrior, running across the rear yard, barking furiously.

Maybe Brad felt bad and had decided to come back, to take her out for a drink or a ride on his Yamaha.

She went to the living room and looked out the front window. No motorcycle. All she saw was a dark car several houses down slowly pulling away from the curb. She let the sheers fall back and went to the sliding glass door in the dining room.

"Warrior!" she called.

The dog raced around the corner of the house, tail wagging with excitement, and charged inside. Tammy knelt down and hugged him. Warrior yipped happily, licking her face and bumping against her. "We don't ask for much, do we, ol' boy?" she said, patting his oscillating backside. "Just a little attention now and then. Just a little love and affection, and to know we're appreciated."

Warrior whined in agreement.

Six

Amelia

Amelia slowly scanned the vacant executive suite. A frown marred her classic features. With long strides, she walked across the large office, high heels sinking into the gray wool carpeting. She reached the windows and looked down. Nineteen floors below on Clay Street people scurried about as traffic moved west in stops and starts.

"You feel we can afford *this?*" she asked Fletcher Kincade, her breath fogging a patch of the tinted window.

Fletcher, thirty years old, five foot eleven — only slightly taller than Amelia if she wore medium heels — had a boyish face with keen, intelligent brown eyes. His sandy blond hair curled over the top of his dress shirt. Today he was dressed in an expensive light blue suit.

"We have to. We need the address if we want this business to fly."

"There are perfectly good addresses in lower rent areas. Christ, Fletch, this is the heart of the financial district."

"I know that, Amelia," he replied coolly.

"Look, honey, I don't mean to challenge your expertise in these matters, but we really don't have all that much capital. My eighty thousand would melt away in no time just paying for office space in this neighborhood."

"Don't forget I'm matching that eighty grand. Amelia, we agreed I would handle the business end. It has to be the best of everything or it's doomed from the start. Global Model Enterprises will be the biggest agency of its kind, internationally, and we can't do that by opening our doors in some tacky, low-rent district.

"Once we've set up shop, the out-of-pocket money will be minimal. The models work outside the office. We send them to Carl Santos for their agency photos. He's willing to do work on the same pay procedure as the models — when the client pays us, we pay them. The only way we can pull that off is to look like we've already arrived. With aplomb, savoir faire."

"Well . . . ," she said tentatively, still staring out the window.

Fletcher crossed to her and embraced her from behind. "With ten years experience in this business, I think I know what I'm doing. Now if you're concerned about your money, if you're having second thoughts . . ."

"Of course I'm not having second thoughts," she snapped. She felt his arms around her stiffen. Patting his hand, she said quietly, sweetly, "I trust you. The money is nothing. I just want it to work. It *has* to work."

She lied about the money being nothing. It was everything. In her eighteen years of marriage to Matthew she had begged and stolen from him to amass her nest egg — her freedom money. Each and every dollar she'd had to hustle for was one dollar closer to emancipation. Early on she had begun to invest in blue chip stocks and it had proven to be a wise move. But it was still risky and too slow. Fletcher had the experience, the contacts and the savvy to make it work. All she had to do was match his eighty thousand dollars. The day she could tell Matthew to go to hell was a day she looked forward to with great exhilaration.

"Seventy models are signed, and a handful more are interested. We've got IBM and Coca-Cola as corporate clients, not to mention the dozen or so smaller companies that have agreed to contract with us."

With a thin smile, Amelia nodded.

Fletcher tucked his chin in the indentation of her collarbone. "I wish you could divorce that asshole now and marry me. I get sick just thinking about the two of you together, his slimy hands on you."

"That makes two of us."

"How do you stay?"

"I have no choice. Not yet, anyway. Until the business starts making money and I can stand on my own, I'm stuck with him. I can't live long on eighty thousand dollars. And that's all there would be since I signed a premarital agreement."

"You get nothing? This is a community property state. Fifty-fifty split."

"He has it all tied up in 'sole and separate' property. Believe me, he knew what he was doing; after all, he was an attorney before becoming a superior judge. I'm entitled to ten thousand dollars, my car, clothes, furs, and any jewelry he bought me, that's it."

"Jewelry?"

"I've long ago had the real stones replaced with glass and converted into cash."

"You're a shrewd woman."

"Survival." She smiled, running a fingernail along his jaw-line.

"Can you get away this weekend? Let's take off Friday afternoon and tour the wine country."

"Ummm, sounds good—oh, damn, I can't. I just remembered I'm scheduled to go on 'City Gallery.' The taping is Friday afternoon. I had hoped to use that spot for free advertising, but since they moved the show up nearly a month, it's impossible now. I don't want Matthew to have even a hint that I'm going into business. He'll do something to spoil it; to make me totally dependent on him again. If that happens, I might as well be dead."

"Talk to your friend on Friday. If she can get us on a future show, we'll plug the hell out of the business and the Honorable Corde can take a fucking leap."

The real estate agent stuck her head in the doorway. "Need more time?"

"Give us another minute," Fletcher said to the agent. He turned back to Amelia. "Well?"

She smiled up at him. "You know what's best."

"You won't be sorry," he said.

I better not be, she wanted to say. "I sold the stock last week. I pick up the check tomorrow."

Fletcher kissed her. "Good. Then I'll open the escrow account. But for now I'll go with the agent back to her office and sign the lease papers. I'll take care of the deposit. You go back to my place and get ready for me."

"I like this business arrangement already," she said in a low voice.

They walked toward the door. Amelia stopped, looking around the room. "When the money starts to pour in, I want to redecorate. I have the most wonderful ideas for this suite."

They parted in front of the building. Amelia walked the three blocks to Drumm, where the Mercedes was parked at a meter. She lit one of her long, slim cigarettes, started the car and pulled out quickly amid a barrage of honking, and merged into the traffic.

As she drove toward the marina, she thought about a weekend with her lover. If they left immediately after the taping on Friday afternoon, they could be across the Golden Gate Bridge and be on their way to the wine country within minutes. Getting away from her husband was no problem. All she had to do was invite Matthew to go to Napa for a visit with her parents. He loathed her parents and he was certain to refuse.

Thinking of her parents made her think of how she had met Matthew Corde. He was one of five judges for the Miss Classic Pageant, and although twenty-year-old Amelia seduced him, as well as the other male judge, she had failed to win the title; had only gotten as close as second runner-up. After Corinne's tragic incident, the crown and title were passed on to the first runner-up, who, fortunately for Amelia, declined the honor.

The top prizes of wardrobe, fur, cash, and new car had already been awarded to Corinne and, in all good conscience, could not be taken away. This Amelia understood with complete agreement. She would never take anything second-hand. She insisted upon, and was granted, duplicates of all the prizes befitting the queen of the pageant.

The most coveted prize had been a screen test at a major

studio in Hollywood. Amelia had taken the test, and been told she showed great promise, but before the contract could be drawn up, the financially faltering studio was swallowed up by a larger, more prosperous one. Her numerous calls went unreturned. In the twelve-month reign, stigmatized by the attack on Corinne, Amelia had been called upon to appear at only a handful of inconsequential functions. Seeing only one way out of her barren, small-town existence, she married the wealthy attorney, Matthew Corde, and moved into his opulent estate in Pacific Heights. She had agreed to the premarital condition because, eventually, she always got her way. "Manipulation" and "persuasion" were words designed for her. There was not a doubt in her mind that once she got Matthew to say "I do," she could get him to say and do anything. On her wedding day she vowed that before their first anniversary he would void that ridiculous agreement.

In less than a week, she realized with utter disbelief as she sped toward the marina, they would celebrate their nineteenth anniversary.

2

He waited. The parking garage was dim and cool, chilly actually; but dressed in wool slacks, sweater, and long coat, with the adrenaline racing through his veins, he hardly noticed the cold. Squatting between two parked cars near the elevator, he donned the black stocking and knit cap. From his pocket he carefully removed the jar. He was certain she would come. In just a short time he'd learned where each one of the women lived and worked, what their routines and daily schedules were. This was Amelia Corde's day to romp with her lover.

3

Amelia left her car in the basement of Fletcher's building and walked, her heels echoing hollowly on the concrete, to the elevator. As she stood waiting for the elevator, squeezing her flat handbag tightly to her side, she shivered from the cold.

"Come on, you damn elevator," she whispered under her breath, looking up at the lights above the doors. She hated these dark parking garages. She jabbed impatiently at the button, shifting from one foot to another. Taking her clutch purse from under her arm, she opened it and took out her keys, finding the one to Fletcher's apartment.

A scraping sound, soles on concrete echoing eerily in the garage, alerted her that she was not alone. She whirled around, and suddenly someone was there, a terrifying figure in black. She got little more than a glimpse of him as his arm swung out from behind his back, coming toward her. She cried out, pulling back, and instinctively thrust her clutch bag in front of her face. The sound of something wet splashed against the leather. A scream, nearly inaudible, escaped from her throat. At her back the elevator door opened and she stumbled inside. The man in black reached out. *He wants the purse,* she told herself rationally, fighting the terror. *Don't be stupid. Let him have it.*

Amelia threw the purse out into the garage and slapped at the elevator buttons. The man in black twisted around at the sound of the leather bag hitting the concrete floor, then turned back to her. The doors were closing as Amelia backed into the corner, one hand striking out blindly with the keys, the other hand over her face; and mercifully, when she had the nerve to look, the doors had closed and she was alone.

Over the clamoring of her heart, she felt the elevator moving. Would he be waiting for her when it stopped on the second floor? He had her purse, but when he saw there was no money or credit cards inside, would he come after her jewelry? She looked down at her wedding ring, a massive tangle of gold and glittering diamonds, and her emerald-cut ruby ring — no longer real stones in either, but the mugger couldn't know that. She moaned, trying to catch her breath. Her heart thumped painfully in her chest, the movement visible beneath the soft knit of her dress. The elevator stopped. When the door opened a moment later, Amelia was rigidly poised, both rings in the palm of one hand — to be given over readily if need be. In the other hand she gripped a sharp key tightly for protection should he want more than the rings.

The man in black was nowhere to be seen.

She rushed from the elevator and down the corridor to Fletcher's apartment. An instant later, she was inside, slamming the door and locking it. Her mind raced. A mugger! She had actually been accosted by a mugger; her purse had been stolen. She had to report it to the police, she thought, slipping her rings back on. Oh God, no, she couldn't. She would have to tell them where it had happened and Matthew would want to know what she was doing, who she was seeing, at this apartment building. Besides, what would she gain by reporting it? There was little of value in her handbag. Makeup, cigarettes and lighter, driver's license, certainly no cash or credit cards.

She felt traces of something wet on her jacket and she grimaced. God only knew what vile stuff had come from that pervert, she thought with a shudder of revulsion. Amelia pulled off the jacket and threw it on the floor. She angrily scrubbed her hands at the bathroom sink, thinking that in addition to losing her purse, something had been tossed on a very expensive outfit. She poured a neat glass of vodka and paced until Fletcher came in an hour later.

"My God, darling, you could have been killed," he said after she told him about the man in the garage. He wrapped his arms around her. "Are you sure he didn't hurt you?"

She was shaking uncontrollably now. Fletcher's concern made her aware of what a close encounter she had had. When she calmed down enough to be left alone, Fletcher went out to retrace her steps. In minutes he was back. No sign of her purse or a man in black, he reported.

They decided, after discussing it at length, that due to the clandestine nature of their relationship, it was best to pretend it never happened.

Seven

Regina

The light on Regina Van Raven's telephone blinked, indicating a caller was holding. She finished up on another line and glanced at the desk clock. Damn, she was going to be late. It was Monday, and Kristy, going straight from work at the Farm House Restaurant, was to meet her at the new apartment to measure the windows and floors. Regina had a key, Kristy didn't.

She punched the lighted button. "Van Raven speaking," she said impatiently.

"That show about the beauty contestants . . ." a low voice began, pausing.

"Yes, what about it?"

"Maybe it shouldn't."

"Shouldn't what?"

"Go on."

Regina rolled her eyes upward and mouthed the word "Lord." Her patience was stretched to the max. "And why not, pray tell?"

"History has a way of repeating itself," he said. Regina was about to cut him off when she heard him ask, "Will Corinne Odett be there? Only one side of her face is burned, shall we try for the other side?"

Regina sat up, her eyes darting around the open production department. She wanted someone to get on an extension and hear this. The only other person in the area was Tom Gansing, the director, and he had his back to her.

"What do you know about Corinne?" Regina asked. She wadded a piece of paper and threw it toward Tom. It fell short, unnoticed.

The line disconnected.

Just as Regina slammed down the receiver Donna appeared, sipping from a bottle of seltzer. "Reg, what's the matter?"

"Someone has a long memory. That was a call about this Friday's show."

"The 'Classic' format?"

"Yes. It sounded like a threat."

Donna stood silently staring at Regina. Then: "Another attack?"

Regina shrugged.

"Man or woman?" Donna asked.

"I couldn't tell. The voice was deep, gravelly."

"A crank, maybe?"

"Sure, it's possible. But what if it isn't?"

"What's possible?" Nolan asked, joining Donna.

"Regina just got a phone threat of some sort. Tell him, Reg."

Regina repeated what the caller had said.

"A kook," Nolan said, grinning. "Forget it."

Donna, her face showing concern, turned to her husband. "Honey, maybe we should discuss it. If Reggie's anxious about it—"

Nolan cut her off. "If it happens again, then we'll discuss it. Okay?"

Donna looked to Regina. Regina sighed. She opened the bottom drawer, pulled out her purse, and stood. Talking to Nolan was a waste of time, she thought. He would welcome threats, even a grisly follow-through if it would boost the ratings. In fact, she wouldn't put it past Nolan to have made the call himself.

Then again, perhaps she was overreacting. They received crank calls all the time. It was her job to deal with them, so why was she making a big fuss over this one? Because, she

65

realized, the subject was much too close to her.

Regina patted Donna's shoulder. "Gotta go. I'm late."

Ten minutes later Regina pulled up to the curb in front of the apartment house behind Kristy's white Rabbit convertible. The top was down and there was no one inside. The dashboard clock read 4:18. Kristy was probably waiting inside the vestibule, she thought, out of the sun. They would have to remember to get the other key from Mrs. Szabo today.

The vestibule was empty. Regina used her key to open the door into the building's wide hall. She climbed the stairs to the second floor. The door to their apartment was ajar and the beat of rock music pounded out into the landing.

Regina pushed through the door, hurried inside, and jabbed at a button on the radio to silence it. She called out to Kristy.

"Hi, Mom. In here," Kristy called back from another part of the apartment, her voice echoing through the empty rooms.

Regina found Kristy and her best friend, Sonya, in the smaller of the two bedrooms. Both girls, still wearing their calico waitress uniforms, had books on their heads and were gingerly crossing the room like tightrope walkers.

"Are you trying to get us thrown out before we even move in? The door's open and the radio's blasting through the place. This is supposed to be a quiet—"

"The door was closed, Mom," Kristy cut in, letting the book drop into her outstretched hands.

"It was *open*."

"I know it was closed because John shut it himself when he went out."

"It was op—*who's John?*"

"John Davie. He's the guy who let us in."

"He let you into the building?"

Kristy nodded. "And into our apartment."

"How the hell does he have a key to our place?" Regina asked incredulously, beginning to feel something between anger and fear.

"He's on good terms with the landlady. I think he's the

66

grandson or nephew or something like that. He gave me the key."

"Oh." Regina felt her muscles unbunching in degrees.

"He's really hot looking. He's about this tall . . . ," she raised a hand several inches above her own head, "and he has dark hair and light blue eyes."

"And there's this groove in the center of his chin," Sonya interjected.

"A cleft," Regina corrected.

"More like a groove," Kristy said. "He's got a rad form too."

"Yeah? Does he go to school around here?"

"He's old, Mom."

"How old?"

" 'Bout your age," Kristy said, and throwing her arms up over her face as if to ward off a blow, she giggled.

"Cute."

"I gotta go. I'm working the split shift. Love your new place, you two," Sonya said, hurrying out.

"Let's get to work." Regina took a tape measure from her purse and stepped to the window.

After measuring all the windows they moved into the living room and stretched the tape across the wood floor.

"It'll fit." Regina was referring to the new cranberry area rug. "Corbin's is delivering the furniture tomorrow."

"This is so much fun," Kristy said. "Mother and daughter decorating together. It's a first."

Regina was as excited as her daughter. When she'd married Leo, he was already established in the big Victorian house in Berkeley with his beloved antiques. She'd sold it all with no remorse, and mother and daughter, sharing a wild compulsion to go light, bright, and cheerful, had gravitated to a contemporary decor; floral designs on plump cushions in cranberry, green, and ivory. For the walls they'd chosen numbered prints and watercolors depicting spring garden florals, bustling street scenes, and cityscapes.

Regina looked around the bright, sunny room with its gleaming hardwood floors. Funny, she thought, how one could live in darkness, like a mole, and be perfectly content.

But now that she had seen the light, so to speak, she wondered how she had managed to exist in such drab surroundings all those years. She couldn't wait to move into the new apartment, with the new furniture, and her new bed and towels and potholders and . . . and new *everything*.

"Mom?"

"Hmm?"

"Can we discuss the model search?"

Regina felt herself sink back into darkness.

"I know it was wrong not to tell you. But I was afraid you'd say no. C'mon, Mom, let's talk about it, okay?"

Regina sat beside Kristy on the windowsill, her hands hanging limp between her legs. "Why do you want to do this, Kris?"

Kristy shrugged. "To see if I'm pretty enough."

Kristy had been born beautiful. Even in her gangling, orthodontal stage, she had been exceptional. She was tall, five foot nine, with a slim, near-perfectly proportioned body. Her shoulder-length, sandy brown hair shone with natural ash highlights. Kristy had inherited her father's light gray eyes. Her full, wide mouth was like her mother's. Strangers on the street stared openly as they passed, some stopping to compliment her. Kristy would blush and laugh self-consciously. She didn't have a conceited bone in her body.

"I would have expected a better reason than that from you. Kris, you're beautiful. So there, now you know."

"Mother," she said in exasperation. "You did it when you were my age. What was your reason?"

Regina stared out the window and said nothing.

"Wasn't it fun?" Kristy prompted.

"There were problems."

"What kind of problems?"

"Weird things. Some serious, some not."

"Like what?"

"Oh, Kris . . ." Regina sighed.

"Tell me. Please."

"Well, the first night there was a banquet for all the contestants. Everyone who ate the seafood salad got food poisoning. I

68

was one of them. During the swimsuit competition one of the girls passed out on the runway, fell off the platform and broke her arm in two places. Another girl overdosed on some sort of drug and nearly died. The list goes on." Regina paused. "And then there was Corinne."

"That could never happen again, Mom."

Regina looked at her daughter and marveled at her beauty — innocent beauty, the purest kind. "How deep into this are you?"

"Sonya and I made the first cut."

"What's it about?"

"The winner will promote tourism for the city for one year. Billboards, TV flyers, magazines. She'll represent San Francisco and all its splendor. Besides, five thousand dollars, a contract with a top model agency, and a new car is nothing to scoff at, Mother."

"Five thousand?" Regina asked, surprised.

"And a car, a 300 ZX. That's only the beginning. There's the money earned on appearances, modeling assignments and commercials," she said. "It's not as if I'm asking to do porn or even a nude layout in a girlie mag."

"I know, but . . ."

"Mom, you take things too seriously. Being attractive isn't a handicap. And no matter how much you try to camouflage what *you* have under those guerrilla fatigues or hide your beauty under a bushel . . . ," Kristy flipped a frizzy lock of her mother's hair, "it's still very obvious."

Regina allowed herself a quick smile before becoming somber again. She picked at a loose thread on her skirt. "The Miss Classic contest was jinxed, and, well, I have this bad feeling . . ." She thought of Corinne and what the acid had done to her beautiful face, and then she thought about the crank call she'd received less than two hours ago. But most crucial of all was the gut feeling she had about the whole affair. Something in the back of her mind screamed *danger*. Something she just couldn't ignore.

"Feelings are just that — *feelings*. Unless you're psychic . . ." Kristy let the words trail off.

Regina sighed. "Yes, of course, you're right."

They sat without speaking for several moments. "Mom, it's not going to happen again."

"I'll make a deal with you," Regina said, pushing away from the windowsill. "Take a couple of days to think about what I said, and if you still want to go through with this, then . . . well, you have my blessing."

Kristy stood and gave her mother a hug. "Thanks, you wonderful, adorable mother."

It was obvious to Regina that Kristy's mind was already made up. Well, it hadn't killed her, so she guessed it wouldn't kill her daughter.

Eight

John

Falwell stared down at the dead eyes of the long-legged beauty and grinned maliciously#!@#?

"Ah shit!" John hissed in disgust.

Everything he'd written that day, John thought, had the ring of a damn clichéd, two-bit detective novel. He took his fingers from the computer keyboard and brusquely scraped a mound of red pistachio shells into the waste basket.

John Davie struggled with his fourth suspense novel. His first manuscript had sold to a small press, then died. His second had been published, but despite a rather handsome advance and decent reviews, sales had not been as great as he hoped. *False Lead,* his last completed manuscript, was about to be released; but this novel, the one he was working on, was to be the blockbuster. He'd written an explosive beginning and the end was equally volatile, but the middle, like the center of a doughnut, was missing.

His fingers poised over the keyboard like predator claws, waiting. The blinking cursor was impatiently prompting him to write something—anything. He leaned forward and meticulously pecked out with a forefinger, in caps, FUCK YOU, then highlighted it in yellow. Rapid-fire now, with both hands on the keys, he repeated the two words across the page until they begin to run together. A series of low creaks overhead made him pause. He dropped his hands to his sides, tipped his chair back, and looked upward.

The new tenants, mother and daughter, were up there doing "getting ready to move into a new apartment" things.

He groaned. His concentration was shot. Anything he wrote that afternoon; he realized, would be forced and stilted. He shut down the computer.

A door softly closed above. John rose and moved to the front window. Directly in front of the white VW Rabbit was the tan station wagon. Minutes later he watched mother and daughter cross the walk to the cars. They stood talking, unknowingly allowing John an opportunity to study them. His attention kept returning to the older one.

In spite of the loose, layered clothing, the lack of makeup, and the uninspiring hairdo, the mother had a certain air about her. John felt that her obscureness was merely a masquerade. She was a very alluring woman.

Where the hell had he seen her before?

He watched them until they entered their respective cars and drove away, his brain still searching for an answer. Forget it for now, he told himself, it'll come. He leaned his head against the window sash and let his mind drift. In an instant, like a multicolored collage, he saw slick images of another striking woman, though this one had blond hair and bright blue eyes. Darlene. Beautiful, sensual Darlene. Fashion model, wife, and mother, dead these past seven years. Time heals all wounds.

He glanced at his watch. It was time to get ready for work.

After a quick shower, John dressed in a pair of dark cotton slacks, a white dress shirt, and a plain dark necktie. He grabbed his leather bomber jacket and went out the door.

He walked the eight blocks to The Bull's Blood on Van Ness, his aunt and uncle's bar. The childless couple, Anna and Charlie Szabo, treated him like a favorite son. In return for their love and kindness, John helped out around the apartment house and tended bar at night. He wrote during the day.

Entering the bar, he saw a smattering of the usual customers. His Uncle Charlie was talking to Babs, the cocktail waitress who waited the seven tables and the piano bar.

"Your Aunt Anna called and said you didn't stop for dinner," Charlie said when John joined him behind the bar. "Why?"

"Wasn't hungry. Besides, I was running late."

"You don't take money from me for tending bar, yet you rush all the time to get here, and then you stay late."

"I told you, it's a rich source for my novels. I'm grateful you don't make me pay to work here." John nodded toward a booth in the back where two lovers were brazenly making out, hands out of sight under the table, then at two denim-clad men arm wrestling at the far end of the bar. "Look, there's romance, adventure, and . . . and local color." He waved at Rosemond, a tall, bony transvestite with an eccentric taste in clothing, who had just sauntered in. Tonight "Rosy" was wearing an Oakland A's baseball cap, a red miniskirt over badly snagged chartreuse tights, black Keds hightop sneakers, and a pink see-through voile blouse. "It's all here, Charlie. Mood, background, characters—"

"Characters we got," Charlie replied, grunting. "Ahhgh, get something to eat. Go across to Dobos' and order a good Hungarian meal."

John shook his head. "Later."

"Go now, while there's no business. Louie has added something. Tell me what you think.

"Added what?"

"Go see. Bring me back dessert. *Palacsinta,*" his uncle called over his shoulder as he headed down the bar to Rosy.

John crossed Van Ness to Dobos', a Hungarian restaurant run by old friends of the Szabos. His aunt Anna and Mrs. Dobos had both come from small villages near Budapest.

The interior of the restaurant was dim and it took his eyes a moment to adjust. Someone approached him, a woman, and though he couldn't make out the face yet, he knew it wasn't the rotund Mrs. Dobos. This woman was tall and slim and walked like a fashion model on a runway.

"Good evening," a soft voice said. The accent was heavy and Hungarian.

Before he could respond, Louie Dobos seemed to come out

73

of nowhere, his voice booming, "Johnnie, Johnnie, hey Johnnie! Good to see you. What you think of our new hostess?" He hooked an arm around the girl's shoulder and pulled her to him. "Pretty, huh? My grandniece Ilona. From the old country."

John's eyes had made the adjustment and he saw that the blond girl was indeed very pretty. She smiled, then looked away shyly.

"Johnnie's a famous writer," Louie said to Ilona.

"Oh, I wouldn't say that."

"Come in, Johnnie." Louie threw his other arm around John's shoulder and steered them into the empty dining area. "It's early, you take any table you want."

John pointed to a small table by the kitchen, but Louie practically pushed him down into a large booth just inside the room, only steps from the hostess station.

"Ilona will take good care of you. *Paprikas* is best tonight," Louie said, then marched off toward the kitchen, leaving them alone.

So, John thought, Ilona was the "something new" his uncle had spoken of. No doubt the girl was straight off the boat and looking to stay, and marriage to an American was the simplest method.

John smiled at Ilona. She returned his smile, and a radiant smile it was.

The long arm of the matchmaker had reached out for its victim.

Nine

Corinne

Corinne finished the beer, tossed the can on the floor, then popped the top of another. Somewhat unsteadily she slid back the closet door. As she silently stared inside, contemplating the contents, she took a drag on the cigarette. Ashes fell across the front of her soiled, wrinkled shift.

It was all there, untouched for nearly twenty years: the Miss Classic wardrobe her mother had hung in the closet for her daughter to wear when she was normal again.

Corinne reached out and touched the sleeve of a burnt orange dress. She pushed it aside and pulled out a houndstooth skirt and jacket. Funny, she thought, how fashions have a way of coming around again. Just yesterday she'd seen Sandy on "The Young and the Restless" wearing an outfit almost identical to the one she held.

She put the jacket to her nose and sniffed. It was hard to tell, her sense of smell wasn't so good anymore, but she thought it smelled musty and smoky.

Flicking ashes on the floor, she stripped the outfit from the hanger and hurried into the kitchen, where she tossed the two pieces into the washing machine.

If it didn't shrink to nothing, it would fit. Over the years she had lost weight. Eating was such a hassle. What weight she managed to keep on was a direct result of all the beer and her daily inactivity in front of the TV.

Between sips of beer, she rolled her freshly washed hair on large metal rollers she had rooted out of the back of the closet. Although the taping for "City Gallery" wasn't scheduled until the following afternoon, she wanted to practice. It had been a long time.

In the bathroom she opened the white paper bag. Her hands shook as one by one she lifted out the tubes, jars, and plastic cases that she'd ordered over the phone. That morning the Avon lady, dressed in bright yellow with a striking array of iridescent eyeshadow from lashes to brows, had delivered it.

Before starting, she popped another Quaalude. Then, working with great care and trepidation, wetting her dry throat with the beer that gave her a warm buzz, she began.

Ninety minutes later, her legs beginning to feel the fatigue of standing, she added the final touches to her face. She had considered wearing one of her eye patches—after all, the patch in itself was a bold fashion statement—but the eye makeup was much too pretty to hide. Following a dusting of Sun Poppy blusher, she outlined her lips, then filled them in with a matching shade of lipstick.

She removed the rollers and brushed her shoulder-length hair until it crackled with electricity. She sprayed the brush with hair spray, a trick she remembered from a time before, and brushed through again, controlling the wispy strands. Holding up a glossy eight-by-ten photograph of herself, taken before the pageant, she worked diligently to achieve a similar hairstyle. One side was swept up and away from her face, the other side fell in waves along the side. It was done.

She closed her eyes, fighting an inebriated wave of dizziness that washed over her, and stepped back several feet. She turned her head to the left, tipped her chin down, lifted her mouth into a coquettish smile, and, opening her eyes, shifting them sideways, she looked into the mirror. It took a moment to focus. She was startled by the effect. More than that, she was astonished. It wasn't possible. No, it just wasn't possible.

Looking back at her was the Corinne of a lifetime ago. Her heart pounded. Her hands trembled.

"Oh, God. Oh, my God," she whispered reverently.

Unable to contain her excitement, she snatched up the can of beer, knocking jars of makeup into the sink, and finished it off, her mind whirling.

All these years she had hated herself. The surgery, admittedly, had made some improvements, but her problem, she realized now, had been compounded by her own damning perfectionism. She had expected too much, had been too hard on herself, had brought on her own failure by refusing to even try to compromise. She had stubbornly adopted the attitude that if she couldn't be perfect, like before, she would be nothing.

Neither stupid nor blind — though definitely tipsy — she could still see the scars and facial damage. And, naturally, the years had taken their toll overall. But it was all relative, wasn't it? Wishing for lost youth and beauty was so damned unrealistic.

Corinne thought about the others. Donna, Tammy, Amelia and Regina. Of all the contestants in the contest, Corinne had feared Regina the most. She had something special that was more than skin deep. When the two of them had stood side by side on the stage, clinging to each other anxiously, waiting for the emcee to name the winner, Corinne had felt an instant choking panic. And then her name had been announced, and suddenly everyone was whistling and cheering, the contestants were hugging her, the crown was being fastened to her head, she thought she would die of happiness . . .

And God, oh dear merciful God, why had *she* been chosen? Why not Regina instead?

Stop it! she told herself. No more negative thoughts. It's over and done with. It can't be changed. Take what's offered now and make a new life for yourself.

In the kitchen she pulled the houndstooth outfit from the dryer, shook it out, and, tossing her shift aside, hastily put on the skirt and cropped jacket. It was loose, but everyone was wearing clothes large these days. She ran into her bedroom and rummaged in her closet for shoes. She found a pair of black patent leather pumps with short heels.

Hopping on first one foot, then the other, she slipped them

on her bare feet. She'd have to buy hose, and shoulder pads, but that was no problem. Nothing was a problem anymore. She'd go to the store, any store she wanted. No more deliveries to the house. No more going without. She hugged herself and spun around, laughing and crying until she had worked herself into a coughing spasm.

She stopped abruptly, gasping. The pain in her lungs concerned her little, it was the fear of ruining the makeup that forced her to gain control. The makeup and its miraculous effects were essential to boosting her confidence. If she planned to go on that show tomorrow, she needed all the confidence she could muster. Twenty years of zero confidence . . .

Twenty wasted years.

"Corinne? What's going on out there? You having some kinda fit?"

Her father. She'd forgotten about the old man. She glanced at the clock on her dresser. It was way past his mealtime.

"Bring an aspirin with my meal. My leg's hurting bad. Cory?"

"I hear you, Daddy," she called out pleasantly. She was too happy to let him spoil her euphoric mood. From now on she would treat him better. There was no reason to be bitter toward him anymore. He was an old man, sick and bedridden with a bum heart and a leg amputated at the knee from complications brought on by diabetes.

Back in the kitchen she made his lunch — a tuna sandwich, a sectioned orange, and a diet Dr. Pepper. She got two aspirin and readied the syringe for his injection.

Looking around the kitchen, she realized how filthy it was. A garbage heap. Dirty dishes crowded the sink and countertops. Trash spilled over the top of a tall wastebasket, filling one corner. The entire joint was a dump. And smelled like one. There was little that could be done about their cheap, plasterboard house, but she could get the inside in shape again like it'd been when her mother was alive.

Walking slowly, the heels of her black pumps wobbling with each step, she carried the tray into her father's room. Without looking at him, she crossed the room to the night table and put

78

down the tray. She could feel him staring at her and she waited in agonized silence for him to say something. Finally, after what seemed an eternity, she met his gaze.

The look on his face was almost comical. His mouth hung open and his red-rimmed eyes, beneath busy, furrowed brows, were filled with shock and disbelief.

She smiled.

He blinked.

She lifted the Dr. Pepper and aspirin and held them out to him.

He ignored them. Then he began to laugh, a low chuckle deep in his throat.

She stiffened. "What the hell's so funny?" she snapped.

"Send in the clowns," he sang out.

She dropped the aspirin on his bed and lightly touched her face. "You're just not used to it. It took me a minute to—"

"A minute? A minute? You wasn't expectin' to go out like that, was you?"

She glared at him.

"Girl, are you a complete fool? Look at yerself. No, not now," he said, when she turned to leave the room. "Wait till you're sober, then have a good long look."

"You're just being mean."

"Lookit yer goddamn eye. Did'ya think no one'd notice that?"

"I'll wear the patch . . ."

Again he laughed dryly, then became solemn. "Cory, your hair . . ."

"What's wrong with it?"

"That cute littl' trick with the waves and curls only makes it worse."

She touched the hair at her temples.

"What's got into you? Christ almighty, daughter, don't you understand? It ain't the eye. It ain't the scars," he said in a quiet voice filled with pity, "It's that ridiculous hairdo and that shitty paint slapped all over yer face. I don't mean to hurt 'cha, Cory. I just don't want you making a fool of yerself and your ol' man. Go wash it off. Wash it off and comb your hair right

79

and forget this crazy notion that . . ." His words trailed off.

"I hate you," she whispered. A rage welled up inside her, destroying the wonderful, dreamy cloud on which, only moments ago, she had floated. A stark, painful realization began to creep in.

She staggered back, dropping the Dr. Pepper to the floor. Foam and amber liquid shot upward across her skirt and jacket. "God, I hate you! It's all your fault I look like this! If you hadn't been such a fucking loser, I'd be normal today! I hate you, I hate you with everything that's inside me. I wish you'd die!" And with that she grabbed the syringe of insulin off the tray and ran from the room.

"Cory, bring that back here!" her father shouted.

In the bathroom, Corinne stepped to the mirror and, without any coy tactics this time, seeing through his eyes, glared hard at herself. Her stomach knotted painfully.

The rose-colored foundation, unblended at the jawline, looked as though it had been put on with a trowel. Clumps of the heavy concealer stood out on the raised, puckered skin. Her eyelids, upper and lower, glittered raccoonlike with rainbow dust. Bright lipstick was pasted on an overly outlined mouth.

Her hair, so meticulously teased and styled, swept forward across her face, covering most of the disfigured portion from hairline to throat.

"Oh, sweet Jesus," she whispered hoarsely, as she dragged the back of her arm across her red lips.

"Cory," her father called out. "Now don't be foolish. Bring me my insulin, honey. I gotta have it, y'know. *Cory?*"

Corinne threw the syringe in the toilet and flushed it down.

Ten

1

Amelia pressed the kohl eyeliner pencil to a tiny brown spot located to the right of her mouth and transformed a mole into a beauty mark. Studying herself in the mirror, she was pleased with the way Garson had worked her dark, mahogany-tinted hair into a dramatic upsweep; sleek and smooth both back and sides, yet full and curly on top. She gave it a final spritz of hair spray.

She'd booked the entire morning at the La Dolce Salon for a massage, manicure and pedicure, a facial, and lastly, hair color and styling, to which all had been billed to Matthew's credit card. Also billed but not received was a permanent wave; the returned cash, her rebate as she so fondly called it, was tucked securely in her eyeglass case. And now, at one o'clock, just hours before the taping of "City Gallery," she sat at her vanity in an ivory teddy applying the finishing touches.

Everything must be perfect, she told herself. For her future success, she wanted her appearance on the TV show to be both spectacular and memorable.

Open on the bed were her crimson weekender bag and matching tote. She had done most of the packing earlier that morning for her trip with Fletcher to the wine country. They had booked a room at the Meadowvale Inn in Napa for tonight and Saturday night. Stubbing out her thin cigarette, she rose, tossed her jewelry case into the bag, then strolled into the enormous walk-in closet that she shared with Matthew.

With the new dress in one hand and the snakeskin pumps in the other, Amelia sensed someone nearby. She turned sharply, startled by the man in the doorway.

"My God, Matt." She put a hand to her chest, feeling the pounding underneath her fingers. Since the man in black had accosted her five days ago, she had been seeing menacing shapes in all the shadows. "Don't sneak up on me like that."

"I'm sorry. I didn't mean to scare you."

"What are you doing home so early? I thought you'd go straight from the courthouse to the club. Don't you have gin rummy tonight? — it's Friday."

He moved forward, reaching out to touch the dress. "Is this what you bought to wear on the show today?"

She nodded. "Do you like it?"

His fingers flicked at the peplum skirt, then slowly moved along its hem to the price tag. He lifted the tag and scrutinized it. "Very much. Your taste, as always, is impeccable."

"Thank you, dear," she said with a slight tightness in her voice. "And your generosity is without parallel."

"Do I get a kiss for the dress and the shoes and — what was it today, the entire beauty works at La Dolce's?"

She tried to make her smile warm, sincere, but she sensed it came off stiff and unnatural. Leaning forward, she kissed his mouth lightly, careful not to smear her lipstick.

Matthew's arms came around her, pulling her to him. His mouth covered hers in a wet, rough, tongue-searching kiss.

The lipstick could be repaired, she thought, trying to remain calm. But when she felt his erection against her stomach she wanted to scream. He was kissing her with fervor now, and she knew there was no escaping what was to come. Saying no to Matthew had its ill consequences. It could mean doing without material goodies for as long as he was hurt by the rejection.

Matthew had unzipped his fly and was pulling at her teddy as he coaxed her to the floor.

Oh Christ, she despaired. Her hair! The intricate upsweep would be destroyed by the thick carpet and there would be no time to have it redone.

"Here. Standing up," she whispered in his ear, hoping at least to spare the coiffure. Naturally she'd have to shower and douche afterwards and fix her makeup, but if she hurried . . .

"I'm yours however you want me," he murmured.

Without another word, he let her undress him. She reached down, took hold of his erection, and guided him inside her, at the same time stealing a peek at her Gucci watch. Amelia knew it wouldn't take long. It never did with him.

Moments later Matthew neared climax. At his moment of glory, his hands came up to cup her face as his fingers wove in her hair, twisting. Amelia felt hair pins loosening. She pulled at his arms, but it was too late, he was beyond anything save fulfilling his own desires. He made a grunting noise, then dropped his hands.

A moment later he stepped back and opened his eyes. "Oh, I've mussed your hair," he said ruefully. "Can you fix it?"

Not trusting herself to speak, she nodded lamely, looking away.

"Well, good." He slipped on a magenta silk robe.

She hurried into the bathroom. When she glanced in the mirror over the double marble sink, she wanted to cry. Without a doubt, she was a total wreck. "Oh, how I hate you, Matthew Corde," she whispered to her mirrored image. "If you can't do me the favor of dropping dead, then at least have the decency to become impotent."

Long ago she had given up any hopes of burying him while she was still young and beautiful. They had no children and Matthew had no close relatives. Although she had never seen the will, and she trusted him as much as she loved him — which was not at all — he had indicated that everything he had was hers. But only if he died. Therein lay the catch. Knowing Matthew as she did, out of sheer meanness he would contrive to outlive her.

Half an hour later, sitting at her vanity, Amelia had managed to finish the repair work. The upsweep wasn't quite the same, but it would have to do. Matthew reclined on the bed, watching her.

"When will you return from visiting your parents?" he asked.

"Sunday evening. I wouldn't even go, but you know I have an obligation."

"Perhaps I'll go with you this time."

Amelia's throat became thick and constricted. In the mirror she watched a vein at the side of her neck throb wildly. "Go with me?"

"We could take the Rolls. The weather is good and, Lord knows I could use some time away from the courthouse."

She swiveled around to face him, forcing herself to look and act normal. "Yes, why don't you come? Mother and father would love to see you. In fact, cancel your card game and we'll leave as soon as I return from the taping." She smiled broadly. "Yes, Matthew, do."

He stared at her a moment, a pleased look on his face, then shook his head. "No. It was just an idea, and a bad one at that. Your father and I don't see eye to eye, as you well know. The man never could fully accede to me, or anyone for that matter, spoiling his little girl as he once did so extravagantly."

Amelia turned back to the mirror, thinking, *My dear and generous husband, if Daddy'd had your money, his little girl would have been spared two decades of vile subjugation as your wife.*

2

Her face and throat were on fire.

Tammy sucked in her breath as she cautiously stroked a cotton pad saturated with a solution of refrigerated witch hazel and white vinegar over her burning skin.

"That sonofabitch," she said between clenched teeth, though she knew she had no one but herself to blame.

Dr. Lampossi had given her a prescription for Retin-A, with instructions to use it with extreme caution. If a little was good, than a lot had to be better, she thought, as she liberally applied the cream twice as often as the instructions had stated. She also ignored his warnings of sunbathing.

84

"Sherry! Kerry!" she shouted. "C'mere a sec."

The twins came through the door together as though joined at the hip. They moved slowly into their mother's bedroom.

Tammy turned to face them. "Does it look any better?"

They glanced at each other before looking down at the tops of their matching Reeboks.

"Well?" Tammy asked impatiently. "Do I look like a lobster?"

They giggled. Sherry said, "You could never look like a lobster, Mom. They're second to nothing in the ugly department."

"You know what I mean," Tammy said. She had turned back to the mirror and was gingerly pressing fingertips into the bright pink flesh. "With makeup, it should be okay."

"You're not gonna put makeup on your burned face, are you, Mom?" Kerry asked incredulously.

"Of course I am. Don't be a lamebrain. All right, you two, go on, get outta here so I can get ready."

The twins hurried out.

From a prescription bottle in her medicine cabinet, Tammy shook out a painkiller. She swallowed it along with a Valium.

Taking her time, she curled her hair with a curling iron, shaved her legs and underarms, and plucked her eyebrows, giving the painkiller and Valium a chance to numb all her senses. Before putting on the makeup, she rinsed her face again and again in a sink filled with ice and water.

As she applied a liquid foundation, she fought back the tears. At last she was done. She combed out her pale blond hair and swept it up into a bright pink banana clip.

"Girls!" she called out.

They took longer to respond this time. But when they came through her doorway, their footsteps dragging, their expressions wary, they suddenly perked up.

"Wow, fantastic!" they said in unison.

Tammy sighed deeply, then smiled. "Really?"

"Honest." Sherry moved in closer leaning forward to stare at her mother's face. "Does it hurt?"

"Like a bitch."

Kerry came forward. "It looks like a sunburn."

"That's all it is," Tammy said matter-of-factly as she began to put on her clothes, "a sunburn. Silly me, I fell asleep while catching some rays."

She wriggled into a sleeveless, mini bodyskimmer in jade green leather. While Tammy crouched down, Sherry did up the zipper and fastened the clasp at the back of the mock turtleneck. She slipped on a pair of pink pumps, pink-and-jade drop earrings that nearly reached her shoulders, and a half dozen plastic bangles.

"Wow!" Kerry's eyes grew wide. "You look like Madonna."

"Yeah?" Tammy said with a wily grin, looking from one daughter to the other. "Not too young for me?"

"Uh-uh. No way," they said with nine-year-old naivete.

"So all's well. What's a little burn on the face — Right?"

3

When Regina left the station at noon to go home to her new apartment, she had no idea that at two o'clock she'd still be indecisive as to what she was going to wear for her television debut. She had planned to wear what she had put on that morning: a white camp shirt under a red safari jacket with a mid-calf, khaki skirt. Donna had teased her, saying the show was a look at yesterday's beauty contestants today, not an endorsement for a safari to Kenya.

Wearing her terry robe, she was tossing clothes on the bed when she heard Kristy come into the apartment. A moment later her daughter stood in the doorway, watching her.

"I knew you'd need me," Kristy said, crossing the room. She picked distastefully through the drab cotton skirts and khaki jackets, then took her mother by the hand and pulled. "Kristy to the rescue."

"What are you doing?"

"Follow me."

In Kristy's pastel room with the white wicker furniture and the floral chintz curtains and matching spread, she sorted

86

through the clothes in her closet.

"Let's get real," Regina said.

"We're the same size. Only I'm proud to be female." She held up a red miniskirted T-shirt dress, shook her head and put it back. She pulled out a three-piece ramie/cotton outfit. "Here we go. You love this."

"On you."

"Try it on."

Regina stared at Kristy for several moments before finally taking the offered outfit. She unzipped her robe, let it fall to the floor, then pulled the teal tee over her head. She stepped into the bronze sarong skirt and zipped it up. Over the two pieces went the jacquard-pattern jacket in a primitive print of bronze, teal, red, and yellow.

"Mom, it looks rad on you."

Regina eyed her skeptically. "Is that a compliment?"

"Have a look." She pointed to the full-length mirror on the back of the door.

Regina gazed into the mirror. She had to admit the outfit did look chic on her — or did she look chic in the outfit? She'd forgotten how thin she was. And she seldom wore skirts that showed all of her calves and a good portion of knee.

"Phase two," Kristy said.

Within minutes Regina was in the bathroom sitting on the clothes hamper as Kristy wound her hair on hot rollers before going to work on her face.

A half hour later Regina stood again at the full-length mirror. She was stunned by what she saw. But she wasn't sure she liked it.

"It's too much," she said about the makeup. "I feel like a hooker."

"You look like a movie star. I should be jealous. You look young enough to be my sister."

She did look younger. The hairstyle had a tame, yet abandoned, appearance. With her hair completely off her face, her hazel eyes, with a light touch of smoke-gray shadow, glowed warm and sultry.

Up to that point Kristy'd had full reign in the make-over of

87

her mother. But Regina had put her foot down concerning the brick red lipstick. She blotted it away and chose a red tinted gloss instead.

"One last thing," Kristy said, digging through her jewelry box. She pulled out a pair of hammered bronze hoop earrings.

As Regina put them on, Kristy lifted the collar on the jacket, then pushed the sleeves to the elbow. Regina turned one last time to the mirror.

"Oh, Mom, you look super sensational. If you entered the Miss Classic Pageant today, you'd win hands down."

Regina laughed, but at the mention of the pageant a dark cloud seemed to pass over her.

She shivered.

4

After twenty-two rings—Donna had counted them—she hung up the phone and sank back in her office chair. Would Corinne show or stand them up?

They taped at 4:00. It was 2:50 and still there was no answer at her house. Donna had started calling moments after coming in that morning.

Nolan appeared in the doorway of the small office. "Anything?"

Donna held fingers to her temples and shook her head. "It's my fault—"

"Nonsense," he said, crossing to her and squeezing her shoulder. "Regina should have arranged for a car, a limo, to pick her up."

"Then we'd have to send cars for the others."

"Piss on the others. I can't believe her, Donna," he said in a hushed tone. "This is goddamned important. We've got cable and major network execs watching, and we don't even know if we have a show."

"We have a show—"

"Not without Ms. Odett we won't," he cut in. "No one wants

to see a handful of aging beauty contestants—present company excluded, naturally—who aren't even winners, for chrissake."

"Darling, this show won't make or break us."

"I put my ass on the line with this disfigured beauty queen angle. It's the kind of show that could boost us up. Treatment of something as sensitive as the loss of a woman's most valuable asset—her looks—might just help us go national. And no one can treat it as sympathetically as you."

Donna blustered some at her husband's sexist remark, but his compliment of her talent softened the barb, as he knew it would. "Corinne told me she had surgery and that she was no longer disfigured."

"She lied. Either to you or to herself. Nobody gets acid tossed in their face and comes out looking normal. No one."

Donna glanced at the wall clock. Three exactly. Nolan's eyes followed hers.

"I hope for both our sakes that she shows. Where's your precious Ms. Van Raven?"

Maxwell Conner, the executive producer, stepped in the office. "Are you having a problem with Regina, Nolan?"

Nolan turned with a guilty start. "No problem. It's just that I feel she doesn't always have the program's best interest at heart."

"Really?" Conner's tone was ironic. "And I'm inclined to think that without her "City Gallery" wouldn't be the show it is."

"Aren't you giving her a little too much credit?" Nolan said, standing behind his wife, his hands on her shoulders. "Or is it that you're not giving Donna enough?"

"Regina's responsible for the format and she's the one who scours the city for those weirdos Donna interviews." Max gazed at Nolan over the top of his Ben Franklin bifocals. "Personally, I find it hard to imagine putting on the show without her."

Donna silently agreed. She realized she had made a grave error by not insisting to Nolan that Regina call on Corinne Odett.

Nolan, his face set, brushed past Max and left without a word.

Max flashed Donna a brief, uneasy smile, straightened his bow tie, and followed him out.

Donna reached for the phone. She hit the redial button and listened to the sound of a phone ringing in another part of the city.

The ringing stopped. It took Donna a moment to react. "Hello? Hello, Corinne? Corinne, it's Donna Lake." She tightened her grip on the receiver. "Please, Corinne, answer me." From the other end of the line she heard the faint sound of someone coughing. Then the connection was broken.

5

John sat at the dining room table with his uncle and aunt. He ate quickly.

"Slow down, Johnnie," his aunt said, "you'll get the tummyache."

"I told Sanders I'd relieve him at four today. His kid's in a school play."

"You go home when I come in at six," Charlie said. "You have taken no nights off in . . . in, I don't know when. I took on a new bartender. He begins tonight."

John looked up, startled. "Why?"

"Business has been good. I know you want to help out, but you are young, you have a life too. Play on the weekends."

"I've got nothing else planned."

"You could find a nice girl," Aunt Anna mumbled.

"I thought that was your job?"

She pushed his shoulder playfully. Then, without looking at him she asked, "Johnnie, have you met Louie's grandniece?"

"I have. She's very pretty. I'm sure she'll make someone a wonderful wife."

Both Anna's and Charlie's heads bobbed in agreement, pleased that he thought so.

"She wants to have children," Anna said. "She's good with

children."

She wants to be a citizen of the good ol' U.S.A, John said to himself. To his aunt he said, "What do you know about the new tenants in 2B?"

"Aghhh," she grunted, shrugging her shoulders. "The girl is just a baby and the woman is . . ."

"Too old to have children?" he answered for her.

"Johnnie, stop. The woman is not *szep*—not beautiful and young like . . ." she let the words die away.

"Like Ilona?"

His aunt shrugged.

"Do you think I should be interested in only young, beautiful women, Auntie Anna?"

"You are interested in women who are not good for you. That Axelrod one was too old. And before her there was the one who drank too much. A good Hungarian girl, a pretty Hungarian girl who is smart and loves children, does not interest you, I suppose."

"They all interest me. I just don't want to marry any of them."

"Six years is long enough to mourn, Johnnie. Aghhh, do what you want," she said, waving a hand. "I don't butt in."

John smiled. He went back to his meal but the memory was too strong to ignore. Ten years ago his family had had no trouble accepting the woman of his choice. Darlene was English, like John's father Eric Davie. She'd had a zest for life and loved children. John was twenty-eight when he met Darlene Goodnight, six years his junior, in London. She was a model on assignment for a fashion magazine. They fell in love, married, then moved to the United States. Fourteen months later Darlene gave birth to a son, Andrew. After four years of living on the California coast, Darlene, homesick and bored, wanted to resume her career in England. With grave misgivings, John put his wife and three-year-old son on a plane to Great Britain. He told himself she would return when reality reared its ugly head. But when her career took off again as though the four-year absence had never happened, John was forced to make a decision: insist his wife come back to him, or go to her. She argued, and justifiably so, that her contacts were exclusive to Great Britain, whereas he could write anywhere. He was still in the process of making a decision when a ferry she and Andrew were on capsized and sank. They both drowned.

A year later he dedicated his book to Darlene and Andy.

Charlie pointed at John with his fork. "At six I will be at the bar and you will come home."

"Okay. Okay. I'll start stripping the paint off the upstairs banister."

Charlie nodded and went back to eating.

Eleven

1

The lounge at KSCO TV was nothing more than a long room with several round tables, molded plastic chairs, a coffee dispenser, and a snack and soft drink machine.

Regina, pacing nervously from one end to the other, looked up to see a tall, dark-haired woman with striking coloring and angular features, dressed in white, enter.

As cool and sleek as the belly of the snake.

"Amelia," Regina said with a grin, moving to meet her.

"Regina, sweetie. We just don't see enough of each other." Amelia leaned in and kissed her on the cheek. "Am I the first?"

"Um-hm." Regina resisted the urge to immediately rub at Amelia's lipstick that she knew was on her face. "Coffee? Coke?"

Amelia eyed the vending machines with disdain. "Thank you, no. Where can I find Donna?"

"She'll be along in a minute."

"I'd like to speak to her in private before the show."

"Is there a problem with today's shooting?" Regina asked.

"No. This concerns a future show."

"Perhaps I can help. I'm in charge of schedul—"

"I'll wait and speak to Donna," Amelia said, smiling.

Tammy entered. From where Regina stood she could see that Tammy had lost a great deal of weight. Aside from her extreme thinness, she had a rather severely sunburned face.

93

The bright green shade of the leather dress tended to accentuate the redness. Tammy's daughters, holding hands, followed her in.

Regina waved.

"Regina!" Tammy said excitedly, rushing forward. "Who's that with you? Amelia? It is, it's Amelia. Long time no see, huh? Goddamn, isn't this just too much?" Tammy hugged Regina, then Amelia. "Amelia, you've never met my kids, have you? Kerry, Sherry, this is Amelia Corde."

Amelia nodded to them, then turned to Regina. "Will Corinne be here?"

"All I can say is that she accepted our invitation."

At that moment the door swung open. "Hi, everyone," Donna said, sailing in. "I'm so glad you could come. Amelia, you look stunning, as always. Tammy—." She stopped abruptly, staring. "My word, Tammy, you've gotten so thin. Are you all right? And what's happened to your face?"

Tammy lightly patted her cheek. "A little too much sun. But I've never felt better. I left Gary a few months back, y'know, and the single life keeps me going, going—too busy to eat."

"How can anyone be too busy to eat?" Donna asked.

"He wants us to reconcile," Tammy went on. "And who knows, maybe I'll take him back for the girls' sake."

Donna gave her a distracted smile, then glanced at Regina and did a double take, but said nothing.

Donna turned back to Amelia and Tammy. "I'd love to visit with both of you, and we will later, but we have a show to put on, so I'd better run through the procedure."

"Corinne's not coming?" Tammy asked.

Donna went on as if she hadn't heard. "Now, what we intend to do is open the show in the usual way. I'll be in the studio and I'll introduce you one by one. As soon as I say your name, a picture of you, taken from the pageant photos, will be displayed on the screen. Watch the floor director. In approximately three seconds he'll give you a cue to enter. That's when you walk out, all smiles, and wow 'em with your mature beauty and charm." She put an arm around Kerry and Sherry.

"We'll put you girls in the audience. Any questions?"

Regina saw Amelia open her mouth, but close it abruptly when Donna said, "Good—excuse us a moment." She steered Regina toward the door and practically pushed her out of the room into the hall.

"It's all falling apart." Donna spoke rapidly, wringing her hands. "She's not answering her phone. She's not coming. Nolan is having a tizzy because he promoted this damn exposé to some bigwigs solely on Corinne's misfortune, and she bailed out. Nolan blames—"

"Stop!" Regina took Donna by the shoulders and squeezed. She had never seen her friend so distraught. "The show will be great, just like you promised me. Did you look at those women in there?" She nodded toward the lounge. "They're beautiful and unique and they're not afraid of the limelight. The viewers will eat it up." With a wily grin she added, "And what about me, don't I look like a very brilliant, successful chick?"

Donna visibly sagged. She threw her arms around Regina and hugged. "Oh, God, you're right. It's just that when Nolan gets . . . y'know—I tend to fall apart. He's blaming you."

"So what else is new?" Regina said lightly. "Go hide out somewhere, take a minute to relax. I'll handle things up here."

Donna, hugging the clipboard to her chest, turned to leave. She turned back and, looking hard at her friend, smiled. "Regina, you're beautiful."

"Kristy to the rescue." Regina stood the collar up on the jacket. "A little makeup, some bright duds."

"It goes deeper than that." With her fingertips she gently rubbed at a spot on Regina's cheek. "Amelia's mark."

The door to the lounge opened and Amelia strode out, smiling. "Donna, I have to talk to you."

"Can it wait till after the show, Amelia? I'm swamped."

"This will only take a moment." Amelia looked to Regina, but when Regina failed to take the hint to leave them, Amelia went on to pitch Global Model Enterprises.

"Terrific," Donna said. "Here's the perfect opportunity to get in a plug."

"Donna, what I want is to be invited on the show in the very near future, along with Mr. Kincade, my business partner, at which time we can go into the entire operation in depth."

"We had something like that featured not too long ago," Regina said. "Model and Talent Productions aired the last week in February."

"GME is not the same as MTP, we have more to offer," Amelia said to Donna.

Donna looked imploringly at Regina.

"I'm sorry, but to us it's the same," Regina said. "In this business we have to be diversified. Maybe next year."

"We need the publicity this year," Amelia said, her voice rising.

"Then you'll have to plug it today. I'm sorry, Amelia, we can't do better than that."

"No, not today!" Amelia said sharply. "Don't you dare mention it on today's show."

"Whatever you say." Donna turned and strode down the hall.

Amelia stared after her with a dark expression on her face.

Regina excused herself and escaped to the production department, leaving Amelia fuming in the hallway.

2

Everything checked out. The panel box had no lock and the switches were clearly marked. The distance from the box to the permanent set of "City Gallery" was less than ten feet. There was a pay phone in the lobby and another in the lounge. The large clock on the wall read 3:06.

They were all here, looking more beautiful than they deserved to look.

There was nothing for him to do now but wait.

Wait and anticipate the thrill of what was to come.

3

Standing at her desk, Regina washed down a Tylenol with cold coffee. Her phone rang as she was leaving to go back to the lounge. She leaned across the desk and picked up the receiver.

"Yes," she said into the phone.

"That show must not go on," a hoarse voice said.

She was suddenly cold. "Which show is th—?"

"If it does, someone will suffer."

"Are you referring to the Miss Classic format on 'City—"

"First will be last and last will be first."

"I don't understand . . ."

"Crucify the flesh with cleansing spirits."

"What the hell are you talking about?" There was something odd about the conversation, it was as if the caller wasn't listening to her, had no concern for what she had to say, was delivering a message and nothing more. "Answer me." The line hummed. "Hello? Hello?"

Damnit, she had to stop the show.

Regina found Donna on the set talking to the director. Nolan was at a table a few feet away. As she approached them a hand closed around her arm, stopping her. She turned to see a tall man with strong-boned, handsome features. Garrick.

Oh, Lord, what more, she wondered? Would she make it through this day?

"Garrick," she said, her heart beating out of sync. "What are you doing here?"

"You look beautiful," the towering, dark-haired man with the full mustache said. "I had to see you. You've moved with no forwarding address. You won't talk to me on the phone, you return my letters unopened. How else am I supposed to talk to you?"

She looked up to see Nolan looking their way. He was casually leaning on a table, his arms folded at his chest and his legs crossed at the ankle, staring intently at her.

97

In a hushed tone she said, "Garrick, this is not the time."

"Then let's make time."

"It's over —"

"It never really got started."

"Okay, it never got started. So let's leave it there. Please, Garrick."

He shook his head sadly. His brown eyes seemed to plead. "Barbara and I split."

"Oh, no. I'm so sorry."

"You don't understand, I left her for us. I know now that's why you wouldn't give us a chance, because of her."

"Garrick, no," Regina said, feeling exasperated. It was always the same. There was no getting through to him. "That was only a part of it. There was more, so much more and you know it. Leo wasn't — Leo — what we did was — oh, God," Regina whispered urgently, close to tears, "will you please go. *Please.*"

Donna turned. "Reggie? Anything wrong?"

Regina shook her head, took a step back.

"Have dinner with me," Garrick said.

"No."

"A drink then."

"Reg . . . ?" Donna called out.

"Okay, a drink. But you have to go now." Regina took another step back.

"I'll call you. Give me your number."

"No, I'll call you," she said. "Where are you staying?"

"The Villa Florence. It's —"

"I know where it is. I'll call tomorrow."

He gazed into her eyes. Finally he nodded and walked away.

Regina closed her eyes briefly, feeling an enormous relief; then she remembered why she had come looking for Donna, and the anxiety returned. She strode up to Donna.

"I want to cancel the show, she said abruptly.

Tom Gansing whirled around, his mouth forming an O.

"We had another phone threat."

"When?"

"Just now. Donna, I can't do it."

"Reggie, it's not like you to get spooked this way."

"I know. Look, we can put on last month's trade show at the Cow Palace. It's already in the can and—"

"What does this mean?" Tom interrupted.

"Acid," Regina said. "Another contestant could be a victim right here on the show."

Tom looked to Donna, his boyish face clearly showing concern. Regina suspected the concern was for Donna. Tom had worked for "City Gallery" since its conception, and his adoration for the hostess had become more overt with each passing year.

"Donna," Tom said, his voice troubled, "if Regina thinks—"

Donna turned to look at her husband. Nolan pushed away from the table, strolled across the room, stopping within a foot of Regina, his gaze unflinchingly meeting hers. "We have a problem?" he asked casually.

Regina hated herself for being the first to break eye contact. He had been privy to the whole scene with Garrick, but she couldn't concern herself with that now. "Another call."

"A drunk playing games," he replied.

"I don't think so. I think we should cancel the show."

"Just because some crank makes a drunken threat, we're supposed to call in the militia? Get serious, Van Raven. Try to show some professionalism here. We have a show to do. So let's do it . . . without the hysterics. Don't let your *personal traumas* influence your decision making."

Ignoring Nolan, Regina pleaded, "Donna, do it for me. Please."

Donna glanced at Nolan, looked rueful. "I can't, Reg. Not this time."

Turning on her heel, Regina stormed from the room.

4

Forty minutes later Amelia, Tammy, and Regina stood behind staggered partitions waiting for the hostess of "City Gallery" to invite them into her little piece of the world. Regina was as anxious as the others. Only for a different reason.

"She hasn't shown up yet?" Nolan asked, coming behind the set. His question was directed at Regina. She knew he meant Corinne.

"She's not going to, Nolan."

"If she shows before the crew goes home, we tape again," he said evenly.

"Count me out."

"I will." He turned and walked away.

Regina looked around to see Amelia staring intently at her. She smiled complacently. "Get ready. Any moment now."

The three women, viewing a backstage monitor, watched Donna stand and say, "Please welcome Miss Classic, third runner-up, Tamara Blanco Kowalski."

Enthusiastic applause came from the two dozen or so people that made up the live audience. Regina suspected the shrill whistles came from the twin girls.

Tammy pulled in a deep breath, waited for her cue, then moved around the partition and onto the set.

Regina glanced at Amelia. Except for a tightness around the mouth, she looked calm and cool. Again Regina was reminded of a snake's belly.

"Nervous?" Regina asked.

"No. You?"

"Scared to death."

Amelia's eyes looked somewhat contemptuous before looking away.

"Miss Classic, second runner-up, Amelia Travis Corde," Donna's voice rang out.

Amelia stiffened. Then with a look of sheer malevolence, she turned to glare at Regina. "You were supposed to be next. I should go *last*," she spit the words out venomously. "*I was the queen.*"

Regina lifted her shoulders and shook her head in confusion. There was a mix-up. Donna was supposed to call them in the order they had ended up, with Amelia claiming the title.

Stork, the lanky young floor director in a tank top and sa-fari shorts, counted down, then gave the cue for Amelia to enter. She stood ramrod straight; not a muscle twitched.

"Amelia . . . ?" Regina said.

"No."

"You've got to go," Regina pleaded under her breath.

"You're not going to gang up on me again," Amelia hissed. She seemed to be in a trance. "I was the queen."

Donna called her name again.

Regina pushed gently but firmly. "Please, Amelia, we'll get it straightened out."

Amelia seemed to snap out of it, and then, smiling broadly, she stepped around the partition and moved onto the hushed set with long, regal strides, befitting a queen.

The applause, sporadic at first, became loud and steady.

Regina closed her eyes and let the air escape in a whoosh from her lungs.

Instead of sitting down, Amelia faced the camera and said, "As Miss Classic 1970, I wish to offer my prayers and best wishes to the lovely contestants of the 1990 Miss Golden Gate Model Search. Good luck, ladies, and may God be with you."

"Ladies and gentlemen," Donna said when Amelia finally sat, "my coproducer and very dear friend, Regina Houston Van Raven."

Stunned by the backstage incident, Regina felt numb, dis-placed. She moved out on cue, just wanting to get the whole crazy affair over with.

In a monitor to her right, inset in the corner of the screen, she saw a black-and-white picture of herself in an early seven-ties swimsuit. As she entered, she saw an image in bronze and teal with a halo of dark brown hair moving across the set, and wondered if that lovely woman was truly she.

5

Technicians, employees, members of the audience milled about the studio, quietly coming, going, sitting, standing, watching the taping. No one took notice of the presence that moved unobtrusively along the wall to the panel box.

In a deep, dark pocket the jar felt cool, hard, filled with an energy that seemed to pulsate on its own. The spirits within had the ability to alter, to cleanse and to purify.

He preferred to work close in, wielding his power behind the straight razor. Seeing the flesh peeling away from the bone, feeling the hot blood. But circumstances were different now, and he would have to be content envisioning the destruction, sensing the shock, pain, and horror.

The four women on the set talked and laughed, unaware that one of them would be changed this day.

6

Regina sat in the club chair at the far end of the semicircle. Donna directed several questions to her, which, thanks to the numb state she was in, she answered without a trace of self-consciousness. The others were brought into the conversation.

Regina heard a rushing in her head, like the sound of a sea-shell at her ear. She looked from one woman to another, seeing but not hearing. Tammy was talking, gesticulating broadly, her lips moving rapidly, her pale brows glistening on her bright crimson face. Amelia sat tall, her legs crossed at the ankles, hands folded neatly in her lap, her porcelain skin a striking contrast to her ebony hair. When she spoke her eyes closed briefly, then fluttered open. Very effective, Regina thought. There was something almost hypnotic about the gesture, making it difficult to look away from her face. Donna leaned into her guests, her expression amiable, benevolent—the peacemaker, the saint, the mother figure who encompassed all others with love and caring. Donna was the security blanket, the chicken soup, the cool hand to the fevered brow.

Regina snapped out of the trance with the following words: ". . . food poisoning at the pageant."

"Yes, I remember," Amelia said, her long lashes lowered,

then fluttered upward. "The seafood at the banquet was bad. More than half of the contestants were gravely ill. I had a touch of it myself."

"I almost broke my neck coming down those stairs on stage," Tammy said. "Halfway down my heel fell off. Just fell off."

"I'd forgotten about that," Regina said softly under her breath, visibly perplexed.

"One more freakish incident to confirm the jinx theory," Amelia added.

"Right!" Tammy said, swiveling around to face Amelia. "The jinx. The media really played that up, didn't they?"

Donna interrupted to announce a station break. The red light on the camera blinked off.

Stork, headgear around his neck, approached. "Donna, there's a lamp out above you. Can I get everyone to move off the set while we change it?"

"Sure, Stork. How long?"

"Five minutes. Ten tops."

"Okay, ladies, stretch your legs," Donna said. "Don't get too far from the set, though. We hate to lose a guest when we're trying to tape a show."

"Would anyone like a soft drink?" Regina asked the three women. They all declined.

Stork hauled a ladder onto the set and climbed to the top. He donned a heavy leather glove and began to unscrew the bulb.

Regina scanned the set before going to the lounge. She saw Donna standing to the left of the ladder reading from the clipboard; Amelia was several feet away, digging through her reptile handbag, and Tammy was standing with her back to Donna, talking to Tom Gansing.

Regina hurried out, passing control rooms with eerie blue and red lights blinking and glowing through the tinted glass. In the lounge she recognized a few people from the audience at the coffee dispenser. A man was using the pay phone at the other end of the room. She inserted change in the soft drink machine, pushed the buttons, and caught the Sprite can before it hit the bottom. She hurried back to the studio.

She was just passing the control room, entering the set, when the large room plunged into darkness.

"Damnit, Stork, what the hell'd you do?" Tom's voice bellowed out in the black room.

"I just unscrewed the bulb, that's all," Stork called back.

"Someone get the friggin' lights," Tom's voice again.

Regina heard shuffling. Someone was moving in the dark, and fast. She gripped the cold can, and trepidation, like a hovering black entity, made the hair at the nape of her neck rise.

And then she heard the gasp, followed seconds later by a nightmarish scream that seemed to paralyze nearly every part of her. Her mind, however was clear and sharp. Word for word she recalled the phone conversation that afternoon in which a gravelly voice said: "Crucify the flesh with cleansing spirits."

Oh, dear God.

She was bumped again. But still she couldn't move.

The endless scream was tearing into her like the razor-sharp claws of a wild and pain-crazed beast.

Twelve

1

Donna heard the screaming, too. It seemed far off and in no way related to her and the agony that, at that moment, was paralyzing her breathing. She could feel, in a thousand different places, beads of red-hot molten steel eating into her. Water! She had to get water. A sea of water in which to submerge and, hopefully, mercifully, drown.

From where she stood in total darkness, clipboard gripped painfully in her fingers, Donna could see bits of glowing red and blue. With the clipboard held straight out, acting as a prod, she hurried toward that panel of lights, tentatively at first, then in ungainly yet rapid haste. She bumped someone, felt fingers pawing at her before she slapped them away and rushed toward her critical destination. The scream followed.

There was nothing for her at the place of the lights; no help, no savior or magic to erase the pain. The lights represented a path out of the blackness and nothing more; a direction in which to guide her toward that precious element — water. Hurry. Hurry. Hurry.

To the right of her now, tiny lights blinked and twinkled. In front of her the green EXIT sign glowed like a rescue beacon. With both arms extended straight out, Donna charged through the wide door into the lighted hallway. The screaming stopped abruptly and Donna, realizing with a dull sense that the sound had been coming from her, felt a diminutive relief. Without the screaming, and with the presence of light, the situation seemed not quite so hopeless. She stumbled across the linoleum, falling to her knees and then coming up, only to fall again. With a strangled cry she lunged through the restroom door, her shoulder bashing painfully against the frame, as she ran toward the row of basins.

With the palm of her hand she frantically pushed the single lever on the faucet. Cold water gushed out and she scooped up a handful, splashing it toward her burning face and throat. The water seemed to intensify the heat. She screamed out, but continued, knowing she had to dilute the oily substance that was eating into her. Moaning in anguish, she pounded the water-saving faucet with both palms, scooping and splashing furiously before it shut off.

Water! Oh God, she had to have water! Lots of it—now! Again she thought of an ocean. Her legs quivered.

The burning was no longer confined to the flesh, it seared deep beneath the pancake makeup and the skin—skin she had so meticulously scrutinized for wrinkles on her birthday only the week before. Her peripheral vision caught fragments in the mirror above the basin. Donna forced herself not to look up. The acrid odor of scorched tissue—her own scorched tissue—made her violently ill. Gagging, she pivoted and ran into the nearest cubicle. She dropped to her knees and with no thought of anything but the reservoir of water before her, plunged her head into the toilet bowl; and as her hands forced the cool water against the raw, fiery skin, she held her breath and prayed.

2

"Get the sonofabitchin' lights!" Tom shouted. "What the hell's happening here?!"

Regina had glimpsed a flash of light from the direction of the hallway. Someone, the screaming someone—and Regina was almost certain she knew who belonged to that wretched scream—had gone through the door. She quickly followed, feeling the taped-down cables and wires under her feet. The way was clear as she made for the door. A red light eerily bobbed behind, seeming to keep pace with her.

There was no one in the hall as Regina charged through the door. Without stopping or even pausing, she rushed into the ladies' room. Her pulse pounded in her brain, making her light-headed. She looked around desperately.

On the floor in the first cubicle was Donna.

Dear God, she prayed, let her just be throwing up.

She rushed into the cubicle, dropped to her knees, and began furiously to splash water over the raw skin. Sensing that the water was already polluted with the burning chemical, Regina pulled Donna to her feet and steered her back to the basin. They nearly collided with the man and his minicamera who had followed her in.

"Sam, get help!" Regina shouted at the cameraman as she pushed Donna's head into the sink. She pressed the faucet button and began to direct the gushing stream where the burns looked the most severe.

Tom Gansing ran in. "What the hell—? Oh God . . . ," he finished weakly.

"Ambulance," Regina said. Her hand slipped off the faucet button, causing her to curse in frustration.

"You heard her," Tom barked at the man with the camera, grabbing him by the back of his shirt and whipping him toward the door. "Call the paramedics!" To Regina he said, "What is it?"

"Acid."

He knelt, allowing Donna to lean against him. He held the button while Regina flushed the burning skin. He softly crooned encouraging words into Donna's ear.

3

The studio exploded with light.

Amelia grimaced and turned her head away from a blinding lamp. She called out Fletcher's name. Through the entire incident while the lights were out—which Amelia figured to be less than three minutes—she had whispered his name and had gotten no response. Fear and anger battled within her. She had seen him sitting in the audience during the taping, but at the break he had disappeared.

Shielding her eyes from the bright lights, Amelia scanned the large room full of people. During the blackout, with the exception of the screaming, the room had been strangely quiet. Now everyone was moving and talking. Where the hell was Fletcher, she wondered?

Tammy rushed up to her, her face more crimson than before. "Jesus, what happened?" Tammy asked, squeezing Amelia's arm.

With a sudden jerk, Amelia freed her arm from Tammy's grasp. "How the hell should I know," she said, still looking for Fletcher. "I can't see in the dark."

"Where's Donna?"

"I don't know, but I intend to find out." She headed toward the door.

In the hall, people milled about, nonplussed, nervous. Amelia went up to Stork and asked, "What's happened?"

The man shrugged, but his gaze flickered toward the restroom.

Amelia spun around, strode to the door, and pulled it open. She made it only halfway in before Regina appeared from inside and gently ushered her back out into the hall. "Go back to the studio," Regina said.

"What happened?"

"Not now, Amelia."

"Who's in there?"

"Stork," Regina called out to the floor man, "stand outside this door and don't let anyone in except the paramedics and the police." And then she pulled the door shut in Amelia's face.

A moment later the paramedics, racing down the hall, wheeled a gurney into the restroom.

The police car, siren screaming, passed John as he walked down Van Ness. A fire and rescue truck followed behind. John was a block from the Bull's Blood and he hoped to hell his uncle's bar wasn't their destination. Both vehicles pulled to the curb at the TV station at the corner.

John slowed. A paramedic van was at the entrance. Curiosity and something more made him turn toward the building rather than go on by. He was thinking as a writer.

He marched through the front door decisively, as if he had every right to be there, and hurried down a long corridor.

At a junction in the building he stopped. To his left he saw a knot of people looking toward a restroom. The restroom door opened. John watched two paramedics backing out wheeling a gurney. Strapped to the gurney was a shoeless woman in a pastel blue dress. Her hair was wet and plastered against her face, and an oxygen mask, along with what appeared to be wet compresses, covered her nose and mouth. The woman was clinging to the hand of the man who hurried along beside the rolling gurney. The man, in his late thirties, with red hair and freckles, turned and spoke to someone standing in the doorway. "Regina, I'm going with her."

The woman, a pair of blue pumps clutched to her chest, dark wet splotches on her bronze-colored skirt, stared trancelike after the departing group.

John thought he recognized her. Where had he seen her before? At the Bull's Blood? On television? Then it hit him—at his apartment house. She was the woman with the teenage daughter who had moved into Wilma's apartment. Regina Van Raven.

Appearing to suddenly snap out of it, she called out, "I'm coming too."

The two attendants wheeled the gurney. The red-haired

man and the woman hurried alongside. As she passed John, one shoe fell from her hand. John swooped it up and handed it to her. Their eyes met briefly. Then she was past him, turning the corner.

From the murmuring group of people, John heard the word, *acid*. He stood frozen, staring in numb shock at the retreating gurney. It was déjà vú and he suddenly felt sick to his stomach.

Thirteen

1

It was obvious to Amelia that they weren't going to finish the taping. Not without a hostess. A policeman had come around asking questions, taking down names and phone numbers for questioning at a later date. Fletcher had managed to miss the entire event, only to reappear in the corridor.

Amelia was about to suggest to Fletcher that they leave when she saw Tammy, an arm around each daughter, eyes red from crying, approaching.

"Oh, Amelia, who would do such a thing?" Tammy asked her in a shaky voice.

Amelia looked to Fletcher. He reached out and touched her hand. Quickly pulling it away, she glanced at Tammy to see if she had caught the gesture. But Tammy, not one to be quick witted on the best of days, appeared to be a million miles away. "I have no idea, Tammy," Amelia said.

"If we're going to leave the city," Fletcher whispered in her ear, "we better be on our way before the traffic gets too unbearable."

Amelia moved away from Tammy and her twins. Fletcher followed.

"Are you insane," she whispered back. "We can't go away together after what's happened here. It's going to be all over the media. Matthew will want to talk to me and the first

111

place he'll call will be at my parents' place in Napa, where I won't be."

"Call him first. Tell him you're all right, then we can leave."

"I can't chance it. We'll go next week."

"Whatever you say," he replied stiffly.

"Besides," she said softly, "I wouldn't miss this bit of news for anything. Can you imagine the publicity this will bring? Someone wanted Donna Lake off the air . . . permanently."

"What makes you so certain she was the intended target? You said yourself that the lights went out. The place was pitch black. Perhaps the assailant got turned around?"

Amelia stared fixedly at her lover; then, through a tightness in her throat, she asked, "Who else would he want?"

2

At the pay phone in the lounge, Tammy deposited a quarter, pressed buttons and handed the receiver to Sherry.

"What do I say?" Sherry asked.

"Just get him on the phone, I'll take over from there."

"Hi, Mae, it's Sherry. Is my dad with a patient?" A moment later. "Hi, Daddy, it's Sher—"

Tammy jerked the phone out of her hand. "Gary, you've got to come and get us." Instant tears sprang to her eyes. "It was horrible. I think it was meant for me, I swear I do. The girls were with me and they could've been hit too."

"What the hell are you talking about?" Gary said, exasperation evident in his voice.

"Acid! Someone tossed acid in Donna Lake's face. It was meant for me, I know it!"

"Slow down and explain—without the theatrics. But first, are the girls okay?"

"Yes, thank God." She began to hiccup. Whenever she became extremely emotional, she got the hiccups. The girls looked at each other and giggled nervously. "We're at the studio, the TV station. Everything was going great, then we

112

broke for station identification and this bulb—"

"Damnit, Tammy, get to the point."

"During the break all the lights in the studio went out and someone threw acid in Donna's face. But it was supposed to be for me. I know it!"

"How do you know?"

"Not on the phone." She waited and when Gary failed to respond, she went on. "You have to come and pick us up. I'm too shook up to drive. I'm scared, Gary. The girls are scared."

Tammy handed the receiver to Kerry and with the other hand she pinched her on the arm.

"I'm scared, Daddy."

And before Tammy could pinch her too, Sherry leaned forward and spoke into the mouthpiece. "Me too, Daddy. Won't'cha come and get us, please?"

"Where are you?" he said in a quiet voice, filled with resignation.

Tammy took back the phone and gave Gary instructions.

An hour later, after dropping the girls off for the night with a friend of theirs from school, Gary Kowalski pulled his Porsche into the driveway of the house in Daly City. Out of the corner of her eye Tammy watched Gary as he glared at her Honda Accord in the driveway. Then he glared at her, his mouth a tight line.

"Too shook up to drive, huh?" he said.

She had lied to him. That afternoon they had taken BART into the city.

"Christ, I was so scared I forgot that we didn't drive in."

Several minutes later Gary was sitting on the La-z-Boy recliner, a tall, frosty glass of iced tea in his hand—he had adamantly refused any food. Warrior sat obediently at his feet, his large black head resting on his previous master's knee.

"Are you ready to tell me yet?" Gary asked, putting down the iced tea untouched.

Tammy paced the room. Warrior, with only his eyes moving, looked from Gary to Tammy.

"I was dating this man—." She glanced at him to catch his reaction regarding her with another man. Gary stared at her, his expression impassive. "I was dating this man when I met another man I liked better. I told Brad—that's his name—that I couldn't see him anymore and . . . well, he sort of flipped out. He's crazy about me. He begged me not to dump him. When he realized it was hopeless, he said that if he couldn't have me nobody could, and that I'd be sorry . . . things like that." The lies flowed effortlessly from her.

"When was this?"

"About a week ago."

"The girls heard him threaten you?"

"Well . . ."

"I didn't think so."

"Maybe they did."

"I'm sure they'll say they did. Look, if you're lying to me—shit," he growled, "it doesn't matter if you are or aren't. The fact that something bad happened to someone else doesn't prove it was meant for you. You're trying to manipulate me again, Tam, and if there's anything I hate more than your lying, it's your manipulating. *Can't you just let me go?*"

"If I'm in danger, then your children are in danger."

"What do you want me to do?"

"Stay with us until he's caught."

"You're being unreasonable. I have a dental practice in the city."

"We can stay at your place."

"Damnit, Tammy, if you're so sure it's this Brad guy, call the police and report him."

"I don't have proof."

Gary heaved himself out of the recliner. "I can't help you. You've made your bed, now you can lie in it."

"What about the girls? Should they suffer because their father hates their mother and doesn't give a gnat's ass about her well-being?"

"Okay." Gary whirled around and, trying to control his

114

temper, said gruffly, "Okay. This is what I'll do. If you're so damned worried about the girls, I'll take them home with me. I'll take *them*, but Goddamnit, I won't take *you*."

She began to cry and hiccup at the same time. This time the tears were sincere. She loved him so much. Couldn't he see that? Couldn't he see how much she loved him and how much he was hurting her?

Gary stood by, his shoulders slumped, his arms hanging listlessly at his sides, a helpless expression on his face.

Tammy went up to him. "I need you, Gary. Hold me," she whispered softly. "Just hold me for a few minutes." She wove her arms around his neck and buried her face against his neck. Her hands moved like silk on his body. Within minutes, against his will, he was responding to her touch.

Then they were kissing. Deep, hungry kisses that sexually stirred her like never before. It can only be this way with Gary, she thought. Because she loved him.

He removed his glasses, the area around his eyes looking stark and somewhat naked, but so familiar, so dear. And then he was undressing her, telling her she was beautiful, kissing her breasts and she felt she would die with the joy of his attention. Then they were on the floor making glorious love. With Gary it was making love; *lovemaking*. With Brad it was a sexual act. Gary was nowhere near as controlled or rhythmic as Brad, but Brad could never make her feel this wonderful. Ten years together had her anticipating her husband's every move, looking forward to it, eager to please him. She chanted "I love you," and he responded with "you're beautiful." And she knew then all of her efforts, the exercise, dieting, breast surgery, had been worth the pain and suffering. Amanda was smart but she, Tammy, was beautiful, and Gary was with *her*. She had him now and she'd make him stay for good.

3

". . . Get help." "What the hell—? Oh, God . . ."

115

Those words came from John Davie's TV. The strained voices of the man and woman in the verbal exchange were too hysterical to be anything but real. The visual was rolling and jerky, another indication it was drama in real life. Following the words ". . . Paramedics!" the camera panned crazily around the interior of the restroom, an angled view of wall, ceiling, and floor, then blackness.

John, with a concentrated expression on his face, reclined on a wing chair in the dark, his stockinged feet planted on the edge of the coffee table as he watched through the opening between his legs. He popped a pistachio into his mouth, rewound the tape on the VCR, then started it again.

Kitty Winter, coanchor on KRNN News, reported the story of the assault on Donna Lake. They ran a sixty-second clip of that afternoon's taping of "City Gallery." The segment being aired had the guests rehashing their ill luck as finalists of the 1970 Miss Classic Pageant.

Then they ran the entire footage of the assault scene filmed by the crew member with the minicam. "Don't adjust your sets," Winter advised the viewers, "the first portion of the film has audio only."

A scream filled the black void.

John felt the hairs at the back of his head bristle.

A moment later the camera picked up light in what appeared to be the hallway, moved toward the door marked WOMEN, and beyond. The lens panned left, then right to a cubicle where two women where bending over a commode. A moment later the women, clinging to each other, stumbled across the room to the row of basins. "Sam, get help!" the brunette called out as she glanced into the lens.

John flipped off the set.

Twenty years ago another woman had gone through a similar experience. Jesus, he thought with wonder, had it been that long ago?

Corinne Odett, a young woman of remarkable beauty, poise, and that additional gift—street smarts—had been a victim of acid. He wondered what had become of her? Had she managed to make a decent life for herself despite the nightmare? He'd heard she had undergone a couple of operations. But Vietnam, college, and a few years kicking around Europe—where he met and then married Darlene—had kept him busy. Eight years after the assault, when he returned to the states with his bride, Corinne Odett was but a dim memory.

He dropped his feet to the floor and rose. He had work to do. He was little more than halfway through stripping the old varnish off the upstairs banister. From the kitchen counter he picked up the can of paint remover, brush, and rags and headed for the door, thinking that he would run through the whole weird "City Gallery" business once more before he turned in for the night.

4

Corinne sat in a tight ball in an overstuffed chair, her arms wrapped around her legs. She rubbed the ridged skin on her face back and forth across the rough denim at her knees. She hadn't moved since watching the news report two hours earlier. In her mind she played it over and over. Kitty Winter had reported the tragedy on the set of "City Gallery." Donna Lake, TV hostess of one of the hottest local shows, had been maliciously burned in the face with acid. Naturally, Corinne had been mentioned, and she'd flushed hotly upon hearing her name. That segment of the news finished with, "The assailant is unknown and the SFPD say there are no suspects at the moment."

Corinne smiled. Her heart hammered in her chest.

It occurred to her she might need an alibi. Her father would supply it. He'd better if he knew what was good for him.

She stood, walked to the coat closet, and removed a long, dark raincoat. She pulled it on, buttoned it to her throat, and flipped up the hood, tucking her hair well inside. Then she quietly opened the front door and went out.

117

The room was cold, gray. The pain was becoming dull at last. She wondered if there would ever come a time in her life when she would not remember the pain at its highest degree. Even now, hours later, heavily drugged, a cooling, soothing medication seeping into the ravaged tissue, she had only to bring to mind the raw sensations she had felt just moments after the liquid hit her to experience the devastating horror again.

Now that the pain had loosened its paralyzing hold on her, she could finally think of other things.

What happened?

Who would do this?

Why her?

Where was Nolan?

Donna forced her weary eyes to stay open, focusing on the wide door. As if by some mystic power, the door slowly opened, and through a narcotic haze she saw a man enter and stand to the side.

Nolan?

Terror suddenly gripped her. What if, instead of Nolan, it was the one with the acid come to hurt her again? She wanted to call, to ask if he was Nolan, but pure oxygen from a breathing apparatus flowed into her, making it difficult to speak.

The man took long, yet tentative steps toward her. Her eyes refused to focus. She stiffened, raised a hand uncertainly. He stopped at the foot of the bed. His gaze flitted around the room, over the contraption that held the intravenous bottles which fed life-supporting fluids into her body, to the tanks of oxygen, to finally settle on her face. His body flinched, as if he were surprised to find her awake.

"I came as soon as I heard," Nolan said in a quiet voice. "They wouldn't let me in to see you until now."

Donna tried to nod, but the movement set off a deep aching under her chin. She moaned.

"They'll only let me stay a moment."

Donna's wan smile was lost to him under the medicated gauze dressing wrapped loosely around the lower half of her face and throat.

A nurse strode into the room, pushing a tray filled with rolls of gauze, tubes, and jars of a milky liquid. She nodded at Nolan.

Nolan began to back away.

"You needn't leave, Mr. Lake. This won't take long." She began to remove the gauze from Donna's face. "It might help to . . . to pass the time if you talked to her while I work."

If Nolan had heard the nurse, he made no acknowledgment. With a grim expression, he pivoted sharply and rushed out.

6

Regina waited in the hospital lounge. She was told that only the immediate family could see the patient, but she couldn't leave until she learned the seriousness of Donna's condition. When she saw Nolan rush out of Donna's room, she hurried to intercept him at the elevators.

"Nolan, how is she?"

Without looking at her he shook his head and entered the elevator.

"Is it critical? Is she conscious?"

Turning to face her, jabbing at buttons, he said hoarsely, "She's conscious. I don't know what her condition is. Ask the doctor. Dr. Hemmer." And the doors closed, leaving her to stand there taking in her own reflection in the stainless steel doors.

She found Dr. Hemmer at the nurse's station.

"Mrs. Lake is in serious but stable condition," he said. "With this sort of trauma we won't know for days. Shock and infection are our main concern. If you'll excuse me." Then he too was gone.

At nine o'clock, before leaving the hospital, Regina called home to Kristy. After only the second ring the answering machine clicked on, indicating a message waiting. Thinking that Kristy may have called in, Regina pressed her code number to receive the message. Background noises filled the receiver, and just when she thought the caller had decided not to speak, a gravelly voice said, "Regina Houston," followed by more background sounds, then clicks and, finally, the dial tone.

Regina hung up slowly, disconcerted. Aside from the show that day, she hadn't been called Houston in many years. And that voice, low, raspy . . . She found it difficult to breathe.

With a growing tension that made her jumpy and impatient, Regina left the hospital and, distracted, failed to take the usual precautions. She had forgotten to take out her key ring—to which was attached a small container of mace in a leather sheath—until after she'd reached the tan station wagon. Now, fumbling in her oversized bag, the nearest street light just far enough away to create distorted shadows all around her, she heard someone walking toward her.

Regina looked up to see a man dressed in layers of clothing—too much clothing for the unusual heat and humidity of the day. The man's hair, gritty looking, stood on end along the crown, like a cock's comb. He was neither tall nor big, but big enough and tall enough to overcome her if that were his intent.

"Got change for a dollar, lady?"

Her fingers curled around the container of mace. She pulled it from her purse and tripped the snap. There was a safety device, she flipped it off. With the mace palmed, she turned to the man. "I don't have any money."

The man looked at her hand held against her stomach. After an agonizing moment, her heart racing, he shrugged and moved away.

Trembling fingers inserted the key in the door and jerked it open. She quickly got in, closed the door, locked it, started the engine and drove away.

Sometime during the fifteen-minute drive home, with the tears blurring her vision before finally flowing down her face, she asked herself *Why?* What reason could someone have for wanting to hurt Donna Lake? Donna couldn't have an enemy in the world. Everyone loved Donna. Damnit! Why?

And then she wondered if a mistake had been made. Had the acid been meant for someone else? For Amelia, or Tammy, or . . . or for her? There had been a warning. And the threat carried out. Had it really mattered to the assailant who the victim was as long as it was a Miss Classic contestant?

Miss Classic.

Beauty contestant.

Kristy.

She wiped her eyes with the backs of her fingers, then pressed down on the accelerator with a renewed sense of urgency. She was still five minutes from home.

7

John dipped the rag into the solvent, then rubbed it along the wooden banister, working loose the old varnish and stain.

Her death was the last thing he wanted. That would ruin everything. It was essential she live to suffer for her transgressions. Dying was too good for her. As he worked he plotted, forming and reforming the perfect scenario in his head.

The door to 2B slowly opened. Kristy Van Raven, Walkman earphones draped around her neck, her expression curious, stuck her head out. A moment later she asked, "What's that awful smell?"

"Paint remover." John held up the coffee can. "I kinda like the smell of it."

"Cheap high, huh?"

He laughed.

She inched out to stand against the door frame. Something in her face told him that she was troubled. She'd no doubt heard about the tragedy at the studio. She probably even knew the victim, since her mother obviously was acquainted with Donna Lake.

"Something wrong?" he asked.

"That's an understatement."

"Wanna talk about it?"

She hugged herself. "My aunt—well, she's not really my aunt—anyway, something awful happened to her today. She has this TV show and some guy threw acid in her face."

"Yeah, I heard."

"Why would someone do something like that?"

"Crazy, perhaps."

"Another understatement."

John had nothing to add so he turned back to the task at hand.

"I wish my mother would get home. She must be at the hospital. I've been calling down there, but they just give me the runaround. Won't tell me anything." Then she sighed, long and deep.

"You look like you could use some cheering up." When she looked up at him, he put down the rag and motioned to her to follow him. Without question she did. She's too trusting, John thought. Someone should talk to her about that.

He walked to a door on the other side of the hall, opened it, and turned on the light. It was the room they used for storage: cleaning supplies, tools, paints, and so forth. Kristy walked in without hesitating.

"There." he said, pointing to a cardboard box on the floor against the wall. "You like kittens?"

Her face lit up. "Love em." She stepped to the box, crouched down, and began to exclaim over the litter, cooing in baby talk.

John crossed the room to a shelf by the window. As he poured paint remover into the can he glanced out.

Their neighborhood, without street lights, was darker than most. But as he casually scanned the street a car passed, illuminating the parked cars. John caught a glimpse of movement behind a van. He became alert, instantly stepping back from the window.

With a quick motion he closed the blinds. Behind him he sensed Kristy watching him, wary at last, but he ignored her. A figure stepped out from behind the van and disappeared between the two apartment houses.

John turned and stared into Kristy's bewildered face. He smiled. "Pick them up if you like. Their mother's outside." Then using the cat as an excuse to investigate the figure he had seen down below, he said, "In fact, I think I'd better let her in so she can feed them."

He hurried from the room, took the steps two at a time, and headed toward the back entrance.

In the laundry room, John put the can of solvent on the floor and was about to reach for the knob to open the back door when he saw it turn slowly, first to the left then to the right. He looked around the tiny room for a weapon. A hammer hung on a nail above the washing machine. He grabbed it, whirled around, and knocked a broom over. The handle fell with a clunk against the door.

He swore under his breath.

Moving to the door, he carefully turned the lock, closed his hand around the knob, and, twisting it sharply, raised the hammer and yanked the door open.

There was no one there.

He hurried down the steps to the side of the building and looked down the narrow walkway. It was clear.

A car door slammed. John ran the length of the building, stopped at the corner, and, keeping his back flat against the apartment house, looked out. Regina Van Raven was hurrying along the walk toward the house.

He waited, watching for signs of a prowler. When she was safely inside the vestibule, he circled the building once before going back inside.

As Regina entered the apartment house, a rush of fore-boding raced through her, making breathing difficult. She quickly looked around but saw no one. So strong was the feeling that she was somewhat surprised to reach the inner hall without dire consequences. She hurried up the stairs to the second level, her nose crinkling at the odd odor she encountered, rushed inside the apartment, and closed and locked the door.

The living room and kitchen were dark. But the lights and radio were on in Kristy's room — rock music pounded to the beat of Regina's heart. Clothes were tossed about in the usual disorder. A glass of cola sat on the windowsill, the ice cubes only half melted. Kristy had been in this room less than an hour ago, Regina told herself. Possibly more recently.

"Kris?" she called, looking in the closet, then the bathroom, and finally her own bedroom. Kristy, in the habit of leaving either a note or a message on the answering machine, had left neither. "Kristy, where are you?!"

She stood in the living room, with panic working its way through her like live electrical wires. Something bad was about to happen, or had already happened. First her best friend, she thought, and now her little girl. What the hell was going on?

Footsteps approached the apartment door, then it was silent. She heard a key in the lock.

Kristy, Regina thought with a flood of relief. She rushed to the door and yanked it open.

Standing at her door was a man. He held a coffee can in one hand and her mace key ring in the other. The man was frighteningly familiar.

Rooted to the spot, her knees threatening to buckle, she could only stare at the coffee can in his hand. The man stepped forward. Over the rushing noise in her head, she heard him say her daughter's name.

He had Kristy.

"Where is she?" she managed in a hoarse whisper.

He turned slightly, tipped his head to the side toward a door across the hall marked STORAGE. The odd way he was staring at her made her want to scream.

"Kristy," she called softly, then louder, more frantic, "Kristy!"

Her own voice released the muscles in her legs. She brushed past the man and ran across the hall to shove the door open. She saw her daughter on her knees, facing the wall.

With tears springing to her eyes, Kristy came to her feet and rushed into her mother's arms.

"Oh, Mom, Mom, thank God you're here."

Regina whipped around in such a way as to shield her daughter from the man in the doorway.

"What'd you do to her?" she demanded.

The man looked from Regina to Kristy, his brows furrowed.

Regina looked at Kristy.

"Mom, what are you talking about?" Kristy said, sniffing and wiping her eyes. "That's John Davie. From downstairs. He didn't do anything to me."

"Then why are you crying? What are doing in here, on your knees?" Regina said in exasperation. "God, will somebody talk to me?"

"Aunt Donna. I heard on the news what happened to Aunt Donna."

"Oh, Lord," the breath rushed out of Regina. "I thought something happened to you, too. I called and there was no answer. I came home and there were no lights on, no message or note, nothing. I had this peculiar feeling . . ."

"You and your feelings, Mom. I just came to see the kittens," Kristy said. And for the first time Regina saw the reason Kristy had been on her knees. In a cardboard box were six black-and-white balls of fur. "I was going nuts alone in the apartment waiting for you to get home to tell me how

125

Aunt Donna is."

Regina turned back to John Davie. She stared at him. What was he doing with her keys? And what was in the coffee can that smelled like a strong chemical?

As if he could read her mind, he said, "I was stripping off the old varnish on the railing . . ." He lifted the can. "I noticed your keys hanging from the lock on your door and I took them out . . ."

Emotions; relief, exhaustion, frustration, and confusion, swirled inside her. Regina nodded—a gesture of understanding, apology—then took the key ring from his hand and steered Kristy out of the room and back to their apartment.

After closing and locking the door, Regina turned, leaned against it, and asked in a hushed tone, "That man—"

"The landlady's nephew?"

"He was at the station today when Donna was attacked. I'd never seen him there before today."

"He's okay, Mom."

"You don't know that," Regina said fiercely. "You don't know anything about him."

"But, Mom—"

"Stay away from him."

9

Alone now in his apartment, the odor of paint remover still reeking on his hands, John could clearly see the face of Regina Van Raven. Although he was staring at it on the TV screen—the action paused at the frame in the restroom when she had glanced at the camera—he was seeing another image. Frozen in his mind's eye was a woman whose soft hazel eyes burned with fear, distrust, and a powerful sense of determination. He was seeing her as she had been less than an hour ago in the storage room, her arms around her daughter, prepared to fight, perhaps even kill, to protect her own.

He admired that.

The compulsion to protect oneself and one's own — at any cost.

It may come to that, he told himself. God help her, it may come to that.

Fear and self-preservation were not strangers to him. He had served his twelve-month stint at the tail end of the Vietnam war and both senses had ridden his back like leeches. Yet he often wondered if the reason he had enlisted instead of waiting to be drafted had been because he had failed to protect his own.

"We've been over this a million times," he said aloud to the badgering part of his subconscious that forever seemed reluctant to let it go, "and we decided there was nothing I could do. Nothing. Right? So fuck off."

John focused his eyes on the TV. It was clear now why both brunettes, the one in the hall at the station talking with the man in the gray suit, and the one clutching a pair of shoes, had looked familiar. They were faces from the past. Although they had never met, and he had seen her only the one time during the contest, and that from a distance, he remembered Regina in particular. She'd been different from the others, showing little interest in her surroundings. It was as if her participation in the pageant had been a job and nothing more. Yet, John had felt she had the best shot to win the title if Corinne didn't.

He pressed the play button on the VCR remote. The two women on the screen became animated again. "Get help!" Regina Van Raven said into the camera.

Get help . . .

Fourteen

1

The following morning Regina sat on the edge of the hospital bed opposite the intravenous pouches and the oxygen apparatus. The room was filled with flowers. The cloying smell reminded her of a funeral home. She held Donna's hand in both of hers. The hand was cool, and the short fingernails, under the clear polish, were pale pink.

Donna's eyes, above the nasal cannula and the saturated gauze dressing, were bright with pain, yet glassy from painkillers. She was staring across the room at her husband, who stood at the window, his back to them.

Dr. Hemmer entered the room and went directly to the bed. Regina was about to rise from the bed when the doctor waved her back down. "Nurse Diehl will give you holy hell if she sees you there. But I won't tell her."

With efficiency and brevity, the doctor checked his patient. "How are you doing with the pain?" he asked. "Is the medication strong enough?"

Donna tried to nod, but instead she stiffened, her eyes squeezing shut tightly.

"Don't move your head. No talking either. Remember the code. One tap for yes, two taps for no."

Donna tapped lightly in Regina's palm.

"Yes, it's strong enough," Regina said.

"You're a very lucky lady, Donna," Hemmer said. "I know that sounds like a damn fool thing to say, but it could have been worse — much worse. Quick thinking and immediate action to dilute the acid spared you the full ravaging effects. Most of the burning, first and second degree, involves the epidermis and part of the dermis. There was some third degree trauma on the right ear and neck that will require skin grafting. I foresee no permanent damage to the mucous membranes."

Without turning around, Nolan asked, "Will she need reconstructive surgery?"

Regina felt Donna's fingers tighten around her hand.

"There are more important things to concern us at the moment. When the risk of infection, dehydration, and hypovolemic shock have been alleviated, we'll discuss reconstruction."

The doctor checked the equipment. "Do you feel up to a visit from the police?"

Donna tapped once.

"I'll send him in."

"I'll do it," Nolan said quickly.

"Don't overdo," Hemmer said to Donna. "I'll look in on you later." He walked out with Nolan.

A few moments later Nolan returned with a black man of mocha coloring. The man moved boldly to the bed, stopping within a foot of Regina. Nolan stayed at the door.

"Ladies, I'm Detective Lillard from the San Francisco PD. I appreciate your cooperation so soon after the incident."

Donna stared at him under heavy-lidded eyes.

"She can only communicate by tapping her finger yes or no," Regina said.

The detective nodded acknowledgment. He opened a notebook and slipped out the pen from the binding. "Mrs. Lake, do you have any idea who did this?"

Two taps. No.

"Any idea why this was done? A motive?"

Donna looked to Regina.

"Other than the fact that it happened to another Miss Classic contestant twenty years ago," Regina answered for Donna, "we don't have a clue . . . except for the phone calls."

"Threatening calls?"

"*I* thought so." Regina glanced at Nolan. He dropped his gaze. She felt Donna tighten the grip on her hand.

"Tell me about the calls," Detective Lillard said.

She pulled a piece of paper from her purse and read the words of the caller. Then she added, "The voice was deep, gravelly, yet it could have been either a man or woman."

"Who'd know about that particular show?"

"The employees of 'City Gallery,' and the guests."

"What about the viewing public?"

Regina shook her head. "On the last program Donna announced another guest for the coming show. When that guest canceled, we moved this one up three weeks."

"That should narrow the field somewhat. Mrs. Lake, do you have any known enemies?"

"Of course she doesn't," Nolan said indignantly. "My wife was a victim of some crazed motherfu—some crazy fanatic. It wasn't Donna that guy was after. It could've been any of those women on the show yesterday. She just happened to be in the wrong place at the wrong time."

Lillard turned back to Donna. "What about hate mail—"

"Open your eyes, mister," Nolan cut in sharply. "Someone makes threats and then strikes on a pitch black set. Unless he can see in the dark, he couldn't be sure who would be the receiver of his little token. Christ man, it doesn't take a brain to figure that one out."

"You were in the studio at the time of the blackout?" Lillard asked Nolan.

"No, I was in the production room going over the budget," Nolan said.

"Mrs. Lake, from the time the lights went out until you

130

felt the acid splash your face, would you say it was less than a minute?"

Donna's eyes were closed. When she failed to open them after several moments, Regina said, "She's more exhausted than we thought. I think I can answer that. From the time the lights went out until I heard her scream, it was within seconds."

"Within ten seconds?"

"I'd say so."

"Where is the breaker panel for the lights on that set?"

"On the wall just inside the door," Nolan said evenly.

"Then it's possible the assailant could see everyone in the room before he or she tripped the switch?"

Nolan shrugged.

"Yes," Regina said.

"I'd like a list of everyone who was on the set yesterday, and if possible, in the entire building."

"That could be difficult," Regina said. "We have an audience of about twenty-five to thirty people. We don't ask them to sign in."

"Who are they?"

"Mostly friends and relatives of the guests and crew. Some regulars . . . some not."

"Give me what you can."

Regina nodded.

"Did either of you see anything suspicious or out of the ordinary? Someone acting nervous or strange? Someone that didn't look like they belonged?" Detective Lillard looked to Nolan first and then Regina.

Nolan shook his head.

Regina remained silent. John Davie instantly came to mind, but she decided to keep his presence at the station to herself until she had a chance to do some checking on her own.

Lillard thanked them and left.

Nolan crossed the room gingerly, as if at any moment he expected to step on a land mine, until he reached the end of the bed. "The boys are anxious to see—to see how

131

their mother is," he said to Regina. "They're with her father today. I'll bring them down tonight. Her father, I'm sure, will want to join us."

Regina rose from the bed and moved back, thinking that Nolan would kiss his wife or take her hand.

He turned and walked out.

Regina stood by silently, wondering what to do. She was about to leave when she saw Donna's eyes open and look over at her. Regina stepped to the bed and took her hand again.

"Nolan will be back later with the boys." One tap from Donna. So she had heard. "We've decided to air reruns until you're well enough to do the show again. Max agrees."

Donna raised her hand and made writing motions.

Regina dug a pen and paper out of her purse. She put the pen in Donna's hand and held the paper in her palm for Donna to write on.

Donna wrote four words. *Go on for me.*

"Nooo," Regina said incredulously.

Donna nodded vigorously. A look of pain sprang into her eyes.

"I can't, Donna."

In her five years at KSCO, Regina had never worked in front of the camera, nor had any desire to. And taking over for Donna, even temporarily, seemed sacrilegious.

Donna tapped the paper.

"Donna, you'll be back on the show in no time."

Donna held the pen up. Regina slipped the paper under it. She wrote, *For me. Please.*

"We'll discuss it when you're able to talk," Regina said, leaning in quickly and kissing Donna's temple. "I'll see you tomorrow."

And she too made a speedy retreat.

Tammy's husband getting out of bed that Saturday morning had awakened her. She rolled over and looked at the clock. 8:50 A.M. Rolling back, she watched him silently. Gary kept his back to her as he slowly buttoned his shirt.

Having him so near gave her a rush of joy. God, how she adored him. She loved his thinness; his long, wiry frame. On Gary, muscles such as Brad's would have been repulsive. She loved his long, finely boned fingers — artist's fingers, pianist's fingers, doctor's fingers. She loved his soft brown eyes behind silver-rimmed glasses and she loved the brown, wispy, receding hair that covered his brilliant mind. He was hers and she couldn't let him go. It had taken her too damn long to find a *normal* man. She had been thirty when she met Gary, and behind her there had been a long succession of geeks and queers, losers and boozers, cheaters and beaters. As far back as she could remember, the oddities were drawn to her. There were so many Brads out there and so few Garys; at least for her. The Garys went for the Amandas. The Brads sponged off the Tammys of the world.

But Gary had married her, therefore he loved her. Men like Gary didn't do cruel, selfish things to women. They didn't use them and then walk. She had driven him away with her lack of self-esteem. Too embarrassed to admit that he'd been turned off by her slobbishness, he'd invented other excuses. And to return to her so soon after she had regained her looks would only make him appear shallow, a cad.

He had slept with her for the first time in four months. There was no question in her mind that they would now reconcile.

She came out of bed and touched his shoulder. He moved away quickly, not looking at her.

"I'll make breakfast. I know exactly what you want."

"I can't stay," he said.

"Of course you can," she said, hurrying out the door to the kitchen. She heard him call her name, but she ignored it.

The twins were sitting at the kitchen table eating Cracker Jacks and sharing a bottle of Pepsi. They looked up, expectant expressions on their faces.

"How'd you girls get home?"

"Patty's mom brought us. We wanted to see Daddy before he went back to the city," Kerry said.

Tammy took pancake mix down and poured it in a bowl. "Daddy's home . . . for good. Why don't you let him know how happy you are that he's back with us. And put that junk away, you'll spoil your appetite."

Kerry and Sherry squealed and clasped each others hands.

Gary appeared at the kitchen doorway, his suit jacket over his arm, the look on his face both sheepish and morose.

"Daddy! Daddy!" the girls cried out in unison, rushing him, their arms flying about his waist as they hugged him.

"We're so glad you're back!" Kerry said.

"We missed you so much!" Sherry said.

Tammy smiled, her eyes misty as she looked on this happy family scene. She took milk, eggs, and bacon from the refrigerator.

"Are we going back to the old house?" Kerry asked. "I hope so. We have lots more friends over there."

"You girls go on out and play, okay? I want to talk to your mother."

Tammy paused in adding milk to the batter. Her stomach tightened. She recognized his tone of voice. Having him in her house, having spent the night together—subjecting him to every sexual thrill she knew he liked—was the closest she'd gotten to him since the separation. There was no way she was going to let him back out now.

134

"I want them here. We're a family, we should be able to communicate as a family." Tammy needed the girls for leverage. Everything was fair in love and war.

"Sherry, Kerry, please go outside."

Tammy put down the bowl, grabbed their hands, and pulled them to her. "You girls stay."

"I'll walk out . . . right now." Gary slung his jacket over his shoulder. "You want to play dirty, then I'm getting the hell out."

Both girls looked up at their mother, confused, uneasy. Gary spun around.

"Okay. Okay," Tammy said, conceding. "Go next door and play with Jimmy. Don't eat anything there. We're having Daddy's favorite pancakes with crumbled bacon."

The moment the door closed behind them, Tammy turned to Gary. "I need you, Gary."

"I'm sorry, Tam, last night was a mistake."

"But you stayed."

"You called me. You made the first move. What was I supposed to do?"

"You said I was beautiful . . ."

"Yes, you are. That's true, but—"

Tears filled her eyes. "Gary, you have to stay to protect me and the girls."

In a quiet voice he said, "That's despicable. You never give up. You never give the fuck up."

"Why should I? You're my husband."

"I don't want to be your husband. I curse the day I ever became your husband. I curse the day I ever laid eyes on you. You suffocate me."

She felt the strength drain from her legs. "You loved me once, Gary, you can love me again."

"I don't think I ever loved you. You caught me on the rebound. You did all the right things. You pampered me, boosted my ego, made me feel like a man again after my divorce. And then, before I could come to my senses, before I could find out what you were really like, you got pregnant."

"You married me. That, in my book, tells me that you loved me, Gary." She reached for him. If she could just touch him.

He jerked back as if burned. "It says I was a stupid jerk for believing your lies. 'Marry me or I'll kill myself,'" he whined in a falsetto. "And for ten years, ten dull, suffocating years, I've been trying to be free of you. The plotting and scheming . . . the suicide threats . . . the lies. Have you no dignity, no self-respect?"

"If you leave now, I'll kill myself."

"Do it," he said calmly. A chill ran through her. "Do it for me . . . and the girls. You'll be doing us all a favor. They can come live with me. Me and Amanda. What do you think about that?"

"I'll kill them too. Amanda and the girls. First I'll kill them and then myself. And you won't have anybod—"

Tammy heard the slap before she felt it. She had failed to see his hand coming, but the force behind it spun her around, nearly knocking her off her feet. She bit her tongue. Her ear began to ring. The next moment his hand was at her throat.

"What are you going to do now?" His eyes were bright, fierce, maniacal. "Threaten me? Touch me and make me want you? Try it. Go on, try it."

He held her by the throat, constricting her air passage. Pain brought tears to her eyes.

"I pity you. Look at you with your new, improved breasts, wearing clothes years too young for you. When will you understand that there's more to a person than good looks? Amanda has brains, common sense, and . . . something that you'll never have—class."

He abruptly released his hold on her. While Tammy struggled for a breath, coughing and wheezing, Gary retrieved his jacket from the floor and stormed out of the house, the door slamming with finality behind him.

She sank to the floor, sobbing.

He loved her. To respond so radically was proof of his love for her.

136

Despite the pain and the panic she felt at the moment, Tammy knew Gary was right about one thing: she'd never have Amanda's brains or social position; therefore, she had only one thing that she could count on in life. Her looks. And the attention it brought her.

As she wept, she thought back to a time when attention wasn't as hard to get. Her father, a deep-sea fisherman, had been lost at sea when Tammy was five. Friends of her father came to her mother's house in San Pedro to help out. On those occasions Tammy would put on her red dress and black tap shoes. To records she danced, her pale hair flying across her face, the full skirt of her taffeta dress twirling straight out, showing off her ruffled panties. The men would clap and press coins into her hand. She catered to them, brought them food, drinks. She rubbed their backs and feet and they said she had magic fingers. All this she did happily, not for the money, but for the attention.

She learned early on that her sweet smile, her magic fingers, her will to please through sex and subservience, attracted men to her. For a while, anyway. They took what was offered and then they went away.

An hour later the phone rang. Tammy prayed it would be Gary. But the caller was a stranger with a deep, gravelly voice, asking for the time schedule of her aerobics class at The Fitness Center.

After hanging up, she called Gary. The answering machine came on. At the beep she said softly, "Gary, honey, pick up the phone. I know you're there. Please talk to me. Gary? Honey?" She rubbed her swollen throat. "Honey, I'm not mad at you. Please talk to me."

3

The man was a psychopathic killer—sociapathXXX

Christ!

The blue screen remained blank save for that one idiotic sentence and that damnable blinking cursor. Another unproductive afternoon.

Holding a red pistachio to his front teeth, he opened it and worked the nut out with his tongue. He chewed slowly, washing it down with coffee. He put his hands back on the keyboard, the fingers stained with the pistachio's red dye, and typed C-o-r-i-n-n-e O-d-e-t-t. He hit the return, then typed the name, Donna Lake. Two spaces down he added three more names: Tamara Kowalski, Amelia Corde and Regina Van Raven. These three ended with a question mark.

His door buzzer sounded. John rose, crossed the room, opened the door, and looked out to the entry. Through the long panes of glass set in the door he saw two men in business suits. One man, oriental, his face to the glass, was peering inside. Their eyes met. John pressed the button to the right of his door, buzzing them in.

John had known instantly who they were. They were both reaching into their pockets for identification. Cops.

"Mr. John Davie?" the thin oriental with the flattop asked.

"Yes."

The badges were flashed. John didn't bother to look.

"May we ask you a few questions?"

"About what?"

Looking into the vestibule, John saw a woman in an off-white jumpsuit enter. There was no mistaking the pretty features of his upstairs neighbor.

One detective turned, nodded his head. "Afternoon, Mrs. Van Raven."

"Good afternoon, Detective Lillard," she said as she passed the three men. For a fleeting moment her eyes met John's before she started up the stairway. John stared after her.

"What do you know about the assault on Donna Lake?" the other detective asked John.

Her sandaled foot missed a step.

"Not a thing." John watched her entire ascent up the stairs. At the top she glanced down at him before disappearing around the banister.

"Come on in."

They followed him inside, their trained eyes darting about the apartment.

John spotted the luminous blue screen of his monitor. From where he stood the white printing was not legible, but if the police should move closer they'd see the names of two Miss Classic finalists—victims of acid. And the three who were not victims—not yet.

He strode across the wide expanse of living room, deliberately using his body to shield the screen, and pressed the "escape" key. The screen blinked before displaying the IBM program menu.

"What was that?" Lillard asked, moving closer.

"A novel I'm working on."

"Writer, huh?"

"Yeah."

"Ever get published?"

"A few times."

"Anything I'd know about?"

"I have no idea," John said leaning on the desk. "You had questions about an investigation?"

"Yeah. Are you acquainted with Donna Lake?" Lillard asked. It appeared to John that he was to be the designated spokesman for the two.

"Never met her."

"Know who she is?"

"I've seen her on TV."

"Ever hear of something like this happening before?"

John waited, knowing damn well the cops knew he had.

"You knew the other one, didn't you, John?"

John stared at him.

"Yes or no, John?"

"Yes."

"You got an alibi for your whereabouts yesterday be-

139

tween four and five P.M.?"

"I can save you a lot of time by telling you that yesterday I was at KSCO."

The two detectives looked at each other quizzically. So they hadn't known, John thought, surprised. He was certain Regina had called them.

"And what were you doing there?"

"I pass the station every day on my way to the Bull's Blood bar where I work."

"What time was that?"

"About four-fifteen. The emergency vans were just pulling up. I felt compelled to see what was going on."

"I see," the detective said. He moved to the desk, picked up several pistachios from the bag and, holding them up, said, "May I?" John nodded. Lillard ate the nuts, then tossed the shells on a red mound in a large ceramic bowl. "It's quite a coincidence that you would be present just moments after a woman gets acid tossed in her face—on two separate occasions."

John sighed. "*This* time it was a coincidence."

"And the other time?"

"I knew Corinne Odett."

From the desk Lillard lifted a copy of John's novel, *Evil Tidings*. He stared at the author's picture on the back of the jacket. "See much of Miss Odett?"

"No."

"When was the last time?"

"Before the assault."

"Why is that, John?"

"It's none of your fucking business," John said, feeling his anger surface. "I had nothing to do with her attack. We went through all this shit twenty years ago. It's over. You can't drag me back into it."

"It's never over. Especially now that we know you popped up at another acid splash. You're back in it again, Mr. Davie."

"Are you arresting me?"

"What's your hurry? Be a sport. Give us a chance to

140

put a good, concrete case together. You slipped through the cracks last time out—no eyewitness and not enough evidence. This time, though, we just might luck out."

The two detectives moved to the door; halfway out, the other one said, "If you think of something you want to tell Detective Lillard, or me, Detective Foyota, call." He dropped a business card on the rocking chair.

The door closed softly behind them. Instead of the footsteps moving toward the front door, John heard them on the stairway, climbing.

4

"My God, Fletch, the publicity," Amelia said excitedly into the cordless phone.

It was late afternoon and Matthew was in the basement tinkering, like King Midas, with his coins and precious metals and whatever else he kept in his room down there.

Amelia was in the closet going through his clothes. Instead of discarding or giving them away, she would sell them to a clothes outlet. With the receiver clamped between ear and shoulder, she dug through the pockets of his suits and shirts. "At first I thought it was a waste of time. But do you realize how much free publicity we've already gotten from that show? My face has been on nationwide TV."

"Adverse publicity, Amelia."

"For Donna, yes, but not for me—for us. When we're prepared to go public, advertisers everywhere will know me. I just can't believe how this is turning out."

"You could show some compassion for the victim."

"Darling, I do. I've just sent her a very expensive floral arrangement with my profound condolences. Will you stop looking at this in a negative light. Everything happens for the best, you know. Something good might even come out of this for Donna."

"I can't imagine what."

141

"I wonder who will be taking over for her while she's recovering?"

"Maybe you could apply for the position."

She didn't miss the sarcasm in Fletcher's voice. "Maybe I will," she said coolly.

He laughed good-naturedly. "Sometimes I underestimate you. You have what it takes to make any business a success. I'm extremely fortunate to have you on my side."

She chuckled low in her throat. "Matthew has a testimonial dinner tonight. I'll be at your place around nine."

"Oh damn, what timing. I made arrangements to meet with Tapperman at his club tonight."

"Who the hell is Tapperman?"

"Elia Tapperman, the promotional manager to RAM Electronics. A contract I promised to deliver."

"Change it to another night."

"It's taken me weeks to pin him down. An invite to his private club is quite a coup, and an indication he's interested. I called him when you canceled the weekend."

"I see. Well, good luck. How is everything else coming along?"

"The lease has been signed and we open the account on Monday. We're about ready to open our doors for business, Mrs. President."

"I like the sound of that." She smiled, pulling a ten-dollar bill from the front pocket of Matthew's wool blazer. "It's so much better than Mrs. *Corde.*"

"How does Mrs. *Kincade* strike you?"

"It strikes me fine," she said sweetly, though deep down she wondered if she'd ever marry again once she'd gotten Matthew's claws out of her. "I'll see you on Monday, Fletch darling." She hung up, and as she stuffed the bill into the toe of a sheepskin boot, she thought of the first time she had met Fletcher.

It had been at one of the endless charity functions that Matthew felt compelled to attend. While standing at the bar waiting for her third vodka Gibson, she had overheard Kincade telling another man that he was looking for a

142

partner to match his investment capital in the modeling business. The other man had shown an obvious interest. Amelia's fingers had trembled as she lifted her drink to her lips. When Kincade stepped to the bar for a refill, Amelia slipped him a note with her phone number and the words "Business Proposition." He'd called the following day. The wheels had begun to turn almost immediately. Both in bed and out of it.

Fletcher was a darling man, handsome and sexy as all hell. But he wasn't the only man in the world. Fortunately for Amelia, the world of stage, screen, and modeling harbored a whole realm of sexy, exciting, and handsome young men.

5

The front door was open a crack. Corinne stood behind it, ready to slam it shut if he tried to come inside.

"Ma'am, please," Detective Lillard said. "Just a minute of your time."

"Go away. I don't want to talk."

"I could get a subpoena and have you hauled downtown."

She thought he might be bluffing, but did she want to take that chance? She'd rather die than be forced to appear at police headquarters where people could stare at her with pity and revulsion. And she sure as shit didn't want any of them snooping around in her house.

"What questions?" she growled.

"May I come in?"

"No." She inched the door closer to the frame.

"Okay, look, we can talk here. Okay?"

"What questions?" she repeated impatiently.

"Donna Lake's assault."

She remained silent.

"She was assaulted, with acid, the same as you. We'd like your help in finding her assailant."

"You didn't find my assailant, yet you want me to help you find hers. Why? Is Miss Donna Lake more important than me?"

"We believe both assailants are one and the same, Miss Odett."

"So? If I had any idea who did this to me, don't you think I'd've told you?"

"Yes, of course."

"I don't know anything."

He cleared his throat. "We've placed John Davie at the crime scene Friday."

Corinne's heart thumped beneath her breastbone.

"Did you hear me, Miss Odett? John Davie admitted to being—"

"Jack?" she whispered.

"Yes, Jack, John. Let me in so we can discuss this."

From behind her, in a room just off the kitchen, a muffled cry reached her ears.

"No!" The door closed a little more. "I can't talk to you now. I can't . . ."

"All right. No problem. Here's my card. Will you call me and talk?"

Her hand shook as she snatched the business card that appeared through the crack. She closed and locked the door, leaning against it.

Oh, Jesus. Jack at the TV station? He lived in the area, so it had to have been a coincidence.

She crossed to a knick-knack shelf and took down a book, the cover worn and grimy from much handling. Years ago, when she'd read that he had become an author, she'd sent away for his suspense novel. His face on the book jacket was that of a serious man with strength and purpose—no trace of the boy she'd had etched in her mind. Yet even in a photograph his charm, his charisma, were apparent. Then she had opened it and had cried when she read a dedication to someone named Darlene. Darlene and Andrew. Wife and son? She never read *Evil Tidings*.

The phone rang. The damn press again, she thought. She snatched it up angrily, barked out a "What?!"

"Corinne?"

She felt as if she'd been gut shot. *Jack*. There was no mistaking his voice. He said her name once more.

"Don't ever call me again," she said low in her throat. "You can't do this to me." She hung up softly. Then she turned slowly, running the palms of her hands over her breasts roughly, shaking her head.

She went to her father's room, leaned against the door frame, and watched him struggle silently on the bed.

Sauntering in, she looked down at him. His eyes watched her warily. With a jerk of her hand she stripped off the silver duct tape from his mouth. He pulled back, but said nothing.

"Well, aren't you going to call out? Shout the house down, maybe? Now's your chance. That was a real, bona fide cop out there."

"You gonna keep my insulin from me?" he asked in a whimper.

"Nooo," she said, as though talking to a child. "You'd die if I did that."

"How 'bout my pills?"

"Don't you want to know why the police were at the door?"

He stared up at her.

"Donna Lake, the TV gal, got a dose of acid in her face. Just like me. What'dya think about that?"

"My legs hurt, Cory. They hurt bad."

"Well, let's have a look." She pulled out one corner of the blanket that was wrapped snugly around his entire body. The stump of the leg that had been amputated was swollen and red, but it looked a million times better than the swollen, discolored foot on his other leg.

"It looks bad, Daddy. Bad like the other one just before the doctors said it had to go. Real close to gangrene, I'd say." She tucked the blanket back under mattress. "Too bad we don't have any money to fix it up. I'll get you an

145

aspirin." She turned to leave the room.

"Cory? Please?" he simpered.

"Now you stop that whining. What good's it gonna do, Daddy?" she replied in a gushy, overly sympathetic tone, mimicking his backwoods grammar. "Even if the doctor does fix it up, it's never gonna be normal. So why waste the money?"

"Cory, baby, I'm sorry. Jesus fucking Christ, how many times I gotta tell you I'm sorry?" Mucus smeared over his stubbled face. "If I'da known how important having those operations was to you, I'da gone and let you have em. If yer momma were alive—"

"Don't talk to me about Momma," she said tightly. "You hear?"

"Why you gotta blame me for everything?"

She downed the rest of her beer, crushed the can, then right hooked it into the plastic wastebasket. "I'll get that aspirin."

6

The stupid woman was making no effort to mask the displeasure that was written all over her face. Carmenita Flores was not a whore—not professionally that is—and therefore not versed in the lies of the trade. But she could damn well make an effort. He had come thirty miles to Novato to see her. This was his second visit and both times she had looked at him as though he were a piece of shit. Not too bright, cunt, not bright at all.

When striking the deal, his instructions to her had been that anything goes, without complaint. She was to display—play act, if need be—how much she desired him, loved him, was dying to please him. This one, this little *puta*, was slow to learn.

"Get yourself ready," he said through clenched teeth.

"This will be the last time," she said defiantly.

He wanted to strike out at her, but managed to restrain

himself. So now that she was off the hook, she intended to stop the play. *There was only one way to end the game.*

As his anger grew into something black and loathsome, he realized how much she looked like the other one, the queen deceiver. The hair, the legs, and, of course, that certain haughty countenance. He wondered how he had failed to see the similarities before.

Yes, this *would* be her last time.

pigeons were eyeing, what had happened to Donna

Fifteen

1

John was on the roof, lying on his back, his toes hooked under the barbell. With one last burst of energy, the tendons on each side of his neck standing out like taut leather straps, he bent forward and touched his toes. ". . . hundred," he wheezed and collapsed back down. Above his head, perched on the edge of the heating unit, two pigeons eyed him curiously and cooed.

It was all coming back to haunt him.

Early in 1970, up from San Jose to visit his aunt and uncle, John met Corinne Odett at a party in a rough neighborhood of Berkeley. She was twenty, he was eighteen. She was the most breathtaking female he'd ever seen. In addition to her beauty, she had spunk and tenacity. She was going to win a beauty contest and go to Hollywood to be a major star. At the time he never doubted that anything she wanted could be hers.

A salty rivulet ran into his eye, stinging. He rolled over on his stomach and shook his head, slinging sweat over his bare arms and shoulders. A brisk ocean breeze cooled his drenched body. He pushed off from the mat, coming to his feet.

It was Wednesday, five days since Donna Lake had been attacked, and that incident, instead of diminishing in his mind, seemed to intensify with each passing day. If his suspicions were correct, what had happened to Donna would not be an isolated event.

There was no putting it off any longer, he thought. He glanced at his watch. 7:35. Regina would be going to work soon. If he hurried he could grab a quick shower, dress, and catch her before she left.

With the towel draped around his neck, he left the roof, jogged down a flight of stairs to the second floor, and nearly knocked Regina over as she rounded the banister to the stairway. Her large leather handbag hit the hardwood floor, its contents spewing everywhere.

She gasped, stumbling back, a stunned look on her face.

He grabbed her arm to steady her. "Are you hurt?"

Stepping back, pulling her arm out of his grasp, she shook her head and dropped down to retrieve the spilled items.

"I'm sorry. I didn't see you." He bent down to help her. She glanced up at him, a mere glance that seemed to take him in from head to toe, but she said nothing. He could imagine what she was thinking. His hair was wet and mussed, and he needed a shave. The only thing covering him was a pair of nylon shorts and a grimy towel. Sweat glistened on his entire body, a body which at the moment was still heaving from his workout on the roof.

"I have to talk to you," he said, awkwardly holding a handful of her things.

She held open her purse, he dropped everything inside. "About what?"

"About what happened to Donna Lake."

"What's your involvement in this? Why were you at the station that day?" She hastily slung her purse over her shoulder and started downstairs. "Never mind, it's none of my business."

"Yes, it is," he said, going down the steps and blocking her way. "It's important we talk."

"Talk to the police."

A elderly man wearing baggy pants, slippers, and a pajama top opened the door to 2D and looked out. "Davie, it's gone and done it again. The sink in the john's plugged. Awful smelling stuff coming outta there."

"I'll be right there, Dutch," John said to the man. To Regina he said, "Please."

She maneuvered around him and made it down another step before he stopped her with a hand on her arm. "You're in danger."

In her eyes he saw fear intermingle with caution. "Why don't you tell the police?" she said.

His silence seemed to confirm her initial fear. She jerked her arm away and continued on.

"Mrs. Van Raven," he said in a quiet voice, "I'm trying to warn you."

Another voice called up to him from the ground floor. "Oh, Johnnie, there you are. Come down." His aunt, standing at her open door with Mrs. Dobos and a slender young woman with blond hair, motioned to him.

"Oh Christ," he muttered, as his gaze went from Mrs. Dobos's smiling grandniece, Ilona, to the retreating back of Regina Van Raven. *Why now?*

2

Half an hour after Regina arrived at the station, Kristy called. "Mom, I forgot to tell you I have a photo session for the pageant at four today. I won't be home till after seven."

A tightness worked at Regina's chest. "Honey, about the contest. Things have changed. It's too—"

"No, Mother. Nothing's changed. Mrs. Nash is picking me up, so stop worrying. Talk to you later."

An hour later Regina was summoned to the office of KSCO's executive producer. Maxwell Conner stood behind his desk and Nolan stood at the opposite side of the room. Their faces looked set, their eyes hard.

She was barely inside when Max said, "I want you to go on for Donna this week."

150

Regina saw Nolan's jaw tighten.

Turning to Nolan, Max continued, "If we don't have a live body in there, then the show goes off the air. Regina knows the format better than anyone. We know she looks good on the tube." Without looking at her, Max held up a palm before she could react to his last remark. "Spare me the sexist crap, Regina — she can walk and talk and ask questions."

"She can't replace Donna."

"No one's saying she will. She'll hold it together until Donna comes back."

"I want that in writing," Nolan said.

"I don't have to give you shit, mister. I want Donna back as much as anyone."

Max turned to Regina. "I've got the perfect show. You remember that psychic we had on last year, Pandora-some-thing-or-other?" Regina nodded. "Well, we do an entire program with her. We set up phone lines to take calls from the viewers, and she gives them psychic readings over the phone. What do you think?"

"You're talking *live?*" she asked.

"Yeah, *live*. Is that a problem?"

Regina looked at both men incredulously, then laughed, short and without humor. "I don't believe this. It's typical, however, considering the way things are run around here." Max stared at her, perplexed. "Am I being promoted, shanghaied, used, or abused? No one bothered to ask *me* how I feel about this."

"I thought you'd be flattered," Max said.

"I've never worked in front of a camera before."

"There's a first time for everyone."

"Not everyone has to carry a thirty-minute talk show the first time out . . . and *live* yet."

"I told you she couldn't do it," Nolan said sourly. "It's too risky anyway. Donna never did a live show."

"I have faith in you, Regina."

"What's my status now? — if I choose to do it," Regina said, ignoring Nolan.

"In addition to producer, you're also talent. Salary for both, naturally. As coproducer, Nolan will help do whatever has to be done to get the show running on all cylinders again."

Regina stepped to the window to think, putting her back to the two men. She would have flatly refused had Donna not already asked her to go on for her. Donna, along with everyone at the station, was acutely aware that "City Gallery" had become an instant local success because of the tragedy. Even with the rerun, the ratings had skyrocketed. Tragedy or not, high ratings couldn't be ignored.

"I'll do it on one condition."

"Yes?" Max asked.

She turned to Nolan. Their eyes met and held. "That I do it my own way." She looked back to Max.

Max glanced at Nolan. "You got it. If you need anything, I'm here." He sat down at his desk. "Oh, Regina, do you have any objections to letting the makeup gal have free rein?"

"You want a face?"

"I want talent uppermost. I'll leave the rest up to you."

With a thin smile, she turned and left the office.

At her desk again, Regina pulled the file with the roster of guests, past and future. She ran her finger down the list of names, stopping at Pandora Cudahay. Pandora never failed to be entertaining. The psychic, a serious, bookish-looking woman in her mid-fifties, had last been on the show shortly after assisting the police in finding a missing child.

Suddenly the realization of what she had just done struck her. She had actually agreed to stand in for Donna on a live show. Was she insane? What the hell, she told herself. As a first-time television talk show hostess, why not go all out?

After calling the psychic and setting up the program, she spotted the list of names for the Miss Classic contestants and, before she could change her mind, she called Tammy and Amelia and invited each to lunch that afternoon. She paused at Corinne's name, then closed the file.

Leaning back in her chair, she thought about her encounter with John Davie that morning. Until that day at the station, she had never laid eyes on the man. What was his involvement? What did he know? Perhaps she should talk to him.

An hour later, sitting at a window table in Perry's Bar and Grill, Regina looked up to see Tammy, in a black miniskirt and an off-the-shoulder red knit top.

"Sorry I'm late, Regina, Gary called as I was leaving the house. The poor man is devastated by the split." Tammy dropped into a chair. "I had to talk to him."

"Is there a chance for reconciliation?"

"Gary wants to, of course, but . . . I'm not sure I'm ready yet," she said, avoiding Regina's eyes.

Regina sensed she was lying.

Tammy changed the subject. "So how's Donna?"

"She's doing very well."

"My God, I just can't believe that someone would do that to Donna. I mean, what'd she ever do to deserve that? What about her face . . . is she . . . you know . . . ? I want to visit, but I couldn't if it's as bad as Corinne's." Tammy finally wound down. "Is it?"

"No, it's not as bad as Corinne's."

Tammy pulled in an exaggerated breath and let it out with a sigh. "There is a God. Christ, when I think how close I was standing to her. Some of that stuff could've splashed onto me—oh, Jesus, that sounded awful. I didn't mean it that way," Tammy sputtered.

"It's okay, Tammy." Regina looked out the window to see Amelia, wearing saffron yellow slacks and a matching sweater, crossing the street toward them. She was the only one Regina knew who made walking look like a painful yet necessary experience.

Entering, Amelia wove her way around tables covered with blue checkered cloths. When she reached their table she paused, looking around as though waiting for someone to pull out her chair. When no one came forth, Amelia gracefully seated herself. "Regina, sweetie, how nice of you to invite me to lunch. How is Donna?"

"The doctor tells her she's very lucky."

"Lucky? Hah!" Amelia exclaimed. "The woman makes a living by her looks. How can she possibly endure, knowing she's going to be horribly disfigured?"

"She has a husband and two children," Regina said. "And many friends."

A waiter took their order. Caesar Salad and a vodka Gibson for Amelia. Vegetable soup and white wine for Tammy. A Reuben sandwich, fries, and iced tea for Regina. The two women eyed her with obvious resentment.

"It's the only meal I'll have today," she said defensively.

"I have to pip," Tammy said. "Anyone else?" The others declined. "I took a diuretic this morning. Bloated, y'know. Can't stop going." She left the table and hurried off to the restroom.

"That girl is on a campaign to kill herself," Amelia said, looking after Tammy. "Bet she takes laxatives, as well."

"Do you think she has an eating disorder?"

Amelia shrugged, dismissing Tammy. She placed her elbows on the table, her chin on her clasped hands, and leaned in toward Regina. "Now that Donna's . . . well, you know—what's become of the show?"

"It'll go on."

"Without her?"

"Until she's able to return."

"Is KSCO auditioning for the spot?"

"No."

"Look, Regina, I'd be very interested in doing 'City Gallery'. I've been at Channel 3 for years."

"That's a public broadcasting station. You're a volunteer."

"It's television. I'm photogenic, articulate, and I know people in this town . . . important people."

"I thought you were in business for yourself. What was it? Global Enterprises?"

Amelia nodded and sipped her drink. "Fletcher Kincade, my business partner, will operate GME, leaving me free to involve myself in other endeavors and, of course, expand my horizons."

"I see." Regina would just bet that Kincade was the man with Amelia that day in the studio, and she'd also bet they were more than business partners.

"Regina, you must have a measure of pull at the station. What are you, assistant something or other?"

"Coproducer."

"Nolan is producer."

"Nolan and I are coproducers."

"My, my. Then you certainly have connections."

Regina bit into a breadstick.

"I'm not going to beat around the bush—"

"You were never one to do that," Regina slipped in.

"Regina, I want that job. Can you help me?"

"I don't think so."

"I know we've had our differences."

"We don't like each other," Regina said.

"We don't like each other, but that shouldn't get in the way of business."

"Amelia," Regina said, losing patience with this conversation, "the position is already filled."

"How firm is it?"

"Firm enough. You're looking at Donna's fill-in." The flabbergasted look on Amelia's face made Regina smile. "A vote of confidence, how reassuring."

"They can't be serious?"

Regina began to laugh. "Oh, Amelia, it's so refreshing in this world of flattery and bullshit, to find someone who's not afraid to speak her mind." She raised her iced-tea glass in a mock salute.

"This is definite?"

"Nothing in this business is etched in stone. You can, of course, call on Mr. Lake and request an audition."

Amelia's only response was a slight lifting at the corners of her mouth as she put her glass to her lips. She sipped, put down the glass carefully, looked at Regina, and asked,

"Then why did you invite Tammy and me to lunch today?"

Tammy returned to the table and sat down, emanating an overpowering cloud of Tabu.

"I apologize to both of you if I led you to believe that we're looking for a replacement hostess for 'City Gallery'." Regina toyed with her utensils. "I asked you to lunch to find out if either of you have received any threats lately?" She glanced up to see Amelia and Tammy staring at each other oddly.

"Why would we get threats?" Tammy asked.

"We had two anonymous calls at the station before Donna was attacked, warning us not to air that show."

"I don't get it," Tammy said.

Amelia was quicker to pick up Regina's meaning. "You aren't implying . . . ? Absolutely not. What happened to Donna was some sort of vendetta. There's no reason to believe—"

"How can you be so positive. Unless, of course, you know who did it and why."

"Don't be ridiculous."

The two women studied each other.

"Hey, you two, what's going on here?" Tammy said. "What are you talking about?"

"I only asked if you'd had any threats," Regina said to Amelia.

"No. Have you?"

"What kind of threats?" Tammy's voice rose in alarm. "Tell me, please!"

Amelia whipped around to face Tammy, her lack of patience obvious. "It's incredible. You haven't gotten any brighter over the years. Regina is implying that whoever got to Donna wants to do the same to us."

"I didn't say that," Regina objected.

"Well, what then?"

"It's a possibility, that's all. The station was warned. There may be other warnings."

"Holy Mother of God," Tammy said in a whisper, her face pale under the peeling skin. "I told Gary I thought

156

the acid was meant for me, but I never really believed—
oh, shit . . ."

The waiter brought their order and for many minutes
they said nothing as each picked and poked at the food in
front of her.

"Corinne . . . now Donna," Tammy said finally. "Both
Miss Classic finalists. Both their lives destroyed. Oh, God,
I can't imagine anything on this earth more horrible than
having your looks wiped away"—she snapped her fingers—
"just like that."

"Well there are worse things," Regina said.

"Oh really?" Amelia gulped her drink. She motioned for
the waiter to bring another. "It's bad enough knowing that
one day our bodies will become saggy and boxlike, and
our faces as wrinkled as a cheap cotton blouse, but at least
there's some degree of control over the aging process. If
you want my opinion, I think Corinne did it. I think she
did it out of spite, to punish us for being pretty when she's
not."

"The thought crossed my mind," Regina said. "And if
that's the case, why stop at Donna?"

Amelia chewed on her lower lip. She slowly nodded
agreement.

"I was standing right next to Donna when it happened.
Maybe instead of Donna it was supposed to be—oh shit,"
Tammy whined. "I don't like this. I wish to hell I hadn't
come today. You two are bumming me out." She pushed
her soup away, dug in her purse until she found a prescription bottle, shook out a tiny yellow pill, and washed it
down with the wine.

"What do we do?" Amelia asked.

"I don't know. Keep our eyes open, report anything unusual to the police . . . move away. Aside from that . . . I
don't know."

3

The furthest thing from her mind, as she lay in Fletcher's bed watching him kiss the soft, white skin of her inner thigh, was a threat or an attack. She had conveniently put the conversation at lunch out of her mind while her lover attacked her with his mouth, giving her a delicious tongue lashing. He had threatened to make her beg for mercy from sheer ecstasy.

She moaned, gripping Fletch's hair as she squirmed on the damp sheets. "Come up here . . . ," she said deep in her throat, barely able to talk, all control gone. ". . . coming, coming . . . want you with me."

Fletcher kissed a feverish path up her sweaty torso to her breasts, then his full mouth found hers as he thrust into her. He bucked and she matched his ride, staying with him. They rolled, turned, found new positions, new sensations, panting and heaving and crying out. They became twisted in the bed covers, pillows tucked beneath them. Fletcher climaxed first, but continued until Amelia, moments later, went over the edge. Then they collapsed back on the bed, their breathing labored. Amelia, heart pounding, gave herself a few minutes to savor the last vestige of the pleasure.

He nuzzled close to her. "You wear me out, pretty lady."

She grinned, stretching.

"Can your husband make you cry out like that?"

"Only from sheer frustration. God, Fletch, I detest him. I loathe the feel of his hands on my body. Thank God he can't last long. Yet brief as his touch is, it's just short of torture. Now you, my dear, know how to make love to a woman the proper way, the lasting way."

He smiled. "It won't be much longer."

"So how'd it go with Tapperman?" she asked.

"Who?"

"Tapperman. RAM Electronics."

158

"Great," he said quickly. "We can count them in."

She rolled over on her back. Looking down at herself, she noticed that her breasts seemed flatter and further apart in this position. She pulled the sheet up to her throat.

"When do we start moving into the office?" she asked.

"Two weeks, when the phones go in. The lease was contingent on the agency fixing a few things. Minor problems, but for that kind of money they damn well better have everything running well.

"Business cards, stationery, office help?"

"All taken care of."

"I feel detached somehow. Maybe if I had something to do."

"There'll be plenty of time for that after you make the break from the old fuck."

"I guess."

"I won't be able to see you for a couple days. I have to go out of town."

"Where? Why?" A jolt of anxiety hit her. With all that was going on in her life, the one and only person she felt secure with was talking about leaving.

"Michigan. It's a private matter."

"Oh? We're starting to have secrets, are we?"

"It's my ex-wife. She's trying to get the courts to allow her husband to adopt my kid."

"What do you care? You never visit him and you certainly don't want him living with you."

"It's the principle of the thing. Billy's an only child, a Kincade. He's the last to carry on the family name."

Amelia was silent. So Fletch was an only child. She also was an only child. A change-of-life baby. A beautiful baby. From the day she was born her parents delighted in entering her in one beauty contest after another. The blue ribbons, trophies, and photographs had filled her room. Black hair, almond-shaped eyes the color of deep sapphires, fair skin that never freckled, were Amelia Travis's claim to fame. And her parents doted on her. Her father, a custodian on the ferry to Oakland, brought home something for his daughter nearly every day. A trinket, a toy, a picture book—these gifts she accepted with glee, until, at the age of seven, she discovered that the items were not new, but things left by other children on the ferry. Without a word, she went through her room, carefully gathering all the used gifts that he'd given her over the years, and, with obvious contempt, dumped them in the outdoor incinerator. In a quiet voice she had said to her mortified parents, "I want new things. Only new things. Never again give me dirty, filthy hand-me-downs."

Both parents worked to supply her ever-demanding needs. In school she had always been the most envied girl, though not the most liked. She lacked the ability to make friends. All her life she'd been too competitive, pitted against other girls and taught that they were nothing more than rivals. Spoiled, conceited, and oftentimes mean and spiteful, she got what she wanted through intimidation and, of course, her looks. The loneliness was overcome by material things.

Later, there was never a shortage of lovers.

Despite the discouraging news that KSCO had a temporary replacement for Donna Lake, Amelia, confident as usual, knew that "show business" was a fickle business. Over the years she had noticed Nolan Lake's gaze sweep over her appreciatively and his fingers linger on hers in greeting. She only had to encourage him a bit. He was extremely handsome, therefore not so easily seduced, but still she was confident. She had, after all, made a screen test that had showed great promise. If the studio had not gone under she would be a star today. If she had looked good to a major movie studio, she could certainly hold her own on a half hour local talk show.

"Leave a number where I can reach you," Amelia said to Fletcher. She sat up and began to dress.

Fletcher left the bed, took a business card from his wallet, and jotted down a number. "This is a hotel in Deerfield."

She tucked the card in her new eyeglass case with the two twenties she'd taken from Matthew's wallet that morning—old habits die hard. God, but she'd be glad when she would have complete control over her life. And the sooner the better.

"I'll go down with you to your car," Fletcher said.

"It's all right. I parked on the street." She refused to use the parking garage. The experience with the mugger was not to be repeated. Thinking about it now, Amelia felt a stab of fear.

4

She opened her eyes to see her father, a grim expression on his face, hovering over her. Under the dressing on her face, Donna smiled, hoping that he could detect, by the brightness in her eyes, how pleased she was to see him there.

"I can't believe something like this could happen to one of my own children," he said gruffly. "A travesty like this could ruin your career. How bad is it?"

Donna rolled her head on the pillow, shrugging her shoulder.

"Well, let's have a look." He reached for the gauze and began to pull it back.

"What are you doing? Stop that!" A nurse rushed in, pushing Stanley Cragg aside. "You could do irreparable damage."

"Then I better get some straight answers," he bellowed. "Is my daughter going to be deformed? I have a right to know."

"Please, sir," the nurse said, her eyes darting from Donna to her father. "If you want answers, ask Dr. Saxton."

"Is he in the hospital now?"

"Yes. Someone at the nurse's station will page him for you."

Cragg leaned over his daughter. "You'll be normal again if it takes every cent I have to make it so. I'll get the *best* plastic surgeon in the states. We'll have you moved to the finest burn clinic. You hear, Donna? By God, you'll not be malformed." He squeezed her hand. Then he was gone.

The nurse smoothed back her hair. "Miss Lake, please don't let what he said disturb you. Some people get so carried away with pain and anger they don't realize what they're saying. I'm sure he didn't mean it the way it sounded."

A tear slipped out of Donna's eye and rolled across her temple.

5

The lid of the chest freezer opened. The gloved hand reached in and began to sort through the wrapped packages of meat, searching. Under the top layer, buried beneath larger packages stamped in blue ink, was one that read "ground sirloin." The hand closed around it, drew it out. The lid closed.

Gary leaned over his daughter. "You'll be normal again
.... I'll get the
....

Sixteen

1

With a strangled cry Tammy awoke. Her hand came up to touch her face. It was somewhat rough from peeling, but no bumps, nothing crawling . . .

She shuddered with relief. It had been so real. In the nightmare she was looking in a mirror at a blemish on her face. She leaned in closer and was horrified to see it moving, wriggling, squirming to work its way out of her skin. The thing from her face dropped into her hand, rolled and twisted on her palm. It was a maggot. Tammy looked into the mirror again. Her entire face was rolling with slimy maggots breaking out through her pores. She wanted to scream, but she could only make a gagging, choking sound.

Through a foggy stillness, Tammy heard the telephone ringing. It stopped before she was really sure she heard it.

She was lying on her stomach at the foot of the bed, fully clothed except for shoes, a pillow balled under her face, the remote control in her hand. She looked around her bedroom, confused, feeling as if she were in a foreign place. Since Gary had left her, she had trouble falling asleep.

The only source of light came from the snowy screen of the TV. Static filled the room.

She rolled over on her side, moaning, and looked at the

digital clock. 2:22. Two was her lucky number. She glanced away quickly and made a wish. She wished for Gary. If she looked back at the clock while it was changing, the wish wouldn't come true.

Sitting up, she began to undress. The phone rang. She paused with her tank top halfway over her head. Who would call this late? Gary?

She rolled over and fumbled the receiver off the hook. "Hello?"

"Tamara Blanco?" a raspy voice asked.

Her maiden name. "It's Kowalski now—hey, pal, do you know what time it—?"

"Last was first. First is last. You're next."

"What?" Tammy asked.

"You're next." The line went dead.

An icy shiver rippled through her entire body. It was then she remembered why she had fallen asleep fully clothed with the TV on. She'd been paralyzed with fear. At lunch that afternoon Regina had implied they were in danger. All the finalists. And what had happened to Corinne and Donna would happen to each of them. She had gone to visit Donna after leaving Perry's, and although Tammy couldn't see the wounds under the dressing, God help her, she imagined what was there.

She went into the bathroom and, as she swallowed two Valium, thought of the girls. She hurried into their room and switched on the light. Kerry moaned. Sherry rolled over, pulling the spread over her head.

She returned to her bedroom and considered calling the police. She lifted the receiver and pressed buttons. She'd call Gary and ask him what she should do. After a half dozen rings Gary's smoothing voice came on the line. It was the same recorded greeting she'd heard a hundred times, but it made her feel better, comforted her. She listened to the voice until the message ended, then forgetting about the police, she hung up, redialed, listened again.

Warrior barked. The dog barked again, the sounds becoming more excited. She rose to stand indecisively at the foot of the bed, then hesitantly she made her way through the house. Her heart pumped a little faster with each step. Probably a cat teasing the dog, she told herself. The neighborhood was lousy with cats.

As she moved through the rooms she switched on lights. On the counter that divided the kitchen and the dining room, Tammy snatched up the receiver of the trimline phone. She held her thumb on the button, prepared to punch 911 if necessary.

The barking had stopped.

The silence clung to her like a web. She shivered. With a shaky finger she drew back the drapes at the sliding glass door. Her own reflection in the glass startled her.

She flipped on the porch light.

Warrior was on the concrete patio. He had his backside to her, and from where she stood she could see his head was down and his shoulders were lowered. There was something between his paws and he was sniffing and licking it.

Tammy slid the door open. Warrior turned his head to look at her. "Warrior, what've you got there?"

At his feet Tammy saw what looked like a ball of ground beef. Puzzled, she took another step forward. Now where would he get a chunk of ground beef at this time of night? Unless . . .

"Oh, shit . . . " she hissed. "Warrior! No!"

He jumped, his eyes widening. Then he quickly went back to the thing at his feet. In two gulps it was gone.

Tammy rushed out the door. Warrior guiltily moved off several feet, head down, tail between his legs.

"C'mere, boy." She stopped, patted her thigh. "C'mere, baby."

The dog whined. Then he suddenly retched, tenuously at first, then violently. Within moments his body heaved in convulsive spasms. The panic in his eyes threw terror into Tammy. She stopped cold in her tracks, frozen, unable to move.

The dog whined, ran in frantic circles. And she knew

165

then that that was no ordinary hunk of meat. It was deadly.

Tammy quickly looked around her. Dark shadows were everywhere. What lurked in those shadows? What was waiting for her to come out in the open to help the dog?

Instinctively her hands moved upward to protect her face. She backed up.

"Warrior." Her voice a hoarse whisper. "Come, Warrior."

The dog continued to run in a circle, moving further away from her and closer to those horrible shadows. It pawed frantically at its foaming mouth and throat.

With a sob, Tammy ran into the house and slammed the slider, locking it. She dialed 911. As she talked to the police dispatcher, she crouched down under the breakfast bar and cried hysterically, hiccuping. Outside, through the loose weave of the drapes, Tammy watched in agony as Warrior, on his side now, thrashing, chest heaving, no longer able to make a sound, fought against the impossible. Then, with a final paroxysmal shudder, he lay still.

A flood of inconsolable pain, grief, and guilt erupted within her. She buried her face in her hands and wailed.

There was nothing she could have done. Nothing except to try to comfort the sweet baby in his dying moments—but at the cost of what? God Almighty, at the cost of *what?*

2

Bells were ringing somewhere and she wished they'd stop. Moaning softly, Regina rolled over and realized the ringing was coming from the bedside telephone. The luminous hands on the clock read 2:44.

Without turning on the light, she lifted the receiver. Before she could speak, a high-pitched voice screeched out, "He was here! God, Regina, that fucking madman was at my house!"

"Tammy?" Regina pulled herself up to lean against the headboard.

"He warned me. Then he killed Warrior. He poisoned my dog and . . . and he was waiting for me to go out there!"

"Tammy, what are you talking about?"

"You were right, Regina. He *is* after us."

"My God, Tammy . . . "

"You've got to come over. I can't get through to Gary, his machine is on."

"Have you called the police?"

"They're on their way."

Regina raked her hand through her hair, holding it off her forehead. "All right, I'll be there soon."

Tammy's hysteria had unnerved her. Her fingers trembled as she dressed in jeans, a bulky sweater, and jogging shoes.

In the bathroom she splashed cold water on her face and pulled her hair into a ponytail; then she went into Kristy's room and shook her awake.

"What's going on?" Kristy leaned up on one elbow, her eyes still closed.

"We have to go to Tammy's."

"Another time." Kristy rolled over.

"Up. I'll explain everything on the way."

Kristy sat up, pulled on the sweatpants and shirt that Regina handed her, slipped her feet into hi-top Reeboks.

They left the apartment and were halfway down the stairs when Regina heard the distant sound of the telephone ringing in their apartment. She paused, putting a hand out to stop Kristy.

"I'll get it." Kristy hurried back up.

Regina waited on the stairs for several moments listening to the tinny meows of the kittens in the storage room. Then she slowly continued down toward the dimly lit stairs to the first floor. Tammy's raving conversation raced through her head: "He poisoned my dog . . . waiting for me . . ." A chilling jolt erupted in her, making her shiver.

From the bottom of the stairs she heard a scuffing sound. It came from the rear of the apartment house. At

167

the back door.

She looked up to the second floor where the kittens' cries were becoming more agitated. The cat? Had the mother cat been locked outside, she wondered, unable to get back to her hungry brood?

Cautiously, rubber soles silent on the hardwood floor, she crossed to the closed door of the laundry room and stopped. She put her ear to it.

There was a metallic scraping on the other side. The knob turned. Suddenly the door was swinging inward. Regina managed to step back before it could hit her, but not quickly enough to get out of the way of whoever was charging through. He was on her in an instant, his body bearing her backward with such force that her feet went out from under her. Then she was going down and the man, clutching at her now, was falling with her. They fell to the floor. An arm, tight around her waist, squeezed the air from her.

The man whose weight bore down on her was breathing deeply, his shirt was wet, and she could feel his heart pounding at his breastbone. Her arms and legs were pinned.

"Don't move—," he began.

She braced her body, then drove her head forward. His words were cut off as the top of her head soundly met the side of his face. He grunted. But instead of letting go, he held on tighter, bringing his head in close so it was impossible for her to butt him again. They struggled silently. She tried to reach for her purse and her canister of mace.

A hand found her breast, then jerked away quickly. A moan escaped from his throat. He released her and rolled to one side.

Regina quickly scrambled to her feet. The man lying on his back on the floor, wearing a dark leather jacket, was John Davie. She watched him warily.

"Mrs. Van Raven, what the hell?—Look, I'm sorry. I thought you were a prowler." He came to his feet, somewhat slower than she. He reached out to her.

168

She backed up. "Don't touch me, all right?"

He shook his head. "Believe me, I'm as surprised as you to meet this way. What are you doing at the back door in the middle of the night?"

"I could ask the same question."

"I tend bar nights. I was coming home. I jog from work, that's why I'm drenched and out of breath. If I hurt you, I'm sorry."

She licked her dry lips, but said nothing.

He reached for her again, but when she glared at him, he dropped his hand, saying, "You have blood on your face. I think it's mine." He pressed the back of his hand to his mouth. It came away bloody. "Yeah, it's mine. Damn, that hurt."

She could believe it. The top of her head, where it had connected with his mouth, throbbed. She swiped at the side of her face. She heard an upstairs door close. Kristy. She backed up several steps.

"Wait. I've got to talk to you. You have nothing to fear from me. If I wanted to hurt you, I had the perfect opportunity a moment ago."

Regina heard footsteps on the stairs.

"Mother?" A whisper.

"Here, Kristy," Regina responded quietly.

Her daughter rounded the banister and walked toward them. "Who's with you?"

"It's me. John Davie."

"Mr. Davie was just coming in," Regina said.

Kristy looked from Regina to John, not trying to conceal a puzzled expression. She reached out and straightened her mother's twisted sweater. To John she said: "You're bleeding, John."

"I did that," Regina said.

"But she promised me two out of three," John said with a straight face.

"Excuse us, Mr. Davie, we have to go." Regina grabbed Kristy's hand and pulled.

He placed a hand over her arm and held on firmly. She

looked up at him. His face was set, at the corner of his mouth, which was already swelling, a bead of blood glistened. "All kidding aside, we have to talk. Are you coming or going?"

"Going."

"It's kinda late."

"A friend is in trouble."

"Does it have anything to do with what happened to Lake and Odett?"

She nodded.

"Let me go with you."

"No. I don't think so."

"You still don't trust me." It was not a question.

"I don't know you, Mr. Davie."

"But do you believe that you may be in danger?"

Regina and Kristy exchanged glances. Regina felt a tingling at the base of her skull. At this moment she was running on nervous energy, compounded by extreme trepidation. But didn't everything seem menacing in the middle of the night after being knocked to the floor in the dark by a hard-breathing, sweaty man in a leather jacket?

She nodded.

He released her arm. "We'll talk later. Be careful, okay?"

She nodded again. She took out her mace key ring and they hurried out the front door to the station wagon.

On the deserted freeway, after Regina had told Kristy about Tammy's call and her bizarre meeting with John Davie, they fell silent for several miles.

"I forgot to ask," Regina said. "Who was on the phone?"

"Wrong number. He wanted a Miss Houston. Hey, that was your name before you married Daddy, huh?"

"What did the voice sound like?" Regina asked with disquiet.

"Deep, sorta sandpapery—oh, there it is, Mom, Daly City turnoff up ahead."

Regina had to grip the wheel to keep it from slipping from her wet palms. Her throat suddenly felt dry.

"Yes, Mrs. Kowalski, dog poisoning is a criminal offense," the uniformed officer said. "But I'm afraid it doesn't entitle you to police protection."

"Warrior was killed because he was a guard dog." Tammy hiccuped. Sherry and Kerry sat on each side of her on the couch. She pulled them closer. "Don't you understand? Whoever did that to him, wanted me to go outside."

"And then what?"

She lost all patience. "And then I would've had acid splashed in my face."

"Ma'am, I think—"

"I was one of the contestants in the Classic pageant," she said in exasperation. She watched the two policemen exchange glances. "The same pageant that Donna Lake was in. You've heard of Donna Lake, I assume?"

The officers nodded.

"Someone's out to get all of us."

"All of you, ma'am?"

"All of the finalists. Maybe all of the contestants, for all I know."

"I see."

The other officer said, "The vet will autopsy your dog. Find out exactly what killed him. Could be he just had a heart attack or a stroke."

"He was foaming at the mouth! He ate—." The doorbell interrupted.

Sherry slid off the couch and ran to the door, a policeman right behind her. A moment later she was back, followed by Regina and Kristy.

Tammy jumped up, rushed to Regina, and embraced her. "Jesus, am I glad to see you. Tell these . . . these policemen about your theory. Tell them how someone wants to make us hideous."

Regina put her arm around Tammy. "Tammy, that's all

171

it is, a theory. I have no proof."

"Christ, my dog was poisoned. That should certainly—"

One officer cut in, "The only thing we know for sure at this point, ma'am, is that the dog is dead. We don't know how it died."

"When will you know?" Regina asked.

"Soon as the vet gets to it."

"Which vet?"

"Over at the Daly City Animal Hospital." He excused himself and went to join his partner outside.

Tammy looked out the slider and saw the young Latin-looking cop dragging a black bag across the patio. Warrior. Such a faithful dog. She turned away and began to cry again.

"I'll get you a pill, Momma," Sherry said.

Tammy nodded, blew her nose.

"Hi, Kristy babe," Tammy sniffed, put an arm around her and squeezed. "It's good to see you again. Jesus, you get prettier and prettier."

The police finished up and left. Kristy took charge of the twins, playing video games with them while the women talked quietly in the kitchen.

After a second cup of coffee, running on caffeine and nervous energy, Tammy said, "You've been great, Regina. Not many people would rush out in the middle of the night to be with a friend. Not a friend, actually. What contact we've had over the years was because of Donna. She's so good for all of us. I never felt threatened by her like I did with you and Amelia. And it's not just because I beat her out in the contest, it's . . . well . . ."

"I know."

"I was too fucking jealous of you to give our friendship a chance."

Regina smiled. "That's honest."

"Weren't you jealous of Corinne?"

"The contest wasn't that . . ." Regina paused, then went on, "Yes, yes I suppose I was."

Tammy realized then that Regina wasn't being as hon-

172

est.

"You were the first runner-up," Tammy said, "and you were supposed to take over as queen."

Regina nodded.

"Why didn't you?"

Regina stared into the coffee mug.

"The truth," Tammy said quietly.

"I didn't have a year to devote to the obligations of the winner."

After a moment of stunned silence, Tammy said incredulously, "God, you came so close to winning. And you didn't even want the title. Or the crown or any of the perks that went with it. How could you do that to the rest of us?"

Regina looked at Tammy. "Do what?"

"Without you I'd've been the second runner-up," Tammy's voice was high and forced, "not third."

"You don't know that for sure."

"Sure enough."

"And what if you had been second runner-up, where do you think it would have gotten you?"

"You're a producer of a TV show," Tammy said, knowing her tone was accusatory, but unable to stop.

"Donna's show."

Tammy understood her meaning; it was ridiculous to think the pecking order would have changed the outcome of their futures.

"Maybe you're right, Tam. Maybe you would have been second runner-up. Maybe—"

"Oh, Regina, I'm such a bitch," Tammy cut in, ashamed of herself. "I wake you up in the middle of the night, drag you from your bed so I can accuse you of screwing up my life. I wish to hell none of us had entered that fucking contest."

They fell silent. Tammy picked nervously at the glittery polish on one long thumbnail, her mind wandering back to Warrior again. Gary would be heartbroken, he loved that dumb mutt. The black Labrador was his, but Gary

173

felt that the girls should have the dog for protection.

"Regina, will you take us to Gary's?"

"Now?"

Tammy nodded. "He has his answering machine on. I can't get through." She failed to mention that Gary always kept his answering machine on.

"Whenever you're ready."

4

At 5:12, Regina double parked the station wagon in front of Gary's house in the Sunset district. Regina and Tammy sat in the front seat, the twins and Kristy in the back.

"I'll wait here till you've gone inside," Regina said. "Just in case there's a problem."

"It's okay. We're always welcome."

"I don't mind waiting."

Tammy, with her arms around her daughters, went up the walk to the front door. Tammy used the knocker, timidly at first, then with gusto.

After several long minutes, the door opened. Regina caught a glimpse of a slender arm and a long royal blue robe. She could not hear what was being said on the stoop, but Tammy looked visibly shaken.

"Oh-oh, looks like trouble," Kristy said.

The girls clung to their mother.

The door opened wider. The woman disappeared only to be replaced in the doorway by a tall, thin, bare-chested man wearing rimless glasses and what looked like a pair of sweatpants. The girls vanished inside, the door closed, and Tammy, left standing on the stoop, began to beat her fists against the door. After several moments she turned and came down the steps, stumbling on the last one.

The rear door opened and Tammy slid inside, closing the door softly. "He had company. Out of town friends. I . . . uh, didn't want to impose. The girls can flop on the living room floor."

Regina started the engine and pulled away.

"Where are we going?" Tammy asked, looking behind her at her husband's house.

"To our place. We all need some sleep."

Twenty minutes later Regina was making up the sofa bed in the living room. Kristy had gone on to bed. Tammy, in a stupor, sat slumped on one of the club chairs, staring at the floor.

It had all caught up with her, Regina thought. The dog's death, the shock, the pills, the rejection. A lot for one person to take in a single night. She found a cotton nightshirt and went to stand before Tammy.

"Here, put this on." She held out the nightshirt. "We better try to get a few hours sleep. Tammy?"

Tammy raised her head lethargically; her eyes seemed glazed and unfocused.

"Tammy?"

With a sudden physical outburst, Tammy began to pound her fists on the top of her thighs. With each blow she grunted in pain and frustration.

"Tammy, stop. Please." Regina grabbed her wrists and held them, dropping to her knees.

"The bastard moved her in," she said vehemently. "She's living in *my* house. Sleeping in *my* bed with *my* husband." Tammy strained, and the strength behind her months of aerobics became quite evident to Regina as she struggled to hold on. Tammy broke the hold and then she did something that took Regina by surprise—she suddenly went limp, fell to her knees, and began to sob; deep, racking sobs. "He loves her. What will I do? Reggie, what will I do now?"

Regina hugged her tightly. "It's okay, Tam. Everything's going to be all right. You'll see. You'll see."

"I don't think so," she cried bitterly, hiccuping now. "Gary threatened to put me back in that nut-nuthouse."

"What nuthouse?"

"They ke-kept me six weeks in a mental ward. Ga-Gary

175

wants me to go back."

Regina held her and rocked. But the comforting words she longed to say wouldn't come.

5

Donna held the mirror with a tremulous hand. She was sitting up in the hospital bed and the room was brilliant with sunlight. Nolan and the boys stood on her right. Her father and Dr. Saxton were on her left.

The doctor leaned in and began to take off the bandage. She kept the mirror turned away, too terrified to watch. She closed her eyes.

The last scrap of gauze came away and she heard some-one draw in a sharp breath. Her pulse pounded and she felt faint. She opened her eyes and saw Nolan. The expression on his face was one of astonishment.

She turned her head to look at her father. The old man had tears in his eyes. He reached out, putting his hand over hers, and lifted the mirror. Slowly she turned her head.

She was perfectly normal.

What was happening here?

She looked to the doctor in disbelief. He smiled, nod-ded.

"It's something new we've been working with." He stroked her jaw. "A drug that rapidly heals without a trace of scarring."

She began to cry. Nolan took her in his arms and shushed her. In her ear he said quietly, "Donna, luv, I can say this now, now that you're okay. God forgive me, I don't think I could have lived with a woman who was . . . "

She cried from sheer relief and happiness.

And as she felt herself awakening, she fought it, strug-gled to go back in, to escape for a bit longer in her miracle dream. But the bright light of day was gradually replaced by the steely dawn, more dark than light. "I'm sorry, Nolan," she whispered.

Fully awake now, Donna wiped her eyes with a corner of the sheet. An overwhelming sadness closed around her. Although her loved ones rallied around her each day, and the room filled daily with flowers from her devoted fans, she'd never felt so lonely in her life. Tammy and Amelia had finally come, and though they were kind and supportive, it was apparent they both struggled to control the revulsion that roiled inside them when they looked at her.

She hated the feelings that had gradually come to replace the apathetic, disjointed ones following on the heels of the assault. Now, along with the incredible loneliness, she battled postattack terror. A new nurse or orderly entering her room sent her pulse racing dangerously. She had become distrusting and hypervigilant.

Not only was she frightened for her life, she was terrified that she would lose her husband's love.

She was about to close her eyes when she sensed someone was in the room with her. Turning her head to the left, she saw a tall figure in a long black coat standing just inside the door. A hood covered the head.

Donna gripped the sheet tightly.

The figure moved forward, one faltering step at a time, until it reached the foot of the bed. With what looked to Donna like a calculated move, a gloved hand reached up and pulled back the hood. Wraparound sunglasses caught the soft night light. Those came off next.

The fact that the figure looking across the bed at her was a woman failed to alleviate Donna's terror. Her breathing became labored.

"Hi, Donna."

Donna recognized the rusty sounding voice. Although the light in the room was diffused, she could make out the dark twisted skin and the black space where an eye should have been. Corinne.

She swallowed.

"Yes. It's early, I know. I don't go out in the daylight."

Donna balled the sheet against her stomach.

177

"You're wondering why I'm here? I wanted to see you." A long pause. "That's all. I just wanted to see you."

Donna glanced at the call button attached to the rail of the bed.

"Looks like you've still got both your eyes." She moved around the corner of the bed and took a step closer. "Does it hurt? Can't talk, huh? Bet you're gonna have plastic surgery. That's no fun either." Another step. "Burns are such a bitch to work on." She chuckled softly. "Course, I wouldn't know. My old man took the money I won, the money that should've gone to fix me up, and paid his bookie with it. He thought his miserable hide was more important than mine. After he pissed that money away and hocked the rest of my winnings, he got deep into them again, so there was never any money for me. My mother worked herself to death to pay his gambling debts and keep him in booze and diabetic insulin. Now we make do with state aid." She was standing alongside Donna's head now, the stale, sour smell of alcohol clearly on her breath. "So tell me, Miss Celebrity, Miss Pollyanna of the Classic women, do you still want me on your show?"

Donna squeezed her eyes shut, afraid to see more.

"What, no pity for me?" Corinne asked lightly. "No, I guess not. Well, save it for yourself. You're going to need it."

Long after those words, though Donna was certain Corinne was no longer in the room, she kept her eyes tightly closed. But behind her lids she saw Corinne as clearly as if she still stood before her. She would end up like Corinne, no amount of surgery could fix her. Whatever the damage, it would be with her always.

Her teeth chattered, making the wounds at her jaw and throat throb.

Seventeen

1

Amelia lay on her side with her eyes closed, feigning sleep. The bed shifted slightly. She held her breath. Cool fingers probed between her legs. She jerked reflexively as a wave of repulsion washed through her.

Oh, how she hated him. Wooing or foreplay were non-existent. Not that she wanted Matthew to kiss or fondle her or in any way prolong the vile act that he called love, but she detested the way he came at her, fingers poking, pinching. The moment he touched her she stiffened, and no amount of self-will could induce her to relax, mentally remove herself, or take on a fantasy lover. If he knew how sick his touch made her, the shock would render him impotent for life. Perhaps she'd tell him when the time was right.

He fit himself to her spoon-fashion, the wiry hairs on his legs pricking at her calves like cockleburs, his erection pressed at her lower back.

"Amelia," he said quietly.

It was no use. He would persist until she could stand it no more, and stalling only wasted time. She turned over on her back and parted her legs. Matthew rolled over on her. In a matter of moments he was on his way.

From years of having to endure, she knew what Matthew liked; what would hurry him along so she could get his bony body off her. She licked her lips and moaned.

"Is it good, Amelia?"

"Hmmm."

"Amelia?"

"Oh, yes, always." She moaned again and rolled her hips just so.

He let out a sharp cry, then collapsed on top of her.

She wanted to push him off, rush into the bathroom and scrub herself with a stiff loofah sponge, but Matthew took his time.

At last he rolled off her. "I have a surprise for you."

Amelia smiled knowingly. Now that the disgusting act was over, it really hadn't been so bad. Especially since he had something for her. Was it the sheared beaver jacket? Or the half-carat diamond earrings she'd pointed out to him at Gump's? She preferred the jewelry. It could always be converted into cash.

"How sweet, darling. What is it?"

"I know you were disappointed that you couldn't visit your parents last weekend, so I've cleared my calendar for a couple days. For our anniversary we'll drive to Napa and stay at the Meadowvale Inn. While I get in a round of golf you can take the car and drive out to see them."

The joy of anticipation drained out of Amelia. She felt cold and sick again. The Meadowvale was the inn where she and Fletcher were to stay. With Fletch it would have been heaven. But with Matthew it could only be hell.

No fur jacket, no diamond earrings. Nothing. Worse than nothing. His surprise? A plush suite where he would behave like a raunchy, insatiable lover.

The timing couldn't have been worse. Fletcher was due back then. And there was one other bit of business . . .

"Is there something wrong?"

"Hmmm?" She brought her attention back to her husband.

"You don't look pleased with my surprise." He frowned. "If you'd rather not . . ."

"No. No, darling," she said quickly. "Of course I'm

pleased. It's our anniversary, after all . . . how thoughtful."
She squeezed his hand and in a distracted voice she added
quietly, "How very thoughtful."

Matthew rolled to the side of the bed and opened the
top drawer of the nightstand. With a self-pleased grin he
handed her a small velvet box.

She took the box, looking up at him; then, tentatively,
she opened it. Against the black velvet the twelve graduated diamonds set in white gold blazed like stars in a des-
ert sky.

"Ohhh," she breathed. "The tennis earrings."

"As I was purchasing these I said to myself, 'There is
only one thing perfect enough to wear with them.' "

The jacket? A matching necklace? Bracelet? Amelia's
head felt light. What else had he bought for her? Perhaps
the ordeal could be somewhat more endurable if . . .

"Bubbles," he said with a pleased expression. "Hot tub
bubbles. I reserved a suite with a Jacuzzi. You, my love,
in a pool of hot, bubbly water wearing nothing but the
earrings." His hand squeezed a breast.

Amelia smiled. Her fingers gripped the box tightly.

Several hours later, just before noon, with their bags
packed and Amelia putting the finishing touches to her
face and hair, Matthew, impatient with waiting, announced
he was going to the station to fill the car with gas. After he
left, Amelia rushed to the phone. Her first call was to Nolan Lake at KSCO. Then she dialed the number from the
card Fletcher had given her. After a half dozen rings a resonant voice said: "Good afternoon, Morse, Blake, Noble
Mortuary. How may I help you?"

"Pardon me, is this 315-555-1010?" She was assured it
was. She hung up.

Damn!

What was the name of the hotel where Fletcher said he
would be staying? Had he even mentioned a name? She
couldn't remember. He had inadvertently jotted down the
wrong number, and she had no idea where he was.

There was nothing to do but wait until he returned.

On his way to the TV station John had made up his mind that he would not take no for an answer. What he had to say was important, more so to her than to him. The tricky part was knowing how much to reveal without scaring her or making her even more suspicious.

He slipped past the station's main desk and took the same route he'd followed the day Donna Lake was assaulted. He passed the restroom from which she had been wheeled and continued on until he came to a large room with desks and tables and unfamiliar equipment.

Regina Van Raven was sitting behind the first desk, her head lowered. The dark brown hair highlighted with streaks of a lighter brown was pulled back into a French braid.

He stopped at the desk, his hands in the deep pockets of his bomber jacket, and watched her. Her lashes were very long and quite lovely. She was wearing makeup today, more than the first time when he'd spotted her out front with her daughter, but not as much as on that fateful day of taping. Today she wore a green cotton shirt, the stiff collar standing up along her jaw, the sleeves rolled to her elbows. Underneath the shirt, which was open to the waist and tucked into a wide faux reptile belt, she wore a gold tank top. The neckline was scooped, and when she lifted her head to look up at him, he caught a glimpse of cleavage, and he knew her breasts would be round and not pointed.

"Hi," he said, meeting her eyes.

She leaned back in the chair, her expression stoic.

"I can't keep chasing after you." He tried to match her detached countenance. "I thought if I took you to lunch, y'know, with people all around, you'd trust me enough to listen to what I have to say. This isn't a pickup."

Without taking her gaze from his, she tossed the pen on

the blotter. She reached into her desk drawer and pulled out her large, shapeless handbag, slung the strap over her shoulder, rose, and said casually, "I've been wanting to try that Hungarian restaurant on the next block."

"'Dobos' will be honored to have the company of one so noble."

She stared at him blankly.

"I was referring to myself. I'm practically family to them."

She laughed then, one of those deep, throaty laughs that sound sexy, yet genuine.

She took the lead.

As they walked through the main lobby, John noticed a tall, slim man, good looking in that sculptured, impeccable way of a model, standing at the main door. The man openly stared at Regina as she stopped to exchange words with the receptionist. An ex-lover, John wondered? Such intense glaring could only come from a jealous ex-lover or a misogynist.

The man opened the door for them, and as she passed him, he said, "We need to talk."

Her response was a quick nod.

Out on the sidewalk John asked, "Who was that?"

"Nolan Lake."

Donna's husband. Curious.

They crossed Van Ness and began walking north.

The heat wave had broken the day before and everything was back to normal, a cool sixty-one degrees with clear skies.

"I've often thought about walking to work," she said. "Especially when the weather's this great. It's only six blocks, but somehow I never allow myself enough time. Where do you tend bar?"

"Across the street from where we'll be having lunch."

She was silent and he sensed some of the mysteries were coming together for her, such as his being in the station the day of the acid attack, and the cops at his door—simple enough to explain. It was the other coincidence that

183

would be tougher to swallow. How would he explain his being a suspect in Corinne's assault? All in good time.

"We have a mutual friend," he said.

"Oh?"

"Wilma Axelrod."

"Wilma . . . of course. It's Greenwood now. She's the one who told me about the apartment. Have you heard from her?"

"No. Have you?"

She shook her head.

They walked a ways in silence.

Stepping in close behind her to walk single file between two cars waiting at the light, John noticed that the sun on her hair made it shine like semiprecious metals—copper and bronze. He marveled at how the intricate braid seemed to alternate between plaits of brown, red, and gold. He was reminded of Black Hills gold.

She stopped suddenly and John nearly ran into her.

She looked perplexed. "Isn't this it?" She tipped her head at the black metal door on the corner.

Somewhat flustered he said, "This is it." He went ahead to open the door. "Prepare to be fussed over. Louie fancies himself a ladies' man, and any friend of mine is a friend of the Dobos family."

The interior was cool and dim. The pungent aroma of cabbage, and unknown aromas—rich, spicy, hearty, and sweet—permeated heavily in the air.

Louie came bounding out of the kitchen, a broad smile on his round face, his arms open. The smile diminished with each advancing step, until, reaching them at last, his face was somber and his arms hung at his sides.

"John, so good to see you," Louie said formally, his eyes darting to Regina.

"How's it going, Louie? I brought a friend, Regina Van Raven."

Louie nodded. "You want lunch?"

"Lunch would be good."

Although there were several empty booths, Louie took

them to a table in the middle of the room.

"May we have a booth, Louie?"

Louie pointed at one. "There. Sit wherever you like." He left them and moved behind the bar.

John waited until Regina was seated before excusing himself and going to the bar.

"Lou, what's going on? You're acting like I brought in the food and health inspector." Louie stared over John's shoulder. John turned, following his gaze. Suddenly it all made sense. Ilona stood in the archway that led to the restrooms. Ilona, the pretty, young refugee who wanted to be an American wife.

How far was this crap going to go? Twice this week, Mrs. Dobos had brought Ilona to his aunt's for a visit. Good manners had dictated that he join them for a cup of coffee, at which time Ilona's knee repeatedly had found his under the dining room table. So far he'd been able to put off his aunt's suggestion that he take Ilona out. But he knew it was only a matter of time before they would be pushed together.

It was obvious he wasn't going to make any points here today. But then points had not been on his agenda. He had serious business to talk over with Regina Van Raven, and old friends gushing over him would only be a distraction.

"I'll take the lady and go," John said to Louie.

Louie grabbed John's sleeve, looked appropriately shamed. His grin was anything but happy. "My manners are unforgivable. You sit down with the pretty *no*." He tapped a finger at John's chest. "You are like family, my Johnnie."

"That's what I told the lady. Right now she's thinking I'm either a liar or a black sheep."

"Go on, sit down. I will take care of you myself."

John slid into the booth. "A little misunderstanding."

Regina smiled weakly and went back to the menu as though totally engrossed in it. She was as uncomfortable as he was, John told himself. That would teach him to be such a fucking blowhard.

"How's the lip?" she asked.

"Lip? Oh, that," he said, touching the corner of his mouth. It was still slightly swollen.

"Does it hurt?"

"No." Lie number one.

True to his word, Louie came offering drinks, appetizers. However, the corner booth to Ilona and the rest of the family nearly ceased to exist.

Between the soup and the entrée, Louie presented them with a bottle of white wine. Although Regina declined, saying she had work to do, Louie poured the wine nonetheless.

"Just take a sip," John said under his breath. "He won't leave you alone unless you do."

"Really, I—"

John held up his glass, waiting. Regina reluctantly lifted hers. Louie smiled and backed away.

"There's an old Hungarian toast that goes: 'Bort, buzát, békességet, szép asszony feleséget!'—Wine, wheat, peace, and a beautiful woman for a wife."

She lifted an eyebrow. "In that order?"

"Here's mud in your eye." He drank, and after a moment so did she.

"It's very good." She lifted the bottle from the ice bucket. "Leanyka?"

"Little Girl."

"You're Hungarian?"

"Half. The other half is English. My body and mind are at constant odds with each other. And you?"

"A little of this and a little of that. A sixth-generation American. I even have a drop or two of Cherokee."

"I see it . . . here." He touched the side of her face. "In the cheekbones."

Sounds of soft violin music came from the bar, gypsy love songs. Louie brought their food. Paprika veal cutlets in sour cream sauce for Regina. A hearty peasant stew for John. She dug right in, seeming to enjoy it. She sipped the wine absently, and when her glass was empty he re-filled it.

Well into the meal Regina lifted the wine glass and stared somberly into it. "What do you think is happening?"

He knew she wasn't talking about the wine or the violins.

"What I think is that someone is out to get you and the other finalists. What I don't know is why. Twenty years ago I thought I knew. But that's another story."

"Twenty years ago?"

"The pageant."

"What do you know about the pageant?" Regina asked.

"I was a journalist." Lie number two. "I covered the contest."

"I see."

"It was my assumption that Corinne Odett was attacked because she had something that someone else wanted."

"The title?"

"Yes."

Regina stared at him, then dropped her gaze to the table. "Then I had the most to gain. The title would have been mine."

"But you declined it. Why?"

She laughed, that low, throaty laugh that made him want to hear it again. "You're the second person in two days to ask me that."

"Did someone persuade you to give it up?"

"I'll tell you what I told Tammy, which is the truth. I didn't have time for it. And frankly, I didn't want it. I entered the contest on false pretenses and I'm not proud of it. By being a finalist I deprived another girl of that honor. It's funny, but until yesterday I never thought of it that way. I hadn't realized how important being a finalist in the Miss Classic Pageant had been to the others." She had a faraway look in her eyes. "Even now, twenty years later, it's still important to them."

He stared at her, waiting.

"I entered the contest because Donna asked me to. I

never in a million years thought I'd get that far. I felt like a heel having to turn it down. But I just couldn't fulfill that commitment." When he failed to comment, she asked, "What's your interest in this now?"

"I hate unfinished business. I don't want anyone else hurt." Not a lie, but not the whole truth either. He wasn't ready to tell her that he wanted to clear his own name and avenge a woman he once loved.

"All right," she said thoughtfully. "What do you have in mind?"

"I think if we find Corinne's assailant, we'll find Donna's."

"That's for the police to do."

"To a certain extent, yes. But I don't think they're looking beyond this one incident. Call the police and tell them you think you're next, then let me know what they say."

He saw something flicker in her eyes. Disbelief? Fear?

She glanced at her watch. "I have to get back to work."

John asked for the check. Louie refused, insisting lunch was on him.

As they slid from the booth, Regina said quietly, "There's a very pretty girl standing at the hostess station who hasn't been able to keep her eyes off you through most of the lunch. Am I in danger?"

Without looking at Ilona, John said, "Yes. But not from her."

3

The scene was the same. A surge of optimism rushed through her. Déjà vú? No, Donna told herself. That had been a dream, this was the real thing.

Her father and the doctor stood on her left. Nolan and a nurse were on her right. The boys were at camp. There was no mirror in her hand.

Donna took Nolan's hand, it was icy cold. "You don't have to see this if you'd rather not," she said to him.

188

"Of course he does," her father said. "He's your husband. He can't hide his head in the sand until the wounds heal and the surgery is completed. Your tragedy affects each of us. We all must bear the pain and unpleasantness."

Nolan stared down at her. "Whenever you're ready, doctor"; his voice cracked.

"Donna is a very lucky lady," Dr. Saxton said as he removed the gauze. "The angle in which the acid was thrown — underneath, instead of full face — well, when I think of the damage that could have been done . . ."

The last of it came away.

Donna watched Nolan. His eyes stared blankly at first, as though they failed to comprehend what they saw. Then his entire body seemed to quaver. He blinked, looking away.

"As you can see," the doctor said, "we've already begun skin grafting on the necrotic tissue where no new epithelization can occur."

"Speak English," Cragg said.

"On the major burn area, the nerve endings, fascia, and the blood supply, were damaged. Little or no chance of regeneration on its own."

"Bring me a mirror," Donna said.

"That's not a good idea," Dr. Saxton said.

"If she wants a mirror," Cragg said, "then bring her one."

"I'm afraid I'll have to pull rank on you, Mr. Cragg. When I feel she's ready to see, then she'll see."

Nolan had backed up a step, pulling his hand from Donna's. His gaze seemed to flit everywhere except at his wife.

"I want to see," Donna said, her voice quivering.

"It looks unpleasant right now," the doctor said. "The healing process has just begun. In a few weeks there will be a dramatic improvement."

Nolan continued to back up.

"Bring me a mirror!" she cried out.

"Damnit, this is ridiculous." Cragg jerked open the drawer on the nightstand, hastily rummaged through Donna's purse until he found the compact; opening it, he thrust it into her outstretched hand.

The doctor moved to grab for the mirror. Donna twisted away, held it up to her face and looked into it. She had only a glimpse before the compact was snatched from her hand. But that glimpse was enough to make her gag. She gagged again, going into a spasm of dry heaves.

The doctor was bending over her. A nurse readied a syringe to inject her. Her father was shouting orders of some sort. Nolan seemed to have disappeared. And through all this, with her stomach heaving and her eyes tearing, she saw a vivid mental picture of a raw, weeping horror. Her throat and the underside of her chin had been turned inside out.

4

Out on the sidewalk in front of Dobos', John pointed across the street to a bar Regina had driven past five days a week for two years. He explained that his aunt and uncle Szabo owned the bar as well as the apartment building.

A breeze had come up while they were inside. It blew wispy tendrils of hair across her face. She brushed the hair from her eyes, and they began to walk.

"John, do you have any idea who the acid thrower is? Do you think it's Amelia?"

"Not really, though I'm not disallowing it. She certainly had that intense drive, determination, and aggressiveness. Corinne had it too."

"Someone called the station with a warning—twice. Amelia wanted to be on the show in a bad way. She had nothing to gain by this attack on—oh Lord . . ."

"What?"

Regina shook her head. It wasn't enough reason, she told herself.

"Say what's on your mind."

"Afterwards, she asked about the replacement for Donna

on 'City Gallery'. But, no. Only a crazy person would try to destroy a woman and her career on the mere chance of taking it away from her." She glanced at John to see him staring intently at her.

"Who is Donna's replacement?"

Regina slowed, then stopped. The breeze had her collar tapping gently against the side of her face. She shivered, hugging herself. "I am."

"Did you tell her that?"

"Yes. At lunch the other day. But I think she's going to try to go over my head and see Nolan."

"What are her chances of getting the job from you?"

"A good chance if Nolan had the power to hire and fire. Which he doesn't."

He put a hand lightly to her upper arm and got her going again. She knew now what he meant by the intense drive and aggressiveness of Amelia. She'd seen it in her eyes the afternoon Donna had refused to invite her back on the show to plug her new enterprise. And she'd seen it again that afternoon at lunch.

They walked the rest of the way immersed in their own thoughts. At the glass door of the station, John searched his pockets, found a scrap of paper, and, with a stub of a pencil, wrote down a phone number.

"Call me as soon as you get home tonight. We need to talk more."

"I'll only be home a few minutes. Kristy, Tammy, and I are going to the hospital to see Donna."

"Tammy?"

"Tammy Kowalski. She's staying with us temporarily."

"That's probably a smart move. Stay together, don't go anywhere alone. And keep your eyes open. My commanding officer had a saying: 'Don't take that step unless you can see exactly where your foot's gonna land. Snakes don't always give a warning.'" He backed up, added, "Call me."

"Look, John . . . ," she began, "the people who should be handling this are the police. I'm not a detective. Are you?"

"No."

"Well, then, neither of us is qualified to track down a criminal, let alone apprehend one. If you want, I'll go with you to the police and we'll run this by them."

"No," he said quickly.

"Why not?"

"I told you. They won't believe us."

"It's worth a try."

"I'm not going to the police." A muscle in his jaw worked, jumping beneath the skin.

"Well then, I don't see how I can help you." She turned to go into the building, but he stopped her with a hand on her wrist. With determination she added, "It's the police or nothing."

He held her wrist for several more seconds, then released her. Without another word, he pivoted and strode off.

He was hiding something, Regina told herself. That relaxed, easy attitude had disappeared. The misgivings she'd had about him before going to lunch today, now came back twofold. What was his true interest in all this? Why had he singled her out?

If he was so gung ho about helping them and solving the crime, he could do it on his own.

At the main desk the receptionist held out Regina's messages. She took them, reading as she headed to her office. One message was from Pandora Cudahay, the psychic, returning Regina's call. The other message was from Garrick. Her stomach tightened. She had promised him she would call. And she would have kept her word if Donna hadn't been attacked the same afternoon. Would it do any good to see him, she wondered? How much clearer could she be? She crumbled the pink slip in her palm.

Nolan approached her in the hall.

"How's Donna today?" she asked when he stopped.

His face visibly blanched. He ignored her question and in a harsh tone said, "So you're going through with it? What are you and Max trying to do, blow the whole thing

192

so that when Donna is ready to come back there won't be anything to come back to?"

"You know better than that."

"We've never done the show *live*. Christ, you don't know a thing about talent and yet you agree to improvise. No one is going to step in and save your ass when you freeze up out there. What you do, good or bad, reflects on Donna."

"I know that. I don't want to take over the show. But I do have to keep it going. For Donna."

"Bullshit. You're doing it for yourself. You got Max on your side. I don't know how you did it, but I can damn well guess."

Regina bit her tongue to keep from saying what she felt. She stepped around him and continued down the hall.

At her desk, she lifted the receiver, dropped her purse in the drawer, dialed the hospital, and asked for Donna's room. The nurse on duty told her Mrs. Lake was not accepting calls or visitors. "She had a little setback today, but she should be better tomorrow."

Nonplussed, Regina hung up, wondering what had happened to Donna. Nolan would know, but she wouldn't give him the satisfaction of refusing to answer her.

Forcing herself to put aside her personal business and get back to work, she dialed Pandora's number.

"Hello, Pandora," she made her voice cheery, "it's Regina. But then you knew that, didn't you?"

The woman laughed. "You give me too much credit, Regina. There are days when I wouldn't give two bits for so much as a hunch."

"Are we on for tomorrow?"

"We're on."

"Do you have a vision of me pulling this show off?" The long silence on the line had Regina's muscles bunching. "Pandora?"

"I'm here," the woman answered softly. "You should know, you're more than a little clairvoyant yourself. Follow your intuition, Regina, it's usually right on."

193

Regina swallowed. "Yes, I will. Well, see you at three o'clock then . . . in the lounge." Regina said goodbye and hung up, feeling, for only an instant, a panic-flash.

5

At two o'clock Tammy unlocked the door to Gary's house and let herself in. Earlier that afternoon, on the back of his motorcycle, Brad had taken her to Daly City to get her car, and after asking her for gas money, he had raced off with a promise to see her soon.

Now, standing in the foyer, she called out, "Hello?" She knew Gary was at work because she had called him that morning to make certain he had gotten the girls to summer school. But it was possible Amanda was still in the house. Tammy speculated on what she'd do if she came face to face with her husband's whore. Her "hello" went unanswered.

In the kitchen she helped herself to a glass of red wine, washing down a Valium with it. Then, carrying the glass and sipping, she quietly wandered through the rooms, saving the master bedroom for last. When she opened the double doors and looked in she saw the bed made and the room neat and clean. A woman's blue robe, draped across the foot of the bed, mocked her.

Tammy moved in a daze to the closet. In the space where only four months ago her clothes had hung, another woman's filled the void. There was something so foreign about the scene. Somber garments of white, gray, black merging into muted shades of red, purple, green, and blue—unlike any Tammy would own—lined the clothes bar. Aside from the unusual colors, there was organization and a degree of artistic design.

She lifted a coatdress in a cobalt blue cashmere-wool and examined the label: Anne Klein. Cottons and denims by Ralph Lauren. She ran her hand across the fabrics of rich leather and suede. She stroked the soft blends of mohair, angora, and cashmere. She sank her fingers in the fur of an ivory, long-haired lamb jacket.

Tammy clasped her hands around the wine glass, locking her fingers together, and slowly backed out of the closet. She stood in the middle of the room, lost and confused. She groaned. Looking into the mirror above the dresser, she wound her fingers into her hair and pulled hard until she groaned again in pain.

What was happening to her life? Everything was falling apart. Someone was out to destroy her looks and her looks were all she had to lure Gary back. But Gary had Amanda, and now he had the twins. Gary was the only man who had stayed with her longer than a few months. Of course she'd had to trap him. But he must have loved her to allow himself to be trapped and to stay with her for almost ten years.

On the dresser were perfume bottles and several jewelry boxes. They belonged to another woman. It was Tammy's bedroom, her quilted spread and matching drapes, but different now in both appearance and smell, tainted by someone else's personal effects.

She stepped to the dresser and pulled out a long, thin drawer. She found neat rows of satin and lace underwear in hues of flesh and peach and ivory. Lifting a full bottle of Joy, Tammy sniffed at the stopper, then dabbed the perfume at her temples and deep into her cleavage. She tipped the bottle. She would get Gary back, she told herself as she watched the perfume dribble out onto the pretty underthings. There was a way. There had to be a way. Gary wouldn't let anything bad happen to her. Then, holding the bottle tightly, she swung her arm, shooting a stream of Joy across the room. This was the smell she had detected when she entered the room. It made her sick. This woman with her sophisticated clothes and scents was ruining her life.

She threw the bottle at the bed and watched for a moment as the perfume gurgled out onto the satin spread. Next she dumped the contents of the jewelry box on the floor and crushed earrings and pins under her shoes. With a strangled cry she rushed back to the closet and dashed the entire contents of red wine over the lamb jacket. She ripped every one of the bitch's clothes from their hangers, tossing them out into the bedroom. She stumbled to the rolltop desk and, with tremulous fingers, grabbed scissors, black felt markers, and a tube of glue.

She giggled as she moved to the pile of clothing. She hadn't done this since she was a little girl. Marking, cutting and pasting scraps of cloth had been her favorite pastime.

Eighteen

1

Amelia drove, oblivious to the terraced hillside vineyards on each side of the highway. Just moments ago she had dropped Matthew at the Meadowvale Country Club. With a lesson and eighteen holes of golf, she estimated he would be tied up for approximately five hours.

She lowered the driver window on the Rolls-Royce and flicked out ashes from her slim cigarette — Matthew, though an avid cigar addict, loathed the smell of tobacco smoke in his car. She hoped she could finish what she had to do and make it back in time. Her husband was not the most patient of men, and to keep him waiting after allowing her this minuscule measure of freedom, not to mention the use of the Rolls, would be unwise.

Five hours. Five glorious hours. Plenty of time.

2

The penguins frolicked in the pool.

John absently shelled a pistachio nut as he stared at the birds without really seeing them. The zoo was a favorite place to lose himself, but today his mind was locked onto something that even the zany antics of the penguins couldn't pry loose.

Damnit. He'd almost succeeded. Then he'd blown it. Regina Van Raven had listened to him, agreeing with most everything; then, with his reluctance to go to the cops, he had lost her trust.

What did it matter if she believed him, he wondered? Why go to *her* with his theories and not Tammy Kowalski? Tammy had just as much to lose as Regina; her risk was just as great. What was it about this woman that made him want to get close to her—to protect her? If he knew that, he wouldn't be sitting here, troubled, preoccupied, he'd be home working on his novel.

She questioned his motives. There were too many mysteries, too many coincidences, and much of them involved him. He'd begun to wonder himself if it was fate or chance. San Francisco was no small community where everyone was acquainted and ran into one another on a regular basis. It had to be fate, he decided, rubbing at the red dye on his fingers.

3

Tammy was at the fitness center, on the platform, struggling to get through her third and last aerobic workout of the day.

She pivoted sharply and her foot twisted under her, bringing her down hard on one knee. The thirty students on the floor paused, several stepping forward as though to help her, but she waved them away, settling down unsteadily to the platform. Sitting now, her legs in second position, in a loud voice that sent screeching feedback over the PA system, she said, "We're going down. Grab your mats."

The music stopped abruptly.

Tammy looked over to see someone—Brad, was it? yes, Brad, she'd recognize those bulging, ropy biceps anywhere. His hand was on the tape recorder.

"What're you doing?" she asked.

"Tell them to go home. You've had it for the day," he

198

said under his breath.

"Brad . . ." She looked out on the floor. Bright leotards bled together like a kaleidoscope. She blinked, trying to clear her fuzzy vision.

"Go home, everyone," he called out. "Your teacher isn't feeling good. She's too dedicated to her work to admit it, so I will."

They picked up mats, water bottles, and gear and filed out slowly, looking curiously at Tammy and Brad.

When the last of them had gone, Brad lifted Tammy off the platform.

"Oooh, you're so strong," she said, arms wrapping around his neck to cling tightly.

"You're damn lucky the boss lady's not in today." He peeled her arms from his neck. "What the hell's the matter with you?"

"I need some lovin'." She reached for him again.

"You're drunk and probably stoned. G'wan home."

"Take me home, Brad. I'm scared. She began to cry, her face twisting unattractively. "Someone's out to get me. They wanna make me hideous. I couldn't live if I was . . . hideous."

"Goddamit, straighten up!" He shook her. "I'm not playing nursemaid to you. Take a cold shower. Get your act together and get outta here." He marched off, banging the metal door against the wall as he went out.

Tammy was too stunned to move. "Brad?" she called out "Brad!" She collapsed against the platform. Everything went black for an instant. She struggled to stand.

What was she going to do? What? She'd call Gary, that's what. He'd come and get her and take her home to their house in Sunset. They were such a happy family. Gary, Sherry, Kerry, and Warrior. Something about Warrior disturbed her, but she quickly dismissed it.

She stumbled, then weaving erratically, found her way into the vast locker room and pool area.

Tammy unconsciously took in her surroundings. A woman was in the swimming pool doing laps, two women

199

were in the Jacuzzi chatting, the window in the door of the sauna was fogged and dewy with condensation. Someone was probably inside.

At her locker she bent down, fished a quarter from her change purse, and, seeing the pills, she reached for them. Better not, she thought. Gary hated it when she was bombed out of her skull. She didn't want him mad at her today. She straightened, clutching at the cold metal of the locker as a dizzy, sickening sensation washed over her. She braced herself, moaning.

At the pay phone she leaned against the wall. She dropped the quarter in and dialed.

4

Regina listened attentively as Tom repeated the cues for commercial breaks and camera-angle changes; cues she knew well on the other side of the camera. Seated in the chair alongside her was the psychic Pandora Cudahay. Since Pandora was accustomed to radio and television and her self-assured attitude could only give Regina a boost of confidence, Max suggested the show open with her on the set.

At the station several things had gone wrong. Some of the crew had been given conflicting instructions, the time of the show had been confused, telephone props misplaced and, too close to airtime to be comfortable, found on another set. Regina suspected Nolan had a hand in these dilemmas.

Lack of sleep had Regina keyed up, tense. Tammy, soused on wine and glassy-eyed from Valium, had kept her awake half the night weeping and lamenting over her husband. When Tammy wasn't sitting on the floor in Regina's bedroom talking about Gary and the events leading up to and after the separation, she was pacing the house, bumping into furniture and walls. Sometime around 3:00 A.M. she had passed out on the couch. Regina had been afraid to leave her alone that afternoon, but Tammy had recovered enough to go to the gym to teach her aerobics class.

Regina was wearing one of several new outfits that Kristy had helped her select when she learned she was to fill in for Donna. This one, a sea green linen skirt and cropped jacket, now seemed too confining. Pinpricks of perspiration broke out on her face and she wondered if the heavy makeup Candie had applied moments ago would come running down her face before the show even got underway.

She looked over at Pandora. The woman's pleasant face, framed by curly ginger hair, the collar of her white blouse buttoned at her throat and encircled with a red and black plaid ribbon tied in a neat bow, calmed her. Pandora smiled and reached out to pat Regina's hand. The instant her fingers touched the back of Regina's hand, her smile disappeared and something disturbing flashed in her eyes. Then she was smiling again and her eyes looked away and Regina felt a slamming sensation in her heart.

"What?" Regina whispered to the psychic.

"It had nothing to do with you, Regina. It was something else. Really."

Regina wanted to believe her. She drew in a deep breath, forcing herself to relax.

The lights keyed up and Stork was snapping his fingers and counting down and suddenly the red light on camera one was on and Stork was pointing a finger at her.

"Hello, I'm Regina Van Raven, today's hostess for 'City Gallery.'" Her delivery had been in a monotone, and her face, she knew, was as expressionless as her tone. She smiled. "Our guest today is psychic Pandora Cudahay. We're coming to you live this afternoon so that you, our viewing audience, may call in with your questions for Pandora."

Before taking the first call, Pandora spoke of seminars and inspirational classes. She talked of predictions that had come true, spiritual cleansings, intuition, metaphysics and crystals; flavoring all with fascinating anecdotes. Regina listened, thankful that this woman was such a pro. Time passed quickly. Regina broke for a commercial.

"Don't look so stricken," Pandora said to Regina when the camera's red light went off. "You're doing great."

"Lord, I must remember to compliment Donna. This is damn tough."

"You're doing just fine."

One by one the buttons on the telephone began to flash.

Regina pointed at the panel of chaotic lights. "Looks like the show's all yours now."

The camera's red light glowed again.

5

Donna stared transfixed at the elevated TV, watching the first live telecast of "City Gallery." Her best friend sat opposite the guest on the set, and Donna had to admit that she was hosting the program quite well.

Regina had wanted Donna to do the psychic show as she was doing it now, but Donna had been terrified of live TV. Though she rarely goofed up, having that extra margin of insurance, the ability to reshoot and edit, had spoiled her.

Donna studied the screen. Regina looked calm and cool and refreshingly lovely in a new green skirt and jacket. What happened to the shapeless layers of drab khaki and the frizzy hair, she wondered with a tinge of sarcasm? It was obvious she had allowed Candie to make her up for the show. She was stunning. Donna felt a rush of envy and distrust.

Why was she thinking such disparaging thoughts? After all, she had insisted Regina fill in for her. What was wrong with her? Since the assault, her sensitivity reared high, her mental state plummeted. She had begun to take it out on the nurses and doctors, snapping and brooding. She felt helpless, irritable, and filled with an inner rage.

She pushed her mean thoughts away and willed herself to listen. Regina was saying that Donna Lake was doing fine, that Donna thanked everyone for their prayers and get well wishes, and that KSCO hoped to have her back soon. Cheers were heard in the studio.

Donna felt tears well up. She looked in the corner at a box of letters. The mail from her fans came in daily. She hadn't felt much like going through it. Maybe tomorrow. Tom had offered to lend a hand. Tom was so helpful, calling every day and bringing the mail from the station. His pleasant face, his warm smile, were like a soothing balm. Until the assault, she hadn't realized just how important Tom Gansing was to her.

6

Steam, thick with eucalyptus essence, rose up around him. Through the tiny window in the door, gray with condensation, he could see into the corridor, see her talking on the pay phone across the hall. She was looking at herself in the chrome plate of the wall phone. Vanity. The woman was scared to death, practically a raving neurotic, obviously bombed out on tranquilizers, yet still she was concerned with her looks. How he delighted in her terror. He had only to plant the seed of the mayhem to come and she quivered deliciously in that gorgeous body.

He turned away, smoothed the hair down flat against his head. He thrilled to the heat of the sauna. The humidity, the heavy air that pressed in around him, reminded him of warm blood and escaping body heat. The straight razor was in his pants pocket in the locker. But he wouldn't be using it on this one. Not unless something went wrong and he was forced to. He almost wished that something would go wrong.

She was absently caressing one full breast. Watching her, he felt a rush of desire.

Patience. He would have to wait to get to her. But picturing the outcome, it was a wait he wouldn't mind.

Tammy heard the ringing, then Gary's voice giving instructions to leave a message. Why did he have his machine on? It seemed lately he always had the damn machine on. A beep. She struggled against the dizziness.

"Honey," she said, "it's me. Pick up the phone."

A moment later a young voice said, "Hello? Momma?"

"Sherry?"

"No, it's Kerry."

She never could tell the two apart on the phone. "Hi, honey. Is Daddy there?"

"Momma, you didn't do it, did you?"

"Do what, honey?"

Tammy heard muffled mumbling on the line. She stared blankly at the woman who was climbing out of the pool. She glanced over to the Jacuzzi. It was empty, the bubbles dying down beneath a layer of foam.

Gary came on the line, his tone hard. "I ought to have you arrested—no, committed. For good this time."

His words made no sense to her. "Honey, I need a ride home. I've had a very bad day and . . . and—come and get me, please."

"What's wrong with you?"

"I just told you I had a bad day. I'm coming down with something. I don't think I can cook tonight. We'll pick up a roasted chicken at Crandall's on the way home."

After a long pause, Gary said. "Where are you?"

"At the center. Where else would I be?" The receiver slipped from her fingers and clanged on the floor. She giggled, hauled it up by the cord, and spoke to Gary again. "Ouch, did that hurt? I dropped you."

"Listen to me. Listen carefully," Gary said. "I'll come, but only if you agree to let me take you to see the doctor."

"Doctor? It's nothing serious. A flu, maybe."

"I'm talking about a psychiatrist."

She closed her eyes, felt nauseated, and quickly opened

them, rolling around to put her back to the wall. The women from the Jacuzzi passed, staring at her, then exchanging glances between themselves.

Tammy waved at them. "Are you coming now?" she said into the receiver.

"Did you hear me? If I come, you go with me to see Dr. Channing. Today."

"I heard, Gary. I heard. We'll get some pasta salad to go with the chicken." She hung up the receiver. There, she already felt better. Gary was coming for her. "Better get dressed," she said aloud to herself. "He doesn't like to be kept waiting."

She chattered on inanely while she dressed. She considered showering, but she had no strength, no will for things of little importance. When she got home she'd have the girls run her a nice hot bath with some of those lilac crystals they'd gotten her for her birthday. Gary would just have to do the dinner dishes or let them go till morning when she felt like her ol' self again. He hated doing anything domestic so he'd leave them for her. Thinking how helpless Gary was in the kitchen made her laugh.

The sound of her laughter echoed throughout the large, humid room. Sitting on the bench in front of her locker, she paused in putting on her shoe. She laughed again, louder this time so she could hear the echo better. She threw back her head and laughed, forcing it out, filling the room with a baying, yet not unpleasant sound.

She wriggled her bare foot into a red pump.

The laughter rolled through the room.

She chuckled at the strangeness of it. The other pump gave her more difficulty, but she worked it on.

Now the laughter was discordant, eerie. Tammy looked up, startled.

"Hello?" she said.

The word hung in the air.

"Brad? Is that you?"

Sounds of water dripping. The ping-pinging din that seemed always to accompany an abundance of water pipes and pumps punctuated the silence.

Out in the other room, where the pool and Jacuzzi were, she heard a door close.

"Brad! Answer me!" She pulled the T-shirt over her head, stood and stepped into the denim miniskirt. Tugging it over her hips, she lost her balance, fell back on the bench, crying out when the corner jabbed into her thigh. She felt dizzy again. "Shit!"

Footsteps.

"Brad?"

She moved into the other room, her heels clicking, wobbling on the wet tiles.

"Brad, I'm going. My husband's coming for me.

No answer. He was ignoring her.

She saw the door to the utility room close slowly.

Tammy felt confused. Something about Brad. She and Brad had been having an affair. Why had she been seeing him anyway? Then it came back to her in hazy bits and pieces. The separation. Her dating Brad. And with that recollection came a surge of anger. He thought he was so fucking great, she told herself. He leeched off her for over a month, eating her food, drinking her booze, and screwing her whenever he got horny. Did he ever consider her? Did he take her out, or buy her one shitty present, or ask her what she liked in bed? Hell no. He just took. Took. Took. Took. Now that Gary was coming for her, what did she need with this sonofabitch?

Tammy stepped unsteadily to the door and pushed it open. The light was off, but light from behind her cut abstract forms out of the darkness. She made out the familiar shapes of mats, weights, and stereo speakers. And standing in front of the shelf with the pool cleaning supplies, with his back to her, was that fucking creep—that brawny brainless bastard.

"I hope you overdose on steroids, you shithead," she said, stepping into the room. "You can't use me anymore, cause I'm—"

The dark figure turned, a unit of black from head to

toe. Not a fraction of color relieved the blackness. A phantom. Her mind reeled dizzily. A nightmare phantom. And through her numbed senses, terror, as she had never felt it before, turned her body to stone. She saw it coming and was powerless to stop it.

A split second before the blinding liquid hit her eyes, Tammy become completely clearheaded. Completely sane.

Panic paralyzed her vocal cords. She whirled around, one hand flew to her face, groping desperately at her eyes, her long glittery nails gouging at skin. Her other hand lashed about in the air, searching for something tangible to give her direction. It smashed into the door frame. So great was the agony in her eyes that she barely felt the pain from the fingernail that was ripped off well below the quick.

She waved a hand in front of her until she found the door frame again, and then she lunged straight through, knowing exactly where she wanted to go. Her pumps teetered precariously, but stayed on her feet.

She moaned, emptying the air from her lungs, and just when she thought that she had somehow missed it, her feet left solid ground and she free-floated for an instant before plunging into the warm water of the swimming pool.

She felt herself going down, down, with blackness all around. Pinging, echoing underwater sounds mingled with the pounding of her heart and the rush of bubbles escaping from her nose and mouth.

She forced her eyes to open. More blackness. Red flashes exploded everywhere. The skin around her eyes stung.

Gary, help me, she pleaded silently.

Oh God, oh no, she thought with a hopelessness. She was going to be deformed. Ugly. Hideous. Gary couldn't possibly love her now. All she'd ever had was her beauty. And now it was gone. Gone with her sight. Blind and hideous.

She felt her body settle in a sitting position on the bottom of the pool. Her chest ached. There was no air in her lungs. She needed to go to the top for more. But she couldn't move. How long could she sit here? Would dying be painful, she wondered? Death would be easier to take than being tossed aside like an old shoe. Death. The thought of it calmed her. Without her looks she would never have Gary, and without Gary she had nothing.

She had to breathe. Had to . . . had to . . . had . . .

She opened her mouth, inhaled, and struggled with the choking panic.

Moments before she lost consciousness, her eyes rolled upward to see light. A blurry dark figure stood in the light—a phantom waiting for her. She would not let him hurt her again.

A sense of peace came over her.

And then, bleary yet discernible, her red high-heel pump floated by, and she wondered about it before the blackness came again.

8

"We'll take another call now," Regina said, pressing a flashing button on the phone. "Hello, you're on the air."

"Hi, Regina. Mine is a voice from the past. Jamie Sue Larson. I was a contestant in the Miss Classic Pageant with you and the others. I saw the clip of the show last week . . . the day Donna was injured. I was one of those ill-luck statistics you spoke of."

Regina frowned. "Jamie Sue . . . . ?"

"It was rumored I'd overdosed on drugs. That wasn't true. Everyone in the pageant knew I was acutely allergic to alcohol, yet someone spiked my drink. There were other incidents."

Regina looked at Pandora disconcertingly. What to do now, she wondered? There were dozens of callers holding to talk to the psychic and time was running out. Yet, this call was something Regina, for personal reasons, couldn't ignore.

Stork signaled for a break, taking the decision out of her hands. She instructed Jamie Sue to stay on the line. To the viewers Regina said, "We'll resume taking calls for Pandora when we return."

During the break, Regina took Jamie Sue's phone number. She felt compelled to continue their conversation. Then they were back on the air.

"We have time for one more call." Regina pressed another button. "Good afternoon, you're on the air." Silence. "Hello? Are you there? I guess we lost that—"

"Van Raven . . ." A voice, low and quiet, come over the airwaves.

"Yes? You're on the air."

Regina glanced over at Pandora. The woman was sitting stiff in her chair, her eyes closed, her arms tight to her sides, hands gripping her thighs.

Regina's mind became stunned with apprehension. She leaned over, placed a hand on the woman's knee, and asked softly, "What is it?"

"Danger." In a hoarse whisper she went on, "I see water and . . . and a tall, dark figure. Not of flesh, but of iron. Atlas—no, no . . . Neptune." Her eyes remained closed. "Yes, Neptune, god of the sea. Black. Black. There is someone waiting—Regina . . ." Pandora clutched Regina's hand. ". . . be careful."

The dial tone came on.

Pandora's eyes flew open.

Regina stared at Pandora, dazed.

Without warning Regina, Stork gave instructions to break away for a commercial.

9

Donna's wandering mind returned to the TV show. She gazed at the two women on the screen. From the tense expressions on both faces she knew something was wrong. Donna quickly focused on their words. "Black. Black . . .

209

Someone is waiting—Regina . . . ," Pandora said, ". . . be careful."

Commercial.

Her mind reeled. What did it mean? Oh God, not another one.

In her mind's eye Donna reenacted the events of her last, fateful show. She saw the lights go out on the set. She heard the scream and felt the terror. The light exploded in her eyes again and Donna saw herself standing on the sideline, staring helplessly at the person who was screaming in agony. Only this time, instead of herself, it was Regina whose face was melting behind her fingers. And Donna felt a rush of gratification.

"Oh, God, no!" she cried out, burying her face in her hands. Don't let anything happen to Reg, she prayed. "Please, dear God, don't punish her for my evil, horrid thoughts."

10

"What does it mean?" Regina asked Pandora.

The two women sat in Maxwell Conner's office after the close of the program.

"I don't know for sure. The person on the phone was linked to you in some way, Regina. I felt you were in grave danger. *Are* in grave danger. But there's something else. Something I can't seem to make sense of. Someone else."

Max stood at the window, looking out at the traffic on Van Ness. "That was one helluva show." He turned to look at the women who gaped at him in astonishment. "That was for real, right? You didn't make it up?"

Their reply was a cold glare.

Without knocking, Tom swung open the door, and in an excited voice said, "Quick, put on Channel Eight!"

Max flipped on the TV and spun the dial. Sam Quinn stood on the steps of the Fitness Center winding up his "on

210

the spot" report while behind him a black body bag was being lifted into an ambulance. . . . drowning. More at eleven. Sam Quinn, Channel Eight."

"What is it?" Max said.

Tom turned to another channel. Sibyl Clayborn sat in the news studio at Channel Four. "Just moments ago the fully clothed body of physical fitness instructor Tamara Kowalski was found by her husband floating in the pool of The Fitness Center on California Street. Details are not available at this time.

"Mrs. Kowalski was a runner-up in the 1970 Miss Classic Pageant, and just last week she was on the same broadcast in which Donna Lake, the hostess of 'City Gallery,' was assaulted with an acidlike substance by an unknown assailant. We hope to have an update on this at eleven."

"Oh my Lord." Regina put a hand to her mouth. "Tammy was staying with me. I just saw her this morning."

Pandora turned to Regina: "Is there a statue of Neptune at the center?"

Regina shook her head dully. "I don't know."

"There is," Tom said. "I've been there dozens of times. It's at the north end of the pool."

"It was Tammy you saw," Regina said to Pandora. "She was the other person."

"Yes. And I saw what she saw. My vision was underwater looking up at the statue. What triggered the image was the phone call in the studio. That person on the line has a strong bearing on what happened."

Max paced. "Can you see him . . . or her?"

Pandora closed her eyes. After a few seconds she opened them again, shaking her head vigorously. "All I see is black. The color black. No images."

The phone rang. Max snatched it up and answered impatiently. He listened a moment, then hung up. "The switchboard is getting calls from astute viewers who are asking if there's a connection between the Kowalski drowning and Pandora's vision. Pandora, would you allow us to interview you for a special broadcast?"

211

"Yes. Of course."

"When this breaks there's going to be one helluva hoopla. 'City Gallery' will skyrocket right off the charts."

Regina's mind was elsewhere.

Tammy had been warned.

Nineteen

1

Wednesday, four nights following Tammy's death, John Davie walked toward the main doors of the hospital where Donna Lake was a patient. The streetlights warmed up to full incandescence. As he neared the entrance, he saw Regina come out, hurry down the steps, and turn in the opposite direction. She crossed the street to the station wagon.

John was about to call out to her when a man strode up to her, grabbed her arm, and turned her around to face him. Regina tried to pull away.

"Hey! Hey, you!" John shouted, as he ran to the couple who were now openly struggling at the rear of the car. "Get away from her!"

"Stay out of this," the man said, putting his back to John. He held Regina by her upper arms. "This is between my lady friend and me."

John clasped a hand over the man's shoulder and attempted to pull him away from Regina. The man struck out blindly, hitting John on the chest with his open hand.

"Garrick, stop it!" Regina cried out.

From behind, John grabbed the man, pinning his arms to his side. "Cool it, fella," John whispered harshly in his ear. To Regina he asked, "What's going on here? Who is this guy?" But before she could answer, the man kicked

213

John in the leg. The pain made him relax his hold. The man spun around, swinging. John ducked, but not before he was hit with a grazing blow along his ear.

More from reflex than anger, John slammed a fist into a firm stomach. His other hand wrapped around the man's throat and he bent him backward over the fender of the station wagon.

Regina thrust an arm between them. "John, don't hurt him, please."

"Don't hurt *him*?" John asked, his shin and ear throbbing dully.

"Please," she repeated.

"You know him then?"

She nodded, not looking at the man.

"I'm going to let you go, then step back," John said to the now passive man under him. "If you move too quickly or raise a limb, I'm going to assume you want to continue the fight."

"Don't do anything, Garrick. Please."

He looked at her. "So he's the reason you won't see me?"

Shaking her head slowly, sadly, she moved around the two men, unlocked her car door, climbed inside, and slammed it shut. She sat staring straight ahead.

John released the man and stepped back, poised for attack.

"Relax, asshole," the man said. And without a second look at Regina, he marched off, got into his car, and drove away, tires squealing.

John stood by the side of the car, waiting. He watched Regina lean over and unlock the door on the passenger side.

He stepped around the car and got in.

Still staring straight ahead, she asked, "Why are you following me?"

"I'm not following you. You're in a car, I'm on foot, how can I follow you?"

"What are you doing here then?"

"I came to talk to you."

"How'd you know I was here?"

"Kristy told me."

"Terrific."

"Don't be mad at her. She trusts me, not like some people I know."

Regina started the car. "It's not that I don't trust you. It's just that . . ."

"Go on."

She opened her mouth to say something, then closed it and looked away.

"Do you think I'd hurt you?" he asked.

"Maybe. Maybe not. Probably not."

"What about that man—what's his name? Garrick? Would he hurt you?"

"No," she answered quickly. Then, more carefully, she added, "I don't think so, anyway. I apologize if he hurt *you*."

He thought she might elaborate, tell him who the man was and what he was to her. Not that it was any of his business, though the guy had dealt John a couple of painful lumps. But she just started the car, shifted gears, and pulled away from the curb without another word.

After several minutes of silence, John said, "How's Donna Lake?"

"She's healing."

"Have the cops contacted you about Tammy?"

Regina glanced over at him. "No. You?"

He shook his head.

She chewed her lower lip.

"I think we should do some checking on our own. What do you say?"

"Not interested. I work in television, not in crime detection. I have a job. I have a daughter. I'm too damn busy to play cops and . . . and, whatever."

"Too busy to want to stop this fiend before he. . . ." He left the words up in the air. He saw her fingers grip tight on the steering wheel. "We have a mutual friend in the D.A.'s office. Wilma would have access to all the reports and files. She'd want to help out a friend."

"You can do that without me."

"I'd like you to be the one to call her."

"You said you knew her."

"I do."

She stared hard at him now.

"You have a reason for wanting to know. Both women were friends of yours."

She sighed, shifted around, tossing her hair back. "What do you want me to ask her?"

John smiled. "For starters, I'd like to know how they're handling Tammy's death. Accident? Suicide? Homicide?"

"And?"

"And then we'll go from there."

2

She made the call to Wilma Greenwood from her apartment. Kristy and Sonya sat on the floor painting each other's toenails and watching the Giant-Dodger ball game on TV. John paced at the bay windows.

"Spill one drop of that nail polish and it's—oh, Wilma, hi, it's Regina Van Raven."

"Regina, how the hell are you? I've been thinking about you. God, I saw the show the other day—*wild*. I get the willies just thinking about it."

"That's partly why I called. Wilma, I'd like your help on something.

"Sure, hon. What do you need?"

"With your connections at the district attorney's office, I wondered if you could nose around . . ." Regina watched John turn his head and look at her, grinning. She turned her back to him. "Y'know, look into a few things for me concerning Tammy Kowalski's death?"

Silence.

"I want to know if the police are treating it as a homicide?" Regina finished quickly.

"That's it?"

"For now."

"May I ask why you want to know? Is it for the show?"

"No." Regina decided the truth was best. "Donna, Tammy and I were contestants in the same pageant. I'd like to know if I should be concerned, that's all."

"Ahhh. Yes, I can understand that."

"Will you do it?"

"No problem. I'll call you back tomorrow. At the station?"

"Yes. Thanks, Wilma. Good-bye."

"Oh, Regina, how do you like the apartment?"

"I love it."

"Have you met John yet?"

Regina glanced over at John. "Yes. I have."

"Enough said then."

Regina wanted to ask what she meant by that, but John was staring at her now and Wilma was saying good-bye.

Regina hung up. To John she said, "She'll call tomorrow."

He lifted his jacket from the couch, draped it over his shoulder, and stepped up to her. Something fell from the pocket onto the carpet.

Regina bent down and picked up three red pistachio shells.

"Some people smoke and do drugs, I'm hooked on pistachios.

"Expensive habit."

He chuckled. "Yeah.

"Coffee?"

"Thanks, can't. I've got to tend bar tonight. I'll be here all day tomorrow. Call." Then he was out the door, closing it softly behind him.

217

Twenty

1

At eleven o'clock the following morning, Wilma Axelrod Greenwood called Regina.

"Good news, dear. Homicide has been ruled out. Of course it's not official yet, but they're leaning toward suicide or possibly an accidental drowning."

"She was fully clothed, Wilma. Not likely to take a swim in her high heels and miniskirt."

Regina heard the rustling of papers. "Medical examiner's report states death due to drowning. No sign of a struggle. The police had gotten excited over a couple deep scratches and facial burns. Turns out the scratches were made by the deceased's own fingernails, and the burns were a result of an anti-aging cream and too much sun.

"There was enough booze and barbiturates in her system to greatly impair her judgment," Wilma went on. "In other words, she was bombed. Two people, a co-worker and her husband, both attested to the fact that prior to her death she was extremely depressed and irrational."

"What about acid?"

"Acid? Oh, you mean acid like with Donna Lake? Nothing here about acid, or any corrosive material, that I can see. I'm sure it would've shown up in the report had there been any."

"I see."

"You don't sound pleased. I thought you were concerned about a connection. There doesn't seem to be one."

"I am pleased. Very pleased. Wilma, does that report give a time of death?"

"Let's see . . . yes, sometime between four and four thirty-five P.M."

"How did the medical examiner determine that."

"Not the M.E. The police report states she was last seen alive by her aerobics class and one Bradley Segal, employee, at four P.M. Her husband found her in the pool thirty-five minutes later."

"I don't suppose they can pinpoint the exact moment she died?"

"Now why—oh, I see. Of course, the *psychic*. I don't believe in that mumbo jumbo, but I must confess it was very convincing what that Cudahay woman did. Look, I'll ask around. Let me get back to you."

"Thanks, Wilma. You've been a big help."

"Anytime."

"Oh, Wilma, about John Davie. What did you mean . . ." But the assistant D.A. had already hung up.

2

At noon, John stirred the pot of chicken soup and tasted it. He added barley, carrots, and a quartered head of cabbage.

He poured another cup of coffee and returned to the living room; to the blue monitor with the cursed blinking cursor. Standing behind his swivel chair he read the five paragraphs that had taken him all morning to write.

Pure shit. Punching function buttons, he deleted the entire text. Then he slapped at the back of the chair, sending it spinning.

Sonofabitch! What was the matter with him? He hadn't been able to write a damn thing since Regina had moved in above him. He knew it wasn't her alone that had robbed him of his creative juices, it was the whole fucking situation. Corinne, Amelia, the acid, his feelings of guilt and inadequacy. And until it was resolved he could damn well forget about writing anything that made sense; or that made money.

John brought up the names of the Classic finalists. To the top of the page, under VICTIM, he added Tammy's name to the list: (1) Corinne Odett (2) Donna Lake (3) Tammy Kowalski. Only two names remained at the bottom of the list, preceded by question marks — Amelia Corde and Regina Van Raven.

He heard a knock on his door, so quietly that at first he thought it was at another door down the hall. He heard it again, louder. It had to be someone who lived in the building, otherwise he would have been buzzed from the entry. He never locked his door and his relatives usually walked in without knocking. Regina?

He cleared the monitor. He pulled his shirt together, buttoned several lower buttons, tucked it into his Levi's, then crossed the room and opened the door.

The young Hungarian girl stood timidly, a plate of strudel in her hands, her gaze meeting his before darting away.

John looked across the hall to see the door of his aunt and uncle's apartment closing softly.

"Hi," he said. "For me?"

Ilona nodded, smiling.

"Bake it, did you?"

"Yes, your Aunt Anna and me. It's sour cherry and walnut."

"That's my absolute favorite." And Aunt Anna knows it, he thought. "Shall we try it?"

She smiled again, moving ahead of him through the apartment.

She was wearing a pastel pink summer dress and sandals. Her honey blond hair hung straight down her back to her waist. Her blond hair intrigued him. The Hungarians in his family, and their friends, were all dark haired.

In the kitchen he poured coffee while she cut the strudel and put it on plates. He pulled out a kitchen chair for her. Then he hoisted himself up on the counter top and sat with his back against the cabinets. After taking a bite, he complimented her baking skills.

"It's very sweet and moist. I judge it delicious. You should make one for your boyfriend," John said.

"I did. He said it was delicious."

"He's a wise fellow."

"Yes."

"So, what's his name?"

"Who?"

"This wise fellow. Your boyfriend."

She smiled at him.

Oh-oh. They had stepped up the operation. So it's come to this—pushing the virgin out the door and across the hall bearing edible proof of her talents. The dress was a nice touch. American men were suckers for the mark of femininity. They had to be very trusting or very desperate to allow her to be alone with him. In Hungary, a good Hungarian girl didn't spend time with men alone in a place with a bed. But this was America.

"How old are you?" John asked.

"Nineteen."

"Nineteen," he repeated. "Do you know how old I am?"

"Thirty-eight."

So they had already discussed his age . . . these match-makers, these conspirators.

"I'm too old for you, Ilona."

"No," she said, shaking her head.

"Then you're too young for me." He looked into her somber brown eyes. "Look, I know a couple of really nice guys. Men closer to your age. I'll talk to Mrs. Dobos first to clear it with her." He slid off the counter, turned to the stove and stirred the soup. In a quiet voice, with his back to her, he added. "I have nothing to offer you."

He heard the scraping of the chair legs as she pushed it back. Soundlessly she moved to his back. Her hand

221

stroked lightly along his arm.

"I like the older man. I like you, Johnnie."

"I like you too, but—." A knock at the door interrupted him.

He expected it to open and Aunt Anna to breeze in. He figured she wasn't desperate enough to leave them alone too long in case he was inclined to sample the girl's other talents.

Another knock.

He excused himself and went to the door. Regina stood there in a pair of white slacks and a navy and white blouse. She looked fresh and crisp and every bit as feminine as Ilona. This was his day for beautiful ladies, he thought. The soup was on and there was plenty of it.

"Hi. Since I'm home for lunch," she said, "I thought you might like to know what Wilma had to say."

"Yes, sure. C'mon in." He stepped back to let her enter.

"Wilma had both the medical and the police report. It seems that—." She stopped talking abruptly, staring over John's shoulder.

He turned to see a barefooted Ilona leaning against the door frame of the kitchen, holding a coffee mug; one thin strap of her dress had slipped off her shoulder.

"Uh, Regina Van Raven—," John said by way of introduction, "meet Ilona Dobos."

"Hello," Regina said.

"Pleasure to meet you," Ilona said, but her eyes seemed to say otherwise.

"This isn't a good time." Regina backed up. "We can talk later."

John looked to Ilona and then to Regina. Ilona disappeared back into the kitchen. In a quiet tone, he said, "Come back after work tonight. I'm serving dinner."

"Oh, no—," she began.

"Bring Kristy with you. That's an order."

"I . . ." She paused, her eyes flickered toward the kitchen. Then, as if accepting a challenge, she said, *"Okay. Six?"*

222

"Anytime. It's soup and it's ready."

She went out.

John stood in the doorway watching her climb to the second level. He glanced across the hall and noticed the door to his aunt's apartment was ajar. He smiled.

"Great strudel, Aunt Anna. *Koszonom.*"

3

Corinne reread the article from the *San Francisco Chronicle*. She clipped the obituary and carefully centered it next to the article in the photo album. She lowered the clear plastic and smoothed it down.

The album was no longer entirely about her. Other beauty contestants, Donna and Tammy, now shared the many blank pages with her. Closing the album, she rubbed fingers over the lettering on the cover. With a black marker she had written *The Thrill of Victory — The Agony of Defeat 1970–1990.*

Thrills and spills, agony and death.

Twenty years ago, she above all had gleaned the greatest thrill, but the agony, to her delight, was to be spread around. Three down, two to go.

The moaning broke through her reverie. The past few days it had become a constant sound, one she'd become accustomed to and rarely noticed anymore. She checked the clock above the stove. Time for his lunch and injection.

She wondered why she bothered with the food. For the most part her father ignored it, despite her efforts to make him eat. A balanced diet was essential to a diabetic. She'd have to remind him of that. He'd never taken care of himself properly, that's how he got in this predicament in the first place. Diagnosed with diabetes in his fifties following a gall bladder operation, he had continued to drink, smoke, and eat everything that was wrong for him. And now this thing with his legs. The crazy fool would kill himself one day.

Well, there was only so much a daughter could do.

4

After work Regina changed into jeans and a short-sleeve sweater. At six o'clock Kristy called from The Farm House.

"Gotta work over, Mom. We're short-handed here to-night."

"Oh, I was waiting for you."

"What's up?"

"We're invited to John's for dinner. In fact we're supposed to be there now."

"Yeah? John cooks?" Kristy said in an amused tone.

"I guess."

"So go on down. What do you need me for?"

"You were invited too."

"I'm sure the two of you can amuse yourselves without the kid there."

"Kristy . . ."

"Mom," her tone was patient, parental, "It's time you learned how to date again."

"This is not a date—"

"So pretend. Practice." She laughed lightly. "John's incredibly sexy, in case you haven't noticed. He's also a nice guy with a great sense of humor. He treats women like they're an important part of the human race. And she tells me he can cook—hell, the man is righteous."

"Your father's been gone less than six months."

"Mom, he's been gone two years and you know it. Two years."

No one knew it more than Regina. The long hospital stay. The many visits when she prayed that he would remember who she was. The anger, confusion, and violence. He had died of pneumonia and Regina had felt the awful pain, but the pain came from a sense of guilt, not loss.

224

Kristy was right, she had lost him two years ago: the day he entered the nursing home.

"You like him a little, don't you?"

"Well, yes."

"Do you think he's good looking, maybe even sexy?"

"Kristy, really." But despite her embarrassment, she did find John Davie attractive and sexy. Very sexy.

"I get off at nine. Tell you what, if you're not at home, I'll drop in at John's to say hello."

"I'll be home. Be careful, okay?"

"Okay. Have fun."

"This is not a date—"

Kristy was gone.

When the phone rang again, Regina figured it was Kristy with something to add. But a soft voice, unmistakably female, said, "There is a very dangerous person out there who has killed and will kill again—"

"Who is this?"

"Don't interrupt. I will not repeat. A *clue*. Listen carefully. Initially, a sea will lead to the assailant."

"Is this a joke?"

The dial tone hummed.

Regina jotted down the message, then sat quietly for several minutes, contemplating the call. At last she dismissed it as merely a crank. Someone had seen her on "City Gallery" and had gotten her phone number. That was one of the disadvantages of being in the limelight; no matter how bright or how dim the "light," people craved contact and they called.

She looked at her watch. 6:15. John was waiting. She rose, went out the door, came back in, grabbed a bottle of red wine; then, wondering if red was appropriate, she grabbed a bottle of chablis. With a bottle in each hand she went downstairs. She tapped on John's door with the neck of one bottle.

Two doors opened at once. Regina glanced at John, then turned to see the landlady standing in the doorway across the hall.

225

"Ahh, I see you are home tonight, Johnnie," Anna Szabo said.

"Regina and I have some work to do."

"Ahh," she said, glaring at the wine bottles in Regina's hands. "How are you, Mrs. Van Raven?"

"Fine, thank you, Mrs. Szabo. And you?"

John gently pulled Regina inside and, after waving to his aunt, closed the door.

"She's not usually a snoop," he said. "It's just that—"

"It's okay. I understand. I have relatives too."

"Where are they? Your parents?"

"In San Diego. My father's a retired fireman and my mother's a travel agent. They travel." She held up the bottles. "Red or white. I didn't know."

He took the bottles from her and suddenly she felt awkward with nothing to hold. She stuck her hands in the back pockets of her jeans. She looked around his apartment. "I like your place. Southwest, isn't it?"

"I call it sunbaked Santa Fe."

He invited her into the kitchen. The table was set for three. Place mats, linen napkins, a fat red candle, a round ceramic vase filled with spring flowers from the garden, and a bowl with a small, black-shelled turtle.

"That's Oliver Tuttle. Ollie for short," John said when she leaned in to look at the turtle. "I named him after a character in my first book. They're both slow, quiet, and thick skinned."

"Hi, Ollie." She lightly stroked the shell.

"Where's Kristy?" He kneeled, peeked through the window in the oven. He had changed into white twill pants and a yellow polo shirt. There was a drop of dried blood in the cleft of his chin where he had nicked it shaving.

"She had to work. She won't be here."

He looked up at her with a tiny smile, his eyes saying a dozen different things He pulled the oven door open. "What do you think?"

She frowned. "About what?"

"Bread, hot out of the oven."

226

She smiled. "Smells great."

She watched him remove the loaf pan from the oven. He has such an easy, relaxed manner, she thought. Nothing seems to faze him. The night they had tangled on the floor at the back door, his mouth bloodied by the top of her head, he'd been able to joke. And only the night before he had come to her rescue, taking a kick and a punch, but nothing more was said of it, as though it happened every day. He was so unlike Leo. Serious, somber Leo, no words wasted, yet Leo had been a warm, caring man, showing his love in a multitude of ways.

John, she felt, was frivolous. Was he even capable of deep emotions, she wondered? This is not a date, she reminded herself.

"You make your own bread?"

He laughed. "Me and Pillsbury. Hungry?"

"I wasn't until I walked in the door. Now I'm starved."

"Would you like a drink first?"

"Wine with dinner will be fine."

"We're having salad, chicken soup, and bread. *The Guide to Serving Wine* dictates white with chicken. I like red, so that's what I'm having. How about you?"

"I like red too."

He uncorked it and allowed it to breathe while he ladled the soup into a large bowl. He set out the salad and placed the bread on a small cutting board. The bowl in front of her had a chip on the rim. He switched with her. He sat down, poured the wine, and lit the candle. The bright kitchen light over the table stayed on.

They began to eat.

"Wilma was helpful?" he asked.

"Very." She told him what Wilma had said.

"Suicide?"

"Or accidental."

"No acid?"

"No."

"You were one of the last to see her alive. What's your opinion?"

227

"I'd have to agree with the police. She was terrified and depressed. She was up most the night drinking and pill popping. She confessed to being committed four months ago in a mental institution for a breakdown."

"Well, that's that then. Looks like I jumped to conclusions."

Regina resumed eating the soup. "This is wonderful. I'd ask you for the recipe, but I don't spend much time in the kitchen."

"I love to cook. I'll give you some to take home, else it goes out to the dog."

Dog? *Dog!* Regina dropped her spoon in the bowl. "Dog!"

John stared at her curiously.

She was hardly able to contain her excitement. "Tammy was terrified because she was convinced her dog had been poisoned. God, how could I have forgotten that?"

"Her dog was killed?"

"Yes. Two nights before she died. That's where I was going when you and I — when we met downstairs. She was hysterical and wanted me there."

"Okay. Back up. Tell me everything."

She told him, beginning with Tammy's phone call.

"And there's something else that bothers me," she added. "When I called Tammy's husband to check on the twins and let him know some of Tammy's things were at our place, he told me she had called him from the center. He had gone to pick her and found her in the pool, dead. She was crazy about that man. I don't think she'd kill herself if she knew he was coming for her. Tammy was scared, but not suicidal."

"That doesn't rule out accidental."

She sank back in the chair. "No, it doesn't."

"The dog, where was it taken?"

"Daly City Animal Hospital."

"Do you want to call, or do you want me to?"

"Let me. I know the details."

"Let's finish our dinner," John said. "There's no hurry."

228

Regina nodded, took a quick gulp of wine, and picked up her spoon.

Their eyes met.

John tossed his napkin on the table. They both rose at the same time.

"I'll get the phone book," he said.

5

Amelia waited until she heard the door to Matthew's study close. Then she picked up the cellular phone, the one that was independent of the house telephone, and dialed Fletcher's number. After a dozen rings, she hung up.

Where in God's name was he?

She'd been trying to reach him for days. Had he been detained in Michigan? What the hell was going on?

If unable to reach him that evening, she decided, first thing the next morning, before going to the TV station, she would go to Fletch's apartment.

6

A switchboard operator at the Daly City Animal Hospital put her through to the doctor on duty.

"Dr. Phillips, my name is Regina Van Raven. A dog was taken there two days ago for an autopsy. The owner suspected intentional poisoning. I wonder if you have the results on that test?"

"The owner's name?"

"Kowalski. The dog was a Labrador, I believe."

"A black lab named Warrior?"

"Yes."

"I did that one myself this morning. It was poison, no doubt about it. The Daly City PD have my report."

Regina felt her heart beat with excitement.

"What type of poison?" Regina watched John's attention

229

suddenly become intense.

"Ground beef laced with arsenic trioxide. A poison commonly used in rat poison, weed killers, and insecticides."

"I see. Thank you, Dr. Phillips." Regina hung up. To John, she said. "Arsenic."

"Looks like your friend was right."

"About the dog, yes. But she didn't get acid. How do you explain that?"

"It's possible she saw her attacker before he or she could use the acid. She may have fallen or jumped into the pool. She could've been held under."

Regina sank into an overstuffed chair. John's theory had merit.

"C'mon," he said, pulling her to her feet. "Get your purse and car keys. We're going for a ride."

"Where?" she asked, allowing him to propel her to the door.

"The Fitness Center. There're some things I'd like to see for myself."

7

A young, brawny man was behind the counter when John and Regina entered the health club.

"Hey, new faces," he said, smiling broadly. "My name's Brad. Brad Segal. I'm one of the trainers."

"Do you mind if we look around the facilities?" John asked.

"Heck, no. Go right ahead. The place looks kinda dead tonight. But it's not always like that."

"Adverse publicity will do that," John said.

The man seemed to blanch. "Uh, yeah. Course that death had nothing to do with the center. She was havin' personal problems and the cops think maybe she killed herself."

"No kidding? I thought they suspected foul play."

"At first they did. That's why it's dead here tonight. No

230

pun intended. The center'd been shut down with yellow ribbon strung up all over the damn place. Didn't do the business much good."

"Were you the one to find her?" Regina asked, knowing the answer, but wanting to keep the topic open.

Brad hitched himself up on the counter. He seemed to bask in the attention. "No, the husband did. I was in the office, though. I was right here when it happened, but I didn't hear a thing. She didn't call out or nothing. I would've heard."

"Was anyone else here?" John asked.

"I don't think so. I didn't see or hear anyone."

"It's okay if we look around?"

"Be my guest. Be careful, though," Brad called out as John and Regina headed back to the pool area. "We don't need no more accidents."

In the main room Regina stood in reverent silence staring at the pool and the cast-iron statue of Neptune. This is what Pandora had seen in the vision, Regina thought eerily, supposedly through Tammy's eyes. She shuddered.

John stepped to the door of the sauna and looked through the small window. The window was clear and dry. The steam had been turned off.

Regina walked into the women's locker room. After wandering around aimlessly for several minutes, she went to the door and asked, "What are we looking for?"

"I'm not sure," John said. He tried the knob on a door marked Utility Room Keep Out. The knob turned, the door opened, and John disappeared inside.

Regina stepped to the door and looked in.

John was squatting down. He lifted something and slipped it in his pocket.

"Find something?"

He started at the sound of her voice. "Oh," he laughed lightly, reaching into his pocket "I dropped this." He held up a red pistachio shell. "Nothing mysterious."

He rose and stood facing the shelves that held what looked like pool cleaning supplies and equipment. He

231

seemed lost in thought. He reached out and lifted a plastic bottle of chlorine. He shook it. It sounded about half full. Regina watched him uncap the bottle and then sniff it. He tipped his head, an odd expression on his face.

He turned to look at her, his body tense, his eyes glaring.

Regina felt the skin on the back of her head tighten. She stared back, puzzled by his strangeness.

His gaze slid from her face to a point behind her. She turned her head and looked at the wall. There was nothing there.

With the chlorine in his hand, his expression tense, he slowly crossed the small room.

Stopping within inches of her, he said, "Something splashed against this wall."

She leaned in, moving so that a glare from the bulb reflected on the wall. Then she saw it. Clean spots. Splashes from some clear liquid.

He bent down on one knee and examined the stack of folded towels. He lifted the top one to his nose. "What's that smell like?" he asked, handing the towel to Regina.

She sniffed. "Chlorine?"

"Exactly."

"You think someone splashed chlorine against the wall?"

He moved Regina to the side and stood in her place, looking toward the shelf where he'd gotten the bottle of chlorine. His hands came up to his face. He turned, and with his eyes closed, one hand out in front of him, he headed for the open doorway. His knuckles rapped the door frame and he grunted, but continued on through the door, stopping within a foot of the pool. He stared down into the water.

Regina watched silently, fascinated. She realized he was acting out some weird scenario.

He came back into the room and busied himself shifting the towels to one side.

"Well?" she said.

"What have we here?" He held something in the palm of

232

his hand. It was a fingernail, broken below the quick, torn skin lining the ragged edge.

"It's Tammy's," Regina said with excitement.

"Are you sure?"

"Positive. Look at it. See the glitter and the special design—the gold stripe? I remember seeing that very design on her nails the night before she died."

"Did you notice a broken nail?"

Regina shook her head, took the fingernail. "That would've hurt like hell. See, it's torn off below the quick. Of course she could have lost this earlier in the week and had the nail mended and repolished."

He looked thoughtful. "There's only one way to find out."

"Hey, what're you two doing in there?" Brad said behind them. "This room's for employees only."

Regina slipped the broken nail into her handbag.

John snatched up a towel, sniffed it, tossed it back on the stack. "Sanitized. That's important. He grabbed Regina's hand and pulled her out the door, hurrying toward the exit.

"You wanna sign up?" Brad called out.

"We'll let you know."

A moment later they were in the station wagon pulling out of the parking lot. Regina started to turn left, changed her mind and made a right.

"Where are we going?"

"The hospital to see Donna," she said. "Do you mind?"

He didn't answer immediately. Then, in a quiet voice, he said, "Mind? No, I'm a fan of hers. Do you have the fingernail?"

"Yes." She pulled smoothly into the traffic. She glanced at him. He was staring straight ahead with that same calculating expression on his face as she'd seen in the utility room. Normally his face was a mixture of hard and soft, brooding eyes over a quick, easy smiling mouth. Now, his features were set. "Tell me what was going through your mind back there at the gym," she said.

"This is purely speculation, mind you, but I think the lady was lured into the storage room and doused with a blinding chemical—"

"The chlorine?"

"Yes. It's not acid, but a dose of it in the eyes could have temporarily blinded her."

"And being blinded, she stumbles out of the room, breaking a nail on the door frame, and falls into the pool?"

"Yes," John said. "Now either she couldn't swim, or she panicked and lost consciousness or she was held under."

"Murder?" she asked incredulously.

"We should have asked Segal if she could swim."

She glanced over at him. "She was a strong swimmer."

Regina found a parking space at the entrance to the hospital. They took the elevator to the fourth floor. The door to Donna's room was open and Regina could see she had a visitor. Tom Gansing, the director at KSCO, stood at the side of her bed. Donna looked past Tom, caught Regina's eye, and motioned for her to come in. They entered. During the introductions, Donna's hand self-consciously went to her throat before dropping to her side. Her throat and neck were unbandaged. Regina noticed that both John and Tom looked Donna directly in the face when talking to her, yet neither stared longer than necessary. Nolan, Regina remembered, didn't seem as comfortable looking at his wife.

"Guess I better be going," Tom said, backing up. "Next time I come I'll bring that book I was telling you about."

"Can you come tomorrow?"

"Sure." He grinned and his face colored, matching the red of his hair.

Tom was more than infatuated. He was in love. Regina had suspected for months that the director had special feelings for Donna. Watching him with her now, the way he looked at her, listened to her, seeing his reluctance to leave her, confirmed it. Tom was a good man. Sweet, considerate and down-to-earth like Donna.

Tom left. Regina moved into his place and took Donna's hand. "How are you?"

"Okay," she smiled wanly. "They'll be doing more skin grafts in a couple days."

"When? I'll come by."

Donna shook her head. "Daddy will be here."

Regina knew how important it was for Donna to have her father to herself. She smiled and squeezed Donna's hand.

Donna looked at John quizzically. "I have this feeling we've met before. A long time ago."

"John covered the Miss Classic Pageant for the *Chronicle*," Regina said.

"Really? That must be it, then. And now the two of you are neighbors. Will coincidences never cease?"

"Donna, the police are planning to rule out foul play in Tammy's death," Regina said.

"That's good, isn't it?"

"Not if it's not true. Tammy's dog was poisoned two nights before she died. John and I went to the gym and found some things that may prove she was assaulted . . . and possibly murdered."

"Murdered?" The color left Donna's face. "But why?" Without waiting for an answer she said in exasperation, "Oh, God, Reggie, what have I done? It's my fault. If I'd have left things alone I wouldn't be here and Tammy . . . Tammy would be alive."

"Stop thinking like that," Regina said emphatically. "No one can say what would have happened. What's important is that we do what we can to stop it before someone else gets hurt."

"Are you going to the police?"

"Yes," Regina said.

John's head snapped up. His eyes bore into hers. She looked away.

"Go see Corinne," Donna said.

"Corinne?"

"She paid me a visit a couple days ago."

"She was here?" John asked, sounding dumfounded. "In the hospital?"

235

"At first I thought I had dreamed it. I'm still not positive she was here. But she said things about her private life that make me believe it really happened."

"What things?" John asked.

"Terrible things about her father. There's so much hate inside her."

"Exactly what day was she here?" John persisted.

"Thursday. Well, actually, early Friday morning. Before dawn."

"What did she want?"

"To see me. Just that . . . to see what I looked like."

"Lord," Regina whispered.

"Was she disfigured?" John asked.

"Greatly."

"But she said she'd had plastic surgery," Regina said.

"I think she lied," Donna said.

"Did she threaten you?" John asked.

Donna shook her head. "But she's a very bitter woman. I'm not at all sure she's entirely sane."

Regina felt cold. She wished she hadn't gotten involved in this investigation. The police were trained for this kind of work. She was too close to it all.

She glanced at her watch. 8:03. Suddenly she felt an urgency to get home. Kristy would leave work at nine, and Regina's maternal instincts took over. She didn't want her daughter coming home to an empty apartment.

8

John stole glances at Regina as she drove. She was quiet, seemingly lost in thought. The radio played a love song by Billy Ocean.

She has a great profile, he thought. He remembered her as a young woman in the contest. She had been beautiful then, but he felt that her beauty had increased over the years. Along with wisdom and a distinctive persona, she had filled out characteristically. Routine movements, such

236

as adjusting the mirror and vents, steering, shifting gears, seemed graceful and sensual when she did them, yet she had a certain innocence that he found quite captivating.

"How long have you been a widow?" he asked. His own question surprised him, coming out of nowhere.

When she remained silent, he figured she had chosen not to answer. He stared out the passenger window. Storefronts and parked cars flashed by.

She leaned forward and turned down the radio, her eyes straight ahead. "Six months."

It was his turn to be silent. Six months. Not a very long time if she had loved him. Six months after the death of his wife and son, he would think of them only half his waking hours instead of all. Then, for many years after that every young boy reminded him of Andrew. Every woman he met he compared to Darlene and none had measured up.

Who the hell was this Garrick character, he wondered?

"What did your husband do?"

"Leo wrote reference books for writers. L. V. Raven. *Nonfiction Handbook, The Craft of Article Writing*, to name a few."

John was familiar with the latter book. "He was good."

She glanced at him, smiling. "Yes, I thought so too. Course I'm biased. I edited and typed his manuscripts."

They withdrew into their own thoughts again.

She braked to a stop at a red light. "I meant what I said about going to the police."

John tried to appear unaffected by her words. His stomach knotted. If he went with her to the police, she was certain to find out who their prime suspect was. The police would like nothing better to pin this *and* Corinne's assault on him, it would save them a lot of footwork.

John touched the pistachio shell in his shirt pocket, the shell he'd found on the floor of the gym's utility room. He had told Regina he had dropped it, but that was one more lie to add to the growing list. If the investigating cops had found it, instead of he, Lillard would be that much closer to making a case against him. Was it a coincidence that the very type of nut he regularly ate was found at the scene of a crime? A crime that in all likelihood was connected to the finalists of the Classic pageant? Or had someone, knowing his habits and knowing that he was a suspect, planted it? It was sheer luck he had come across it.

And his luck had held regarding Donna Lake. She had recognized him from the pageant all those years ago, but fortunately she had believed he'd been a journalist covering the event. Unlike Regina, Donna had come in contact with him twice during that fateful pageant. The first time was at the hotel the day of the final judging. He and Corinne had fought that afternoon. Corinne, angry that he would not be present for the crowning, had screamed at John, slapping his face when he had turned to leave. Donna had been within hearing. His second contact with Donna was at the hospital the following day. Corinne, though heavily sedated, adamantly refused to allow John to see her. He had waited all night, endlessly pacing the corridors, praying she would change her mind and let him share her pain and anguish. In the morning Donna had shown up, along with the police detective who took him away for questioning.

"I think they should know what we know," she added.

"I agree," he lied again. "But the police will only tell us to stay out of it. And I don't think I can do that."

After several moments of silence, Regina said, "Wilma, then."

He suppressed his relief. "Yes. What time?"

"Eleven. I have a light load this week. We're doing the show Saturday, live again with open phone lines."

"You're very good in front of the camera. Your face comes across sensationally on the screen. As well as off."

"Thank you. Pancake makeup works miracles. At least I wasn't asked to have a face lift."

"There was no reason to."

He saw her glance at him as if checking his sincerity.

"Well, I won't mind in the least turning the program back over to Donna."

"She's coming back?"

"Of course. Why not?"

He shrugged. "Why not."

At 8:30 they pulled up to the apartment house.

9

Corinne had been sitting in the old, gray-primered Packard on the quiet residential street for nearly an hour. She stared at the lighted window on the ground floor, hoping to catch a glimpse of him.

She was nervous, like the two other times this week she had come here to spy on him. So strong was her compulsion to see Jack Davie that she did so at the risk of being caught. Last night she had come close to being discovered when, sitting in the car at three in the morning, staring at his dark windows, Jack had surprised her by jogging by within yards of her, and by some miracle he hadn't noticed the hooded woman in the parked car. Minutes later she was watching him move around in his apartment and she'd filled her eyes, her aching heart, with the wonderful sight of him.

Tonight the light was on in his apartment, but there was no movement. She felt empty, unfulfilled. Perhaps she was too early, she thought. She would leave and return after midnight.

Corinne reached over to start the car when she saw a station wagon pull up across the street. She jerked her hand away, sat back, and slid down on the seat, pressing herself into the dark corner. With pulse racing, she watched as a man stepped out of the car. There was no mistaking Jack's silhouetted profile. She watched a woman get out of the car a second later. *Who was the woman with him?* she asked herself, watching the two of them enter the apartment house. *Not a mate, don't let her be his mate.*

239

In the light of the vestibule, she recognized the woman with John. Regina.

Corinne was relieved to see that the two hadn't touched each other. Not lovers, she thought. Thank God.

10

In the hall, Regina headed for the stairs.

"Why don't you come in," John asked, unlocking his door and pushing it open. "It's early."

She paused indecisively.

"Kristy's not home yet. She has to pass here to go upstairs. I'll leave the door open."

"Well . . ."

"We haven't had dessert yet."

Regina smiled weakly, then walked past John into his apartment.

"Sit down. Make yourself comfortable," he said, disappearing into the kitchen.

She stood in the middle of the living room and leisurely took in her surroundings. His apartment was furnished in a potpourri of new and old, store bought and scavenged. The furniture consisted of a bone-colored leather sofa and a matching armchair, a weathered pine rocker, a straight-back pine chair, and an upended antique leather trunk topped with a round piece of glass. The coffee table, rich-toned mahogany, was one half of a scarred double door, intricately carved, the hinges and handle intact. Opposite the sofa was a wall unit stereo system with television and VCR. On the floor were large throw pillows, cacti in terra-cotta pots, and baskets made from thick, gnarled twigs woven into crude shapes, containing potted plants and magazines. On the walls were sketches of deserts and Indian and Cavalry portraits and paraphernalia. The pastel color scheme of sand and sunsets contrasted boldly with the deep, rich accents. The room was warm, western, and very pleasing.

Against the far wall was a work area. She crossed the room to the desk. To one side of the computer system she saw a group of photographs. There were pictures of John's aunt and uncle, pictures of him standing with strangers, both men and women. There was a portrait, done by a professional photographer, of John, a baby cradled in his arms, and a stunning blond woman. His wife and baby? Where were they now?

"Sugar? Cream?" John said from the kitchen doorway.

She spun around, embarrassed to be caught peering at his little gallery of pictures. "A little milk, please."

He stared at her a moment before nodding and disappearing back into the kitchen.

One entire wall, from floor to ceiling, held shelves of books. Books upon books; fiction, nonfiction, reference, but mostly fiction. Three books had the same title. *Evil Tidings* by — she lifted the book to read the name of the author — John T. Davie. She turned the book over to see his photo on the back. Inside she read the dedication: "To Darlene and Andrew with eternal love." She closed the book, staring at his picture.

John entered the room carrying a glazed terra-cotta tray with two steaming mugs and two squares of a sugar-glazed pastry. He put the tray down on the coffee table.

"This table," he said. "was once the door from a Spanish mission in California. A friend sent it to me as a gift. The freight nearly bankrupted me."

She turned with the novel in her hand and said, "Why didn't you tell me?"

He shrugged. "It's no big deal."

"I'd like to read it."

"Take it. It's yours."

"I'd rather buy one."

He smiled. "I appreciate that, but I doubt it's still in print. Take it. A gift."

"Thank you."

"Let me know what you think. If you hate it, lie."

She laughed. "Any others?"

"There's one coming out in the fall."

"I'll buy that one." Bringing the book back with her to the sofa, she sat and picked up the coffee mug.

John sat on the other end of the sofa. He handed her a plate of strudel.

"Looks delicious. What is it?"

"Sour cherry and walnut strudel."

"You and Pillsbury?"

"This is homemade and I had nothing to do with it."

She took a bite. It was delicious.

"Can you get a list of the contestants from the pageant?" he asked.

"You think it may go beyond the finalists?"

"It's possible."

She remembered the call from one of the contestants in the studio Saturday. Jamie Sue had nearly died from an allergic reaction to alcohol. Regina felt an iciness inside her. "I have a list at the office. I'll bring it home tomorrow."

He rose, came around to her side of the sofa, took her hand, and pulled her to her feet. "Come," he said.

She put down her plate and allowed him to lead her across the room. He pulled out the desk chair for her. Over her shoulder he activated the computer and pointed to the monitor.

Materializing on the blank screen was a list of names. Under VICTIMS, she read: Corinne, Donna, and Tammy. She saw Amelia's name, and finally her own. Question marks followed the latter two. The icy feeling returned.

John pulled up the pine chair and sat beside her. On the keyboard he typed, CHEMICALS: Acidlike substance: Rat Poison: Chlorine.

"Those chemicals — assuming chlorine was used — can be bought in most hardware or building supply stores. If the dog was poisoned, then the killer was in her yard. He or she could have dropped something by way of evidence. I doubt the police did anything beyond remove the animal

242

and file a report. We'll check it out."

Regina positioned her fingers on the keyboard and typed, *Telephone warnings before both assaults.*

"How many knew about that scheduled program?"

"The employees, the guests, and, of course, whoever they told."

"That should narrow it down. Have you personally had a warning?"

"Not exactly."

Over her shoulder he pressed function buttons, saving the latest text. She became acutely aware of his body close behind her. She could smell some vague after-shave, musky, yet light. When he reached around her to shut down the computer, his arm grazed her arm and she felt a slight current of electricity run through her. They were just inches apart. She sensed he was staring at her. She held her breath. Time seemed suspended. She had only to turn her head and . . .

He pulled back.

She rose quickly only to find he had also risen. They stood facing each other. She breathed deeply and was filled with his scent. His hands came up to cup her face lightly. Their eyes found each others and locked.

Her heart began to pound. She hadn't kissed a man in a long time. The thought both excited and terrified her. She lowered her eyes and felt his lips, warm and soft, lightly touch hers. Her lips parted.

The sound of the street door closing sent a jolt through her. Someone was coming. The inner door open and closed. They broke the kiss, and, like deer caught in the blinding light of a car's high beams, stood facing each other, frozen.

"Hi," Kristy said cheerfully from the open doorway. "What're you two working on?"

Her voice broke the spell, sending John in one direction and Regina in another.

"Kristy," Regina said, her voice cracking. "You're home."

Kristy looked from her mother to John, a sly smile

working at her mouth. "It's after nine."

John consulted his watch and then as if that wasn't proof enough, he double-checked by staring at the wall clock. "So it is. Say, Kris, how about some strudel?"

"Love some. But first I want to change clothes and check the machine for messages."

"I'll go with you," Regina said. She felt uneasy, shy—vulnerable.

"Don't bother," Kristy said. "Oh, by the way, Uncle Garrick called for you this morning."

Regina stiffened. "He called here? At the apartment?"

"Yeah. I told him you were at the station. I'll be right back," Kristy said, hurrying out.

Regina glanced at John. He was watching her, an enigmatic expression on his face. She was certain he was wondering what "Uncle" Garrick was to her. And she wondered how the hell Garrick had gotten their private number.

John went into the kitchen. She picked up her coffee mug and drank. It was cold. She took the two mugs into the kitchen. John stood at the counter cutting the strudel.

Regina began to clear the abandoned dinner dishes from the table.

"You don't have to do that."

Oh yes I do, she wanted to say. "I don't mind." She filled the sink with soapy water.

He poured fresh coffee for them and milk for Kristy.

Behind her she could feel his presence, unmoving, yet overpoweringly absolute. She sensed he had his back to her. It took every ounce of willpower for her to not turn and look at him. What was he doing? Why was he standing so still? Would he touch her again? Kiss her again? She forced herself to stop before she could finish the thought.

She scrubbed a soup bowl, the dishcloth going around and around. From the corner of her eye she saw him move, and then he was out of her peripheral sight. She swallowed. Her body tensed. She anticipated his touch.

244

Waited for his touch. Longed for his touch.

And when she felt his hand at her waist, she jerked, dropping the bowl in the sink and breaking it. He stood close, the heat of his body warming her. She closed her eyes and leaned against him, her head bent forward. His lips came down on the nape of her neck, making her shiver. His fingers played the vertebrae along the length of her back.

Feelings she had forgotten she possessed rushed through her like a flash flood. She hadn't felt a man's special touch in . . .

A voice inside her head said, *He's been gone only six months.* Yes, yes, I know. *Six months.* But it's actually been years. Years.

"Momma?" Kristy's voice, strained and shaky, spoke from the kitchen doorway.

Regina spun around.

John stepped away.

Kristy's face was pale, her brow furrowed. "Momma, there's something I think you should hear."

Regina shook the water from her hands and hurried to her daughter. "What is it?"

"On the answering machine. A message."

"Uncle Garrick?"

Kristy shook her head.

John was already out the door and climbing the stairs when Regina and Kristy came out of his apartment. They took the stairs two at a time. When they entered the apartment, John was standing in the living room looking around, confused.

"Bedroom," Regina said, and rushed down the hallway to her room. She activated the machine.

The voice, low and gravelly, said, "The prettiest shall be last. Which one is the prettiest?" Rushing air, the dial tone, then a final beep before the cassette rewound itself.

"I've been warned," Regina said softly.

11

In a fit of jealous rage, Corinne pounded her fists on the metal dashboard. Oh, God, why hadn't she driven away before Jack came home? Then she wouldn't have had to see him tenderly kissing another woman the way he used to kiss her.

Regina Houston. The bitch. The only woman Corinne had feared. The only one who could compete with her. Then she laughed ironically. There was no competing now. Regina had won again. Regina always won.

She put her forehead on the steering wheel and cried: deep, choking sobs that tore into her frail lungs and throat.

12

Many hours later, after John had returned to his apartment and Kristy had gone to bed, Regina, keyed up, yet exhausted, finally managed to fall into a deep, druglike sleep. Sometime in the night she awoke to her own voice, the memory of ringing still echoing in her head. The voice was coming from her answering machine. It beeped.

Groggy, she struggled to wake up.

The gravelly voice repeated the message left on the cassette. ". . . be last. Which one is the prettiest?"

What was happening? Oh my God, what was happening?

The phone rang again. Regina reached for the receiver, then decided to let the machine screen the call. After the greeting a raucous tone warbled in her ear. A recorded voice began, "We're sorry, your call cannot be completed as dialed. Please check the number and dial agai—"

"Momma?" Kristy cautiously slipped into the room, rubbing her eyes. "What's going on? Who keeps calling? Is it him?"

"I don't know."

"I'm scared."

So am I, Regina wanted to say, but instead she patted the bed and said, "Get in, sweetheart."

Kristy slid under the covers. Regina clasped hands with her daughter. Kristy fell asleep quickly. Finally, exhausted, Regina followed.

Twenty-one

1

Donna wondered about it. She wondered about it a lot lately.

Would it hurt? Could she do it without making a mess of it? The last thing she wanted was to live indefinitely in a comatose state, a burden on her family, her brain fried by the overdose of drugs.

Why me? That was one of a dozen questions she asked herself. How could this happen to her? What kind of monster would do this? What would the future bring? Depression, fear, anger, those were the emotions that carried her through each dreary, pain-filled day. Although she wanted to lash out, to cry and scream and vent the pent-up rage that twisted at her insides, such behavior from someone so habitually kind and optimistic would shock those who knew her. And she was a conformist to the bitter end.

Donna pulled her hand out from beneath the covers and slowly opened her fingers. The bottle was nearly full. Percodan. Painkillers prescribed for her last winter when she'd injured her back skiing.

Donna's aversion to any drugs stronger than aspirin stemmed from the fear of becoming dependent upon them. For as long as she could remember, her mother had been addicted to one prescription drug or another, in addition to nicotine, coffee, and alcohol.

Nolan had brought Donna the Percodan the night before.

Poor Nolan. He could never tolerate ill health, mental or physical. Just showing up at the hospital each day had to employ a great deal of effort. He came every day, though his visits had become shorter and shorter. He seemed gravely discomforted and wired, pacing the room, standing at the window nervously snapping the band on his wristwatch, until she too wanted him away from her.

The worst was his inability to look directly at her. He looked at the top of her head, her hands, her pillow, everywhere but at her face and throat. Occasionally he slipped, casting his gaze where he had so carefully avoided, and the instant flash of repulsion, no less a reflexive action than if he had been punched in the stomach, would leap over his face.

Her father insisted she would be normal again. Dr. Sexton said there would be a dramatic improvement, and that with makeup, high collars, and the right lighting, it would be difficult for the TV viewers to discern the burned flesh from the unburned flesh.

But Nolan would know. And he would react to it, his eyes displaying horror and revulsion.

She opened the bottle and spilled the contents out in her hand. She'd have to wait and take them after the nurse did the evening medication rounds. From ten to seven should be plenty of time for the pills to do their work.

She heard footsteps in the corridor. Someone was coming. With tremulous hands, she poured the pills back into the bottle and pushed it under the sheet. It was probably Nolan. He had taken to coming early in the morning, using the excuse of the station as a means of breaking away sooner.

As the door opened slowly inward, Donna felt a sense

of hopelessness sucking painfully at her insides. She pulled the sheet up to her chin.

"Hi," Tom Gansing said with a warm smile, holding up a book.

The room seemed to brighten.

Donna smiled back, the sheet slid down unawares.

2

Amelia circled the block until a parking space in front of Fletcher's apartment building became available. She still refused to use the parking garage. She used a key to open the wrought-iron gate at the entrance. She smoothed the skirt of her black-and-white tweed suit, and then, in thin-heeled, sling pumps she cautiously climbed the steps to the third floor, avoiding the elevator as well.

At the door of 31 she raised her hand to knock, changed her mind and used her key instead. She slipped in silently and closed the door.

The apartment had an unoccupied smell, devoid of coffee and other cooking aromas. She crossed the living room to the hall that led to the bedroom and bath. She found herself breathing deeply, trying to detect the smell of Fletcher's toiletries. She smelled a slight musty odor.

In the bedroom an unmade bed and the usual clutter of a bachelor awaited her. Had he slept in this bed the night before? she wondered.

She went to the closet. His clothes were there, five suits, a dozen shirts, and nearly as many pairs of slacks. In the dresser drawers she found underwear, the bikini briefs in vibrant colors that he preferred, socks, and T-shirts. On the dresser top was his watch—not the gold Pulsar, but the less expensive Calvin Klein.

She strode to the telephone on the night table and lifted the receiver. The dial tone confirmed that it was in working order. With the receiver tapping lightly against her chin, she stood stiffly, her gaze sweeping the room. Everything was as he'd left it. So goddamnit, where the hell was the sonofabitch?

She scribbled out a note telling him to call her house and use the code of two rings. She'd get back to him as soon as she could. She signed it with a large A. As an after thought she squeezed in the word "love" over the initial.

3

In a tiny, cramped office in the courthouse, John watched Wilma Greenwood squeeze honey from a small plastic package into her coffee mug. She stirred it as she looked from him to Regina, then again at him. She smiled. John, somewhat self-consciously, returned the smile.

He had met Regina that morning at the station and she had seemed reserved, avoiding his eyes, jumping at his casual touch, talking quickly and nervously. She'd had plenty of time to think about what had happened between them in his apartment last night, and he suspected she had deemed it a mistake. A faux pas not to be repeated. Her husband had been dead six months. Only the widow could decide how long was long enough to grieve. She had enough problems without adding guilt and shame He wanted her, but he wasn't the only man who did, and Garrick so-and-so certainly wasn't faring well. The next move was hers. He could wait.

"How do you like married life?" Regina asked Wilma.

"I like it. Clyde's a loner like me, so we respect each other's privacy. And he has warm feet." She sipped her coffee. "I have a feeling the two of you are about to enhance my life. Or should I say my work load?"

John looked to Regina. She cleared her throat. "Wilma, we suspect Tammy Kowalski may have been

251

murdered."

"Pretty strong word . . . murder," Wilma said.

"Yes, it is."

Wilma leaned in, forearms on her desk. "So tell me."

Regina explained about the poisoning of Tammy's dog, the chlorine at the gym, the fingernail they'd found, and, finally, the message on her answering machine.

"You have that message?" Wilma asked.

"Right here." Regina dug in her purse and extracted the cassette. "Isn't there something police use, like fingerprints, to identify a voice?"

"A voiceprint analysis. But it determines identity through comparison. We need a voice to compare it with."

"If we got a voice?" John asked.

She nodded. "It could be done. Anyone in particular in mind?"

"Not yet," John said.

"Where's the fingernail?"

Regina went back into her purse and pulled out a sandwich-size ziplock bag. She held it up.

Wilma stared at it a moment, then she rose, and before going out the door she said, "Sit tight."

She was back within minutes with a file folder. She sat behind her desk and opened the folder. John saw photographs and reports.

"May I?" Wilma said, holding out her hand.

Regina handed over the plastic bag.

"Humm." Wilma handed John the bag along with one of the photographs.

Regina leaned toward him. Her hair, smelling of scented shampoo, tickled the side of his neck as she looked at the color picture.

In the picture two hands were displayed, obviously female by the slim contours and the long painted fingernails. The left hand, ring finger, was missing a nail. Something red—torn flesh, John guessed—ran across the edge of the nail. He didn't have to compare the nail in the bag with the hand in the picture. The bright color, the diagonal stripe and glitter told the story.

Wilma read from the report. "Lacerated finger above nail bed. Trauma, fresh. Contusion on upper thigh, fresh. Lacerations on face determined to be caused from the fingernails of deceased."

"We found the broken nail in the utility room," John said.

"What about the bruise on her thigh?" Regina asked.

Wilma shuffled papers. "Uhh, according to the police report the bruise and broken nail likely occurred when she went into the pool."

"Not only was Tammy a strong swimmer," Regina said, "she was physically strong as well. I can't believe she couldn't have saved herself, impaired or not."

"Regina, people have been known to drown in inches of water."

"What about the dog?" John asked.

"And the phone threats?" Regina added.

"I must admit there does seem to be an aura of mystery surrounding this case. Beauty contestants, psychics, animal poisoning. Look, you two should contact the detectives that are working on the Lake case. If you feel there's a connection, they're the ones to notify. Make sure they get that cassette with the voice."

"What if they refuse to see a connection?" John said.

"Then, should that happen, I'll do what I can to help you if you want to carry on with your own private investigation. Sound fair?"

"More than fair," Regina said.

John had expected as much from both Wilma and Regina. So now he had to convince Regina that she had to talk to the police without him. He knew he should tell her about his involvement with Corinne and the fact that he was a suspect in both cases, but something held him back. Something that even he didn't understand. Sure he was attracted to her, and if he had to speculate, he'd have to say he was afraid she might turn away from him. But would that be so tragic? He felt his stomach tighten at the thought.

On the street in front of the courthouse, Regina put on her sunglasses, then scanned the block. "The police station's not far," she said, "shall we walk?"

"I'll walk you down, but I won't go in with you."

She turned to look at him. "Why?"

"I have my reasons. I'd rather not say just yet."

"What is going on?" Her voice betrayed exasperation. "Are you running from the law? Is that it?"

"I'm not running from the law. They know where to find me if they want me."

"Then what? What is it?"

He turned and started to walk in the opposite direction.

"John," she called out.

He stopped, but didn't turn.

She came around to stand in front of him. "Damnit, you dragged me into this and I can't do it alone."

He stared at her a long moment before looking away.

"Okay," she said. "We'll do it your way. But there's one thing I have to know: Will you ever tell me why you're being so evasive?"

"I'll tell you when the time is right." When it won't matter anymore, he thought.

He saw her frown, and puzzlement flicker in her eyes.

She sighed, thrust the car keys at him, and said, "I'll meet you at the car in an hour." Then she walked away, her strides long and smooth.

4

Detective Lillard escorted her to his desk along the far wall. She declined his offer of coffee and sat in the straight-back wooden chair. She told him everything she and John had told Wilma, only she didn't mention John. She showed the detective the fingernail and produced the cassette, explaining that she assumed it was a threat.

He sat facing her, his legs parted, the cassette in one hand and the plastic bag with the fingernail in the other. He looked curiously at first one and then the other.

"Are you going to listen to it?" she asked, nodding at the cassette.

He swiveled around to a small tape recorder on the desk and fitted the tape into the machine. He pressed a button. There was a beep, a dial tone, and then a recorded voice intoned, "We're sorry, your call cannot be completed as dialed. Please check the number and dial agai—."

She sat straight up. "Rewind it."

He rewound the tape, pressed play again. The same message repeated.

Stunned, Regina could only slump back in the chair. "How?" she whispered. "It was erased. But how?"

The detective's brow formed a deep V.

"It was there, damnit."

"What did it say?" the detective asked.

She struggled to think clearly. " 'The prettiest shall be last. Who'—no—'which one is the prettiest?' "

"You say it was somehow erased?"

She nodded. It was coming back to her now. The two calls in the middle of the night.

"Who's the prettiest?"

"What?" She brought her attention back. "Oh, I think what he—or she—is referring to would be the finalists, there are only two of us left. Amelia Corde and me."

"So who's the prettiest?"

"Excuse me?"

His brow furrowed. "Isn't Amelia Corde the raven-haired siren with the blood-red lips and steely eyes?"

Regina wanted to laugh, his description was so clichéd,

255

yet so apt. "That's the one."

He popped the cassette out of the recorder, handed it to her. "You're prettier."

Regina said nothing. There was no comfort in knowing she would be last on this maniac's list.

"How'd you know the Kowalski's dog was poisoned?" he asked.

"I was there the night it died. I called the animal hospital and was told by the doctor on duty."

She watched him scribble on a pad.

"She was a friend of yours, this Kowalski?"

"Yes."

"What would you say was her state of mind prior to her death?"

"Confused. Scared. Terrified, actually."

"Depressed?"

"I don't know."

"Suicidal?"

She shrugged. "She didn't say. But I don't think so."

"What do you think happened that day at The Fitness Center?" His tone was soft, patient, patronizing.

"We—I . . . I think she was attacked by whoever attacked Donna Lake."

"There was no corrosive material."

"No, but . . . there was—I think she had chlorine thrown in her face. It momentarily blinded her. She fell in the pool and for some reason couldn't get back out."

"What reason?"

"I don't know that. Someone held her under? She panicked?"

"Why would this someone use an acidlike substance on—what was the first one's name? Oh, yes, Corinne Odett—Odett and Lake, and then use plain ol' chlorine on Kowalski?"

Regina bit her lower lip. This was going nowhere, she told herself. She was wasting her time.

"Mrs. Van Raven, our investigation in the Kowalski

256

death was quite thorough. The Center was gone over with a fine tooth comb. We missed the fingernail. But even if it was hers—"

"It was."

"—it has little relevance to the case."

"The dog?"

"A nuisance to the neighborhood. Barking dogs make enemies and are silenced in cruel ways."

Regina thought she knew better. But what did she have? A cassette tape without a threat. A psychic's vision. The gut feeling of a man whose own evasiveness was somewhat suspect.

"I hear you took over the 'City Gallery' show."

"Temporarily."

"I bet the publicity hasn't hurt the ratings none. Saturday's program with the psychic claiming to be tuned in to the drowning of Miss Kowalski went over pretty big, huh? And this on the heels of Miss Lake's well-publicized attack."

With his implication utterly clear, she stood, took the bag from his hand, and stuffed both bag and cassette back into her purse.

"This doesn't mean we won't continue to investigate the Lake case," he said.

"What about Tammy's case?" she asked flatly.

"You bring me something solid indicating foul play and I'll be happy to hear you out."

He said something else, but his words were lost to her as she marched through the door and out of the detective division.

5

"It was erased," Regina told John as they climbed into the car.

"The tape?"

"Yes." She started the engine and pulled away from the curb.

"How?"

"I'm so dumb," she said, hitting the steering wheel with the palm of her hand. "I should've taken the tape out of the machine last night. It never occurred to me that another call would come in the middle of the night and erase the message."

"What happened?"

She told him about the two calls.

"Don't blame yourself, Regina. You were upset. I should have thought to remove the tape." John turned to her. "You say you heard the warning message repeated before it was erased?"

"I think so." Then it dawned on her what he was asking. "My God, the only way I could have heard his message first was if he used my code number to retrieve it from the tape. How would he know my code?"

"He'd make it his business to know everything he could about you and the others."

Regina felt a heaviness bearing down on her.

"Forget it for now. What did Lillard say?"

As they drove through the midmorning traffic, she related the conversation with the detective. "He practically accused me of fabricating the whole thing for the damned publicity."

John's only response was a slow shake of the head.

When she pulled to the curb at the TV station, John looked at her quizzically.

"You wanted the list of the pageant contestants. It's in a file in my desk."

John nodded.

In the rearview mirror Regina saw a dark blue Mercedes pull up behind her. She recognized the driver.

Amelia. She hadn't wasted any time, Regina thought. To John she said, "Amelia Corde just pulled in behind us. I don't want her to see me." She slid down in the

258

seat until her head was level with the back of the seat.

Without a word, John moved over on the seat and put his arm around her, shielding her from view.

"Is she still there?"

He looked in the mirror. "She's putting on lipstick. Would she be coming to see you?"

As close as he was to her, Regina could detect the fine stubble on the side of his face, smell his after-shave and the fresh-laundered scent of his knit polo shirt. "I doubt it. I'd say she's come to see Nolan about a job."

"She has the look of a predator," he said, his breath tickling her ear, causing her stomach to flutter lightly. "A look I remember well. She's coming now."

Regina heard a car door close and then heels clicking off into the distance. She watched John's face, waiting for a sign. He looked down at her, his eyes strangely masked; then he leaned back and helped her slide up on the seat.

Before leaving the car Regina adjusted her clothes and shook her hair out. "I'll check Nolan's office. Maybe I can catch some of what they're saying."

She went into the building, picked up her messages at the main desk, and hurried back to the production department.

Nolan's office was the cubicle he shared with Donna. There was no one inside.

Regina went through the files in her desk, looking around as she pulled out the Miss Classic file. With the folder under her arm, she strolled through the department, peeking in other offices.

The door to Max's office was closed, which was odd because it was rarely closed, even when he was out.

She lifted the phone and buzzed the receptionist.

"Suzie, is Max in?" Regina asked.

"Sorry, Regina, he left for lunch about ten minutes ago."

"Is Nolan here?"

"Yes, someone just came in to see him."

Ten to one, she told herself, Nolan and Amelia were behind that closed door. Oh, to be a fly on the wall.

"I could kill him easily," a voice behind her said, making her stiffen. Regina turned to see Tom Gansing standing at her desk, his hands made into tight fists. "It's only been a couple of weeks and already the bastard is scouting for a replacement."

She could think of nothing to say. Tom rarely showed impatience and never anger. This was so unlike him.

"He doesn't deserve her. Donna was always too good for him. But he does deserve that one." His chin jerked up in the direction of Max's office.

Regina laid a consoling hand on Tom's arm.

With a look of chagrin, he said, "I'm sorry, Regina. I didn't mean to unload on you like that. Forget I said anything." And with that he turned and walked away.

6

"I'm for you all the way, Amelia," Nolan said. "Regina has her special skills, but hostess, and *live* for crissakes, is not one of them."

They sat on the Naugahyde sofa in Max's office.

"Who, aside from Regina, would oppose my filling in for your wife?"

"Well my wife for one. But don't concern yourself, I have control in that department. Max is the other. Regina is sleeping with him so that could be a problem."

The corners of Amelia's lips curled up. She saw no problem there. Only when someone was beyond sexual manipulation was there a problem.

"I'll take care of Max," she said in a deep, self-assured tone. She saw something flash into Nolan's eyes. Caution. Wariness. She had to be careful. He was looking for another stooge to lead around. The reason he wanted

260

Regina out was because she couldn't be led. There was plenty of time after she got the job to rebel and pull the rug out from under him if he became difficult.

Her voice softened, became submissive. She placed a caressing hand on his thigh. "If you could just endorse me, then set up a meeting for the two of us, I think I can help persuade your boss."

He stared at her for a long moment. Then he smiled.

7

John looked over the list of Miss Classic contestants as Regina drove toward Daly City.

"Twenty-eight women made the initial lineup," he said, reading. "This was cut to ten, and finally four runners-up and the winner. How many days did the pageant run?"

"One week. Because there was no talent competition, we could only parade around in various stages of dress and undress for so long." She turned to him. "Don't you remember? You covered the contest for the newspaper."

"It was a long time ago," he said, looking out the passenger window, avoiding her eyes.

"What paper?"

"The *Chronicle*," he said without hesitation, and hoped to God the *Chronicle* had assigned someone that piece. She would know.

As he slid the list back into the folder a pink message slip fell out. John picked it up, glanced at it, then read it slowly. The message read: Someone with an alibi is lying.

"What's this?" John asked, holding up the pink paper.

"What?"

"A message slip fell out of the file folder."

"I picked that up at the station this morning. What's it say? I didn't have time to read it."

"It says, 'Someone with an alibi is lying.' "

"Who is it from?"

"It doesn't say."

"Odd." After a moment's silence, she said reflectively, "Last night a woman called and said there was a dangerous person who had killed and would kill again. She gave me a clue."

"A clue?"

"That's what she called it. I thought it was a crank. I don't know if I can remember what she said."

"Try," John said.

"Something about an ocean. An ocean will lead to the assailant. No, it was a 'sea'. Yes. A sea will lead to the assailant."

"That's it?"

"There was something else. Ultimately, a sea—no, wait—Initially, a sea will lead to the assailant. That was it."

John wrote it on the back of the pink message slip. "We'll go over this later."

She looked back to the road. "Tammy's house is right up here." She turned right, then made a left on the first street and pulled up to the second house from the corner.

"Have the cops been out here?" he asked.

"They were out the night the dog died. But that was the Daly City police. I don't know if any came out after her death."

"Probably not, since she died in the city and they were quick to rule out homicide," he said. "Where two jurisdictions are involved, one hand never seems to know what the other hand is doing."

They walked up the driveway to the front door. John rang the bell.

After several minutes he strolled around to the side of the house. He opened the wooden gate and stepped through. Standing just inside the yard, he paused to take in the scene. He heard Regina come up behind him.

"Tell me what you remember about that night. Where was the dog?"

"On the patio."

Scrutinizing the ground in front of each footstep, John slowly walked to the edge of the concrete slab. About two feet in he saw a foamy substance resembling hardened egg whites tinged with what looked like blood. He pointed at it. "There?"

"I think so."

He scanned the ten-by-fifteen-foot patio. In the center he saw something dark. Flies crawled over it. He walked to it, bent down in a crouch, and stared.

It was dried meat. Bits of raw ground beef that had stuck to the rough cement. He looked around. The fence was about twenty feet away.

John walked back to the gate. At the top he saw fresh scratch marks in the weathered wood.

"What is it?" Regina asked.

"The dog got pretty excited about something. Whoever poisoned him must have stood here. See the gouges? And then tossed the hamburger—probably a ball of meat with the poison inside—on to the patio. Big dogs aren't known to be finicky eaters."

"Then Tammy was right," Regina said. "He wanted her to come out in the open. He could have dropped the poison right here, but he wanted to make sure Tammy saw the dog and felt its suffering."

John opened the gate and went out between the two houses. The narrow space comprised a concrete walkway and grass. He dropped his gaze to the ground and began scanning outward.

Trapped in the corner, where the house and fence met in a right angle, was a pile of windblown debris: leaves, twigs and bits of paper. John bent down and, with a twig, poked through the litter. A piece of white paper caught his eye. He worked it out and picked it up by the two edges.

Regina had crouched down beside him, watching.

"What's that look like to you?" he asked.

She leaned in closer. "A tab—no, wait—tape. Butcher tape?"

"Umm." He held it up. "Can you make that out?"

There was something printed on the tape in blue, but most of it had been torn away. Regina studied it, turning her head this way and that. "It looks like an emblem of some kind . . . a sun, or . . . ," she shook her head, "I don't know, John, I can't tell."

"We'll find out. Do you have something to put this in?"

Regina reached into her purse, brought out an appointment book, and opened it. John dropped it between the pages. She carefully put it back in her purse. "It could have been there a long time."

"It's not weathered. It hasn't been there long."

A sense of being watched made John look up. Over the top of the fence he saw gray hair and a pair of pale blue, watery eyes. The head disappeared.

"Hello," John said, moving to the fence. "Sir?"

The head came up again, slowly. A tiny man in his early seventies, with a pair of eyeglasses pushed up through his sparse, yellow-gray hair, glared at him, eyes squinted.

"Afternoon, sir. We're from the Humane Society and we're investigating the death of Mrs. Kowalski's dog."

The limpid eyes, filled with suspicion, went from John to Regina and back to John. Suspicion strained the voice as well. "Mrs. Kowalski's dead too. What's the big deal about the dog?"

"We're not the police. We're following up on a report of animal poisoning. Could you answer a few questions, please?"

"Don't look to me. I didn't do it." He rose higher, so that his entire head cleared the top of the fence.

John moved to the fence and looked over. He saw that the man, in lamb's wool-lined bedroom slippers, was standing on a weathered step stool that looked as if it had been in that spot a long time. Around his neck hung a small pair of binoculars. "We're not accusing anyone. Did the dog bark a lot?"

"Naw."

"The night the dog died, did he bark?" He assumed this neighbor was aware of the all the particulars of the dog's death. Anyone who used a step stool to see over the fence and carried binoculars knew what was going on around him.

"Yeah."

"Did you see anyone out here that night? Possibly right where I'm standing now?"

"Couldn't have. When the dog started barking I was in bed. I got up, but I didn't go outdoors. There's no window on this side of the house, don't you know."

"Before you went to bed that evening did you see anyone at all?" Regina asked.

"Nope."

John stepped back. "Well, thank you for—"

"Saw a car though."

"A car?"

"Parked around the side of my place. It was there a long time. Never saw it before in the neighborhood."

"What kind of car?"

He shrugged.

"Color?"

"Dark. Blue, black, brown."

"New? Old?"

His mouth went down and his shoulders came up. "Hard to say. It had one of those hood ornaments. They don't seem to make hood ornaments these days."

"What did the ornament look like?"

"Couldn't see it good. That's the night I misplaced my glasses. Mostly I saw the lights, y'know, from the street

265

lamps, reflecting off it."

"Did anyone get in or out of the car?"

"Not while I was looking."

"Did you see anything else out of the ordinary? Not just that night but any time in the past week or two?"

The man shook his head. "Just that weirdo she was seeing what drove that infernal motorcycle. The noise liked to wake the dead, coming and going odd hours of the day and night."

John looked to Regina questioningly. She shrugged, shaking her head.

"What's become of those two little girls?" the man asked. "The twins?"

"They're with their father," Regina said.

The head disappeared.

John watched Regina take a pen and paper from her purse. She spoke aloud as she wrote. "Dark car with hood ornament. Friend with motorcycle. Do you think there are fingerprints on the butcher tape?" she asked.

"It's not likely there'll be a clear one. And again, as with voiceprints, it's a matter of comparison."

"How do you know so much about crime detection?"

"I write suspense novels. It's my business to know. Of course it's a lot easier to solve a crime when you know who the bad guy is." He put a hand on the small of her back and said, "C'mon, let's get back to the apartment house. We have follow-up work to do."

8

Back in Regina's apartment, John sat on the couch scanning the phone book for meat markets while Regina, sipping a Corona, was on the phone calling from the list of Miss Classic contestants. The women from the original list had since married, moved; two had died—one of cancer, the other from an overdose of barbiturates; and more than half of the twenty-eight had disappeared without a trace. She reached Jamie Sue, the contestant who had called in to Saturday's show with her tale of near death from alcohol poisoning. Jamie Sue then went on to tell of several other oddities; contestants plagued by freakish accidents and mysterious illnesses. Regina brought up the food poisoning at the banquet.

"Amelia lied on the show," Jamie Sue said. "She said she'd had a touch of food poisoning. She didn't."

"Are you certain?"

"Yes. She hates shellfish. I do too. We talked about it. I also saw her doing something with a pair of aqua dyed-satin pumps, and that evening Tammy, coming down the stairs, lost the heel on one of her aqua pumps."

"Lord."

"Amelia had vodka stashed in a rubbing alcohol bottle in plain sight in the changing room. She offered me a swig and that's when I told her I was allergic to booze."

Things were falling into place. Not jinxed, but sabotaged. The two women talked several more minutes, then said good-bye.

John only nodded when Regina passed on Jamie Sue's information.

She opened the refrigerator and pulled out two cold Coronas. After cutting wedges of lime, she pushed them, peel and all, down into each bottle. "Any luck?" she asked, pointing to the open phone book on the table in front of him as she handed him a beer.

Shaking his head, he stood, stretched, then stepped to a rattan bookcase and began to peruse the titles.

Seeing him looking at the books reminded Regina she had forgotten to get the novel he'd given her. "I didn't forget *Evil Tidings*," Regina said. "In all the excitement with Kristy and the answering machine . . ."

"I know."

"I'd like you to autograph it for me, if you will?"

"It's already been done."

She smiled, then began to pace. "John, I've been thinking. Assuming we're not dealing with a copycat criminal, who would have the most to gain?"

"It's my guess the same person committed the assaults on Corinne, Donna, and Tammy."

"Corinne had a motive. Jealousy and hate or, as Donna suspects, sheer dementia. And since she visited Donna in the hospital the same night that Tammy's dog was poisoned, we know she goes out of her house."

"Perhaps only at night. The two other assaults happened in broad daylight."

"Amelia then. But I just can't picture her stalking women and tossing acid in their faces."

John drew in a deep breath. "There's something we're not seeing yet. Something there, but indirect and . . ." He went to the counter, opened the file folder, and took out the pink slip on the back of which he had written Regina's message. "Initially, a sea will lead to the assailant?"

"A sea. Water . . . ," Regina began.

"No, not 'sea,' " John cut in excitedly. "A. C. They're initials. *Initially*. *A. C.* will lead to the assailant?"

"Amelia Corde," Regina said quietly. "John, are we grasping . . . twisting things to make them fit?"

"What do you know about Amelia?"

"She's married, has no children, and recently she started a modeling business with a man—" Regina stopped abruptly. "That man with Amelia . . ."

"What is it?"

Regina began to pace faster. "Her partner, Fletcher Kincade, was at the station the day Donna was splashed. Tammy overheard them talking about going to the wine country together. She said they sounded like lovers." She turned to stare at John.

"What part of the wine country?"

"I don't know. Is it important?"

"It could be."

"Maybe I can find out." Regina picked up the phone and dialed. She got the Corde residence, spoke to a woman with an oriental accent and asked to speak to Amelia. She sipped at the beer while waiting. Amelia came on the line.

"Regina, I was about to call you," Amelia said guardedly. "How dreadful to hear about Tammy. The poor dear. Is there word of a funeral date?"

"No, nothing yet. There's the inquest still. Amelia," Regina said carefully, "the peculiar way Tammy died is one of the reasons I'm calling. First Corinne, then Donna, and now Tammy—"

"Really, Regina, I refuse to listen to any of this doomsayer propaganda. It was obvious the woman was on a rapid course of self-destruction. You saw how she acted at lunch last week."

"I had a warning last night. Donna and Tammy also had warnings."

"Oh?"

"A message on my answering machine."

"Did you recognize the voice?"

"No. I'm sure it was disguised. But I intend to have it analyzed," Regina lied. "Have you had any threats?"

Another long pause. "They can do that? Analyze a voice?"

"Yes. They match speech patterns like fingerprints. About the threats . . ."

"No, no one has threatened me."

"Where were you when Tammy died?"

"I was—I resent this line of questioning. I don't need an alibi, Regina."

"An alibi? According to you, Tammy self-destructed."

"Damnit," Amelia said impatiently, "I wasn't even in the city when it happened. If you don't believe me call the Meadowvale Inn. In fact, at the time of her death I was at my parents' home in Napa."

"Amelia, I only called to tell you to be careful."

"I appreciate the concern. Good night." A soft click punctuated the line.

"The Meadowvale Inn in Napa," Regina said to John, pausing to drink. "She was visiting her parents when Tammy died. She's had no threats. She seemed rather fascinated about the voice analysis."

John had the phone directory draped over his knees. "Too bad it was erased. It'd be interesting to compare it to Mr. Kincade's voice. Hey, look at this, Regina." He rose quickly, bringing the book with him.

"You've found something?"

"Blue Ribbon Meats. Where's the butcher tape?"

Regina got it and handed it to him. John inspected it. "It could be . . . yes, it could be." He handed it back. "Does that resemble a blue ribbon?"

Regina studied it. Only half the emblem was there, but yes, she agreed silently, it could be a ribbon. She looked up and nodded.

"First thing tomorrow we buy us some meat."

"Speaking of meat," Regina said, sipping her Corona, "I'm starving. I haven't eaten since this morning. If I don't get something in my stomach soon, I'm going to get drunk. Drunker." She held up the empty bottle.

"Come down to my place. I'll fix you something."

Regina looked at her watch. 8:28. Kristy would be home in half an hour. "Let's eat here."

9

There was no screen and the window was unlocked, yet when he pushed, it refused to budge. With the heel of both palms, he butted the bottom rail until he heard a sharp snap as the dried paint cracked free. He eased the window sash upward and hoisted himself through the opening into the kitchen.

The apartment was dark. He stood quietly, listening.

Taking out a flashlight from his deep coat pocket, he clicked it on and followed the circle of light into the living room. The beam played over the photographs on the wall above the desk. A hardcover book sat atop the monitor. He picked it up, turned it over in his gloved hand, and saw the photograph of the man who lived in the apartment. John Tyronne Davie.

He opened the cover and read the personal autograph inside: "To Regina, a 'Classic' woman then and now, from a longtime admirer, John." He returned the book to the monitor.

Moving down the hallway, he turned into the bedroom, the flashlight beam crawling over the furniture. In no hurry, he looked into the closet, then crossed the room and entered the bathroom. It was a long, narrow room with a second door off the hallway. After checking the medicine cabinet, he went back into the bedroom, moved to the dresser, and began silently going through the drawers. Nothing. He crossed to a nightstand, gave a framed photograph of a woman and child, similar to the one in the other room, a cursory glance, then pulled out a drawer and began rifling through it. The .38 Smith and Wesson was a pleasant surprise. Ignoring the cigar boxes of quarters and silver dollars, he lifted the gun and shoved it deep into the pocket of his black trenchcoat. Before closing the drawer, he carefully lifted out several books of matches and pocketed them as well.

He looked around the room, satisfied with what he had found. The man in black was about to leave the bedroom when he heard tapping at the front door. In a crouched position, he stiffened. Moments later he heard the door open and close softly. A light went on in the hall. Reaching a hand into his pocket, his fingers wrapping around the butt of the .38, he backed up into the dark bathroom. After making certain the door into the hallway was closed, he positioned himself behind the door off the bedroom.

271

He heard movement in the living room and a light step coming down the hall. Looking through the space between the door hinges, he watched a young blond woman, in her late teens, enter the bedroom. With a sashaying step, swinging hand flipping the limp gauze skirt at her side, she moved about the room leisurely, surveying everything, touching one item after another. She leaned in to stare at the photograph on the nightstand, the one with the woman and little boy, and in a heavy foreign accent, she said aloud, "It's my turn now. When he is mine, I will never leave him the way you did."

The man in black watched the girl through a sheer veil of black nylon as she tossed her fabric drawstring purse onto a chair and, in a fluid movement, like a cat, poured herself onto the queen-size bed. On her back, arms spread out, she stretched, arching her back and sighing. Then she slid off the edge of the bed, kicked her shoes off, and stood. Her long, tapered fingers went to the waistband of her skirt, and as she walked toward the bathroom, she undid the buttons, pulled the skirt down, and stepped out of it. At the doorway she pulled her cotton tank over her head and tossed it on the bed. In her bra and panties she entered the bathroom. When she switched on the light, he readied himself to attack should she close the door and discover him.

She was out of sight now, on the other side of the door. He heard bare feet padding on linoleum, then a click and the gushing sound of water pouring into the tub.

He saw her pass by again into the bedroom, and he took that opportunity to leave the bathroom through the other door. In the hallway now, standing flat against the wall, he saw her go to her purse, take out a pink packet, and, gripping the packet in her teeth, twist her long hair on top of her head, fastening it with a clip. Then she removed her bra and panties and returned to the bathroom. Moments later, over the running water, he heard a slight splashing sound and detected a flood of fragrance. Jasmine. The cloying smell triggered something dark and painful inside him. He closed his eyes, rolling his head against the rough plastered wall.

Over the sound of rushing water the girl began to sing sweetly. He moved along the wall and reentered the bedroom, his eyes near slits behind the nylon mask.

10

Regina opened the freezer and pulled out a large plastic container. "I don't cook often, but when I do, I make enough for an army. Spaghetti sauce." She moved to the cupboard and took down a package of pasta. The container of frozen sauce went into the microwave and she started a pot of water to boil.

"What can I do?"

"Just sit and watch." She pointed to a rattan stool at the breakfast counter.

"It'll be my pleasure."

Regina glanced at him. Their eyes met and held. That feeling of longing that she hadn't experienced in ever so long, surfaced again, making her breath come out shallow and tight. Regina broke eye contact first.

Quickly opening the refrigerator, she pulled out lettuce, tomatoes, feta cheese and black olives for a salad.

From a magnetic hook on the stove she lifted an apron and tied it on.

As she cut up the vegetables, she felt his eyes on her. She avoided looking at him. In her tipsy state she feared she might expose the passion that had lain so long under the thin veneer of her being.

The water began to boil, huge bubbles erupting lethargically at various points on the surface. She lifted the pasta and held it in her hand in front of the pot, waiting for the water to come to a full boil. While waiting she unconsciously ran her palm up and down the material of her apron where her hip and thigh joined. She watched the bubbles, her eyes staring trancelike, powerless to move. The bubbles became smaller, breaking the surface with an urgency that she found mesmerizing and very pleasant. I'm getting drunk, she thought, and felt herself smile.

With her face tipped to one side, her gaze swept sideways to look at the man sitting on the rattan stool. He was watching her with a somber expression, his eyes intense, almost brooding. He smiled, slow and easy, and she realized he was smiling back at her. Then he was standing and moving, as in slow motion, toward her. The pasta was taken from her hands. Out of the corner of her eye she watched as he dropped it into the water. Her hands were still poised before her, holding nothing, with nowhere to go.

He stood before her, his eyes asking a thousand questions as they took in her face, one feature at a time, until they found her eyes and became locked. His hands lightly cupped hers. She turned, feeling the cool solid surface of the refrigerator at her back, her palms pressed flat to the smooth enamel. He moved in, his body melding lightly against her breasts and stomach. His lips touched her temple, then her eyelid, then the corner of her mouth. She twisted her head and his mouth brushed across hers. She came forward into the kiss, her lips parting. She tasted him. Found him wonderfully delectable. As they kissed, boiling water from the pot skipped across the stove top and pricked her skin.

She heard the hissing, sizzling sound of water boiling over on the electric coils. It might have been coming from the radio or television for all she cared.

John pulled away to reach over and turn off the burner. She leaned her head back on the refrigerator, eyes still closed, waiting for his return.

The buzzer on the microwave oven went off. Regina

opened her eyes and glanced at the clock above the sink. It was nine o'clock. Kristy would be home soon.

John reached for her again, but she stiffened.

He looked at her questioningly.

"Kristy. She'll be walking in any minute." She turned the burner on again and moved around him to finish the salad. "I'm sorry," she said, sounding flustered and breathless and on the verge of tears, "I'm sorry."

He stood behind her, his fingertips drawing hair from her face, caressing the back of her neck.

"Sorry for what?"

Sorry because she wanted him. Sorry because there wasn't time. Sorry because she felt herself caring for him. She shivered.

"Sorry for what, Regina?" he repeated.

"I don't have any red wine to go with the spaghetti," she replied morosely, as though it was something to grieve for.

He took hold of her arms and forced her to look at him. "Hey, what's the matter?"

"Nothing," she answered without conviction, staring at the cleft in his chin. "Nothing."

But everything was wrong. Leo was dead only six months and she wanted this man more than she had ever wanted any man, including, she thought grimly, her own husband. How could this happen? I've only known him a few weeks. I don't know anything about him. Of course what she was feeling for him was purely physical. Like with Garrick. It had been so long. And the last few times with Leo, before he had gone into the hospital, it had been unpleasant. Unpleasant? It had been bad. Very bad.

"There's half a bottle of wine downstairs," John said, kissing her mouth lightly. "I'll run down and get it."

11

While the girl reclined in the tub, humming softly, oblivious to another presence in the apartment, the man in black went through her handbag. From an identification card he learned her name was Ilona Dobos and she was nineteen. He found a key that he assumed opened the main door of the building; this he pocketed.

He dropped her handbag back on the chair and stepped closer to the bathroom. Through the doorway he saw a long, slim leg covered in bubbles, toes tracing a pattern on the tiles above the faucet. Her upper body was hidden from his view. He bent, lifted her panties; and, feeling suddenly light-headed, confused, he rubbed absently at the silky material beneath his gloved hands. Then, with the stealthiness of a predator, he moved toward the dulcet voice.

12

John opened the door of his apartment and immediately heard someone inside. The sound he realized, was a woman humming. Puzzled, he followed the sound.

The bedroom was dark, but light from the open bathroom door cut a pattern across the threshold, revealing a trail of feminine clothes. He cautiously stepped toward the bathroom.

What the hell?

"Johnnie?" a woman's voice whispered.

Ilona. He'd recognize that accent anywhere. Christ, why now? he asked himself.

John reluctantly moved to the open door, his tone mildly irritated. "Ilona, what are you doing in my—."

The sound of the floor creaking behind him interrupted

his sentence. He started to turn, saw a flash of black, then a brightness so intense it was like an explosion behind his eyes. He went down on his knees, his head ringing and ringing.

Twenty-two

1

John heard his name over and over. The room spun and he flailed out, searching for a solid hold. His knees buckled, but he managed to stay upright. He heard someone retreating down the hallway. Groaning, he fell against the door. Who the hell had hit him? And with what?

"Johnnie!" the voice cried again. He pulled himself back to consciousness just before he could succumb to the blessed darkness. He touched his head at his brow and felt skin growing taut over a throbbing knot. His fingers came away wet and sticky.

"Please, Johnnie, answer me."

He moved in ungainly steps to the bathroom. At the doorway, the light pierced his brain, intensifying the pain above his eye.

He found her in the tub, bubbles clinging like a white feather boa to her naked breasts.

With confusion and dismay clouding his brain, he went to her. What was she doing here? Was he dreaming, hallucinating? he wondered. He had come downstairs from Regina's to get the red wine, and now here he was standing in his bathroom, his head pounding, about to black out any second, gaping stupidly at a naked girl in his tub.

"What . . . ?" he asked, seeing blood, his own, drop on the linoleum at his feet.

"Johnnie, your head. You're bleeding."

"Ilona." He leaned against the door frame. "What are you doing here? What . . . what the hell . . . ?"

Swiping at the blood that was working into his eye, he reached back, pulled down two towels, handed one to her and pressed the other one to his brow.

"Please . . ." He turned, leaving the room. "Come out of there."

"I wanted to surprise you," she called out. "I didn't mean to frighten you, to make you hurt your head. What happened?"

He fought a wave of nausea, unable to answer.

"You ran into something. It's my fault," she said sadly, coming into the bedroom, the towel wrapped around her. "I surprised you too much. Johnnie, I'm sorry."

It was obvious she had no idea what had taken place here. Not that he was too sure either. But someone else had been in this room and Ilona hadn't been aware of it. There was no point in scaring her, he decided. Ignorance was bliss.

"Ilona, you don't just walk into people's apartments and take a bubble bath." He picked up her clothes and handed them to her.

She stuck out her bottom lip in a pout.

John looked around. Except for Ilona's clothes scattered about, nothing else seemed out of place. What had his attacker wanted in his apartment? Could he have been looking for a way to get to Regina? It hurt his head to think.

Ilona straightened up and let the towel drop to expose two high, pointed breasts.

John stared long enough to show appreciation before he turned his back and went to the doorway. "Ilona, please get dressed."

He heard her call his name again as he left to follow what he assumed was the path the intruder had taken.

In the kitchen he discovered the open window. On the closed-in brick area that served as his patio he found two tipped-over flower pots.

He went out, righted the pots, and cursed under his breath. He was certain Donna and Tammy's attacker had been here. But why? Why?

When he reentered the bedroom, Ilona had put on her skirt and top, but her feet were still bare. She sat on the edge of the bed, hands limp in her lap, her head bowed.

Going to her, he knelt at her feet, lifted her foot, and slipped on her sandals.

"How did you get here?"

"I walked."

The Doboses lived above the restaurant eight blocks away. It was dark now. He couldn't just send her out to walk home alone. "I'll call a cab for you."

"No!" she said, rearing back as if he'd slapped her. Tears welled up in her eyes. "I cannot go home yet."

"Why not?"

"My relatives believe I am at school for my class in English. If I go home now, they will know I lied."

"The cab can take you to the school."

"There is no class tonight. It is canceled."

John sighed. "What time is the class usually over?"

"Tiz."

"Ten o'clock?"

She nodded.

He looked at his watch. It was 9:15. His aunt was at her sewing group. Regina was waiting for him upstairs. He cursed his rotten luck.

She began to cry softly.

"Please don't cry."

"You hate me. I have made a fool of myself and now you hate me."

"That's not true, Ilona."

"You only want to get rid of me. Out of your head." She shook fingers through her hair. "Like that."

"Stop crying, please."

"I want to die. You think because I take off my clothes I am not a virgin?"

"It doesn't matter to me whether you're a virgin or not."

280

She cried harder.

"Look I'll take you home at ten o'clock. Okay?"

She sniffed swiping roughly at her eyes. She nodded, smiling weakly.

"Good."

"Do you have wine?"

At the mention of wine he was reminded of the reason he had come downstairs in the first place. Regina was waiting for him to bring the wine that would accompany their dinner. "Ilona, I have to run upstairs. You'll be all right till I get back. It'll just take a few minutes."

He hurried into the kitchen, grabbed the bottle of red wine, and went out the apartment door. He nearly careened into Kristy, who had just come in.

"Hi, John," she said. "Hey, what happened to your head?"

"Barbell fell on me," he said, touching the cut that had now stopped bleeding but still hurt like hell.

"You shouldn't press weights without someone to spot for you."

"You're right. It was dumb of me."

From inside his apartment, Ilona called out to him. "Johnnie, where are you? Johnnie?"

Kristy stared at him.

He handed her the wine. "Give that to your mother, will you? And tell her I can't make dinner tonight. Something's come up. Tell her I'll call her as soon as I can."

"Sure, okay," she said, puzzled.

John went back into his apartment and closed the door.

Ilona was standing in the doorway of the bedroom. He motioned for her to come into the living room as he paced impatiently, glaring at his watch.

2

Regina had eaten little of the meal she'd prepared, though she had drunk a good portion of the wine.

Back in the living room, Regina picked up the list and the phone. She dialed, but hung up before it could ring. Without John, she realized, she had lost her enthusiasm for investigating.

After dousing most of the lights, she went to the window seat. She leaned against the inner casing, her knees drawn up to her chest, looking out at the tiny red lights atop the Bay Bridge as she listened to the distant, soft love songs from Kristy's radio.

Again she wondered what had happened to prevent John from coming back upstairs. Kristy had handed her the bottle of wine and delivered the message from John. But there was something odd about the whole thing. Kristy had avoided her eyes through dinner, and after cleaning the kitchen had disappeared into her room.

What could possibly have come up in the short span of time it took for him to run down to his place for a half bottle of wine? A death in the family? An accident? A change of heart?

Don't be a fool, she told herself, one kiss does not an affair make. Something important had come up and it had nothing to do with her.

She found herself studying her shadowy image in the windowpane. Her looks had meant little to her for so many years. Leo had praised her in everything except her appearance, actually discouraging any notions of vanity. She thought of Corinne and Donna, beautiful women now marred for life, and suddenly she felt a sense of panic. Would John have looked twice at her, she wondered, if she hadn't been pretty?

She heard the exterior door open and close. A moment later she saw two people standing on the sidewalk. It was a man and a woman—lovers, she surmised. They turned left, heading west. The woman had a youthful air about her. Her step was light, and her free arm swung back and forth, whipping the filmy gauze skirt about. She held onto the man's arm, her head against his shoulder.

A car turned east onto the street and as it passed the

couple, its beams bathed them in light.

Regina recognized the woman as the young Hungarian girl she'd met in John's apartment.

The man was John.

No wonder Kristy couldn't look her in the face at dinner. Regina suddenly felt sick to her stomach.

3

From the dark front seat of the old Packard, Corinne watched the couple walk down the street. The woman clung possessively to John's arm.

Corinne waited until they reached the corner before leaving the car. She followed, keeping close to the building fronts. After a half dozen blocks the pair ahead of her reached Van Ness Avenue. They crossed.

Corinne couldn't decide whether to continue or turn back. The busy avenue was well lighted by traffic and street lamps. Standing on the corner, her hood pulled across the scarred side of her face, she decided to wait, watching until John and the young woman disappeared from view. But to her surprise, they stopped in front of a restaurant kitty-corner from her.

A man lumbered out of a bar several doors down and looked up and down the street. He stopped to light a cigarette and paused when he saw her. With the unlit cigarette dangling from his mouth, he walked toward her, swaying drunkenly.

"Hey, babe, you lost?"

Corinne turned her head away and said nothing.

"Need an escort home?" He reached out and plucked at the sleeve of her coat.

She backed up and he pursued. More angry than frightened, she pushed at him. He was interfering in something very important.

"Let's see what you look like behind that mysterious hood," the man said, cigarette bobbing between his slack lips. He pulled it away from her face.

The cigarette dropped from his mouth and he frowned before stepping backward, his eyes widening. Without another word he swiveled around and hurried off the way he'd come.

Corinne collapsed against the cold concrete building, fighting an array of emotions. She hated the man for reminding her how ugly she was. Then she remembered why she was there and, pushing her hate and anger aside, looked across the intersection.

John and the girl stood facing each other, then suddenly they merged as one. Corinne realized they were kissing. She didn't know whether to laugh or cry. She wanted to laugh because the woman he was now kissing was not Regina, therefore it was obvious he didn't love Regina. But she wanted to cry because the woman he was kissing was not her, Corinne.

4

John reached up and pulled Ilona's arms away from his neck. Without warning she had embraced him, kissing him with brash, inexperienced force.

"You're going to get into trouble doing things like that," John said, holding tight to her wrists.

She smiled and came forward again, rising on her tiptoes to kiss him. John turned his head and her mouth brushed his jaw. "Good night," he said, opening the door, turning her, then propelling her through. He pivoted quickly and strode away.

A little more than halfway home, he sensed he was being followed. He slowed, listened for footsteps. His head hurt where he had been hit. There was still a slight ringing in his ear and he wondered if that was responsible for the sounds he was hearing; making him think that someone was behind him, keeping pace. He spun around quickly and he swore he saw, just a flash, a dark figure being swallowed by shadows.

Less than an hour ago he had been bashed on the head and he realized then that if someone was following him, there was a strong possibility it was the same person. His heart hammered. He was curious to know who that person was, but not enough to risk, unarmed, another confrontation. He hurried on, looking back often. Minutes later he reached his apartment house. The sidewalk behind him was clear for as far as he could see.

Looking up to the second floor, he thought he saw a figure in the dark upstairs window of Regina's apartment. He entered the building, climbed to the second floor, and knocked softly several times. When he received no response, he went down to his apartment and called her on the phone. After four rings the answering machine greeted him.

Perplexed, he hung up without leaving a message.

Twenty-three

1

John called Regina's apartment at 7:30 that morning. Kristy informed him that Regina had already left for work. He called the station. After holding on the line for an interminable amount of time, she finally came on.

"Hi," he said softly.

"Hello." Her tone was cool and businesslike.

"Look, I'm sorry I couldn't make it back for dinner last night. Something unexpected came up and I had to take care of it."

"I understand," she said flatly.

"What time can you break away?"

"I'm sorry. It's impossible today."

"What do you mean? We have the butcher tape and—"

"Can't you do it without me?"

"I can, yes, but I don't want to. Regina, this is important. It won't take long, I promise."

A pause. Then, "All right. I'll pick you up in an hour."

He hung up slowly, staring out the window. Her cool reception had him wondering if she now regretted the intimacy they had shared the night before. He'd made a promise to himself not to come on to her until she was ready. But the look, the smile she had given him as she stood at the stove, could have been interpreted only one way, and damnit, he had responded in kind. However, he sensed her reluctance to go with him today was an ex-

286

pression of anger rather than remorse. More than likely Kristy had mentioned the woman in his apartment or she had seen him walking Ilona home.

He had decided not to tell her about the intruder. She was frightened enough as it was. So she would just have to think the worst. Trying to explain why Ilona was in his apartment, in his bathtub, wouldn't be any easier.

After two cups of coffee and no breakfast, he showered and dressed. He paced for several minutes, then decided to go to the station instead of waiting. Deep down he was afraid she wouldn't show.

The morning was overcast and chilly. He buried his hands into the pockets of his bomber jacket and walked briskly, covering the six blocks in minutes. He found her car parked on Lombard, a block from the station. Leaning against it, he waited, watching the entrance.

At exactly 8:30 she came out of the building, walking briskly toward him. Her hair was up today, held by two large tortoiseshell combs, and loose tendrils of hair, from the dampness in the air, curled against her cheek and neck. She wore a gray, knee-length straight skirt, split up the front, a fuchsia V-neck sweater under a matching oversized cardigan, and pearl gray pumps. A silver rope chain swung between her breasts as she walked.

She stopped to get something from her purse. John watched her, thinking how different she'd become since the first time he saw her outside the apartment building. Was the change entirely due to her new job as talk show hostess? He wanted to believe that his recent emergence into Regina's life might have something to do with her sudden desire to play up her looks.

She pulled her mace key chain from her purse and resumed walking. When she spotted him, she seemed to waver slightly; then she continued to the car.

"I thought I was to pick you up?" she asked, unlocking the door, not looking at him.

"I need the exercise."

She got in the car and unlocked the door.

John climbed in.

"Where to?" she asked, starting the engine. Her gaze darted to the cut at his brow, but she said nothing.

He directed her to an area south of Market Street. They were both silent as she drove.

The Blue Ribbon Meat Company was a large gray building not far from the Mission District.

"This doesn't look like a butcher shop to me," Regina said, parking.

"It isn't. It's a wholesale place. Better for us. Now we can be relatively certain that someone didn't pop in off the street for a pound of ground round. Whoever had that package probably buys their meat in bulk. Let's find out if it's Amelia Corde."

They entered a door marked Office. The small room was empty. A button on the counter read, Ring Bell for Service.

John buzzed.

A middle-aged man with a pot belly and short legs pushed through a swinging door. "Help you?" he asked.

"We're interested in buying some beef."

"You with a market or a restaurant?"

"Neither. It's for private consumption. We're looking to buy a hindquarter."

"Half's the least amount we handle. Could sell you two hindquarters though."

"Then you do sell to the public?"

"If it's in bulk."

"Any chance of us trying a couple steaks before we make a decision."

"I'll have to charge full price."

"Sounds fair. Two porterhouses. Thick."

The man smiled, nodding. He pushed through a swinging door into the plant. Several minutes later he was back with a package in white butcher paper.

"Came to a little more than two pounds. That'll be—aw, what the heck, I'll give it to you at wholesale price. Call it an introductory offer."

288

"Thanks," John said paying for the meat. It wasn't the discount that had his heart beating soundly, it was the tape with the little blue ribbons stamped an inch apart.

"Friends of ours recommended Blue Ribbon," Regina said. "The Cordes. Do you know the name?"

The man shook his head. "I don't do the order taking or the billing. But tell them we appreciate the recommendation."

Out on the sidewalk John handed the package to Regina. She looked at the tape, looked up at him, and for the first time since they met that morning, her eyes became bright. She smiled.

"We know where the meat was purchased," John said, "but we still don't know by whom."

"I've been to Amelia's house. There's a freezer." Regina said. "It's in a utility room off the kitchen."

"Let's go." John took her arm and began walking.

"Where to?"

"Back home. There's something I want to look into."

A half hour later they were in John's apartment. Regina sat in the rocker, her legs crossed. The split in the straight skirt exposed her leg to mid-thigh. John's gaze kept returning to her legs as he paced the room, talking into the cordless phone. The nylons she wore were sheer, and he saw the white line of a small scar on the kneecap. He wondered how she had gotten it.

The information operator gave him the number for the Meadowvale Inn in Napa.

"What did you say Amelia's husband did for a living?" he asked Regina as he dialed.

"He's a judge."

A female voice said, "Meadowvale Inn. Desk. Rachel speaking."

"Rachel, this is Judge Corde in San Francisco. I have before me an invoice from your establishment. It seems there is a discrepancy regarding a number of long-distance telephone calls made from the room my wife and I were said to occupy."

289

"Which room was that, Judge Corde?"

"That, I believe, is another problem. The room number on this invoice is not the same room we occupied. And the dates, I fear, are off. We checked in on the eleventh and checked out the fourteenth. Now, if you'll just pull your copy so we may get this straightened out."

John heard papers rustling. "Your dates are correct, Judge Corde, and according to my records there were no long-distance calls charged to room nineteen."

"That was my opinion, as well. Am I safe to assume a mistake has been made in billing and I may, therefore, dispose of this invoice?"

"Yes, of course. I'm sorry you had to be inconvenienced, sir. We have a new girl in accounting."

John pushed the antenna in. He turned to Regina. "Damnit."

"What?"

"They were there from Thursday to Sunday morning."

"But she still could have driven into the city on Saturday," Regina said. "She may have lied about visiting her mother."

"Or she could have had someone else go to the Fitness Center. Kincade." John paced. "If I could just get a look in their meat freezer." He whirled around to Regina. C'mon. He pulled her up from the rocker. "I have an idea."

2

Donna stood at the window, looking out across the hospital parking lot. A sense of sadness was all that remained of yesterday's deep depression. She'd been a fool to consider suicide. Tom, so levelheaded and compassionate, had convinced her she wasn't to blame for Tammy's death, or for her own attack. And she realized that had she succeeded in killing herself, the burden of her death would fall on Nolan. After all, he had brought her the

290

pills, though, naturally, he hadn't dreamed she would use them in that way.

A gunmetal gray BMW pulled into the side entrance and she wondered if it was Nolan's car. He had called that morning to say he would be in, but he'd been vague about the time. He'd hinted that he wanted to discuss Regina.

She thought about Regina. They'd been friends for so many years. Regina, who didn't have a jealous bone in her body, had been content to stay in the background and cheer her on. Nolan had never liked Regina and though she'd asked him about it many times, he refused to give a reason for his obvious animosity. She suspected it was because she and Regina were too close. Nolan was comfortable only if he had complete control. To Nolan, Regina was a threat. Though, unbeknownst to him, she never interfered. "He makes you happy," Regina had told her once when Donna felt a need to explain why she put up with Nolan's dominating manner. "And if you're happy, that's all that matters."

He makes you happy.

Did she make *him* happy?

At one time she did. Could she say the same now? How much had changed? Surely Nolan still loved her despite what had happened.

She thought of Corinne . . . alone now and bitter. Had someone loved her before she had lost her beauty? Had he turned his back on her, repulsion and guilt clouding his eyes? Corinne had had a boyfriend. Donna recalled a young man, a street kid actually, whose light blue eyes glowed like blue topaz against his tanned skin. A boy who looked a lot like—

Oh, sweet Mary! Could it be? Was it possible?

Only now did she remember where she had seen that man before. John Davie, Regina's new friend and neighbor, had come to the hotel on the day of the crowning. He and Corinne had argued under the stairway. Donna had heard a slap, then the one Corinne called Jack had stormed off. Donna had seen him again the following morning when she'd come to the hospital to check on Corinne. He had looked wretched, like a tormented soul committed to hell, a glint of desperation glowing feverishly in his brooding, bloodshot eyes. A plainclothes policeman had come then, and together they had gone to the police station. Of course Davie had been a young man then, practically a boy, but she could never forget those eyes.

Did Regina know about Corinne and John Davie?

Donna moved to the phone and dialed Regina's number.

3

They sat across the street from the Cordes' three-story house in exclusive Pacific Heights. The house was set back on the property amid a growth of mature shrubs. A narrow driveway on the right led to a three-car garage.

At a market they had bought six pounds of ground meat wrapped in one-pound packages. John had filled a cardboard box with bags of cat litter—for weight—before arranging the packages on top. Regina had called the Corde house; the housekeeper informed her the Cordes were away.

"Well, here goes," John said, climbing from the station wagon. With the heavy box, he crossed the street. By the time he traversed the long driveway and reached the back door of the house, he was breathing hard, a thin film of sweat across his forehead.

He rang the bell.

He was about to ring again when it swung open. A young Asian girl stood there looking tiny in the oversized uniform.

"Special order from Blue Ribbon Meats. Where's the freezer?" He stepped forward, one foot perched on the doorstep.

292

The door closed to his foot.

"You no can come in. Missus no home."

"How about the Mister?"

"Mister no home. You come back later."

" 'Fraid I can't do that. This meat needs to be put away now. Here," he said, thrusting the box at her, "take it yourself then."

She automatically took the box and nearly buckled from the weight of it.

He grabbed it before it hit the ground.

She looked stricken, then mumbled something under her breath and backed up.

"Much heavy. There—" She pointed to a room off the service porch. "You put away. Then you go."

"No problem. I'm running behind. Can't stay for tea."

"No tea," she said sharply.

He carried the box into a room that had to be a pantry. Rows upon rows of shelves, stacked with canned, boxed, and packaged goods, covered three walls. The large chest freezer took up the fourth wall. Putting the box on the floor, he lifted the heavy lid. A cloud of frost rose up to sting his eyes and chill his breath.

He reached in and lifted a package wrapped in white butcher paper. The words "prime rib" were stamped on the side. A lovely roast, he thought. Enough for eight guests, sliced as thick as the steaks he had bought that morning. The tape holding it together was also white. He brought it close to his face. No markings. No little blue ribbons standing in a row. Just plain white butcher tape.

He felt disappointment course through him. He dropped the roast and picked up another package. The same plain tape. Tossing packages from side to side, he reached deep into the freezer. His hand came up with a package marked "ground sirloin." It had a strip of tape with blue markings on it. John rubbed frantically at it, erasing the thick layer of frost. He stared at two and one half blue ribbons. His pulse accelerated. Reaching down deep again, he pulled up another small package. Again he saw the blue ribbon trademark. He pulled the tape off and shoved it in the pocket of his jacket.

Hurrying now, he moved aside several layers of meat and stacked the ground round that he had brought. He covered it with the Cordes' meat. In a deep cupboard to the right of the freezer, he stashed the two bags of cat litter. The empty box he took with him.

The Asian girl was in the kitchen. She saw him, but stayed at the center island, chopping green and red peppers.

John raised a hand and smiled. "Sorry, can't stay for the tea. Maybe next time."

This time she giggled, her hand covering her mouth.

John practically ran down the long driveway. At the station wagon, he tossed the box into the back and jumped inside, gesturing for Regina to drive. When they were half a block away, he whooped.

"It was there?" Regina asked incredulously.

Without answering, he dug into his pocket and pulled out the tape, holding it up. Regina pulled to the curb and stopped. He put it in her hand.

"I had to dig for it. But it was there. By God, it was there."

Regina was quiet as she stared at the tape in her hand.

"That's pretty concrete, isn't it? I mean, the odds of finding butcher tape from the scene of a crime and then finding the same tape—not the same tape, but—well, you know what I mean . . ."

"Yes, I know what you mean. And yes, this is very conclusive evidence."

"Then the police will have to believe us now, won't they?"

John looked into her eyes. There was something there he couldn't quite read. Fear? And if so, fear of what? The assailant? Of finding out for sure who it was? Or fear of him, John Davie?

John looked away. "It's conclusive, but only to us. I'm

294

afraid we've screwed up the evidence. We can prove that Amelia Corde has a freezer full of Blue Ribbon Meats, but so what? The police don't know about the tape we found at Tammy's. *We* found it, not they."

"I see," she said quietly. "Then why are we doing this?"

"Because somebody has to. The police want to write Tammy's death off as an accidental suicide. I don't believe that, and neither do you."

"What's in this for you?"

"I told you. I think there's a crazy person out there who's directly or indirectly hurting people. And we're getting close to finding out who that person is. If Amelia is behind this in some way, then you're the last of the finalists. She certainly isn't going to give herself a dose of acid."

"And it's our job to solve this mystery?"

"*I* have to. I'd like your help. What was Amelia's maiden name?"

"Travis."

"What's the name of the business she and Kincade are in?"

"GME . . . Global Model Enterprises."

She turned the tape in her hands over and over. "What now?"

John stared out the windshield. "How'd you like to go to Napa?"

4

Amelia rode the elevator to the ninth floor of the California Building, unaware that she was grinding her teeth. The pain along her jaw and neck had been with her for days. It was Friday, eight days since Fletcher had left for Michigan. She hadn't heard one word from him.

The doors opened. She stepped out, turned right, and, in long, even strides, made her way down the wide corridor. The office she and Fletcher had leased for Global

Model Enterprises, a corner suite with a spectacular view of the city and bay, was at the very end. As she neared suite 917 her apprehension intensified.

Through the open door, she saw men in coveralls working and a telephone repairman installing phones. She exhaled the pent-up air. *Thank God.* Everything was going to be all right. Fletcher had not lied to her after all. Plans to equip and occupy the office were underway just as he had said.

She stepped over an extension cord and cables and entered the smaller reception office. Several file cabinets and a desk were already in place. The man working on the phone glanced up when she passed him to enter the main suite. A tiny woman in a gray linen suit, clipboard in hand, was instructing two men where to move a massive mahogany desk.

The woman turned to Amelia. "Hello, may I help you?"

"I'm Amelia Corde."

"Yes? What can I do for you?"

"Who are you?"

"Janet Swenson."

The name meant nothing to her. "Janet, have you seen Mr. Kincade?" Amelia asked.

"Kincade? No," the woman said shaking her head. "I don't believe I know the man." She turned back to the men, "Too close. It's too close to the wall."

"Fletcher Kincade. He leased this office for Global Model."

The woman turned slowly, her long forehead furrowing. "Oh, I'm afraid you've made a mistake. This space has been leased to Satellite Investors."

"That's not true." Amelia felt a stabbing pain behind her eyes. "This is Global's office—my office."

"Check for yourself, hon. The papers were signed a week ago today."

"But that's when . . ." The words died away. That's when Fletch was supposed to sign the papers, she

296

thought, her stomach quaking.

Amelia felt the rush of blood to her head, making her dizzy and nauseated. Don't panic, she told herself. A misunderstanding, no doubt. Fletcher had rented another office somewhere else. Perhaps in the same building. There was something he didn't like about this particular suite. That's right, she remembered him complaining that something had to be fixed or changed. Instead, he had just decided to take another office. Of course, that was all.

What was the name of the real estate outfit that he had worked with? Channing . . . Chamber . . . Chamber Properties—yes, that was it. The agent was Rose Arnold. She would just give the agent a call. Clear everything right up.

She whirled and rushed from the office. In the outer room she snatched up the phone. She'd call Miss Rose Arnold right now and straighten things out. Fletcher had to have leased an office; otherwise he had lied, and if he lied about that then he could have lied about . . .

There was no dial tone. She banged on the disconnect button with the side of her hand.

"Ma'am," the repairman said, "the phone isn't hooked up yet."

She pushed the receiver into his hands and stormed from the office, stumbling over the cables.

She had no recollection of going to the elevators, but she found herself inside, pounding on the G button. The doors closed and she felt her stomach swoop when the elevator began to descend. Her stomach continued to swoop and heave after she rushed out on the ground floor and made her way to a bank of telephones in the lobby.

In the phone book, she found the number for Chamber Properties and dialed. Rose Arnold answered. Amelia, in an effort to control herself, asked her questions in a monotone.

"I remember you and Mr. Kincade," the agent said.

"No, he did not lease from us. I called Mr. Kincade several days after that and he informed me that something had come up and he was no longer interested in an office. Has that changed? Are you looking again?"

Amelia hung up.

She drove to his apartment and let herself in. Everything was as she had left it the day before. She sat on the edge of the bed and flipped through the phone directory.

She called RAM Electronics and asked to speak to Elia Tapperman. There was no such executive employed with the firm.

She called the Business Licensing Office and was told there had been no new business license issued to a Global Model Enterprises.

There was only one call left to make and she couldn't bring herself to do it yet. She rose from the bed. Meticulously, she went through every drawer, cupboard, and shelf in his small apartment. She realized now what she hadn't before. Everything was replaceable. Clothes, inexpensive jewelry, books. Nothing personal. Nothing precious or valuable or important. Nothing with his name on it. The entire contents of the flat could be bought for a couple thousand dollars in one afternoon at any department store.

She called the bank and was told that the joint account had been closed out.

"All of it?"

"Closed, Mrs. Corde. Every cent taken out."

"When was that?" Amelia said, her voice cracking.

"Thursday the fourteenth."

The day he was supposed to leave for Michigan.

Her life was over.

5

Regina had flatly refused John's suggestion to go to

298

Napa. She had Kristy to consider, not to mention airing a live show the following day. Besides, she saw no reason to go.

She had dropped John at the apartment house before going back to KSCO to finish out the day. But unable to concentrate, she had turned everything over to the production secretary, left the station, and walked aimlessly for hours.

At 3:30 that afternoon she collected her mail and climbed the stairs to her apartment. She was tired. The morning's tension and excitement had carried her through the afternoon, but now, coming down at last, she felt drained.

She sorted through her mail and opened first the plain white envelope with no return address. She expected it to be from Garrick. He knew her phone number, so it stood to reason he also knew her address. She hadn't spoken to him since that fateful day at the station when she had promised to call him. Of course she hadn't.

The envelope contained a newspaper clipping and nothing more. The headline on the article read:

Novato Woman Murdered

Carmenita Flores, 27, was found dead this morning in her duplex in Novato, California. The body was discovered by her roommate when she returned from a weekend trip to San Francisco. Novato Police Sgt. Larry Hawkins said the woman's throat had been slashed from ear to ear. No weapon was found.

There is evidence the victim had been bound and gagged and sexually assaulted before she was killed. Neighbors on the quiet residential street neither saw nor heard anything suspicious prior to the discovery of the body. Hawkins declined to comment on the similarity of this slaying and the attempted murder of a woman a week ago in Mill Valley. There are no suspects.

What the hell was this all about? she wondered? Who was Carmenita Flores? And who had sent this? She suspected it was from the same person who'd called her at home and again at work with those curious clues and tips. At the bottom of the clipping, an address had been penciled in.

She put the clipping in the Miss Classic file folder. Taking a glass of wine, Regina began to unzip her skirt as she headed for her bedroom. The answering machine on the nightstand was beeping. Regina pressed the button.

"Regina, it's Donna. Call me, it's important."

Regina removed her clothes and wrapped herself in a turquoise kimono, then called the hospital. A nurse informed her that Mrs. Lake was recovering from surgery.

Surgery? The skin graft, of course, Regina thought. Donna would be in no mood to talk. She made a mental note to call again in the morning.

Regina took her wine and reclined in the low armchair, her bare feet on the ottoman. She closed her eyes. Behind her lids John's face materialized. Something tugged inside her. She opened her eyes and stared out the window.

This man was getting to her. This handsome, personable, clever man was getting to her in a very serious way.

She closed her eyes again, reliving the two times he had kissed her. She felt a burning flush radiating through her body at the memory. Was he that good, that sensual? Or was it only that she was starved for sex and the touch of a desirable man?

The door suddenly burst open. Startled, Regina nearly spilled the wine. Kristy and Sonya rushed in.

"Mom, guess what?" Kristy said, her eyes bright, her cheeks rosy. "We made it! Sonya and I both made it!"

"Made what?" Regina managed to squeak out.

"The second cuts, that's what. Miss Golden Gate. We're in, Mom. In like skin."

300

"Both of you?" Regina asked, trying to show an enthusiasm she did not feel; could never feel. "That's wonderful."

"There are ten of us now. We do a fashion layout on and around the bridge next weekend to determine the final contestants," Sonya said.

"Mom, Sonya and her folks are going to Lake Tahoe for the weekend, they want me to go. Can I?"

"What about your job?"

"I'm not scheduled till Monday."

"Please, Regina," Sonya pleaded.

"When will you leave?"

"As soon as Kristy gets her stuff . . . if it's okay, that is."

"All right, yes. Go." Regina realized she would feel better if Kristy was out of town.

The two girls clasped hands and spun around.

"God, can you believe it? We're in the top ten. There's no stopping us."

"Congratulations," a male voice said.

Regina twisted around in the chair to see John leaning against the door frame.

"Hey, John, you heard?" Kristy said. "Isn't it rad?"

"If inherited looks count for anything, you'll make it to the finals." He glanced at Regina.

"We're just thrilled we got this far." Kristy turned to Sonya. "If we don't go any farther, we'll be satisfied."

The two girls looked at each other, paused, then shrieked, "Yeah, *right!*" Then they laughed, threw arms around each other, and hurried off to Kristy's room.

John shook his head and chuckled as he sauntered into the room. "Great kids."

Regina pulled her kimono tightly together, self-conscious with him standing over her. She uncrossed her ankles only to cross them again.

He laid a hand on the back of her chair. His finger traced the pattern of a brocade flower. In a quiet voice he said, "I'm going to Napa tonight. Come with me."

"John," she started with a tone of exasperation. "Kristy—"

"—Is spending the weekend with Sonya and her parents," he cut in. "She's in good hands and you know it."

"I have a TV program to put on tomorrow."

"We'll get back in plenty of time."

"Yes, but—"

"I'm going with or without you. If you go with me then I won't have to worry about you . . . *alone* here."

"That's dirty pool," she said tightly, feeling a sudden coldness at the back of her neck.

"That's how desperate I am." He took a wisp of her hair between two fingers and rubbed it softly.

"What good will it do to go to Napa. If she has an alibi—?"

"That's just it, on the afternoon that Tammy died she doesn't have an alibi. I called her mother in Napa. She saw her daughter for only a few minutes on Saturday morning. Amelia, it seems, had to cut the visit short to meet a business associate."

Regina sat up. "You can't possibly believe that she drove into the city, went into a health club, and killed Tammy?"

"No. But I do believe she rendezvoused with the killer that afternoon. Why else would she lie? I checked on this guy Kincade. There's no such person. There's no Global Model Enterprises."

Biting down on her lower lip, she swung her legs to the floor, stood, crossed to the kitchen counter, opened the file folder, and pulled out the pink message paper. "Someone with an alibi is lying," she read aloud. Then she picked up the newspaper article and took it to John.

She watched his face as he read. He looked up to stare solemnly into her eyes.

"I'll meet you downstairs in half an hour," she said.

They took Highway 101 to Novato and reached the address on the clipping at 5:45 pm. 433 Arbor was a brick duplex surrounded by concrete and colored gravel. On a narrow strip of grass that lined the driveway, a pretty young woman in a bikini lay on a beach towel, reading.

"This is the unexciting part of investigating," John said, eyeing the woman. "The interview."

Regina's smile seemed weak, unamused. They left the car and walked up the driveway to the woman, who had put down her book to watch their approach.

"Hi," John said.

"Hi."

"My name is John Davie and this is Regina Van Raven. Do you live here?"

She nodded, her hand shading her eyes. "Beverly."

"Beverly, we're private investigators from San Francisco. Was Carmenita Flores your roommate?"

"That's right."

"Mind if we ask a few questions?"

"I guess not." she gestured for him to step left.

He shifted until his shadow fell across her face. "We read about Ms. Flores's murder in the newspaper and we wondered if there might be a connection between her death and several other crimes committed recently in the city. Did your roommate receive any warnings? Was anyone harassing her? Did she say anything to you that would indicate she felt she was in danger?"

"Not really. Carm was quiet. Kept her thoughts to herself. I met her after her little girl died, and she was bitter—y'know, sort of hard."

"What happened to her daughter?"

"Defective heart. She was only two when she died. That was eight months ago."

"Did Carmenita date or have a steady guy?"

303

The woman shook her head. "No, not that I knew of. She was very pretty, but just didn't seem interested." She thought for a moment. "I told the police there was one peculiar thing. A few days before she was killed, I'd picked up the extension, not knowing she was using the phone. Anyway, this guy says 'now that you're off the hook, don't think you can cross me.'"

"Off the hook?"

"I think she'd been in trouble at some point in her life."

"You're sure it was a man?"

"Well, I thought so at the time. The voice was very deep, raspy sounding."

Twenty-four

1

John and Regina entered the lobby of the Meadowvale Inn at 6:30 P.M. and made their way to the registration desk. A plaque on the counter read Sorry, No Vacancy.

"Is that for real?" Pointing at the sign, John asked the young woman behind the counter whose name tag read Rachel. She was probably the one he had spoken to on the phone when he called impersonating Judge Corde.

"Yes, sir. Unless you have a reservation, we're booked. The Napa Valley Chateau may have accommodations."

"We had our heart set on staying here. The Cordes rave about this place."

"Judge Corde?"

"That's right. They said they were coming sometime in June, but for the life of me I can't remember which weekend."

"You've missed them, I'm afraid. He and Mrs. Corde were here last week."

"It's just as well. You see, we've just come from that little chapel down the road and we don't really relish company." John took Regina's hand. "But if there's no room available . . ."

Rachel's large brown eyes looked remorseful. The phone at her elbow buzzed. She excused herself and answered. A moment later she was smiling at them as she slid a guest registration form across to John. She hung up. "Your luck is changing. That was a last-minute cancellation."

Ten minutes later they were in room 142. Regina put her handbag on the dresser and turned to survey the charming room with its French country decor, its terrace, fireplace, and queen-size bed.

She noticed John's gaze had swept the room to end up where hers had — on the only bed.

"Hungry yet?" he asked, breaking the silence.

"Before we eat we should see Amelia's parents." On the drive to Napa they had devised what they hoped was a plausible excuse to talk to the Travises. Regina lifted the phone directory, sat on the edge of the bed, and opened it to the Ts.

While she scanned the directory, John put on a dark red necktie. Over his ice blue shirt and charcoal gray slacks, he slipped on a gray plaid sport coat.

She tapped the book. "They're in here. 599 Winecastle Court number 5. Amelia mentioned a retirement complex."

"Ready?" he asked.

"Could you give me a minute?"

"Take as long as you like. I'll meet you in the lobby."

She waited until he left, then she rose and crossed the room to the French doors. Leaning against the frame, looking out over the verdant, landscaped golf course, she watched the sun's rosy glow shimmer through the tall trees, like a black on red filigree design.

They hadn't discussed the room arrangements beforehand. The decision, as it turned out, had been made for them. She couldn't blame John. Besides, she told herself, sharing a room didn't mean they had to sleep together or anything like that. *Oh Lord, Pollyanna, who are you trying to kid?*

Minutes later she entered the lobby to find John standing at the grand piano, one hand in his pants pocket and the other hand softly tinkering with the keys.

The parking valet brought the station wagon around. Regina got behind the wheel and pulled away.

They headed west into the setting sun. Ten minutes later they reached Winecastle Court. The retirement complex was nothing more than a trailer park, and a rather austere one. The Travises single wide mobile home sat five in from the dusty highway.

A skeletal woman dressed in hot pink with hair dyed a harsh, unnatural black, answered the door. Her dark eyes glared out of sunken sockets.

"Mrs. Travis?" Regina asked. "My name is Francie Simpson. Mr. Davidson and I are with the public relations department at KSCO TV. We're working up a biographical profile for the station on your daughter Amelia."

"My heavens, Amelia mentioned KSCO when we saw her last. Come in. Don't stay out there baking in the sun. Come in."

"Who is it, Wanda?" a voice called out from inside the trailer.

"It's some folks from the TV station Amelia's going to work for, y'know, that 'City Gallery' show."

John and Regina exchanged glances as they stepped in.

In the tiny living room, after introductions were made and they were seated, Regina asked, "Does Amelia come to Napa often to visit?"

"Not that often. Only when the lord and master deems fit to bring her," the woman replied with a sarcastic edge.

"You mean Judge Corde?"

"Yeah, his honor, his majesty, his—"

"Now, Wanda . . .," Mr. Travis warned. To Regina and John, he asked, "Do you know her husband?"

"We've met," Regina said.

"Amelia met him at the Miss Classic pageant. He was a contest judge." The woman chuckled. "It seems he's always a judge of one sort or another."

307

"He's got plenty of money. Old San Francisco money," Mr. Travis interjected, clearly impressed. "Money's kinda important to our Amelia. She likes nice things. I wasn't surprised when she drove up last Saturday morning in that old Rolls."

"Rolls? Like in Rolls-Royce?" John leaned forward.

"Yes sir," Mr. Travis said.

"She came alone?"

"Yeah, but she couldn't stay long. The judge had a golf date and she had an appointment to meet with someone from the TV station. Wanda, what was that man's name?"

"Well, let's see now . . ."

"Kincade?" Regina prompted.

"No, not Kincade," Wanda rolled her eyes upward, thinking. "It was something to do with water. Spring? Pond? Nooo. Lake, that's it. Rolan Lake, the producer of the show."

Regina felt a jolting shock.

"She drove back to the city to meet him?" John asked.

"Heavens, no. They met for lunch up the road here at that new resort. The Napa Valley Chateau."

"She'll get that job," Mr. Travis said. "When our Amelia sets her mind to something, it's done. She could've been a motion picture star, but the damn movie studio folded up. Television's where it's at today. A TV personality isn't anything to be ashamed of."

Regina risked a glance at John. He was watching her, an unreadable expression on his face.

Regina stood. John followed. "Our time is limited today, but may we contact you soon for an in-depth interview?"

"Of course. No one knows a person better'n her parents," Wanda Travis said. "Say, we got plenty of photos of Amelia, if you—"

"We'll be in touch," Regina said, going out the door with John.

308

Amelia paced the master bedroom, sipping straight vodka and smoking one long, slim cigarette after another. She lifted the rock glass to her lips and tilted her head back. A last drop fell on her tongue.

"Shit."

She debated going downstairs for another shot of vodka. But she knew she would just gulp it down like the last one, and if Matthew found her drunk in the afternoon, just hours before their dinner party for ten, he would sure as hell wonder about it. What could she say? *Matthew darling. I've had a shock. I've just been screwed out of all the money I stole from you. Money that took me eighteen miserable years to nickel and dime from you. Money that was rightfully mine. Money I worked for, on my back, in a thousand one-minute performances.*

God, she needed that drink. Desperately her mind whirled, played, rewound, like a malfunctioning cassette, revealing snatches of information — Fletcher . . . Global Model Enterprises . . . Joint Business Account. Gone. All gone. How could she have been so trusting? So stupid? But was it really her fault? Could she have prevented it somehow? Fletcher had shown her his check, a cashier's check, for the matching money. Her eighty thousand and his eighty thousand — one hundred and sixty thousand dollars comingled to make up the initial operating capital for Global Model Enterprises. She had insisted on the joint account rather than an escrow account as he had suggested. But he had won out in the matter of the single signature disbursement, making it possible for either party to draw funds from the account; *making it possible for either to close out the account.* But only one party had.

It was a nightmare. She would wake up and discover none of this had really happened. It had to be a nightmare or some ridiculous mistake. Because if it was true then what would become of her? Where would she be? She was forty. She didn't have another nineteen years to amass her freedom funds. She would either have to leave Matthew and chance it on her own—without all the wonderful things she loved—or she would have to stay with him, allowing him to own her like one of his collectibles; to use her like a common whore. Or she would have to—no, don't think about it now.

She had to have another drink. To hell with Matthew.

She hurried down the stairs, her white silk wrapper flying out behind her, and rushed into the dining room. The sight of the table, already set with their best bone china, crystal, sterling flatware, and pink tulip floral runner, twisted at her insides. How was she ever going to get through this night? How could she possibly entertain guests without screaming or throwing whatever came into her hands?

At a liquor cart she quickly poured vodka into her glass. She took a long gulp, refilled the glass, then hurried back upstairs. At the bedroom doorway she heard the front door open, then close soundly. Matthew's voice called out.

She froze, not breathing. Her hand gripped his maroon smoking jacket hanging on the back of the door.

"Amelia, where are you? If you're in the bedroom, stay there." He chuckled lightly. "I'm coming up."

She growled deep in her throat, her fingers crushing the soft velvet of the jacket. She wanted to weep, to wail, to kill.

3

They drove to the Napa Valley Chateau.

A valet took the car and they went inside, crossed the lobby, entered a cocktail lounge, and sat at a table just inside the room. The Napa Valley Chateau was small compared to the Meadowvale Inn. John seemed pleased about that. He ordered two drinks, paid for them, then stood.

"I'll see what I can find out," he said, and left the lounge.

Regina watched him cross to the registration desk. A young man in his early twenties looked up with an eager smile. John spoke. The desk clerk responded with a shake of his head. John reached into his pocket and brought out his wallet. The clerk stared at it, shook his head again, only this time there was little conviction in the gesture. John extracted several bills, laid them flat on the counter, and, with his hand over the money, pushed them toward the clerk. Regina sipped her wine nervously. Then, just like in all the detective movies she'd seen, the money changed hands. The clerk was talking, his mouth moving rapidly, his eyes darting about furtively.

"I'll be damned," Regina said under her breath.

A few minutes later John joined her. Without sitting down, he lifted his Tanqueray and tonic and neatly tossed it back. "Ready?"

Regina quickly finished her white wine and stood.

In the car on the drive back to the inn, John said, "It was no lunch. They checked in around noon under the name of Williams. No luggage. Cash transaction. Checked out at five-thirty. Left in separate cars."

"How do we know it was Amelia and Nolan?"

"I had only to mention the Rolls and he was off and running. He described both of them. And if that's not enough, the man had a gold money clip with the initials N.A.L."

Nolan Alan Lake. Regina had been with Donna the day she'd bought the money clip for Nolan.

So Nolan and Amelia are having an affair, Regina thought dismally. While Donna lies suffering in the hospital, her husband is cheating with the woman who is

311

making moves to take her job. Her job *and* her husband. Christ.

"I'm sorry," John said, stroking her arm. "I know how much you care about Donna."

She nodded. She didn't want to think or talk about it now. "And I'm sorry that the reason we came here turned out to be a bust. Amelia didn't meet Kincade. She didn't sneak into the city. We're right back where we started. Worse, she now has a solid alibi."

They drove the rest of the way to the inn with less than ten words passing between them.

4

From her car Corinne watched the delivery boy from Fong's press a buzzer in the vestibule of John's apartment house. A moment later he disappeared inside. She left the car and rapidly made her way into the building. In the vestibule, with her long dark coat tight around her, the hood that covered her head pulled across the side of her face, she glanced through the two long panes into the wide hallway. It was empty.

The air in the small space was permeated with the smell of Chinese food. The pungent odor made her already queasy stomach knot up. When she saw the boy coming back toward the door, she shifted and stood facing the row of mailboxes.

He came through the door quickly. Corinne caught it before it could close, then moved through casually. The boy was out of the building without a second glance at her.

At the door of 1B she tapped lightly, waited, then tapped again.

John was out, she reasoned. It was early, barely nine o'clock. She wondered if she should wait or come back later. The sound of footsteps coming down the stairs prompted her to make a decision. She took hold of the knob and twisted. It turned and the door opened. She slipped inside.

5

In the lobby, John stopped to read the menu at the door of the Oak Room. "I'm starving. What do you say we drown our disappointment in a bottle or two of Pinot Noir along with a rack of lamb or chateaubriand?"

"I'd like to change clothes first." She ran her hands over her denim jumpsuit.

"You look fine."

"*You* look fine, I'm underdressed for chateaubriand. Why don't I meet you in the bar in thirty minutes?"

"You don't need any help with zippers or hooks?" he asked with a straight face.

She felt a fluttering in her stomach. "I learned to dress myself a long time ago," she said with a thin smile.

"Pity."

Regina went to the room, took a quick shower, freshened her makeup, ran a brush through her hair and then put on the only other thing she had brought, a Calvin Klein bare-back halter dress in a soft white linen. As she reached up behind to tie the dress at her neck, her gaze settled on the bed.

What was she doing in a hotel room with a man she'd only known a couple of weeks? Oh, she knew why she had come here, she'd come to help John investigate — which they had done with disappointing results. Amelia had an alibi, so their work here was done.

She stepped into a pair of medium-heeled sandals, grabbed the black-and-white plaid shawl, tossed it over one shoulder, and went out the door.

She found John standing at the bar in the Sword Room Lounge. He smiled, watching her as she crossed

313

the room to him.

"You look beautiful."

"Thank you."

"What would you like?"

"Martini," she told the waiting bartender.

She looked around the dim interior of the lounge at the rich, dark wood paneling, the upholstered club chairs, the endless hanging plants and candles on small round tables reflecting a multitude of glowing red in gold-veined mirrors. It was meant to convey a cozy, romantic atmosphere.

They finished their drinks and ordered another. The maitre d' stepped up to them, announced that their table was ready, lifted Regina's martini and John's Tanqueray, and led them to a corner table in the dining room.

After sitting down, Regina said. "What now?"

"Now we eat." His attention was diverted to the menu in front of him.

They decided on the rack of lamb. The waiter came, took their order, and left.

"You had more than one shock today, didn't you?"

Regina stared blankly at him, not understanding.

"Amelia. 'City Gallery.'

"Oh. That."

"Would it really bother you?"

"Yes. Not for me, but for Donna. No one can take Donna's place."

"You can."

She shook her head. "No, not even me."

"But especially not Amelia."

"Right." She felt anger flash through her. "How could Nolan do that to his own wife?"

"What's in it for him?"

"Control. He doesn't know how much power I have, or whether I have any at all. But he doesn't want to take any chances. If he can get someone to follow orders like Donna did, then he has a job. If not . . ."

314

"I get the picture."

The salads were put in front of them, red wine poured.

"Nolan thinks it's so easy. He blusters around, giving orders that no one pays attention to and the show goes on. It goes smoothly *in spite* of him. Even Donna knows that, but she'd never admit it. And now he wants to cut her out—just like that."

"She's really a good friend of yours, isn't she?"

"The best. We go back a long way."

"Is Nolan giving you a hard time."

"He'd like to. But no, Max is on my side on this one."

"Will the psychic return for tomorrow's show?"

She shook her head. "Tomorrow we have a dream analyst."

"Do you believe in that stuff?"

She looked him straight in the eyes and said emphatically, "Yes."

"I knew you'd be wishy-washy about it."

She laughed.

He stared at her, one corner of his mouth turned up. "God, I love the way you laugh."

She laughed again. This time she heard the nervousness in it.

Their entreé was served. They fell silent, eating and sipping wine.

Regina asked herself why she was here in this beautiful resort inn, in this cozy restaurant with a man who had stood her up the night before. It dawned on her that living in the same building, having to pass his door to come and go, could be very awkward if things didn't work out between them. She would have no choice but to move.

She cleared her throat. "John, I've been thinking. There's really no reason for us to stay the night now. In fact, we could probably do more good in the city."

John looked up at her "The room is paid for," he said

quietly. "But if you want to go, we'll go."

She felt a profound sense of disappointment that baffled her. Had she hoped he would try to convince her to stay? Yes, that was it and she couldn't deny it. Why the game playing, she asked herself? You want to stay. You want to make love with this man. He's here with you, now, not with the other one. There's an incredibly romantic room down the hall, waiting, with open arms . . . like a lover.

"We'll go," he said with finality.

"I insist on paying for half—," she began before he cut in.

"It was my idea to come here. It's on me."

She nodded, looking away uneasily.

He poured wine into her empty glass. "Let's enjoy this fine food and drink, shall we?"

"No more wine for me. I'm driving."

"Drink up, I'll drive." She looked up at him, eyebrow raised.

"What?" he asked.

"I'm trying to picture you behind the wheel of a car. It's difficult."

"I'm a good driver. You'll be safe."

To prove that she trusted him, she drank her wine down quickly and held out her glass for more. John obliged by refilling it.

"Tell me about you," she asked. She sipped the wine more slowly.

"There's not much to tell."

"You were married and had a child." It was a statement, not a question. "I saw the picture on your wall in your apartment The boy looks like you.

John told her about meeting Darlene in England, marrying her, and moving to America. He then talked of their son Andrew. As he spoke Regina focused on his mouth. He had a way of speaking slowly, and softly, his lips moving only slightly, revealing white, slightly crooked

316

lower teeth. Upon recounting a pleasant slice of his life, one corner of his mouth lifted in a half smile. Completely captivated by his voice and the easy way in which he related his years as a husband and father, she was stunned when he finished with: "A week before I was to join them in London, they both drowned in a ferry accident."

Regina stared at him, saying nothing. She was awe-struck by his serious countenance, unusual for this man who made light of most everything. She felt a strong tugging deep inside. She sensed that there was something more than grief behind those sad eyes. Guilt. There's guilt there. He feels it, too. A sense of guilt enmeshed with the sorrow. He thinks that if he had done things differently, his wife and son would be alive today.

Guilt.

Regina knew the feeling well. Of course, there was nothing she could have done that would have changed the course of Leo's dementia. Blaming herself for that would be absurd. Her guilt stemmed from the relief of his death—but mostly from her betrayal.

They had finished eating. Neither wanted anything more. The waiter brought the check and John paid with cash.

"Ready?" he asked.

"Yes."

Regina led the way into the lobby. She looked at the clock above the registration desk. 10:20. If they checked out now they would be back in San Francisco before midnight.

"If you want, I can get our things from the room and meet you here," John said.

"That's all right. I'll go with you. I want to change out of this dress."

Their walk to the room was devoid of conversation. John opened the door to room 142 and stood aside for Regina to enter.

After taking only a few steps inside, she paused, drawing in a deep breath. The room was dim, yet it glowed richly from the blazing wood in the fireplace. While they had been dining, the beds had been turned down, and on one pillow lay a long-stemmed red rose. Fresh rose petals were scattered over the satin dusty-rose comforter. On the nightstand to the right of the bed, next to the radio that was playing love songs, was a bottle of champagne chilling in a silvery ice bucket.

"The newlywed treatment," John said quietly behind her.

She swallowed, nodding.

"What a shame to waste it."

"We could open the champagne, I suppose."

"It's the *least* we could do."

As John uncorked the bottle, Regina moved to the fireplace and stood gazing at the burning logs. She heard the cork pop. John came up behind her and reached around to hand her a glass of champagne. She took the glass. He was close enough for her to feel his warm breath in her hair and the crisp fabric of his shirt against her bare back. She flushed and shivered simultaneously. Hot and cold. Cold and hot.

She continued to stare at the fire. She smelled the scent of sweet flowers nearby, and realized why when she felt the velvety petals of the red rose he was holding caress her bare shoulders, then the side of her face. She closed her eyes. She was unaware of how tense she was until he whispered in her ear, "Relax . . . relax."

Exhaling, forcing her muscles to unwind, she leaned back against him. From the two martinis and the red wine at dinner, she was tingling, floating. She felt his lips press lightly to her neck, over a throbbing pulse below her ear. His fingers stroked her throat, lowering to trace the skin at the edge of her halter dress, along the side of her breast. His wrist lightly brushed across one breast and, beneath the thin material of the bodice, her nipple

318

become erect and highly sensitive.

The glass was carefully taken from her. His other arm came around her at the waist, his splayed hand pressed against her abdomen, fingertips lightly kneading. She felt his erection against her lower back and she wanted to reach back and touch him, but her arms seemed paralyzed, useless appendages at her side. His hands moved in lazy circles at the most sensual areas of her body. Wild currents of pleasure crackled through her. Electrical charges, like ragged streaks of lightning, sparked a savage intensity of feelings.

He gently tugged on the cord tied at the back of her neck. The cord loosened and the bodice slid down to her waist, exposing her breasts. John cupped them.

She moaned, turning in his arms, hungry for his lips on hers. Their lips met, moist and warm and with an urgency that made her frantic with desire. She had no control, nothing existed except what was going on in a core of her that had become universal . . . all-powerful . . . all-consuming.

Somewhere in the back of her mind she experienced a pang of shame for her desperate abandonment. What must he think of her? Then the shame was gone.

As he undressed her, she became aware of how little she had on. The dress, shoes, and sheer panties. Had she subconsciously dressed for lovemaking? Then he was naked, lifting her and carrying her to the bed, where he lowered her slowly. Atop the cool satin spread of rose petals, he entered her, thrusting all the way into her until she gasped from a mixture of pleasure and pain, pain that was so brief she wondered if she had imagined it. And then, filling her up, not moving, he kissed her with a fevered passion, saying her name.

She began to rotate her hips, reflexively, as waves of ecstasy spread outward from that pulsating core. She had forgotten how good it could be. Had it ever been this good? Yes. No. *No. never!* It was building, beyond slow-ing down, beyond stopping. And then she cried out with an abrupt, gripping orgasm. She rode the waves for what seemed an eternity as John glided into her, seeking his own release. Minutes later, when he shuddered in climax, Regina, again cresting the wave, cried out.

John kissed her earlobe, her temple, her swollen lips. Without speaking they lay in each others arms, sweaty, spent.

6

In John's living room, with the cool blue rays of a full moon illuminating the interior, Corinne sat stiffly in the straight-back pine chair. She had unbuttoned her coat, letting it fall open, but the hood remained up, coming far forward on her head. From where she sat she could read the digital clock on the VCR. 1:16. Four hours ago she had entered his apartment and sat down to wait.

Coming here had been a hard decision. John had called her twice since Donna's attack, and both times she had refused to speak or listen. But she couldn't hide from him forever. It was only a matter of time before he would seek her out. Try to come to her. She wanted him nowhere near her place. He would be shocked, disgusted by the filth and squalor. He wouldn't understand about her father. So she had come to him.

These past few weeks, seeing him through his window, watching him on the street, had brought him despairingly close to her again. After all these years her love for him had not dissipated. It had, she realized, only been smoldering, like sparks on a bed of wood shavings, waiting for a breeze to rekindle its fiery life.

She allowed herself to think of him. It was impossible not to anymore. Their time together before her attack had been so brief, a few precious months, yet Corinne could recall, with crystal clarity, everything about him.

The way he looked, smelled, spoke, and laughed. The way his hands felt on her skin, his lips against hers in a kiss. And now to see him again, practically unchanged, perhaps even more handsome and alluring . . .

She felt sick with love and desire for him.

She rose slowly, her cramped muscles screaming in agony, her gaze sweeping the room. She was desperate for a cigarette, a butt would do, but it was clear by the absence of ashtrays that John had given up smoking.

Corinne walked around the room, her hands buried deep in the pockets of her coat. She had to use the bathroom.

Minutes later, with the moonlight reflecting off the white tiles, she stood at the sink and took in everything. John's toiletries stood on the back of the commode, and more stood on a shelf above. She touched nothing, though God help her, her fingers ached to hold something of his. On the back of the door hung a blue wraparound towel. Reaching out, her fingers brushed against it and she felt a slight dampness before she jerked her hand away, as if burned, and thrust it back into the pocket of her coat.

She pivoted, stepped to the doorway of the bedroom, and stared into his room. John's bed. It was so big. Big compared to hers, that is. She went to the bed, taking hesitant steps, then leaned over and ran a hand across the ribbed clay tone comforter. Her hand traveled upward until she tentatively touched his pillow. She lifted it, squeezed the downy fullness to her chest. Then she rested her cheek to it and closed her eyes. A picture of John materialized in her head. John then and now. And she felt a painful ache deep inside her.

The pillow went back on the bed and Corinne gingerly followed. She lay stiff, her legs drawn tightly to her as she tucked the pillow close. It smelled of him. A smell she hadn't forgotten. She would just lie here a minute to ease her cramped muscles.

7

Sometime in the night John and Regina awoke to make love again. No words were spoken.

8

She sensed the light. Coming awake abruptly, she sat up, confused. It took her a moment to realize that she had fallen asleep on John's bed. The faint light of dawn had awakened her. The clock read 4:50.

She had to leave.

Back in the living room, as she buttoned up her coat, with the early light bringing the room into focus, she spotted the note on the large mahogany coffee table.

> Aunt Anna,
> Gone to Napa. Back on Sat.
> Feed Ollie, please,
> > Thanks,
> > > J

On the note was a small canister of turtle food.

Out of town? She had worked up the nerve to come to him and he had been out of town.

Out of town alone?

Rushing to the window, she looked up and down the street. The station wagon was nowhere in sight.

No. Please, no.

She came back to the note and read it again.

Napa. The romantic wine country. A night under the stars in the valley of the moon.

Reaching into the bowl, she took hold of the turtle and lifted him out. His head and feet disappeared into the greenish-black shell. She placed him on the palm of her hand, staring intently at the creature.

John had gone away with her. *Her* . . . Regina.

She closed her hand around the turtle, the tendons along her wrist stood out, stark against the purple veins. Her hand trembled. *John and Regina were together this night. In one another's arms.*

Corinne put her hand back into the bowl and gently released Ollie.

Twenty-five

1

He stared at her face, thinking she was as radiant asleep as she was awake. Her lips were parted slightly. A wisp of dark hair fell across her cheek to lie curled at the corner of her mouth. John gently lifted it away. She stirred, but didn't wake.

Carefully, he slipped out of bed, gathered his clothes. While he dressed, he watched her sleep. She was on her side, one hand on the pillow where he had been.

It was 7:05, too early to wake her. Too early for him, actually, but he had awakened abruptly, his mind troubled by something unfinished. *Posers*. The clues that the anonymous informant had given Regina hadn't gotten them any nearer to a solution.

The newspaper clipping had enabled them to discover that prior to her death Carmenita Flores had spoken to a person with a deep, raspy voice. True, there was a good chance that that person was the same one who had made warning calls to the finalists, but it brought them no closer to disclosing the identity of the killer.

Amelia's original alibi had been shattered, only to be replaced with a more solid one.

Was someone sending them on a wild goose chase?

All that aside, John had a poser of his own: If Amelia's only crime was to sleep with another woman's husband, was it then merely a coincidence that butcher tape found at Tammy's house and also in the Corde's freezer came from the same meat company, a company that did not sell to the general public?

He found it hard to believe that neither he nor Regina had thought of that the night before, but then for *him*, other things — such as the impression of her nipples beneath the thin material of her dress, her rich laugh, the depth of her thickly lashed hazel eyes — had clouded his reasoning.

In the bathroom he splashed water on his face and ran a comb haphazardly through his hair.

Before going out the door, he looked once more at the woman sleeping beneath the satin comforter. She had turned over on her back, an arm draped across her forehead, one lovely, full breast partially exposed above the sheet. He had known her breasts would be round, but what he hadn't known, what he couldn't know, was how fantastic being with her — making love to her — would be. She had seemed wanton in her desire, yet somehow inhibited, as though trying to hold back — wanting, though ashamed of her need. Perhaps the fact that her husband had been dead so short a time had something to do with it. Afterward, as they lay in each other's arms, he had waited for her to speak first. When she remained silent, he followed suit, afraid to break the spell. Thinking about her now he felt a fluttering in his gut. He was tempted to hold off on the investigation and return to bed.

Instead, he strode to the door and went out quickly and quietly.

2

Regina heard the latch click. She opened her eyes to a room filled with soft morning light. A room not her own, smelling of roses, cedarwood smoke, and sex. She lifted herself up on her elbows and looked around. She was alone.

She propped her back against the headboard, drew her knees up, circling them with her arms, and hugged herself. The champagne cork lay on the spread beside her. She lifted it and turned it around in her fingers, breathed in the scent of it, and allowed thoughts of John to come into her mind, filling it with the images of the two of them together. She sucked in a deep breath, exhaled it slowly. Then she began again, at the beginning, with John bringing her that glass of champagne. . . .

She smiled, hugging her knees tighter.

He was a gentle, yet bold lover, one who derived great gratification in pleasing his partner. Physically she had soared to great heights, yet she had held back emotionally. On an emotional plane she was still a cripple, afraid to run, afraid of falling. The sheltered one. The one who had known only one man . . . until— *not now*, she thought brusquely, *don't spoil it with thoughts of Garrick* . . .

But thinking of John now felt wrong. She reached over and, without knowing why she did it, dropped the champagne cork into her purse as she lifted the phone. After pressing 9 for an outside line, Regina dialed her home number. Kristy was with Sonya, but it wasn't Kristy she was calling. The answering machine clicked on. Regina dialed the code to retrieve any messages that might be on the machine. Donna's voice came over the line. "Reg, call me as soon as you hear this message, no matter what time. Call."

She glanced at the watch that was still on her wrist. 7:15. Surely, Donna didn't mean this early? But she'd sensed an urgency in the tone. So, getting an outside line again, she dialed the hospital and asked for Donna's extension.

Donna came directly on the line. "Reggie," she said, her voice anxious. "Where have you been?"

326

A red flag went up. "What's wrong? Is it Kristy?"

"No. No, it's you. I mean, it's you I was worried about."

"Me? Why?"

"Reg, that man you brought to the hospital, John Davie. I remembered where I'd seen him before. It was a long time ago, but I know it's him. He was with Corinne."

"What do you mean 'with Corinne'?"

"They were a couple. He didn't tell you that, did he?"

Regina was confused. John and Corinne? Donna was mistaken.

"I saw them together on the day of the crowning, I heard them arguing in the wings. She called him Jack. I heard a slap. I can't say who slapped who. Then he stormed off."

"He said he was a reporter."

"I doubt that. He was a just a kid, no more than eighteen, nineteen. Our age."

"But why would . . ." Regina didn't bother to finish. What was going on? Why would he lie to her?

"Reg, that night, after Corinne was attacked, I told the police about the fight. He became the number one suspect, and they took him in for questioning, but for some reason they never arrested him."

"Lord."

"I don't mean to scare you, but I thought you should know." The phone line hummed. "Reg?"

"I'm here. I'll . . . ah—I'm glad you told me. I know what to do." Her voice sounded leaden, emotionless. "I'll try to come by this evening."

"I'd like that."

They exchanged good-byes.

Regina couldn't think straight. Too much was coming to her all at once. Where was John the night Corinne was splashed? Where was he when Tammy died? She already knew where he was when Donna was attacked—at

327

the station. Corinne . . . lover? John . . . suspect?
Donna. Tammy. Suspect. Suspect . . . lover . . . suspect
. . . Jesus!

With her heart racing, she picked up the phone, called
the desk, and asked to have her car sent around. She got
out of bed and quickly dressed in the denim jumpsuit.
Then she stuffed her clothes into the overnight bag and
ran her fingers through her hair. Looking around the
room, she saw the clothes John had been wearing last
night still lying on the floor in front of the fireplace. She
saw the rose on the mantelpiece. And she felt as though
she'd been slapped in the face.

She snatched up her things and hurried out the door.

3

John found Rachel at the registration desk. He paid
the bill, then brought up the Cordes again, saying how
sorry he was to have missed them by only one week.
"The judge promised to give me a pointer or two on the
golf course. My chipping's the pits."

"According to Judge Corde, his chipping wasn't so
good either. He had me make an appointment with the
pro at the golf course that Saturday."

"Morning or afternoon?"

"Had to be morning, because that afternoon I saw him
board the courtesy shuttle."

"Courtesy shuttle?"

Rachel pointed to a Poster of a minibus. "Twice on
Saturday the Meadowvale runs a shuttle into the city.
Just another courtesy service we offer our guests."

John read the time schedule: Departs 8:30 A.M. and 1
P.M. — Returns 6 P.M.

Was it possible that while Amelia and the Rolls-Royce
were at the Napa Valley Chateau, the judge was on a
shuttle going into San Francisco? Five hours. Plenty of

time to tour the city, drown a woman, and be back before dinner.

"You're sure he was on that shuttle?"

"Oh, yes. It leaves right out there," she pointed. "At the main entrance."

John turned just in time to see Regina pushing through the double glass doors. He saw her gesticulating to the doorman.

What the hell . . . ?

"Excuse me," he said, and rushed across the lobby to the main doors.

Regina was climbing behind the wheel of her car when he pushed out onto the portico. He called her name. He saw her glance over at him, her face a mask of perplexity; then the car shot forward and sped away.

Baffled, he hurried back to their room. Had she left a note to explain where she had gone and why? Had something happened to Kristy? To Donna? Christ, whatever it was, he thought, she could have taken a moment to inform him.

Regina's things were gone from the room. There was no note.

What the hell happened?

Had she awakened filled with remorse for their night of lovemaking? That was hardly a reason for running off without a word. What then? he wondered.

John sat slumped in one of the two wing chairs facing the fireplace. He stayed that way for a long time, thinking, trying to sort it out. When he heard a key slide into the lock, his heart skipped in his chest. She had come back! But it was only the maid wanting to clean the room.

He looked at his watch. 8:25. He had a shuttle to catch.

"Looks like the alternator," the mechanic said from under the hood of the station wagon.

Regina sighed with frustration. She had pulled into the Shell station on Highway 101 just outside San Rafael for gas. After filling up, the car had refused to start.

"Can you fix it? I've got to be in San Francisco this afternoon."

"Ball Automotive in San Rafael should have an alternator. I'll send one of the boys over for it. Should have you outta here by noon."

It was 9:00. She had three hours to kill. She needed coffee and, though she wasn't hungry, felt she should get something in her stomach. She crossed the street to a coffee shop.

She used the pay phone to call Max at the station. "Max, I'm in San Rafael. My car broke down. It's being fixed now."

"How soon?"

"Noon." She heard voices in the background. Max was talking to someone else.

"Regina, Nolan—"

"Max, I'll be there."

"Nolan wants to call in a backup."

Regina knew perfectly well who the backup would be and she was about to protest, but thought better of it. "Okay, let him. But if I'm there in time, I go on."

"That's a promise," he answered. "Say, what are you doing in San Rafael?"

"It's a long story. I'll talk to you later."

She was sitting in a small, dingy room; the sparse furnishings around her were old and cheap. In the gray light she could make out a lumpy sofa, straight-back vinyl chairs, and a scarred Formica dinette table, pieces Amelia would be loath to touch, let alone own. But they were hers, that much she knew. The view from the window was as depressing as the interior she wished to escape. Shrouded in a bone-chilling ocean fog, the blank structures of factories and dock warehouses loomed like things from a deadly holocaust; only the mournful horn of a freighter in the harbor gave life to the dismal scene.

Amelia cried silently, alone in her despair. A ringing telephone broke through the quiet, confusing, yet bringing a ray of promise and hope.

She was dreaming. Thank God, that dreary existence was nothing more than her subconscious fear come to torment her. Amelia nearly sobbed with relief. But as she pulled herself out of the dregs of the nightmare, she suddenly felt a deadness inside.

Oh God, nothing had changed since the night before when, after that endless party, she had taken two Demerols and had finally fallen asleep just before dawn.

The phone rang again. Amelia rolled on her side and groped for it. A hand closed over hers.

"I have it, dear," Matthew smiled, lifting the receiver. She lay back down.

Matthew listened, then said, "Yes, that is curious. I'll tell her. Good day." He hung up, turned to Amelia. "That was the cleaners. It seems a linen jacket you took in practically disintegrated. It's beyond repair."

"What?" Amelia sat up alarmed. "I don't understand."

"The woman on the phone said some sort of caustic substance must have splashed on it. The fibers broke down completely during the dry-cleaning process. What could it have been?"

"I have no idea," she said, sounding mildly perplexed while her heart thumped madly. "No idea at all." But she did know. She had been wearing that jacket the day she was accosted in Fletcher's parking garage. She vaguely recalled something wet splashing against her purse before it was lost to her. But the jacket had been splattered, too. *Acid.* She had been a victim after all. The *first* victim. And she couldn't tell anyone now because, fearing Matthew would be suspicious, she had kept the attack a secret. It had to have been Fletcher. He was the only one who knew she would be in the garage at that particular time. But why? Where was he now? Would he come after her again?

The phone rang again. Matthew answered.

"Yes, Mrs. Corde is in. May I ask who's calling?"

She propped herself on her elbows.

Matthew handed her the phone. "It's a Nolan Lake."

Amelia felt the blood rush to her face as she watched her husband leave the bed. Why was Nolan calling her at home on a Saturday? First the acid and now this. It was more than she could stand in one morning.

"Hello."

"Amelia, this may be a break for both of us. Regina has a show this afternoon and her car has broken down north of the city. There's a chance she won't make it here in time."

"Oh?" She looked up to see Matthew going through one of his drawers, seemingly moving garments around without purpose.

"I want you here in case she fails to turn up at airtime."

Amelia worried her lower lip. She could feel Matthew's gaze on her now. "I, ah . . ."

"Perhaps this job isn't as important to you as you led me to believe, Amelia."

332

"Yes," she said in a rush, glancing at Matthew. Their eyes met, held; she looked away. "Yes, I'll be there. What time do you want me?"

"You'd better come as soon as you can so we can go over the format. Even if she shows, we might be able to squeeze her out."

"Yes, all right." She hung up.

Matthew folded his arms over his sunken chest. "Nolan Lake. Isn't he the husband of your friend? The producer?"

She nodded.

"What could he possibly want with you?"

She cleared her throat. "Regina, who has taken over for Donna, may be indisposed. He wondered if I might host the show in her stead." She couldn't believe how calm she sounded.

"Oh? And you agreed?"

She nodded.

He slowly unbuttoned his pajama top. "I don't understand," he said quietly, beginning to pace. "How is it that you were even considered as a replacement? Have you been keeping things from me?"

"It was only a germ of an idea. Nothing concrete. I didn't think you'd be interested."

"Not interested in what my wife does?" He pulled off the top. "Would this be a steady replacement?"

She forced herself to look at him. "Perhaps."

"Perhaps." His head bobbed slowly. "I thought we had an agreement that I would support you, meet all your needs financially, and you would be a homemaker. I know the word has a less than admirable distinction nowadays, but the home you oversee is certainly not a hovel. It's been in my family for half a century."

"It's a beautiful house."

"Of course I can't order you to stay home. If you want to work there's no way I can forbid it."

"Matthew—"

333

He held up a hand. "I feel as though I've failed you in some way. Have I, Amelia?"

"No."

"Then can you explain to me why you feel the need to take a job? I had no objection to you offering your services to that PBS station as a volunteer, but this appears to be a career move. Am I correct?"

"It's not the money. You've been very generous to me," she lied. "It's—I . . ." She realized there was nothing she could say to rectify the situation. Matthew would feel threatened by any answer she could come up with. "I've committed myself for today. I must go."

"You do what you must," he said stiffly, putting on his dressing gown.

"I won't be needed for hours, Matthew, if, indeed, I'm needed at all. Come back to bed." She pulled back the bronze satin sheet.

He stared solemnly at her, not moving.

"Please," she whispered seductively, undoing the row of tiny buttons on her white chemise. "There's plenty of time. I feel in the mood to play act. How about you?"

He stood quietly, a reflective expression on his face.

"Which one, darling?" she said coaxing. "You decide."

Finally: "The naive virgin—no, cancel that." He backed up to the black-and-silver chaise and leisurely reclined, grinning. "The famished war refugee, I believe," he said softly, letting the dressing gown slide open to expose his body. "And today, utterly desperate, she will do anything for food and shelter."

6

Donna heard footsteps in the hall and wondered if they belonged to Nolan. They passed. She missed Nolan terribly. Something had come up at the station the day before and he had been unable to visit her before the surgery.

He had probably come later that night, but with the anesthesia, she would have been too groggy to remember.

Nolan. Poor, dear Nolan. To have something like this happen to him just when things were going so well was sheer bad luck. There was nothing he wanted more than to have the show syndicated nationally. And they'd been close, so very close, before the assault. The dream was still possible. They'd had a setback was all. The doctor said the scars, in time, would be undetectable on camera. Nolan would just have to be patient for a little longer.

More footsteps, and this time the door opened. Donna's heart began to beat faster. Nolan? But when she spotted the red hair and wide grin, she smiled wanly, feeling mixed emotions: let down that it wasn't Nolan, yet pleased to see Tom.

"Hi," Tom said softly, stepping into the room. "It's just me."

"Hi, just me."

"How are you feeling today?" Tom seemed uncertain what to do with his hands. He finally shoved them in the pockets of his slacks. "What's this about you going home in a couple days?"

"They're throwing me out. I heal quickly. At least the outer wounds are healing."

"What do you mean?"

"I'm seeing a counselor. He's coming this afternoon."

"A psychiatrist?"

"Dr. Saxton suggested it. And I think it's a good idea. He says it will help with the fear and depression. Victims of crime tend to have trouble coping, I'm told."

"I had no idea," Tom said quietly. "You always seem so optimistic. If there's anything I can do . . ."

"Your visits help." She smiled. "You're here early today."

"We've got the show this afternoon, so I thought I'd drop in before."

"How's it going—the show?"

335

"Ratings are great, but it's not the same without you." He lifted the grocery bag. "More cards and letters from your loyal fans. They're biding their time till you're back where you belong."

"Thanks, Tom. How is Regina working out — I mean, she's great on camera, any one can see that, but is she getting her way with Max and . . . ?"

"Nolan?"

She nodded.

"Look, Donna, it's not my place to interfere, I'm only the director, but . . ." He let the words trail off.

Donna pressed the button to raise the bed. "What is it?"

"You know the last thing I want to do is upset you."

"Tom, please."

"Well, that woman, the one on the program the day you were attacked? She has designs on taking over."

"Amelia?" Donna asked, knowing the answer.

"Yes. The two of them are cooking up something to knock Regina out and put her in."

"How do you know this?"

"The station grapevine. And it's not an idle rumor. Nolan called her in today."

"What does Regina say about it?"

"Not much she can say, since she's out of town. Her car broke down somewhere on 101, but she promises to make it in time to get the show on. If she doesn't, Nolan has insurance."

Donna felt sick. Why was Nolan doing this? They had discussed it and he was aware of her feelings regarding anyone taking Regina's place. Especially Amelia.

"Sure, the woman is beautiful, but she has the warmth of an Eskimo Pie."

"Where does Max stand?"

"Max is loyal to you and Regina, but hell, Donna, he has to think about the show. Regina's acting real strange. She hardly showed up to work at all last week, then she leaves town right before a show. I'm not saying she can't pull it off, but to a power-hun—to an ambitious guy like Nolan, it gives him a foothold."

"I'll talk to him," she said without conviction.

"I'm behind you a hundred percent. I'll do what I can."

She forced a smile and patted the edge of the bed. "Why don't you read me some mail from my fans. I need to know someone still cares about me."

He stared at her, a softness in his light blue eyes. "I'm your number one fan. I have been for many years. I—we all love you." He lowered his gaze.

She touched his hand and waited until his eyes met hers again, then she swallowed and said quietly, "You're always here, aren't you?"

He squeezed her hand.

Twenty-six

1

At eleven o'clock Regina left the restaurant to return to the service station. The temperature had climbed rapidly, and although it was still relatively cool, she knew the mercury would reach well into the nineties by noon.

Fifteen minutes later her car was fixed and she was on the road again. At noon she was at the apartment house. She sat in the car a moment, reluctant to go in. Then, taking a deep breath, she climbed out and quietly entered the building, hoping she could make it upstairs without intervention. But the moment she passed John's door it opened.

He stepped out, grabbed her hand, and said evenly, "I think you owe me an explanation."

She tried to pull free but he held both her arms.

"I don't owe you anything," she replied. Anger and fear surged through her. "Let go, please."

"Not until you tell me why you ran out on me this morning."

"Look, just leave me alone. I never wanted to get involved in this. It's over."

"What's over?"

"Everything. Everything that has to do with you and me."

He pulled her toward his door. "Let's talk about it at

least. You owe me that much."

"Damn you," she practically hissed. "Stop saying that. I don't owe you anything."

He had an arm around her now, forcefully propelling her inside his apartment. The door across the hall opened. Mrs. Szabo poked her head out.

"Johnnie?" the woman said.

"It's okay, Aunt Anna. Go back inside."

The head withdrew and the door closed firmly.

"Regina, please. I won't hurt you, you know that."

"You lied to me."

She expected him to deny it. To lie again. But he looked her in the eyes and said sadly, "I know. I'm sorry."

She opened her mouth to say something, then closed it.

"We have to talk." He backed her into the apartment and quickly closed the door.

She pressed her back to the door, her body stiff, unyielding. She stared at him defiantly.

"I can't trust you," she said quietly. "If you can't be trusted to tell the truth, then you can't be trusted at all. I'm not one of those people who you had to lie to to get the information you needed. I went along with you. I trusted you. We . . . I let you—oh God." She struggled in frustration. Tears filled her eyes and rushed out, and she tried to avert her face.

John placed a hand on each side of her face, urging her to look at him. "You ran out on me because you found out I lied to you?"

She nodded.

"And no other reason?"

She shook her head.

"You weren't sorry about . . . last night? You weren't having second thoughts about us?"

"I wasn't at the time. I am now."

"I can explain everything."

"I don't want to know. I don't care to know. I just want my life back again. The way it was. Uncomplicated."

339

"I'm afraid that's not possible. You can erase me from your life, but you can't erase the one who's after you. He's out there and he's very real. And I think I know who it is."

"Yes, of course," she said caustically, "Fletcher Kincade."

"No."

She looked at him, swiping the tears from her face.

"I think it's Matthew Corde."

"Amelia's husband?"

He nodded.

Regina felt a chill from head to toe. She wanted to laugh in his face; tell him how ridiculous he was being; how he must be grasping desperately—but she couldn't. She couldn't because she felt a horrible, insane logic behind his words. Nevertheless, she found herself saying, "He's a judge, he wouldn't . . ."

"He would and he could. I don't know what his motive is, but he has the means and the opportunity. He was also one of the few people who would've known about the 'City Gallery' broadcast that day. Amelia would have told him."

"That's crazy," she said without conviction.

"Remember the message, the one that said 'a sea will lead to the assailant—Regina, it wasn't A. C. for Amelia Corde. It was, 'a C will lead to the assailant.' C for Corde, yes, but not Amelia."

Her silence prompted him to say, "Regina, we found the butcher tape at Kowalski's and in the Corde freezer. Both Amelia and her husband were in Napa, but on the afternoon of Tammy's death, the judge took a shuttle into the city."

That horrible logic intensified for Regina. Matthew Corde. The pageant joke. The vile, bug-eyed man who'd leered at all the contestants as if they were strippers. He had come on to her the first day of the competition. Although young and naive, Regina, interpreting his lascivious advances for what they were, had feigned ignorance. And after the first encounter, she'd managed to stay away

340

from him.

"Regina?"

True, the man was a creep, but that didn't mean he was capable of such vicious acts.

She started to answer when it suddenly dawned on her that the assailant was not the issue at the moment. John Davie, the man she feared she was hopelessly in love with, had lied to her. She suspected that he had lied more than once.

For all she knew, John could be the assailant. It made sense that he'd try to steer her in another direction. He'd been the number one suspect in Corinne's case. He had lied about knowing Corinne. If he lied once he could lie again and again. He could be the informant, as well. He could have planted the butcher tape at Tammy's house and then again in the Corde's freezer. He could have lied about everything. She hadn't been there for any of it. It was John, after all, who'd pointed a finger at Amelia and Kincade. And perhaps he'd continue to point fingers, as long as they were pointed away from him.

"Stop looking at me like that," he said. "Christ, Regina, surely you don't suspect me?" She continued to stare silently at him. He turned and walked several feet into the room. "Are you going to let me explain?"

She nodded, once.

He sat on the arm of the couch. "I didn't tell the truth about Corinne—it is Corinne we're talking about here, isn't it?"

"Yes. Unless there was something else you lied about."

"I figured if you knew Corinne and I had been friends—"

"You were *lovers!*" she said.

"All right. I was afraid if you knew we had been lovers and that I was a suspect in her assault, you wouldn't trust me."

She opened her mouth to protest, but he put up a silencing hand.

341

"I wanted you to get to know me first. To realize I was incapable of doing something like that to a woman I cared about . . . to any woman, for that matter."

"I got to know you. My God, I went to bed with you," she said vehemently. "How much time did you need?"

"I know. But it just never seemed to be the *right* time."

"Why are you involved? Why is it so important for you to solve this case now, twenty years later?"

"To clear my name. To avenge Corinne. To . . ."

"Go on."

"To protect you."

"I was in just as much danger then as now."

"I wasn't in love with you then," he said softly.

Regina stared into his eyes. There was no teasing glint. They were serious, brooding. Something twisted slowly inside her.

"What about Wilma. Did you and she . . . ?"

"We shared a bed and that was it," he answered. "We're friends."

"And the Hungarian girl?"

"There's nothing to tell you about her. She—"

"Oh Christ!" Regina said in exasperation. She whirled around, grabbed the knob, had the door halfway open before he, bounding across the room, slammed it shut again. He pulled her away and blocked the door with his body.

"I saw you two," she said. "Do you hear me, I saw you two walking, like lovers, down the street after you'd stood me up." She paced to the couch, turned and came back, pushed at him. "Get out of my way."

"I know you saw us. I didn't lie to you about walking Ilona home. I just didn't mention it. Regina, Ilona could have been attacked that night. Right here in my apartment. Attacked by him, the one we're looking for."

"What are you trying to pull now?"

"Ilona was taking a bath. I had no idea that she was here in my apartment, in my tub. I was with you, re-

342

member. I always leave my door unlocked and she came in and made herself at home. When I came down to get the wine I heard her calling my name. He bushwhacked me — that's how I got this." John rubbed the bruised lump on his forehead. "Then he ran out. And that's not all. The night Donna Lake was attacked, I saw someone prowling around the building."

"Why didn't you call the police when he broke into your apartment and hit you?"

"And implicate myself even more? This is my apartment. Ilona had no idea what had happened. She saw only me."

"Why didn't you tell me?"

"I didn't want to scare you. If you'd known he'd been this close . . ."

Regina tried to swallow and found it difficult to do so. She cleared her throat and tried again.

He reached out to touch her face, she pulled away.

"Regina, what can I say or do to make you believe me?"

"I want to see Corinne," Regina said.

He stared at her for several long moments. "I don't think she'll be receptive to a visit."

"I want to try."

"When?"

"After today's show."

He nodded. Their eyes met and held. "Regina . . .," he moved in, his mouth coming forward to brush against hers.

She turned, opened the door and rushed out of his apartment.

2

Regina arrived at the station at two o'clock, two hours before airtime. Though she hadn't seen them yet, she

343

knew that Nolan and Amelia were together somewhere in the studio, ready to take over.

At 3:20 she got the call to see Max.

"Shut it," he said when she entered the office.

An eyebrow went up, but she said nothing as she closed the door.

"I feel like a ref at a tag-team match."

"Only I don't have a teammate," Regina said.

"You got Tom. And you got me. He dragged deeply on his cigarette and forgot to blow the smoke out. "This is a helluva note. Donna wants you, and Nolan wants Amelia. Donna usually does what Nolan wants. But everyone does what I want." The smoke finally came out, reminding Regina of the worm with the water pipe in *Alice in Wonderland*. "What do *you* want, Regina?"

"I want what Donna wants."

"Any problems, other'n those created by Nolan and that woman?"

"You mean with the show?"

"Course I mean with the show. Since when have I started butting in on your personal business?"

"No problems."

"Ratings are up. I can't argue with that."

Regina looked down at her hands in her lap.

"Well, go on and do whatever it is you have to do before airtime. If Nolan gives you any trouble, tell him to come to me."

"Thanks, Max." She rose.

"What's your opinion of that Corde woman? Do you think she's got screen appeal?"

"She looked good on the tape."

"Looked good, huh?"

"Max, I—"

"Oh, don't fret, I'm not thinking about her for host on 'City Gallery'. She's too tightass for that. I was thinking about that two-minute beauty spot at the end of the show." He pounded out his cigarette. "It's just a thought."

344

"You're hopeless, Max." She laughed lightly. "No, I wouldn't have a problem with that."

"Yeah, well, it was just a thought."

He crossed to the door and opened it. Regina was about to go out when she heard raised voices coming from the control booth. She and Max exchanged puzzled looks, then followed the voices. Nolan and Tom were facing each other, their bodies rigid with anger.

"You stay away from my wife," Nolan said to Tom. "Just stay the hell away from her or I'll have your ass."

"Look, you sonofabitch, Donna may be your wife, but you damn well don't deserve her. How can you do that to her? She's given you two hundred percent of herself. She's off the show temporarily and you panic, start latching onto what you see as another meal ticket. You'd toss away a wonderful woman like Donna for a handful of power?"

"Mind your own business, mister," Nolan shot back, pointing a finger at the director. "What I do is none of your fucking concern."

"If Donna wasn't so goddamn blind with love for you, she'd see you for the crud you are. The only reason I haven't told her about you and that woman is that it would break her heart. And God knows she's suffered enough."

"So tell her. You think she's going to believe you? It's obvious to her, and everyone in this studio, that you want her for yourself."

"You're damn right I want her. I love her. Hear me? I love her! That's more than you can say."

"You're pathetic, Gansing. She's feeding off your sympathy. Do you think she would have had anything to do with you before she got her face messed up by—"

Nolan's words were abruptly cut off by Tom's fist to his jaw. Max ran into the room and pulled Tom away.

As Regina turned sharply to leave the room, she caught a glimpse of Amelia ducking back into Nolan's cubicle.

3

John wondered how Corinne would react to a visit from him after all these years. She had adamantly refused to let him see her after the tragedy, and when he had called her after Donna's assault, she had told him never to call again. He doubted that anything had changed. Maybe he hadn't been as important to her as she'd been to him. After all, at eighteen he was little more than a street kid, no job, a school dropout, into booze, low-level drugs, and fighting to get and keep what he wanted. The only thing he'd wanted that he hadn't been able to fight for had been Corinne, and only because she herself had turned him away.

He picked up the phone in his apartment and dialed her number. After a dozen rings the phone was answered. The voice that spoke a lethargic greeting was deep and hoarse.

"Corinne, it's Jack. I have to talk to you."

There was a long silence before the voice, a raspy whisper, said, "Stay away." Then she said no more.

After many minutes, with John gently coaxing her to speak to him, the line was disconnected.

4

As Donna looked at her two sons that Saturday afternoon she felt a great emotional rush of pride and love. So handsome, both of them. She had missed them terribly these weeks in the hospital.

It was 5:20. The three of them had watched "City Gallery" on the elevated TV and now both boys were engrossed in cartoons about transformers. Junior, the oldest, sat across the room in a Naugahyde club chair. His brother, Nigel, was curled up on the bed beside Donna, his fingers rubbing absently at the satin trim around the sleeve of his mother's bed jacket.

Donna thought of Tom and she felt a poignant stirring in her stomach. Tom was so sweet, so kind and caring. It was obvious he loved her, had loved her for a long time. For the first time since she'd known him, she allowed herself to think of him in a way other than a good friend and coworker. She remembered how his hands had held hers tenderly, squeezing affectionately, and she had squeezed back. When he left, he had bent down to kiss her forehead, as was his usual departing gesture, and she had surprised herself by lifting her face until their lips met. The kiss was brief, chaste, yet filled with wonder and excitement.

She smiled dreamily.

At the commercial Nigel turned to his mother. "How long do you have to stay in this place, Momma?"

"I can leave tomorrow, I hope."

"Will you be as good as new. Like before?"

Donna smiled. "Not quite. Better than now, of course. I have to heal first. Then the doctors will fix me up *almost* as good as new."

"Will you go back to work on the show."

"I'd like to."

"Daddy says no," Junior mumbled from the corner, his gaze still on the TV screen.

Donna turned to him. "Daddy says no to what?"

"He says you'll never be right again. And that you won't be on TV no more."

Donna's stomach felt queasy. "He told you that?"

"Not me. To someone on the telephone."

Donna was finding it difficult to breathe. She took Nigel's hand and squeezed. "What else did your dad say?"

Junior shrugged.

"Who was he talking to?"

No answer. He studied the screen with great interest.

"Junior, stop watching cartoons and answer me."

347

"What?" he said, glancing impatiently at her.

"Who was he talking to?"

"I don't know. Some lady."

Donna turned to Nigel. "Do you know anything about this?"

Her sensitive child, with his large eyes full of concern as he stared back at her, shook his head.

She turned back to Junior. "Was her name Amelia Corde?"

The boy ignored her.

"Junior, damn you, pay attention!"

"What?" he replied with obvious irritation.

"Amelia. Was it Amelia?"

"I don't know. I guess."

Donna reached for the remote control and flicked the set off.

"Hey! Whadya do that for? I was watching that." Junior jumped from the chair, strode to the bed, and turned the set back on.

Donna flicked it off again. When he reached for it, she pushed his hand away.

"I don't have to watch TV with you," he said, his tone hard. "I hate it here. It stinks and everybody is crippled or sick. I hate it and I wish I never had to come!"

Donna grabbed Junior by the arm and yanked him around. "Now you listen to me—"

"—Oww. Let go. I want outta this cruddy place."

He tried to twist free, but Donna held tight. Was it possible to dislike your own child, she wondered? Before her stood a miniature of his father; so young, yet already prejudiced and narrow-minded.

"You're going to learn some manners, some respect," she said. "You're not going to be the way he is. No son of mine will be bigoted and, and—." Tears sprang to her eyes, rolled down her face, but she was oblivious to them. "—Not like him . . . not like *them*."

She realized then that all her life she had put up with

the intolerance of the two men most important to her. She had worshiped them — first her father, then her husband — allowed them to use her or dismiss her, depending on their whims. Her father, after all these years, had finally taken an interest. Not because he realized he loved her, but because he could not tolerate deformity of any sort in his family. To her husband, as long as she was useful and served a purpose, she was number one. No longer the star, Nolan had switched allegiances. He had already replaced her for an unflawed specimen. Her husband was cheating on her with Amelia Corde.

Junior continued to struggle, his face red, twisted in anger. "Lemme go. I'm telling Dad."

"Stop it," she said sternly. "Don't make me more ashamed of you than I already am."

"Who cares? You're ugly now!" he pulled back and shouted. "Ugly!"

Donna let go of his arm, but before he could move away, her hand flew out and struck him hard across the face. The sharp sound reverberated in the room. She felt a tearing in her throat, then excruciating pain. Something oozed across the burned skin.

Nigel began to sob, hugging close to Donna's other arm.

Junior ran to the door. He grasped the handle; then, turning to look at his mother, stooped over, his breath coming in ragged gasps, his face crimson where he'd been slapped, he opened his mouth wide, as though to shout, but no sound came out.

Donna stared back, her chin quivered. She had a strong urge to beg him to forgive her. She had never struck out in anger before and she never wanted to do it again. But she held her position, sensing a turning point in her life. Would she, this day, she wondered despairingly, lose her son as well as her husband?

Well, so be it.

Junior's mouth still worked silently. Then, in a cracking

voice filled with emotion and pain, he cried out, "Why did *that* have to happen to you?"

Donna continued to stare at him. She ran tremulous fingers through Nigel's hair.

"Momma . . . ?"

Donna, salty tears stinging the wound at her jaw, moved her head slowly from side to side as she contemplated her oldest son and *his* pain.

Suddenly his face crumbled, the stony reserve, uncharacteristic of a nine year old, gave way to a child, heartbroken and pathetic. He rushed across the room and threw himself to his knees at the side of her bed. He buried his face in the stiff sheet and sobbed.

Donna pulled him up. She held him to her chest and rocked both Junior and Nigel, cooing softly, the pain under her chin no more than a dull ache now.

The door opened and her husband and father entered. Both men stopped at the foot of the bed. Neither came close enough to kiss, let alone touch her.

"You saw the show today?" Nolan asked Donna.

She stared solemnly at him before nodding her head.

"Your best friend seems to like being on that side of the camera. I believe she has designs to stay there."

"Really?" Donna said with unmistakable irony.

"Is there something wrong?" Nolan asked, looking curiously from Donna to his sons.

Donna turned to her father. "Dad, will you take the boys home now? I want to talk with Nolan—alone."

"We have things to discuss first," her father said gruffly. "The cosmetic surgery—"

"Later," she said, cutting him off.

The boys went to their grandfather. Nigel took his hand and pulled him toward the door, his large, expressive eyes silently coaxing.

When they were alone, Donna turned off the TV. "Are you sleeping with Amelia?"

Nolan could only stare at her. Not directly *at* her, she

realized, but at some point above her head. She felt she could forgive his infidelity, if only he could look her in the face, if only he could care for her despite her deformity.

"I'm coming home tomorrow," she said quietly. "I don't want to find you there."

"You can't mean that," Nolan sputtered. "You're being irrational. This whole tragedy has changed you. You're not yourself—"

"Don't you mean I'm not your puppet any longer? All these years you were the ventriloquist and I was the dummy. The dummy broke, and now it's time to find a new one."

"Donna, that's crazy talk." He glanced at her, glanced away.

"Look at me. Look at my face. My throat. Take a good look at my wounds, damnit!"

Nolan looked. And for a moment he was able to mask his disgust; then he dropped his eyes and whirled around, putting his back to her.

"I'm certain Max will accept your resignation at KSCO. And the sooner the better," she said.

"Now you wait a minute," he said whirling around. "You can't force me to resign. Without me you'd be nowhere. I gave you 'City Gallery'. If you think they're going to let you anywhere near the set looking like . . . like that, you're crazier than I thought. Even with your father's money and all the plastic surgeons—"

"To hell with my father and his surgeons!" she shouted, raising her voice for the first time. "He's not running my life anymore! And neither are you!" She rolled over in the bed, putting her back to him. "Now get out, I can no longer stand to look at *your* face."

They were heading toward Potrero Hill. Regina stared out the window at boarded storefronts, vacant lots overrun with weeds, abandoned cars. John drove. Although he drove well, maneuvering through traffic as if he did it every day, he looked odd sitting there—belonging, yet not belonging.

John had met her at the station after the show. The program had gone extremely well. The phone lines remained lit to the end of the show with callers eager to talk to the "dream doctor."

As they rode in silence, Regina found herself stealing glances at John. She had a score of questions, but she'd made up her mind to wait until he opened the portal for conversation. John, however, seemed preoccupied and uncommunicative.

Why were they doing this? When he'd met her at the station she had indicated that it was not necessary to go to Corinne's; that she had changed her mind. But John had insisted, saying it was something *he* had to do.

He pulled up to a clapboard house, the yard long ago gone to weeds and junk. A front window had a wedged-shaped piece of glass missing, duct tape covering the opening.

"This is it," John said. "This is where she lived when I met her."

"How do you know she still lives here?"

"Where else would she go? Winning the pageant was going to get her out of the slums."

John got out, came around and opened Regina's door, and they both started up the walk. In the driveway at the back of the house, Regina saw an old car. It was large, as cars in the fifties tended to be, and a dull black. There was a bulky hood ornament above the grill. Regina put out a hand to stop John. She pointed to the car.

John gave it no more than a cursory glance before moving on.

Regina bit down on her lower lip, but kept quiet. She followed.

On the cracked, concrete slab that served as a porch, an old stove, thick with grease and grime, sat to one side of the front door. Plastic garbage bags filled with trash littered the area.

John knocked.

Regina saw a corner of the curtain flicker.

They waited. John knocked again, louder. Again they waited.

John put the side of his face to the thin door. "Corinne, it's John Davie. Regina is with me," he said gently but firmly. "We just want to talk. Please open the door."

A voice close to the door responded. "Get outta here. I have nothing to say to you . . . or her."

"I have something I want to say to you," he said.

Silence.

"Corinne, you're not alone anymore. Two others have suffered like you."

"So what?"

"Let's talk, okay?"

They waited.

John looked at Regina, looked away. "Please, Cory."

Regina thought she heard a sob from the other side of the door. She definitely heard the click of a deadbolt turning. After several moments John reached a hand to the knob and turned; the door opened a crack. He pushed slowly, stepping inside. He motioned for Regina to follow.

Regina had a bad feeling about this. The open door had unleashed a putrid odor from inside the house. The heavy, cloying smell of stale cigarette smoke and beer, and the underlying stink of filth, rot, and decay.

John took her wrist and pulled her along with him before she could turn and leave this place. What had she expected? she asked herself. A doll house, with shiny linoleum, chintz curtains, and knickknacks in shadow boxes?

The cluttered room lay deathly quiet in a haze of cigarette smoke. Mounds of butts were piled in a half dozen ashtrays; and beer cans, each one crushed, were littered about.

No one was in the room.

John closed the door and everything, blessedly, faded in the darkness. A panel of light glowed under a closed door that probably opened into the kitchen.

They stood just inside the front door. Regina breathed shallowly. She wanted to take John's hand; wanted to feel his arm around her, giving her strength.

Neither moved.

From a dark doorway Regina saw the silhouette of a tall figure.

"Sit down somewhere," the hoarse voice said. "Excuse the mess. It's really not as bad as it looks. Nothing a can of gasoline and a match couldn't put right."

Regina and John stepped to the sofa and sat.

The figure moved into the room. Regina could vaguely make out a woman in a shapeless shift. A towel was wrapped turban style around her head, a corner dropped down to cover one side of her face.

"Hello, Cory," John said quietly.

"It's been a long time, huh, Jack?"

"A long time."

She sat still, not speaking. The silence grew heavy with tension.

"I'd offer you some refreshment," Corinne said flippantly, "but I'm afraid the cupboard is bare. If I'd known you were coming, Jack, I'd have stocked up on those red nuts you like so well."

"Cory," John said carefully. "Donna was attacked like you—"

She cut into his words, "Not like me. I saw her. A mere flesh wound." She laughed at her pun.

"Tammy wasn't as lucky," Regina said.

"Luckier than me." She lit a cigarette, turning her head away at the flare of the match. "Three down, two to go. Who will be next?"

"We hope no one," John said.

"Why are you here? You think I did it?" Corinne asked.

"No," John said.

"Then why? To tell me I should feel better because I'm not the only freak?" She snorted sardonically. "Sure I feel better. But not much. I had twenty years to live with this. My life was destroyed before it got started. Donna, Tammy, Amelia, and you Regina, all had a life. Beautiful people doing beautiful things while I sat here in this hole rotting both inside and out. Shit, now that you're finally beginning to get old and wrinkled, what's a little acid when you've got all those good memories."

"Cory—"

"Stop calling me that," she snapped at John. "Say what you came to say and get out so I can get back to what I was doing. What I do best. Which is being alone."

Regina remembered Donna telling her that Corinne resented her father for gambling away the money that would have gone to reconstruct her face. Disturbed by the fetid odor and the deathly silence of the house, Regina asked, "Where's your father, Corinne?"

"I don't think that's any of your business, Regina."

"Corinne, do you have any idea who did that to you?" John asked.

"Maybe you did it, Jack," she said.

Regina felt John stiffen. In the dim light she could see the astonishment on his face.

"Is that what you think?"

Regina caught John's quick glance.

Corinne laughed with wry humor. "Oh, poor baby. They came after you, didn't they? The cops. Someone told them we'd argued that day. And you had no alibi. It

355

looked bad for you." She rose and moved slowly to the window. She adjusted the drape so that the slice of light became a mere laser stripe down her front.

"Is that why you wouldn't let me near you? Why you shut me out? Because you suspected me?"

"You're such a fool, Jack." She whipped back the drape, light flooded in, making her squint. The towel was flung from her head to expose the matted hair beneath. Then she turned her head so they could get a full view of her scarred face. "Look at me," she said deep in her throat. "Would you have loved *this?* Would you have stayed with *this?*"

John stared unflinchingly at Corinne, his expression neither shocked nor repelled, only sad. "I don't know, Cory. You never gave me the chance."

"I'm giving you the chance now. What do you say, Jack?"

John was silent as he rose and moved toward her. He reached out to touch her.

She jerked back violently, letting the drape fall. "Don't touch me. I'm only blind in one eye. I can see that you love *her.* I can see that much."

Corinne's words caused Regina's stomach to flutter.

Corinne turned her face away, her voice softened, yet still bitter. "And that hurts. God, it hurts so bad. No one cares about me. I might as well have died. There were just two people who seemed to care. Momma," she paused, "and . . . and you, Jack. Only I couldn't let you see me.

"That man in there," she spun and pointed a finger toward a closed door, "killed my mother! He went through all my money. I was forced to depend on him for everything. Well now he has to depend on me. It's his turn to hurt."

"Cory, don't do this to yourself. Let us help you. Let us help both of you."

He reached for her again. She raised her arms, her fists

356

clenched, and then she let them fall and began to cry. "Oh, sweet Jesus, why? Why me?" Deep sobs were torn from her ravaged throat and she collapsed against John, burying her face against his chest. His arms went around her, holding her tight. He smoothed her hair, rocked her gently.

"Stay out of it. It's not your concern. He doesn't deserve to live," she cried. "God is punishing him. God made him sick. And if he dies, it'll be God's will."

Regina looked down to see a photo album on the floor at her feet. On the cover, with a black felt marker, were the words, *The Thrill of Victory — The Agony of Defeat 1970–1990.*

With the toe of her shoe she lifted the cover. She saw a grainy black-and-white picture of Donna Lake and a newspaper clipping of the assault. There was one of Tammy, as well. Regina, her leg now shaking, let the album close.

John looked over at her and, with his eyes, gestured toward the closed door.

She shook her head vigorously. John continued to stare.

Regina surreptitiously reached into her purse and wrapped icy fingers around her mace container. Holding it tight in her hand, she rose slowly and crossed the room. Her heart thumped in her chest as she turned the knob and opened the door. The smell that assaulted her made her reel. The odor was unmistakably body waste and decaying flesh. She breathed in short, shallow breaths as she slowly entered the room and stepped to the bed. The man in the bed was pale, his glazed-over eyes were partially open, and Regina knew without touching him that he was dead.

Oh, Lord, what had she and John walked into? She backed out of the room, returned to the living room where John still held a sobbing Corinne. He looked at Regina inquiringly.

"He's dead," she whispered. "We have to call someone."

Corinne pushed away from John. "Get out of my house. This is none of your business. No police! Do you hear? No police!"

"Cory," John said, "We have to—"

"Nooo!" she said, her face twisting. She pushed at John, her fists swinging, hitting him on the chest. "Why'd you have to come here? God, I hate you. I hate you all!" And before John could stop her, Corinne grabbed her long black coat from the sofa and fled out of the house.

John cursed. He seemed uncertain whether to go after her or let her go. The sound of an engine revving, then a car racing down the driveway, took the decision out of his hands.

Regina felt an overwhelming sense of oppressiveness. She couldn't stay another moment in this awful place. "I have to get out of here," Regina said, pulling him toward to door.

"Are you sure her father's dead?"

"Yes, positive," she replied, on the verge of hyperventilation. "John, there's nothing we can do for him. Please."

They went out the door, leaving it open, and hurried to the station wagon.

Twenty-seven

1

They drove across town in relative silence, not unlike the ride to Corinne's earlier.

"Would you mind dropping me at The Bull's Blood," John said. "I'll call the police from there."

Without taking her eyes off the road, Regina asked, "Will you tell them who you are?"

He shook his head. "I'll tell them I think someone needs medical attention at that address, and that's all. They'll find out when they get there that he's dead."

She glanced at him. It was clear he didn't want to be to be the one to set the cops on Corinne. She wondered if he was doing the right thing.

"John, we have to talk about Corinne. Back there at the house I saw an album, a scrapbook, with newspaper clippings of Donna and Tammy—mementos. She drives an old, dark-colored car with a hood ornament. She has a black hooded coat. Her name begins with a *C*. John, anyone who is capable of letting her father die is capable of anything. She could have gotten into the Corde's freez—"

"It's not Cory," he cut her off brusquely.

At the next corner she turned left, made another left on Van Ness, and pulled up in front of the bar, double parking. John sat a moment, looking straight ahead. In a quiet tone, as though talking to himself, he said, "You and I

359

. . . where the hell are we going?"

Before she could respond he climbed out, leaned down to the window and said, "Be careful." Then he closed the door and strode off.

A horn honked behind her. Flustered, she pulled away and drove home.

She let herself into her apartment. Without Kristy, the place seemed empty. She wondered if her daughter was having a good time in Tahoe. She hoped someone was having a good time. Donna was laid up in the hospital frightened and in pain while her husband made plans to replace her with his mistress. Tammy was in the morgue awaiting a coroner's release before she would be settled into her final resting place. Corinne was in her own private hell. And Amelia . . . ? Amelia, she assumed, was the only one of the five oblivious to pain and suffering.

2

Amelia had been offered the two-minute beauty spot on "City Gallery"—a crumb compared to the cake she had hoped for, but she was in no position to complain. Once she was in, it was only a matter of time before she'd have whatever she wanted. Nolan was on her side, and now the producer, Max, was beginning to weaken.

Only a matter of time.

She hoped the executive producer was a better lover than Nolan. Max wasn't much of a looker, but that could prove to be in her favor. The pretty ones, such as Nolan, oftentimes were vain and selfish, especially in sex. Nolan, to her initial delight, had made all the right moves in their prelude to an affair; romantic manor in Napa, champagne, words expressing appreciation for her beauty, a little kissing and heavy breathing and breast fondling, but when it came down to the sex, his mind ran on one track and one track only—to take his pleasure and to hell with

360

his partner. The second time they made love, Amelia had guided him, seeking her own sexual release, but his attempts to bring her to climax had been so impatient and halfhearted that, to get it over with, she had pretended.

They were too much alike, therefore an impossible match. Fletcher, on the other hand . . . She sighed with regret —

Then again with pleasure. Now, in her bedroom, on her stomach on the massage table, a bath towel and a fine patina of scented oil the only things covering her body, she relaxed under the firm hands of the masseuse as she worked the tightness from between Amelia's shoulder blades.

She had decided to leave Matthew. She'd sell off what she could around the house; some silver and crystal. The jewelry was all gone, sold ages ago, the money turned over to Fletcher, but she had the diamond earrings Matthew had given her last week. They were worth a couple of thousand. She would wheedle the credit card out of him one last time and go on a shopping binge.

The decision to leave Matthew had been an extremely difficult one. But she reasoned that if he touched her one more time she would go berserk; tear his eyes out, take a knife and rip him to shreds, castrate him. The night before when he had come at her — she always thought of it as coming *at* her, not *to* her — it was all she could do to keep from biting off his slimy tongue when he lapped at her, leaving her sloppy wet and physically sick.

She was still a beautiful woman. Still desirable. Fletcher had valued money over love. A sad excuse for a man. Gay, most likely. There were plenty of other men out there, and many of them were rich. She would just have to learn to live with less until the right one came along.

The hands left her just when the tension was beginning to ease.

"My neck and shoulders, Katie," she said, her words muffled in the flat pillow under her head. "And then my feet."

The hands touched her calves, then moved along the back of one thigh before diving between her legs.

Amelia's eyes flew open. She jerked her head up, a protest on her lips. But instead of Katie standing over her, she saw Matthew, his bulbous eyes watering. He smiled wickedly.

He bent down, his tongue invading her ear, sopping her hair. She shuddered involuntarily.

He reached for his fly.

Amelia rolled over and sat up, covering herself with the towel. "Not tonight, Matthew," she said petulantly.

He looked at her in that particular way of his, a mixture of wounded pride and anger.

That was stupid of her, she realized too late. Now she could forget the damn credit card.

3

Regina sat in the window seat, in the dark, staring at the faraway winking, shimmering lights. This had become her favorite place to sit and contemplate. And lately she had plenty to contemplate.

With the telephone in her lap, she called Donna, apologized for not visiting, and asked straightaway. "Has Judge Corde ever propositioned you?"

"You mean lately?"

"Anytime."

"Why do you ask?" she said, her voice sounding evasive.

"Please, Donna, it's important."

"Several times. I considered them bribes."

"Why didn't you say something?"

"The first time I was just a frightened young girl in a beauty pageant where he was a judge. I was afraid. The last time was a couple months ago at a dinner party at their house. I told Nolan. He said I shouldn't make waves, that the judge had a lot of influence in this city. God, I was blind where Nolan was concerned. But my eyes are open now. Reg . . ." Donna paused, then said, "Nolan and I are separating."

"Oh, Donna . . .," Regina said quietly.

"It's okay. It was my decision. There are going to be a lot of changes in my life. Good changes. I'm coming back on the show—when I'm fully recovered, that is. And I want you to cohost with me."

"Donna, I don't know what to say, I . . ."

"Say yes. I've already talked with Max. Nolan will be off 'Gallery'. Don't think I didn't know what you had to go through with him over the years. And I appreciate your silence, your patience. Now, with just you, Tom, and me, it'll be one helluva show."

"You still care for Nolan?"

"Of course I do, but I'll get over him." She sighed. "My decision has little to do with his sleeping with Amelia. Nolan was like a mood-altering drug. Before the attack, he made me happy, but he wasn't good for me. I can't get well with him around. Although he doesn't mean to, he makes me feel ugly, like damaged goods."

"Donna, how are you doing? If you need company, I can be there in twenty minutes."

"Frankly, I'm exhausted." She paused. "Regina, I'm going to be fine. Really fine."

"Of course you are," Regina said.

Regina offered to drive Donna home the following day, but Donna said Tom Gansing had insisted.

They exchanged good-byes and hung up.

So Donna knew about Nolan and Amelia. Tom Gansing also knew, but she doubted he had been the one to enlighten Donna. More than likely Donna had simply sensed the rat abandoning ship.

Thinking of rats, her thoughts wandered indiscriminately to Judge Corde. During the Classic pageant, the judge had used his lofty position to bribe at least one contestant, though she suspected there were more. In exchange for sexual favors he had promised to tip the scales. But he was only one of six judges. How much influence could one man have? The accidents. Had they really been accidents, or cleverly executed eliminations? Corde was without a doubt guilty of bribery at the pageant, but did that automatically make him the culprit to all the rest?

What of Corinne?

Regina tracked another course, trying to make sense of what was happening, but no matter where her mind ventured, John was there, crowding out all else.

She wished she had his novel now. Reading it would bring him close to her for a time.

The phone in her lap rang, startling her. She let it ring again, then answered.

"Regina," John said quietly, letting her name hang in the air.

"Hi." Why was her heart going crazy?

"Just wanted to make sure you got home safely and that everything's all right."

"Yes, thanks." Silence. "John?"

"Yeah, I'm here."

"John, Corde propositioned Donna. Bribery seems to be consistent with him."

No response.

"Did you hear me?"

"Yes, I heard." Another long pause.

"It's awfully quiet in the bar," Regina said.

"I'm not at work. I'm downstairs."

"Oh."

"Well . . . good ni—"

"John . . . ?" She couldn't let him go. "The copy of your novel you gave to me . . . maybe tomorrow I can—"

"It's on my desk. If I'm not at home, go on in, the door's always open. Get it whenever you like."

"Thanks. I will."

"Good night."

"John?"

He was gone.

She pressed the receiver to her chest and hugged it, reluctant to give up the instrument that had carried his voice to her. He was home, yet he hadn't invited her down. But then she hadn't invited him up.

She cradled the receiver, rose, and with weary steps, went into her bedroom. Although it was early, she was exhausted. She had to shut off her brain or she would go crazy.

She undressed, dropping her clothes to the floor. In the bathroom she took a clean towel from under the sink, and shaking it out, she paused. John's words in the car as she dropped him at The Bull's Blood came back to her: *You and me . . . where the hell are we going?*

Where, indeed?

And then she knew. She knew where *she* was going.

Wrapping the towel around her, she strode out of the room and didn't stop until she reached the closet in the entry. There she paused only long enough to exchange the towel for her gabardine coat, cinch the belt together, and rush out the door.

4

He poured himself a gin on the rocks, took off his shoes, socks, and sweater, and popped the top button on his Levi's. After flipping off all the lights and turning on the stereo, he slumped down in the high-back chair, his bare feet propped on the mahogany coffee table. He thought of Regina as he sipped his drink and listened to Roy Orbison singing "Oh, Pretty Woman."

He'd been in love twice before in his life. First with Corinne and then with Darlene. What he was feeling now was strangely like that, only he wasn't young and naive anymore. After Darlene, there'd been women, but nothing

365

serious. He wondered if what he was experiencing now was only the wants and needs of a man lusting after a desirable woman . . . a woman who hadn't fallen all over him because he was single and charming and easy to look at.

It was one thing to lust after a woman, quite another to love one—especially another career-minded woman. Commitment was scary. Regina had been married half her life. A good marriage? Probably.

He couldn't think about their night at the inn without feeling a pleasant, erotic stirring. He wondered if he would ever make love to her again. At that moment as he sat in his chair, he wanted her badly. Wanted to hold her in his arms and stroke her satiny skin. Wanted to hear her breathy cries in his ear, feel her fingers gripping him as she shuddered with sexual release. But to go to her, to seduce her again with soft words and tenderness, was to imply an obligation he wasn't ready for.

Across the room he heard a slight scraping sound. Then the door opened slowly and someone, a woman, silhouetted from behind by the low-watt outer hallway light, slipped inside.

John's pulse quickened. He recognized Regina by the cut of her hair, her profile, her posture. Casually, without disclosing the excitement he felt, he lifted his glass and sipped again, the cut-crystal rock glass reflecting fragments of light. He watched her as she closed the door. With her back against it, moonlight raking over her gray coat, she stood quietly staring at him.

He put down his drink, lowered his feet to the floor, stood, and then moved toward her. She waited. He stopped within a fraction of an inch, his bare chest grazing the stiff fabric of her coat lapels.

She untied the belt and let the coat fall open. Moonlight poured over her nakedness. John's pulse began to throb with the pace of the music. There was no question as why she had come. No games. No words. Touched by her need for him, greatly aroused by her provocative approach, he resisted the urge to crush her to him and take her right there in the entry.

Instead, lifting his arms, one on each side of her, his hands flattened to the door above her head, he leaned in and gently pressed his lips to hers. They kissed, savoring the touch and taste of each other. Her breasts felt warm and silky against his chest. He pushed the coat off her shoulders, letting it fall to the floor. He turned the deadbolt, locking the door.

Her hands moved between them and, one by one, she released the metal buttons on the front of his Levi's, the backs of her fingers caressing his fast-growing erection. All restraint gone now, John pulled her in his arms and kissed her with a barely controlled fierceness. In an instant he was as naked as she. Without parting, he backed them up until they were in front of the fireplace, where he lowered her to the floor to lie on a lamb's-wool rug. She inhaled sharply—from the erotic touch of the fleece, or the hardness of him as he entered her, or both, he didn't know. His own senses were wild with anticipation and pleasure, wanting her and knowing that afterward he would want her again.

They rolled on the fleece, each experiencing the sensual softness of it. She was breathing rapidly now, emitting low, moaning sounds deep in her throat. He was approaching orgasm too quickly. Against a muffled protest, he slowly pulled out before he went over the edge. He began to kiss her, taste every part of her, his fingertips caressing her warm, damp skin. Lifting a corner of the rug he rubbed the soft fleece lovingly along her hips and waist to her full breasts, across nipples hard and erect. She moaned.

"John . . . now . . . please," she said, taking hold of him.

He moved between her legs and she guided him into her. This time there was no mistaking the reason for the sharp intake of breath. She locked her body to his, as though fearing he would leave her again. They moved together in perfect sync, the perfect couple fitting together in perfect harmony, lost in the superheated flashes of complete and total passion. He wanted it to go on and on, yet was fearful that it might, fearful that he'd be stimulated beyond reason and driven deliriously mad. He sensed her sexual tension and the instant he felt her first orgasmic contraction, he erupted. Both cried out in unison, holding tight to each other.

5

It was time. This one had avoided the acid long enough, which meant the other one, the queen bitch, would soon have her turn. He preferred it go in order. He was an orderly person. From four to one. The screw-up of number three — the freak drowning — had the police ruling out foul play. Now he had to reestablish credence, get the law on the right track again, make it look as if some nut was attacking the four finalists one by one.

From his place in the deep shadows he stared fixedly at the lighted upstairs window. It had to be now. He casually crossed the street at the corner and slipped into the shadows of the tall hedge that ran along the side of the property. At the back door he took out the key he'd taken from the Dobos girl's purse and slid it into the lock. It fit. He opened the door and went in. He made his way to the staircase and climbed to the second floor.

The hallway was empty. Moving fast now, he crossed to the apartment at the other end. From his pocket he withdrew the black stocking and knitted cap and pulled both over his head. He unscrewed the cap on the jar. There was no peephole on her door, and he doubted that she would take special precautions inside the building. He would knock, wait for her to answer, then throw the acid.

But when he reached her door he paused, confused and

wary. The door was open a crack. He looked around. With the tips of his thin leather gloves, he pushed the door open far enough to see into the living room. The window seat was empty. He quietly slipped inside the apartment. Moving quickly, but cautiously, he searched the other rooms. She was nowhere in the apartment. She had left the front door open.

She would be back, soon.

6

Regina hugged herself deliciously.

"Cold?" John asked, rising to look at her.

She shook her head. "No."

He kissed her throat, her chin, her nose, then rose to one knee and began to build a fire in the fireplace. A moment later it was blazing nicely.

"What a rotten host I am," he said. "You're a guest in my home and I've yet to offer you anything."

"I haven't gone without," she replied.

He kissed her again. "What can I get you? Wine, beer, cognac, brandy?"

"Brandy sounds good."

He draped his sweater over her shoulders, the long sleeves partially covering her breasts, then got them each a snifter of brandy and returned to the floor. She accepted both with a smile. The sweater smelled of him.

John stretched out on his side, braced himself on a elbow, and pulled her down to lie beside him. She felt herself instinctively burrowing in closer, searching for the warmth of his flesh, the security of his nearness. She had a million things she wanted to say, yet she said nothing. They lay that way for a while, John's fingertips moving over her body affectionately.

"Was it pretty bad for you?" he asked out of the blue.

"What?"

"The death of your husband."

"No." She was unable to see his face, but she sensed his surprise. "His death was the easy part. It was the last four years of his life that tore me apart."

"Cancer?"

"Alzheimer's. Leo was much older than me."

"It was a good marriage?"

"Yes. For the most part it was very good. It turned sad."

"Care to talk about it?"

She snuggled in closer. Regina spoke slowly, choosing her words carefully. "One year we were the perfect couple; lovers, companions, parents, and then suddenly we became strangers. Maybe it wasn't so sudden, but it was fast enough for me to know that he was different and that nothing could ever be the same for us again."

Silent for several moments, she cleared her throat and continued. "I sometimes wonder if our love, and all those special memories, make any sense at all. Memories only I carried. I had ceased to exist for him. At the end, when he did seem to recognize me, it was to call me by his first wife's name."

John, working his fingers in between hers, waited for her to go on.

Regina sipped the brandy. "Do you have any idea what it's like to witness the slow degeneration of the person you love?" She spoke quietly. "His mind . . . brilliant—little by little, like an inch worm nibbling a leaf, was eaten away. He turned hostile and abusive, drawing into himself and shutting us out. We kept him at home as long as we could, until the outbursts began to be a major part of his existence. He was still physically strong. We . . . I . . . was afraid that he . . ." She was unable to go on.

John wrapped his arms around her, holding her tight. "Regina, I'm sorry, I didn't realize . . . ," he whispered into her hair.

"I only hope that someday I can remember him as he was before the disease struck him."

370

"You will, honey, you will."

"The man I knew died—for me, anyway—more than two years ago. Sometimes, brief as it was, he'd come back, you see, and be the man I married, and it was those times that made it so hard overall."

"You feel guilty about his death. Why?"

"Can we change the subject?"

"Maybe you should talk about it. What you went through, how you felt, is only natural. You have no reason to blame yourself or feel guilty—"

"Oh, John, I have every reason to feel guilty. I *am* guilty."

"Because you wanted to end his suffering?"

"Because," she blurted out, "because the night he died I was in the arms of another man."

She felt his body stiffen.

Pulling away, drawing in her knees, she covered herself with his sweater. She turned her head away. "My husband died alone, without any of the people he loved, and it was my fault."

John was silent. She wanted him to say something, anything. Regina felt vulnerable, exposed. She hadn't meant to speak of her dead husband, of her infidelity. What must he think of her? His silence was so damning.

"The man at the hospital? Garrick?"

She nodded, swallowing.

He reached for her at the exact moment she struggled to her feet, his sweater sliding off her shoulders.

"I have to go," she said, striding across the room.

"Regina, wait . . ."

In the entry she retrieved her coat and put it on. John stopped her before she could leave.

He held her. No caressing, no kissing. He just held her in a way that made her feel both wonderful and wretched.

"Stay," he whispered.

She shook her head, biting back the tears. And before she could change her mind, she gently pushed him away

371

and hurried out the door. She felt his eyes on her as she rushed up the stairs.

At the top of the landing, she stopped to catch her breath. Her chest felt tight, constricted. She brushed at the tears on her face, then she continued down the hallway. As she approached her apartment, she was suddenly overcome with a quaking sensation of dread. The door to the storage room was slightly ajar. Through the opening she saw darkness, the dark giving sanctuary to an unknown terror. Had it been open when she left her apartment? She felt a cold numbness in her legs. Hurrying now, she rushed inside her apartment and hastily closed and locked the door. The feeling hung on.

In the entry she hung up the coat, then swooped the towel off the floor and loosely wrapped it around her. The tension that had been building the past twenty-four hours had dissipated with just one hour with John. But now it was back again, along with a sense of loss. She had spoiled everything with her confession.

She wouldn't blame him if he never wanted to see her again. Why did she have to move into this apartment and meet him? She could have gone the rest of her life without falling in love again. It was the price she had to pay for being unfaithful to a dying man.

She went directly into the bathroom and turned on the shower. Within moments, a steamy vapor filled the stall. She stepped in and let the hot water beat down on her, soothing the taut muscles of her shoulders and thighs. She stood there, her head back, her eyes closed, letting the hot water massage her body.

She heard a noise, thought she saw a movement on the other side of the shower curtain. Her heart began to beat wildly, making her light-headed. She looked out. The room was thick with steam. No one else shared it with her.

She began to wash herself. The lather was slick as she worked it along her arms, breasts, stomach, and thighs. Again she stood still as the water rinsed away the soap.

And as abruptly as she had gone into the shower, she was out.

As she dried herself off, she looked out the small bathroom window to the ground below. She saw light spilling out onto John's patio. She felt a sense of longing deep inside her.

With the towel wrapped around her like a sarong, she stepped back into the bedroom. Lethargically, Regina bent down and gathered up the clothes on the floor. With the bundle in one arm she went to the closet and, as she reached for the knob, her hand paused in midair. There was something wrong. Very wrong. She reached for the knob again when suddenly she stopped and drew back her hand. A heaviness bore down on her. She stood facing the closet, staring at the rows of slats in the door. The air seemed thick and oppressive.

An icy chill racked her body.

The door, a fold-back louvered type, stood open a crack. The blackness beyond whispered to her to run, to scream, to do anything but open that door. The clothes in her arms fell to the floor. She began to hum softly, backing away, fighting the panic as she gripped the towel around her until it cut into her flesh.

Before she could reach the hallway, she heard the sound of hangers rattling, then the closet door crashed open. A figure in black lunged out, a curse erupting through the black nylon stocking covering his head as he reached for her. She tried to scream but managed only a strangled cry. She ran. The intruder was close enough to rake a hand down her back. Tracks of pain seared along her spine. The towel came away, but she continued on, staggering before regaining her footing. She made it into the bathroom, slamming and locking the door seconds before his body smashed against it. She shot the slide bolt home. She heard footsteps. The other door!

She spun, ran to the far end of the bathroom, and slid the bolt on that door moments before it banged with a jarring thud. He was in her bedroom again. Her mind raced. Could she make it out the hallway door and escape from the apartment before he could reach her?

The next thump came from the door in the hall. If she were to go out any door, it would have to be the one into the bedroom. And that was exactly where he wanted her.

A barrage of bangs sounded against the door. Oh my God, she thought, he was going to force his way in! As she frantically looked around for something to use as a weapon, she spotted Kristy's cotton shortie nightgown draped over the hamper. She grabbed the nightgown and struggled into it.

Through the door she heard his labored breathing, as though his mouth were pressed to the crack. The door banged again. The wood around the slide bolt gave with a creak, but held.

Regina looked around desperately for something to fight back with. The only razors she had were disposable, the blades locked permanently into a cartridge. She pounded at one with a jar of moisturizer, whining in frustration. The razor shattered, but the cartridge held onto the twin blades.

The door banged, the wood screeched, the screws in the bolt inched outward. Another ear-splitting bang. One screw flew out and landed at her feet.

She ran to the window, pulled it open. It was too narrow for her to get through. And even if she could, it was a straight drop down two stories to the brick and concrete of John's patio.

"John!" she screamed.

With each bang at the door she started. When another screw pulled free from the wood, she screamed for John. Backing up into the corner between the tub and basin, Regina crouched down, the broken razor clutched in her hand. She was to be burned like Donna and Corinne. The noise outside the bathroom door intensified. Her attacker was becoming enraged, growling and grunting as he threw himself against the door. Still she screamed, watching the slide bolt as the last two screws worked out of the door.

An instant before the door came crashing open, Regina threw the jar of moisturizer at the overhead light, smashing bulb and plunging the room into total darkness.

The door slammed into the opposite wall.

She heard her name. Biting down on her lower lip, she crouched into a tight ball, trying not to breathe.

"Regina, damnit, where are you?" Glass crunched underfoot. "Regina?"

John!

She cried out with relief, lunging forward into his arms. They clung to each other, Regina crying, John hushing her as he planted kisses on her tear-drenched face.

"Where is he?" she managed to gasp out.

"Gone."

"Are you sure?"

"Yes. He went out a bedroom window and dropped to the ground below. Don't move, there's glass on the floor." John swept her into his arms and carried her into her bedroom, where he placed her on the bed.

"What happened?" he asked.

"He was in the closet. Waiting."

"Jesus Christ."

"He jumped out . . . and I ran into the bathroom. And then, thank God, you came."

"I heard banging. I came up, knocked, and when I heard you call out to me, I had to run back down and get the pass key from Aunt Anna. Was it Corde?"

"I don't know. He was wearing a stocking over his face. His features were distorted."

"His size?"

"Average. Five-ten or eleven, a hundred and seventy pounds."

"Could it have been Corde?"

"Possibly." She was trembling.

John picked up the phone and began to dial.

"Who are you calling?" she asked.

"The police."

"Wait." She grabbed his hand.

He stared at her.

"Not the police. I don't want the police," she said.

"Why not, for God's sake."

"Even if we know for certain who it is, we don't have any proof. Do you know what they'll say when we accuse a superior judge."

"We won't tell them who we suspect."

"Then why call them? John, you might have to go with them."

"Regina—"

"Right now you're probably the number one suspect. You said so yourself."

"Yes, but—"

"If they took you in for questioning, I'd be alone and he'd come back for me." She realized she sounded paranoid, but she couldn't help it.

"That's why we have to call them. You need protection. More than I can give you."

"They won't protect me. John, Lillard practically accused me of fabricating a killer to boost ratings for 'City Gallery'. I don't want them called," she said, her nails digging into his arms.

"Regina, I don't know what to do."

"Don't leave me." She clung to him, crying. "Just don't leave me!"

He brushed the hair from her face and kissed her. "First thing in the morning I'm calling Wilma."

"Okay. Okay, good," she said absently. She folded back the covers. "Stay with me tonight."

He bent, lifted her in his arms and deposited her under the covers. He touched a spot on her back and she jerked with pain. He looked at her back. Without a word, he went into the bathroom. A moment later he was back with absorbent cotton and hydrogen peroxide. He cleaned the welts carefully, gently. Then he undressed and slid in beside her.

His fingers plucked at a raw edge of the nightgown. "Your nightgown's on inside out."

Regina looked down. Not only was it inside out, it was backwards as well. She thought back to when, in the bathroom, she had frantically crawled into it because she didn't want to die naked. And then she began to laugh. The sexy, melodious quality was still there, but woven in, unmistakably, was an underlying note of hysteria.

7

The anger bordered on rage. When it got to this point he sometimes lost it; lost the control, the orderliness. Things got messy. Perhaps it was just as well the attempt was aborted.

He forced himself to breathe deeply, to regain a degree of discipline.

He had ruined his chance to do what he had gone there to do. He'd had several opportunities to toss the acid, but had tarried, waiting for the perfect chance. It had come when she stood just inches from him, on the other side of the closet door, her body gleaming with moisture from her shower. He had decided, then and there, with lust barely in check, to have this one before splashing her.

And then she had bolted like a frightened doe.

Now, sitting in his car on a dark street several miles away, he thought about what he would do to her next time, how the acid would look as it ate into her pretty flesh. He smiled, imagining it would be much like the dying snails, only better.

It had begun with the snails. Disgusting creatures. As a child he had delighted in pouring salt on the viscous undersides to watch the slimy bodies foam, wither and dissolve before his eyes. Next to feel his wrath were the small

377

animals, neighborhood pets, then anything or anyone who dared give him trouble.

Of the five finalists, this one, Regina, had given him the most trouble. He was an orderly person and she was throwing everything off. She would pay twofold. Unlike Odett and Lake, Van Raven would have no opportunity to reach water and dilute the acid. Before dousing her face with acid, he would render her immobile. At long last he would have his chance to witness, firsthand, the ravishing effects of the chemical.

Twenty-eight

1

Regina slept fitfully. Only when John held her tightly in his arms did she doze.

At seven o'clock she awoke in the circle of those secure arms. Turning her head to look into his face, she saw his eyes were open, watching her. She smiled tentatively. He returned the smile, pulling her closer.

She ran her hand down his side to his hip and then around to his taut belly. His full erection flexed against her hand when she touched it.

She silently rose to her knees and pulled the short gown up her torso and over her head. John rose to his knees facing her. His fingertips moved over her warm, sensitive flesh, caressing. He took her into his arms and kissed her. Within minutes she was lost in an intense pleasure that dulled her awareness of the problems past, present, and future, lost to all but the quiet scream of feelings at the core of her being.

Afterward, lying quietly in each other's arms, Regina finally spoke. "I'd like to try to explain about Garrick."

"Regina, it doesn't matter to me. What you did was not a terrible thing. What's terrible is the burden of guilt you've been carrying with you since your husband died."

"I'd like to try anyway."

He took her hand, kissed the palm. "I'm listening."

"Garrick was Leo's son. From a previous marriage." She heard John's sharp intake of breath, then managed to continue speaking. "He's my age, married with two children. When Leo first learned he had Alzheimer's, he asked Garrick to look out for Kristy and me. And that's what Garrick did. He lived in another state, but when his father started to get violent and uncontrollable, Garrick temporarily moved in with us to help out. Nothing happened between us at that time. Eventually we had to commit Leo to a home. Garrick went back to Washington to his wife and family. Then Leo's health started to deteriorate and we feared he didn't have long to live. Garrick came back and moved in with us again. We spent long periods of time at the hospital with Leo. Many times he came so close to death, only to pull through. This went on for months. Garrick was a great comfort to Kristy and me, as we were to him. And one night after a particularly long bout with Leo, with both of us about to explode from sheer exhaustion and tension, it happened. It was just the one night, but it was to be Leo's last night on earth."

"Do you love this Garrick?" John asked in a strained voice.

"No." She sat up, hugging her knees. "That's what makes it so awful. I don't love him . . . that way. I just fell into bed with him and let my husband die alone."

John folded his arms around her. "Stop it, Regina. You couldn't have known. And even if you did, your husband was gone long before that."

"But what about Garrick? He had a wife . . . children—"

"That was his problem, not yours. You were vulnerable. Both of you were. It happened. You can't let it eat at you any longer. Let it go, Regina."

"I can't. Garrick left his wife for me."

"You have no obligation to the man. None whatso-

380

ever. He's using your guilt and shame to manipulate you. Unless the feeling is mutual . . ."

"It's not." She could only love one man at a time, she thought, and that man was with her now.

"Let it go," he said with finality.

Neither spoke for several moments. Then Regina asked, "John, what did you and Corinne fight about that night? The night she was attacked with the acid?"

"She was angry. Accused me of abandoning her on the most important night of her life. The day of the crowning I got a call that my mother was in trouble. My stepfather was a mean drunk, and when he got tanked up, he took it out on the family. I went to San Jose to bring my mother and sister back to my aunt and uncle's, then rushed back to the city. I arrived at the hotel just as the ambulance was pulling away."

Regina said nothing.

"I've lived with guilt all these years, blaming myself. If I'd been there, at the coronation, maybe I could have prevented what happened to Corinne."

"Oh, John, there's no way you could have known about something like that."

John rose up on an elbow and stared knowingly at her. "I've finally come to realize that," he said. "Now it's time for you to do the same."

She stared at him. Then she nodded, smiling.

At eight o'clock John swept up the glass on the bathroom floor. Then they showered together, soaping, caressing, bringing each other to a breathless climax with nothing beyond an erotic touch.

Back in the kitchen, as Regina poured two mugs of coffee, the phone rang. It was Kristy.

"Did you have a good time?" Regina asked. "Where are you?"

"At Sonya's. We just rolled in. I'll be home in a bit."

"Honey, listen. Can you stay with the Newmans another night or two?"

381

"Yeah, I guess. Why?"

"Someone broke into the apartment last night."

"What'd they take? Did they get my Walkman?"

"It wasn't that kind of break-in."

Silence.

"We think it was the same person who attacked Donna."

"Are you all right, Mom?"

"Yes. John chased him off." Regina looked up at John. Their eyes met.

"Did the police come?"

"No. We didn't call them. Look, Kris—"

"Is John there with you now?"

"Yes."

"Will he stay with you tonight?"

"Yes, he'll stay the night."

A pause. "Okay. Cool."

"Yeah, cool." She smiled at John, raised her eyebrows. "If you need to come home for clothes or anything, make sure I'm here. I don't want you in this apartment alone. You hear?"

"I hear. I won't need anything for a couple days. I can borrow from Sonya, and I have all my makeup and stuff with me."

"Good."

"You sure you're okay, Mom?"

"Honest, honey, I'm fine. Are you working tomorrow?"

"All day."

"I'll come down and explain everything. And I think we should discuss your going to San Diego to stay with Grandma and Grandpa."

"Oh, Mom, I can't. The pageant awards are this Friday night. Have you forgotten?"

She had. And in remembering, she felt a knot in the pit of her stomach. "We'll talk about it tomorrow. Bye, Kris." Regina lowered the receiver.

Looking out the window, she said, "I'm sorry she en-

382

tered that damn contest. I have a bad feeling about it."

"If it *is* Judge Corde, why would he do it?" Regina asked John. But before he could answer, she added, "I mean I see a motive for attacking Corinne—to put Amelia closer to the crown—but why Donna, Tammy and me?"

They sipped coffee, facing each other over the break-fast counter.

"Rejection?"

"Twenty years later? It doesn't make sense."

"It's possible something happened to trigger the latest attacks," John surmised.

"*What?*"

"It's hard to believe someone could attack a woman with acid and then go on to lead an exemplary life for twenty years and—"

"Maybe it wasn't so exemplary," John cut in.

Regina stared at him. "You think he's attacked other women within those years?"

"Why not?"

"Lord."

Regina lifted the phone and dialed. "I'm calling Wilma." She reached the assistant D.A. and explained that she and John were still privately looking into Donna's assault.

"Any new developments, Regina?" Wilma asked.

"No, not really," Regina lied. She considered carefully before asking, "Wilma, what do you know about Judge Corde?"

Silence.

"Wilma?"

"Judge Corde? Why do you ask, dear?"

"John and I have reason to believe that the judge may

. . . well . . ." Regina plowed on, "may know something, or may in some way be involved in what happened to Donna and Tammy."

"What makes you think so?"

"He was a judge in the 1970 beauty pageant and he married one of the finalists."

"Yes, go on."

"Wilma, I . . ."

There was a long pause. Then Wilma said, "We're friends, right?"

"Of course."

"But more important, we're both ethical. You didn't hear this from me, and I'll deny it if you say otherwise, understand?"

"Yes." Regina felt a flutter of excitement. She glanced at John and squeezed his hand.

"Talk to a woman by the name of Marilyn Keane. K-E-A-N-E. She lives in Mill Valley."

"Who is she?" Regina jotted down the name and city. "What does she have to do with Corde?"

"Just contact her. I can't say any more. Are you working with the police?"

"No."

"With John?"

"Yes."

"Be careful. Both of you."

"Wilma . . . ?"

The line was disconnected.

John leaned across the counter, looking at her intently.

"She gave us something, but I'm not sure what."

She dialed directory assistance and asked for the number in Mill Valley, then dialed it.

"Keane residence," a woman said.

"Marilyn Keane, please."

"Who's calling?"

"My name is Regina Van Raven. Are you Ms.

Keane?"

"Marilyn is not taking calls. If you'll leave your number and state the nature of your business, I'll pass it along to her."

"It's rather personal. Would you ask her if she will talk to me, please?"

"Ms. Van Raven, my daughter is recovering from severe post-traumatic stress. She is not receiving any calls." The line was disconnected.

Regina hung up. She told John what the woman had said. "What do you suppose it means?"

"I don't know." He paced the kitchen. "But right now I'd welcome any halfway sensible clue if it would get us closer to nabbing Corde. All we have so far is butcher tape and a shaky alibi."

"This is a long shot, a real long shot," Regina said, picking up the phone again, "but we're desperate, right?" She dialed. "Pandora? Hi, it's Regina Van Raven." They exchanged greetings. "Pandora, you mentioned once you could see certain things about a person by touching something that that person had touched. Is that correct?"

"Correct. It doesn't always work. But my track record is pretty good. There's someone you want to learn about?"

"Yes. Could I impose?"

"It's no imposition. What do you have and when can you bring it by?"

"Well, I don't have anything yet. But soon. Today, perhaps."

"The more personal the item, the stronger the images. Bring it by as soon as you can. If I'm out, the doorman will see that I get it."

"I appreciate this, Pandora."

"Anything I can do to help."

Regina said good-bye and hung up.

"Where are we going to get this 'something'?" John asked.

"At his house."

"It's too risky. He might be there."

"We'll make sure he's not." Regina found Amelia's number in her address book and dialed. The Asian housekeeper answered, then called her employer to the phone.

"Regina," Amelia said tightly, "if it's your intention to call me names or try to make me feel guilty, I'm not in the mood. Donna's my friend too. It's only a two-minute beauty spot. I'm not hurting her or—"

Regina interrupted. "That's why I'm calling. Max wants a personal profile on you. I'm stuck doing it."

"Oh."

"I'd like to get it over and done with. Will you be home in the next hour?"

"Yes, of course."

"And Matthew, will he be at home?"

"Why do you need him?" Amelia asked warily.

"I don't actually. But I thought he might want to put in his two cents. His feelings about his wife's debut in commercial television and so forth."

"He's out. I don't expect him home until late this afternoon. I'd rather we do this without him."

"Whatever. I'm on my way," Regina said and hung up.

They drove to Pacific Heights and parked across the street from the Corde residence. After adjusting the rearview mirror to see behind him down the one-way street, and the side mirror to reflect the Corde house, John slumped down in the seat to wait. Regina, wearing a navy blue jumpsuit and low-heeled shoes, went up to the house. She was shown inside by the housekeeper.

Ushered into the study, Regina hastily scanned the room for something to take. She saw a humidor on the cherry wood desk. A heavy lead crystal ashtray held the butt of a cigar. Regina felt a surge of excitement. There was no doubt in her mind that the cigar had been smoked by the judge. It was on his side of the desk. Regina reached for it.

"Would you care for tea or sherry," Amelia said behind her. "Or perhaps a cigar for your boyfriend. They're not Cuban, I'm afraid. Even Matthew is without connections in some things."

Regina jerked her hand away and spun around. She smiled wryly. "Nothing for me, thanks."

Regina took a slim notepad from her purse. She dug around inside the deep leather bag. "I don't seem to have a pen. May I?" Without waiting for a reply, she pulled the pen out of the holder on the onyx desk set. "Now then, where were you born?"

3

In the rearview mirror John saw the shiny hood ornament above the double Rs on the solid barred grill of a black Rolls-Royce. He slid down farther in the seat. The car turned into the narrow driveway of the Corde estate and disappeared.

John's heart slammed in his chest. Regina was in that house and soon the judge would be in there with her. Amelia was home, but John couldn't be certain she wasn't also involved.

John slid across the seat, opened the passenger door, and climbed out. He wished he had thought to bring his pistol. If it came to a confrontation to save Regina from harm, he'd kill if he had to. He hurried across the street and, staying low, carefully made his way down the long drive. The Rolls sat near a side gate, empty.

What could he do? He feared putting her in jeopardy by showing himself unnecessarily. He glanced at his watch. 10:44. If she wasn't out by 11:00, or if he heard a scream, he would go in after her.

He ran his hand along the glossy paint of the judge's car, his pulse continuing to race out of control. He wondered how Regina would react when she saw Matthew Corde, a man she suspected of mayhem and murder.

4

Regina shot questions at Amelia, giving her no more than a few seconds for each one. She had taken a club chair in front of the desk. Amelia sat behind the desk, tinkering with a silver cigar cutter.

"Well, this should be enough for now," Regina said, closing the notepad and standing.

"I've hardly begun," Amelia said, protesting.

"I'm short of time today. I'll get the rest tomorrow."

"What's the matter with you? You seem very nervous."

Regina gripped the pen until her fingers cramped. "I have a lot on my mind."

"That reminds me," Amelia said, rising. "Are you still of the opinion that Tammy was murdered?"

"No," she lied. "I saw phantoms where there were none. You were right. Tammy was hysterical and she passed it on to me."

"No more warnings?"

"No. None."

"Warnings?" a deep voice said behind her.

A sharp gasp escaped Regina. She whirled to see a balding man wearing red slacks and a white pullover sweater standing in the doorway. Regina felt light-headed.

"Darling, I didn't expect you back so soon." Amelia came around from behind the desk. "You remember Regina?"

"I do. It's been a long time, Mrs. Van Raven. If I remember correctly, I saw you last at the Heart Ball some ten years ago." He extended his hand. "It's always a pleasure."

Regina clasped his hand with the enthusiasm of han-

388

dling a python. It hung heavy in hers. "Thank you, Your Honor."

"Please, none of that. You're a friend of my wife's, therefore a friend of mine." He held onto her hand. "Heavens, your hands are like ice, my dear."

Regina gingerly pulled her hand away. She smiled wanly.

"Excuse me for interrupting, but I've forgotten my cigars. Filthy habit, but unfortunately I can't make it a day without them." He moved to the desk, opened the humidor and extracted four cigars. "Amelia, is my tux out of the cleaners?"

"Your tux?"

"Have you forgotten? I have that judicial banquet at the Embarcadero Hyatt Regency."

"Tonight? Oh, dear, I'm afraid—"

"Don't fret, Amelia, your radiant company is not required this evening."

Amelia looked greatly relieved. "Your tuxedo is in the closet."

Regina took this opportunity to leave. "I must go. Thanks, Amelia, for your cooperation." Regina backed toward the door. "Judge Corde, good to see you again. I'll let myself out." She turned, strode down the hall, and crossed the living room to the foyer. With her heart pounding, her hands trembling, she grabbed the knob and turned. The door refused to open. She shook it, twisted again. A hand with coarse black hair at the knuckles covered her hand on the knob. Regina whirled around and stared into the bulging eyes of Matthew Corde.

His gaze was cool and penetrating. Regina involuntarily drew back.

A thin smile curled his lips. "I believe you have my pen, Regina."

"Your pen?" she replied in a voice that cracked. She looked down at her hand with the notepad and pen.

"Oh, of course. I'm sorry."

His smile widened. He took the pen, turned the dead-bolt and opened the door a crack. "It was my father's. I'm very partial to it."

Regina nodded, then hurried out the door. She didn't slow down until she had passed the Rolls-Royce. A hand came out of nowhere and grabbed her wrist. She nearly screamed before she realized it was John. He pulled her down the driveway, and together they ran across the street and into the station wagon.

John helped her into the passenger seat. Within seconds they had left the Corde house behind.

"Lord oh Lord oh Lord," Regina said under her breath, visibly shaken. "I almost died of fright. I didn't get a damn thing. It was all a terrifying waste of time."

"No it wasn't," John said, tossing a black leather driving glove onto her lap.

5

John, double parked, watched Regina as she talked to the doorman at Pandora Cudahay's high-rise apartment building. Regina handed the gray-uniformed man a bag containing the glove taken from Corde's Rolls. John hadn't been surprised to see a cellular phone in the judge's car. Convenient for making warning calls near the scene, he thought.

Regina joined him in the station wagon. "Pandora's out. The doorman will see she gets the glove. What now?"

"Marilyn Keane."

In Mill Valley, less than a hour later, going to an address found in the phone directory, they arrived at the house of Marilyn Keane. An attractive, gray-haired woman answered the door.

"I told you on the phone that Marilyn was not taking

calls or seeing anyone."

"Mrs. Keane, we just want to ask her a few questions."

"Absolutely not."

"What happened to Marilyn?"

"Mrs. Van Raven, my daughter was attacked by a maniac. She was raped and severely disfigured. It's a miracle she's alive."

"I'm sorry."

"Mother, who is it?" a voice from inside called out.

"No one, honey. Go back to bed."

From behind Mrs. Keane, another woman appeared. With the sun shining on the screen door, John could only make out a tall, slim figure in a long robe.

"I know you," the woman said to John. Her voice was soft and lilting, her manner of speaking unhurried.

"Could you refresh my memory?" he said, squinting to see her inside the dim foyer.

"We met at your first autograph signing. I have both your books."

John was taken aback. He rarely ran into people who recognized him as an author. "Thank you, I'm very flattered."

"You've come about the attack?"

John nodded.

"Come in."

The mother opened the door. Regina and John entered. Marilyn had turned and was walking into the living room. Her long black hair shimmered with blue highlights. She crossed to a peach-and-gray sofa and sat in the corner, gracefully folding her legs up under her. She looked up at her mother, an angelic smile on her face. "Momma," she said, "Would you mind getting our guests iced tea, please."

John found himself staring at the young woman. Marilyn Keane's face was crisscrossed with slashes. Angry, red, weltlike slashes punctuated by hundreds of stitch marks. Despite the jagged slashes, the beauty of her face was apparent.

With radiant sapphire eyes Marilyn looked over at him, smiled sweetly when he self-consciously dropped his gaze. "It's all right. People stare. Most don't mean to be rude."

"Miss Keane, can you tell us what happened?" he asked.

"He broke into my house and attacked me," she said in that soft, even tone. "I was raped and cut." She lightly touched her face, her breasts, and her legs. "He said crazy things. Things that I thought had nothing to do with me. But I understood."

"What do you mean?"

"It was a message. I was the chosen."

"What did he say?"

"He called me by someone else's name. His words were foul, filled with hatred."

"Did you know him?"

"No."

"What was the name he called you?"

"I can't remember."

"Did they catch him?"

She shook her head.

"Would you recognize him if you saw him again?"

Again she shook her head. "He was a black apparition."

Regina bent forward. "You mean he was dressed all in black?"

"He was a black apparition. The evil one. *Satan.*"

Marilyn's mother stood in the arched opening of the dining room with two glasses of iced tea. "Honey, maybe you should rest."

Marilyn ignored her. "He was sent to punish me for my vanity. I was the chosen."

John and Regina exchanged glances.

"Marilyn," John said, "do you know of a man by the

392

name of Matthew Corde?"

She tilted her head, appeared to think, then shook her head negatively.

"Did you receive a warning?"

"Warning?" she asked with a puzzled expression.

"Before the attack. By telephone."

She shook her head.

"Marilyn was on the phone to me when she was attacked," Mrs. Keane said. "Darling, say good-bye to our guests. It's time to rest."

Marilyn unfolded her long legs and rose. John caught a glimpse of red and purple gashes across her thighs. "Thank you for coming. It was kind of you," she said, then left the room.

John and Regina stood. Mrs. Keane set the glasses on the dining room table. "The cuts will heal eventually. Her mind may forever be scarred . . . childlike."

"I'm sorry," John said.

"She said she had been punished for her vanity," Regina said. "What did she mean?"

"My daughter was a contestant in a beauty contest. She's certain that her vanity had something to do with this monster's attack."

"A beauty contest? Which one?"

"A model search, actually. The Miss Golden Gate Model Search."

6

Pandora Cudahay entered her eighteenth-floor apartment. In her spacious, high-ceilinged, Italian marble foyer, she hastily sorted through the day's mail. She would barely have time to shower and change before she had to go out again. She was to give a speech that evening to a group from the San Francisco Society of Psychic Research.

The doorbell rang. Looking through the peephole, she saw the full-cheeked, mustached face of Carl, the building's doorman. She opened the door.

"Sorry to bother you, Miss Cudahay, but I forgot to give this to you." He held up a brown bag with a note clipped to it. "A Regina Van Raven dropped it off earlier. Said you were expecting it."

Pandora took the bag, thanked the doorman, and closed the door. After stepping out of her shoes, she removed the paper clip and opened the bag. She reached in and pulled out a man's black leather glove. She held it in both hands and, closing her eyes, slipped her fingers inside. She stiffened, feeling the vibrations immediately. Violent sensations of rage and dementia, the bizarre thoughts of a madman, as well as the frantic thoughts of his victims, rushed at her. The razor slashing. The cold smile. Those *eyes*. The face that belonged to the glove stood out so clearly in her mind's eye that she opened her eyes to eradicate the brutal, piercing effect. Her knees suddenly felt weak. She lowered herself onto the brocade cushion of a settee.

"My God," she whispered. She sensed the horrible violence inside the man. Something told her his fury was intensifying day by day, growing like a cancer, eating away what conscience he may have originally possessed. Soon he would be out of control.

Pandora rose unsteadily to her feet and crossed the living room to the phone. She dialed Regina's number and cursed silently when a recorded message came on. At the beep, unable to bridle the tremor in her voice, she said, "Regina, it's Pandora Cudahay. Call me, it's urgent. I'll be at home until six-thirty." Barely audible, she added, "I saw his face."

He dialed, patiently listened to Regina Van Raven's recorded message, and, at the tone, pressed the two digit-code that would retrieve any messages on the machine. He heard the message from Pandora Cudahay. The words "I saw his face" pounded in his head. Pandora Cudahay. Who was this woman? The name was familiar. Cudahay? And then it came to him: the psychic from the "City Gallery" show. Was it possible that through telepathic means it was his face she had seen? Impossible. He refused to believe in such garbage. But, he told himself disconcertingly, he could not afford to take any unnecessary chances.

He reached for the phone book, turned to the Cs, and ran his finger down a column. There were three Cudahays. He dialed the first number. After only two rings the phone was answered. The woman, sounding breathless, said hello several times. He hung up. He had heard enough to know hers was the voice on Van Raven's answering machine. He noted the address, then left the house.

8

At 6:38, no longer able to wait for Regina's call, Pandora slipped on a white angora cardigan, tucked her clutch purse under her arm, picked up the folder containing her notes for tonight's speech, and walked to the apartment door.

Since touching the glove, she'd had an unrelenting premonition of danger and doom. So overwhelming were these ominous vibrations, that her stomach quaked and her head throbbed. As her fingers touched the doorknob, a shower of black images exploded in her head. The razor slashing wildly. Those sadistic eyes. That horrid grin. A wave of dizziness passed over her, and she wondered if she would be able to make the presentation after all. None of her visions had ever been this intense, this internal.

Stop! she told herself. Put it from your mind. The killer was a madman, but Regina would survive. This she strongly sensed.

Before she could change her mind and cancel her speaking commitment, Pandora grabbed the doorknob and twisted, pulling the door open quickly.

The razor came at her from the other side of the threshold. Pandora's first stunned impression was that it was suspended in air, slashing at her throat on its own volition. But then she realized through a haze of terror that the blackness on the other side of the razor was human, and he was pushing his way inside.

Her scream was nothing more than a foamy gurgle of blood.

9

On the way back to the city Regina could hear John talking, but she found it difficult to concentrate on his words. After a time he too fell silent. They stopped for an early dinner at an Italian restaurant on Redwood Highway. In a secluded booth, over eggplant rigatoni that Regina was too preoccupied to enjoy, they talked quietly, their tone somber.

"Marilyn Keane had never heard of Corde," she said.

"There must be a connection. Why would Wilma give you her name?"

"It may have nothing to do with Corde. Wilma knew Marilyn was a contestant in a beauty contest and that she was attacked, not with acid, but in a manner just as effective." Regina sipped her red wine. "Objective was to disfigure. A coincidence?"

"The attacker raped this victim. And from what Marilyn said, he appeared crazed, cursing and striking out in a frenzy. The M.O. *is* different."

"The woman in Novato," Regina said, rubbing her aching temple as she stared off in the distance, "she was slashed. Her throat cut."

John was silent.

Back in the car, John hesitated before starting it. He reached over, slipped his hand into hers, and squeezed. "You're worried about Kristy, aren't you?"

She looked at him and saw deep caring in his light blue eyes. She returned the pressure of his hand and nodded. "I've denied her very little over the years," she said solemnly. "Fortunately, she asked for little. But this time I have to renege on a promise. Kristy will drop out of this contest, or by God, I'll send her to my parents until this bastard is caught."

"What about yourself? He's after you, you know."

"Do you want me to go?"

"I don't want anything to happen to you. I couldn't stand it if I . . ." John pulled her to him. He cupped her face and kissed her. His lips, tender at first, turned fierce. Regina sensed in his kiss an urgency of bonding rather than desire, and she felt a longing of such absolute magnitude that she moaned low in her throat.

"Nothing will happen to me as long as I'm with you," she whispered in his ear.

10

Forty-five minutes later they crossed the Golden Gate Bridge and drove to Twin Peaks. They found a parking space on the next block and walked to Pandora Cudahay's high-rise. At the double glass doors, the doorman asked who it was they wished to see.

"Cudahay, 1806. I'm Regina Van Raven. I dropped off a glove, earlier, remember?"

The doorman smiled. "Yes so you did. I took it upstairs myself and gave it to her."

"Could you ring her apartment, please?"

He lifted the phone, pressed buttons. Regina could hear it ringing. "Sorry, no answer. She must be out."

"She left no message for me?"

He shook his head.

"Any idea when she'll he back?" John asked.

"No, sir. Though she's not one to stay out late."

"Do you see her leave?"

"No, sir, I did not."

"May I use your phone?" Regina asked.

The doorman stepped aside.

Regina called home, coded the machine, and listened to Pandora's tremulous message. She disconnected, went through the same procedure again, then handed the phone to John. As he listened to the same message, his gaze locked with Regina's.

"Corde?" she said softly.

John hung up the phone. To the doorman he said, "Did a man in a black Rolls-Royce come here?"

The doorman chewed his moustache a moment, then shook his head. "There have been no Rolls-Royces here tonight. And no one, aside from yourselves, has called on Miss Cudahay today."

"C'mon," John said to Regina, grabbing her hand and pulling her in the direction of her car.

"Where are we going?" she said, running to keep up.

"Wilma's."

Minutes later they were in the Marina, knocking on the door of a large Victorian house. They had come unannounced, yet Wilma Greenwood greeted John and Regina as though she had expected them. She settled them in the den, then listened to what they had to say regarding their visit with Marilyn Keane.

"Why did you send us there?" John asked.

Wilma said nothing for a minute. Finally, looking from one to the other, she replied, "First tell me everything you know. Don't leave out a thing."

John and Regina took turns talking. Twenty minutes later they were recapping that day's events: going to the judge's house and taking the glove; the psychic; Marilyn Keane; the message from Pandora on Regina's answering machine.

"And then we came to you," Regina finished.

Wilma stood and began to pace the room, her fingers plucking at the strand of pearls at her throat. She stopped at the window and gazed out. "Judge Corde is capable of doing everything you've told me."

"You suspected he had something to do with the attack on Marilyn Keane, didn't you?" John said.

Wilma nodded.

"And yet you did nothing?"

She began to pace again. "You have to understand that the courthouse grapevine is phenomenal. There are spies and loose-lips everywhere. To investigate a judge is to alert him that he is under suspicion."

"And you feared that if he suspected you were on to him, he'd stop before you could prove anything?" Regina said.

"I wish that were all. It's much more complicated than that." Wilma returned to her desk.

"Someone else was suspicious of—." John stood, an expression of revelation on his face. "It was *you*, wasn't it? You were the one planting the clues and directing the show, prodding, keeping us on the right track? The anonymous informer."

Wilma dropped her gaze, toyed with a crystal paperweight on the desk blotter.

"I should have guessed when you gave Regina Marilyn Keane's name. You suspected him all along, yet for some unfathomable reason, which I damn well want to hear, you wouldn't get involved? Christ, we have here a regular Watergate 'Deep Throat,'" John said, his voice rising angrily. "What is this shit?" He slammed his fist on the desk. "Wilma, I'm a suspect in the acid attacks. Regina is an intended victim—"

"I know," she said quietly. "That's why I decided to use you. You both had motives for wanting to find the perpetrator, and I took advantage of those motives. I'm sorry, but I didn't know what else to do."

"Why the hell didn't you just tell the cops that you suspected Corde? What gave you the right to withhold information? To play cat and mouse? To jeopardize lives? Innocent women are being slashed, burned. Regina could've been burned—worse, she could've been killed."

"I realize that now. It's true, I was wrong, but I had my reasons. Unfortunately, when you hear them, you won't think any better of me. I kept quiet to save my own skin. I hoped that you and Regina could flush Corde out. I wanted him found out. Yet it was essential I be far removed from any investigation."

Wilma pulled in a deep breath, exhaled slowly. "For Matthew Corde it started many years ago with bribery, blackmail, and extortion. His victims are women. I, regrettably, was one of the first."

Regina and John waited.

"I wasn't long out of law school. Corde and I were assistants, working in the public defender's office. I did something that could have resulted in my disbarment. I fell for this guy, a land developer, and . . . well, I destroyed evidence that could have convicted him on a tax evasion charge. Although it's not relevant, and certainly doesn't change anything, I'm positive Corde had me set up. He offered an ultimatum. Become his sex slave or suffer the consequences. I'll spare you the sordid details."

"The other victims?" John asked.

"Young, attractive women, always. Women about to go before him in court with charges ranging from simple misdemeanor to felony. He knew which ones had the most to lose by a jail-term decision. Women with children, with good jobs or reputations, first offenders. No decent woman wants to spend time in jail for a stupid mistake. And God knows he had the power to put them there."

"The woman in the newspaper clipping?" John asked.

"Yes, Carmenita Flores. A lovely girl in her late twenties. She was scheduled for trial on a health insurance fraud charge. Her two-year-old daughter had a congenital heart defect and the medical bills were astronomical." Wilma went on. "Judge Corde gave her probation."

"They struck a deal between themselves," John said matter-of-factly.

"Precisely. Sad thing is she would probably have gotten probation no matter who the judge."

"Isn't what he did illegal?"

"Not if he doesn't take money. It's more a matter for the ethics board."

"So why did he kill her?"

"I wish I knew. Though I suspect she didn't want to play his nasty game any longer." Wilma's face was drawn and pale as she twisted at the string of pearls. "I'm scared to death of the man. He'd kill me in a second if he suspected I talked to the authorities about him." There was a popping sound. A shower of pearls danced across the stained desk blotter and bounced to the floor. Wilma ignored them.

No one said anything for several drawn-out moments. Then, almost as though she was talking to herself, Regina said, "How do you go after a judge?"

"It's not easy. Blackmail victims don't talk. There were no witnesses in the Flores murder, no physical evidence, either. And in Marilyn Keane's case . . . well, you talked to her. She thinks she was attacked by the devil."

"There must be something we can do," Regina said.

John stood. "The man is after Regina. He's already made at least one attempt to get to her."

Wilma sighed heavily. "You're right. I can't stay out of it any longer. And I no longer have the luxury of trying to build a solid case against him. There's too much at stake now. Give me tonight to get what I have together. First thing tomorrow morning I'll go to Detective Lillard and fill him in. It's not likely Corde will do anything crazy before morning."

"Should we warn Amelia?"

"We can't take that chance. She may be in on it and she'd only tip him off."

"I still have to talk to Pandora Cudahay," Regina said. "She saw his face."

"I can't use psychic visions in a court of law, but I'd be interested to know what she saw. *Who* she saw. Let me know when you hear from her."

Regina nodded. She rose to stand beside John.

Wilma, a weak smile on her lips, said, "You two make a nice couple. Take care of her, John."

His arm went around Regina protectively. "I intend to."

Twenty-nine

1

At 6:30 in the morning, careful not to wake John sleeping beside her, Regina slipped quietly from bed, went into the kitchen, and called Kristy at Sonya's.

"Kristy, you have to get out of that contest."

"What?" Kristy said, her voice shrill.

"Sonya, too."

"Mom, I don't believe you. The winner will be announced in five days."

"I don't care if it's today. You're in danger. One of the contestants was attacked and—"

"I know that."

"What do you mean you know that? How could you know?"

"The police interviewed all the contestants. It was a random assault. The pageant committee said so, and so did the police."

"You knew and you didn't tell me?" Regina tried to control her voice.

"I know how protective you can be, Mom. You were already paranoid just remembering *your* pageant. This has nothing to do with that. No one else has been hurt."

"Damnit, Kristy, you listen to me. There's a madman out there and he's hurting, and now killing, women. I know who it is—." A hand touched the back of her neck.

Regina gasped and spun around.

John stood behind her. He reached out, touched her face apologetically.

"Mom? Mom, are you all right?"

Regina inhaled deeply. She smiled at John, patted his hand. "I'm all right. Look, Kristy, just promise me you won't do anything until we have a chance to talk. That goes for Sonya too. I'll meet you at The Farm House at noon."

"Okay, sure, Mom."

"Promise?"

"Yes, I promise."

She hung up. The phone rang under her fingers. It was Wilma.

In a solemn tone she said, "Regina, I'm afraid I have bad news."

"He's killed again?"

"Yes." Wilma paused. "Your psychic friend."

"Pandora?"

"Yes."

"Oh, no."

"She was found in the foyer of her apartment. Killed with a—like the Flores woman."

Regina felt weak, sick to her stomach. Pandora had died trying to help her. She was caught in a swirl of emotions: anger, sorrow, fear, and guilt. *This maniac had to be stopped before another innocent woman died.*

She felt John's hand on her shoulder and she squeezed it.

"Lillard will want to talk with both of you today. Can you make yourselves available?"

"Yes. Yes, of course," Regina said. "Wilma, does he know our suspicions about Corde?"

"We'll go over all that when you get here. I'll call."

Regina hung up. John turned her around, folded her in his arms and held her securely, gently swaying as he stroked her hair and back.

"A hundred and fifty," the jeweler said, putting down his loupe.

"You mean fifteen hundred?" Amelia said.

"I mean one hundred and fifty dollars."

"But those are diamond earrings."

"Cubic zirconia is what they are."

Amelia was too stunned to speak. Matthew had never given her imitations before. There had to be a mistake.

She had come out into the damp, drizzly morning to sell the earrings. As always, she was prepared to take much less than their actual worth. She was unprepared to discover they were practically worthless.

"They retail for approximately a hundred and fifty." He handed the case with the earrings back to her.

She took them absently. The earrings had come from the same high-priced jewelry store where Matthew bought all her jewelry. The "love gifts," always genuine. Why cheap imitations this time? He could certainly afford the real thing.

"A pawn shop might give you twenty, twenty-five dollars for them," the jeweler said.

"Hardly worth the effort, is it?" she said snidely.

The man shrugged.

She shoved the case into her gray lizard handbag and strode from the store. Out on the street she stood at the curb, nonplussed, oblivious to the light drizzle, wondering what to do next. It was half-past ten. She had an appointment with Max Conner at the station at four, without Nolan.

Nolan was of no use to her any longer. He had called her that morning, obviously shaken, to say that Donna, released from the hospital the day before, had suggested a trial separation. Without his hold on Donna, Amelia realized, the man had no ground to stand on. She had gone around him to the executive producer. Max would be a pushover.

She walked to the end of Maiden Lane, stood on the sidewalk taking in the green of Union Square with its hundreds of greedy pigeons and the surrounding chic boutiques and department stores. She sighed audibly. After the rejection on the massage table, Matthew, naturally, had withheld the credit card. And there was no telling how long before he would relent and give it to her. There was only one sure way to dissolve his anger and that was to play the victim. The "victim"—where she allowed herself to be bound, gagged, and totally at the mercy of his sick sexual appetite—was the role she consented to only when the stakes were extremely high.

Well, perhaps just one more time.

3

At eleven on the dot, Amelia arrived back home. As she entered the house, she wondered if there was a way she could get into Matthew's room in the basement. The room where he kept his secret goodies was as secure as Fort Knox. She imagined it held countless coin collections and other things of great value, else why would he forbid her access?

In the foyer she sat on the mohair bench and pulled off her wet boots.

"Kelly!" she called out to the housekeeper.

"I gave her the day off."

Startled, her head snapped up. Her husband stood looking down from the second floor banister.

"Matthew, you're home?" she said, her voice high and breathy.

"Trial was postponed. Where have you been?"

"Window shopping."

"In the rain?"

"It's just a figure of speech, darling. I was browsing in Saks."

"Find anything?"

"Many things. Unfortunately, I am without funds."

"Perhaps something could be arranged."

She smiled broadly, disguising her true feelings. "I'm glad you're home."

"Are you?"

"Of course."

"How glad?"

"How glad do you want me to be?" Her tone was sultry, teasing.

His eyes stared into hers. One side of his mouth pulled into a grin. "Why don't you come up and we'll find out?"

He was offering her a chance to right things between them. The option she had considered when she discovered the earrings were fake was, conveniently, being presented to her. This could be her last opportunity before she left him. The victim game never failed to elevate his mood and loosen his purse stings. And by God, she swore, this time when she got hold of that credit card she'd max it out. That would teach the bastard to give her phony jewels.

She continued to smile as she crossed the parquet foyer, climbed the curved staircase, and walked ahead of him into their bedroom. Without a word, she went to her dresser drawer, took out several pairs of panty hose, and handed them to him.

The look on his face was both surprised and pleased. She rarely submitted voluntarily to the victim role.

He grinned, leaned against the wall, and waited.

She began to undress.

A moment later, completely nude, she turned to him, an inquiring look on her face. She waited for him to tell her which outfit she was to wear: the garter belt, black hose, and spiked heels, or the long flannel nightgown, or the plain cotton dress with no underwear and bare feet, or the child's chintz pinafore with knee socks and Mary Jane shoes?

Matthew grinned again. "Just as you are."

He never started with her entirely naked. Although she was taken aback, she feigned nonchalance, nodded, and moved to the bed.

On the bed she held out her hands, fingers clasped, waiting for him to tie the hose around her wrists. He did, jerking the knot tight. She winced but said nothing.

"Lie on your back and be very still," he instructed.

When she had done as he said, he left the room. She heard his steps going down the stairs. A few minutes later he returned upstairs, went into the bathroom, then finally joined her again.

She hadn't moved. She watched him, wondering why he was being so quiet.

He smiled at her.

A flicker of apprehension passed over her.

He sat on the edge of the bed and took the other pair of panty hose, made a slip knot, then quickly worked it over her head before she could protest. She tried to sit up, but he firmly pushed her back down.

"Matthew, don't do that. You know I can't stand anything around my neck."

"Except expensive jewelry. Don't talk and don't move or you'll spoil it for me." He tied the end of the nylon stocking to a slat on the headboard. He reached into his pocket and brought out a straight razor.

"What — ?"

"Sssh."

He lifted her bound arms above her head. Her flat, smooth stomach heaved.

In the past he'd used a whip made of soft strips of cloth, or occasionally a fabric belt or hairbrush. He'd never brought out something as lethal and terrifying as the blue steel razor.

He opened the razor and moved it toward her. Amelia bucked, tried to get up. The nylon around her throat squeezed tight, making her cough.

He slipped a finger under the knot and loosened it. "Be careful," he said. "You'll choke yourself."

408

"Matthew, release me . . . now! I don't want to play this sick game of yours."

"Not even for jewels and furs?"

"No. Now free me."

He laid a velvet box on her abdomen, the lid open. Inside she saw the glittering earrings. "These were in your handbag," he said. "Why were they in your handbag?"

She swallowed over the tightness in her throat. "I took them to the jeweler for repairs," she lied. "The clip on one is too tight, it pinches."

"You didn't take them to sell?"

Her fear intensified. "Of course not," she responded indignantly. "Why would I want to sell my new earrings?"

"Why indeed."

He left the room again. She thought she heard him in the den midway down the hall. He returned to the bedroom carrying a document and a portable tape recorder. He sat on the edge of the bed, pressed the "play" button, and watched her intently. Amelia recognized her voice immediately, but the shock came when she realized the other voice belonged to Fletcher Kincade. The two voices filled the silent void. Amelia's resonant voice was saying, ". . . Eighty thousand and it took me nineteen endless years to accumulate it dollar by miserable dollar. . . . The fool never suspected."

She looked at him, forcing her face to remain stoic. But beneath her bare breasts her heart pounded. She said nothing, only stared at him.

Corde pressed the stop button.

"Have you nothing to say?" he asked.

"You hired a detective?"

"What does it matter. I want the money back. All of it."

"It was my money. Money I saved and invested."

"Money stolen from me. The jewelry, the credit cards, the out-and-out thievery of cash from my wallet. Imagine, a woman of your class and caliber, going through her husband's pocket like a common fishwife. It's all on this tape." He tapped the recorder. "So where is it?"

Amelia stared silently at him.

"Return it to me and I'll forget it ever happened. You have my word. You'll not be punished or made to suffer in any way. I'll even give you an allowance so you won't feel the need to lower yourself to such a level of degradation."

She shook her head. He was lying. He would never forgive or forget. But what difference did it make, she had no money to return to him.

"And if you really want that position at the TV studio," he continued, "I won't object. Ahh, I see by your expression that you don't believe me."

"No.

Matthew unfolded the document in his hand and placed it in front of her to read. "It's our premarital agreement. I'm willing to tear it up, Amelia."

"Why?" she asked suspiciously.

"Isn't it obvious? I don't want to lose you. I'm willing to change, but I must have back the money you took from me . . . as a sign of good faith. For future trust."

Would he do all he said? she wondered. Let her work, give her an allowance, void the premarital agreement? Even if she had the money to give back, she asked herself, would she want to stay with him now?

"Fletcher swindled me. Took the money and ran."

After several moments of silence Corde began to laugh.

"We could get it back," she said, a note of hopeful desperation in her voice. "You hired a detective to follow us, so you must know where he is."

"Oh, I know where he is." He continued to laugh.

"What are you laughing at?"

"I have my money back. All of it, and with interest, I might add."

She glared at him.

"You invested well with the money you stole from me. Blue chip stocks and the like. I was impressed. Unfortunately your last investment was a bad one. Bad for you, good for me."

Then she realized what he had done. There was only

410

one way he could have gotten both the taped conversation and his money back. "You hired him to set me up," she said flatly.

"Precisely. Your lover is now on the East Coast, happily spending a handsome fee which, my dear, came from you."

Corde fast-forwarded the tape. Amelia's voice came through the recorder again. ". . . detest him. I loathe the feel of his hands on my body. Thank God he can't last long. Yet brief as his touch is, it's sheer torture. Now you, my dear Fletch, know how to make love to a woman the proper way, the lasting way."

She jerked her head, forgetting the noose around her neck. It squeezed, making her gasp.

She glared at him with hatred and contempt. There could be no living with him now.

"You fucking bastard," she managed to croak out.

4

John and Regina met Wilma Greenwood in the detective department at police headquarters.

"Detective Lillard has been detained at the morgue," Wilma said. "He'll be here as soon as he can."

"I'm supposed to meet Kristy at noon," Regina said.

"I think John and I can handle it ourselves if it comes to that. John?"

"Sure, no problem."

Regina and John sat on contour plastic chairs holding hands while Wilma paced the floor, sipping coffee from a Styrofoam cup. She looked harried, as though she'd had little sleep, and Regina thought she knew what her friend must be going through.

Regina synchronized her watch to the large clock on the wall. 11:27.

They waited.

He looked at her, wondering at the strangeness of her face. It was noticeably changed from just a moment ago . . . before he had struck her with the back of his hand. The cheekbone, eye and nose were beginning to swell out of shape, distorting her beautiful features. It was a shame to mess up such an exquisite face, especially since he had to look at it, but she should never have called him a foul name.

Her voice on the tape played on. This was the same cassette tape he had listened to in his car the night he viciously attacked the Keane woman, the woman who was so very much like Amelia. That night, in a black rage, with the tiny bird fluttering above him, it was Amelia's face and body he slashed with the straight razor.

His wife was crying softly. Not so defiant now, he thought. But her tears only heightened his cruel temper. He wanted her to beg and plead, grovel and crawl to him on hands and knees—if and when, that is, he decided to free her from her bonds.

He had thought she was different from the others when all along she was not only the same but worse. She'd been the only one to take from him. The cool, materialistic bitch deserved to be punished for her years of lies, deceptions, and infidelities.

She had thought she could live in high style under his roof, steal his money to buy a young cock and a fashionable business, and then walk out on him. But he had again knocked her back down and there was more to come. The *best* was yet to come.

He hadn't meant to reveal his hand so soon. But Amelia had been exercising her independence and he feared she would slip away from him, cheating him out of the coup de grace. The reason, the only reason, behind the acid assaults was to set up Amelia. The others were only pawns, to be sacrificed, to cover and protect him, affording a motive, however bizarre, for what he was about to do to his wife.

The attack in the parking garage had been a ruse — to scare her, to establish a pattern of mayhem against the pageant finalists, and to remove suspicion from Amelia. But it had all gone for naught when the bitch chose to keep quiet about the attack.

The next time would be for real. But Van Raven must come before Amelia, establishing the proper order — the final order as it had played out in the 1970 pageant.

He had her where he wanted her now, off guard, terrified to be found out by him: without her security nest egg. She would beg for forgiveness and an opportunity to start over. He would pretend to relent, granting her all the conditions he had promised. And then, some months later, when her confidence had returned, when she had secured a solid place in the TV world, "the splasher" would strike again. Corde smiled at the image. Let her try to hold a position in television with her face a ravaged horror. Disfigurement, for Amelia, would be the ultimate hell.

A delicious surge of elation washed over Corde. Since early childhood, with his grim, bug-eyed countenance, he suffered abuse and cruelty from those around him. Too weak to defend himself outright, he learned to attack through acts of terrorism. Time was of no consequence. In fact, the longer he waited for retaliation, the sweeter the reward. His first act of revenge, at the age of five, was directed at the family cat, for scratching him. Several weeks later he doused the cat with lighter fluid before tossing a match to it. Then came the girl in his fourth grade class who repeatedly called him Mr. Toad. One frigid day after school she unknowingly donned a death cap of black widows. And that was only the beginning.

Matthew tenderly stroked the swelling flesh on the side of his wife's face. "I'm sorry, my dear," he said with solicitude. "I'm afraid I lost my head. To have my wife call me such vile names, well . . ."

Amelia looked up at him. Her dark sapphire eyes were unreadable, though he thought he saw a glint of remorse, perhaps even hopelessness.

"Now, what should I do with you? How should we resolve this problem?"

She brought her bound hands up, wiped a tear from her face.

"You don't deserve a second chance, but I do care for you, Amelia. Convince me that I should be charitable."

"I'm leaving you," she said quietly.

That was the last thing he had expected to hear. Where were the pleas, the conditions, the promises to toe the line? After all, she wasn't getting any younger and she no longer had money of her own.

He was surprised by his next words. "I shall be gracious and repeat my first offer. An allowance, the right to work, and the nullification of the premarital agreement."

"Untie me." Her tone was hard.

"Not until this is settled," he said sharply. It wasn't going according to plan. It made him livid when his well-laid schemes went awry.

She turned her head away, the nylon rope straining at her throat.

"I won't stand for this . . . this insubordination, this lack of respect," he responded harshly. "Who do you think you are? You're nothing but a one-time beauty queen. A beauty queen who, incidentally, won by default. Not even my influence could assure you the title. But I married you, made you something. Without me you are nothing. Nothing!"

Her head snapped around. She glared at him. "I'd rather be nothing than married to you. What I said on that tape was true. I can't stand your touch, your voice. I can't stand the sight of you. Do you know what you are? Laughable, that's what!" she screamed out, laughing. "Utterly laughable!"

In a rage he grabbed her by the shoulders and shook. Her laughter changed to gasps as the pantyhose around her throat pulled taut. A moment later her eyes began to register the fear he so wanted and needed. "Laughable?"

414

With one hand he ripped at his own clothes, discarding them. He climbed on the bed and fell on her, entering her with force.

She twisted, struck out with her bound hands. Her fists pounded his face. He heard a crunching sound as pain exploded in his face. Rage and pain blinded him momentarily. He swore, pulled her forward, putting more strain on the hose around her neck. He crushed her to him, pinning her arms between them as he thrust into her. With his face inches from hers, blood now flowing from his broken nose onto her lips and chin, he said, "You're lying. Tell me you're lying. Tell me!"

Amelia's mouth gaped open, her jaw working frantically, oblivious to the blood dripping from his nose, mingling with her saliva. Her eyes were wide and staring into his.

"You whore! From the beginning I stood behind you. I knew it was you sabotaging the other contestants. Not only did I keep quiet, I helped by taking care of Corinne for you. I would have done the same to Regina, or anyone who stood in your way, don't you see that you owe me? Don't you see? Tell me you love me! Tell me!"

She continued to struggle, refusing to answer him. After a while he hoped she wouldn't say what he demanded. He reveled in her panic and fear. He was locked in an intense paroxysm of pleasure, with her naked body in his arms, her head bent back exposing the graceful line of her slim neck, her eyes pleading now, begging him to . . . to what? — to allow her to love him, to please him, to worship him? Plenty of time for that, he told himself, his body thrilling to her helplessness. He stared back at her, waiting for the pleasure to ease so he could release her and let her say what he wanted to hear, but the pleasure seemed only to increase with each passing moment, making it impossible to let her go. At last he cried out at the explosive release, squeezing her in viselike arms.

She stiffened, shuddered, then collapsed limply in his arms, her eyes still open, though no longer glowing with fear.

He released her. She dropped heavily to the bed. With haste he groped at the panty hose cutting deep into her throat and attempted to slide a finger under it. The flesh-colored nylon resisted. Desperate now, he shook her, called her name. Her head lolled strangely.

Nooo, it can't be. She couldn't have cheated him. Not after all he'd done to make it perfect.

With the straight razor he slashed at the length of tightly stretched hose between the headboard and Amelia's neck. He clawed at the noose, loosening it, whimpering, cursing.

The panty hose was off, but still she lay limp, lifeless, his blood bright against her ashen skin.

No, goddamn you. Wake up!

And then he realized the bitch had outwitted him after all. He had wanted to burn her face, make her live out her natural life with a hideous deformity as Corinne Odett had done. But she had forced him to kill her.

He shook her again.

It was all the fault of that cunt, Van Raven. It was she who had spoiled everything. By thwarting his efforts, she had thrown the plan out of kilter. Van Raven was to be before Amelia. Now, without Amelia, what reason did he have to continue?

What reason indeed? It was all her fault. He couldn't let Van Raven get away with this. He had to punish her. She, above all, would pay the ultimate price.

And he knew exactly what that price would be.

Stanching the flow of blood from his nose with a hand-kerchief, he hurried to the den, opened a folder on his desk, ran his finger down the roster of Golden Gate Model Search contestants until he found the one he was looking for. There were two phone numbers listed. He picked up the telephone and dialed.

416

At 11:55 Kristy stood under the awning in front of The Farm House. She watched for the gray-and-black Oldsmobile, the one her chaperon, Mrs. Nash, drove, and hoped that her mother wouldn't arrive first.

Her mother had insisted she not do anything regarding the contest until they'd had a chance to talk, and she rarely disobeyed a direct order, but jeeze, how could she possibly know she would get a call to do a last-minute photograph session? Her mother, who was obviously being paranoid, just didn't know how important this was to her. No one wanted to hurt the contestants. What could happen at a photo session? As soon as she arrived at the photographer's studio, she'd call. Her mom would be pissed, but she'd get over it.

The parking lot roiled with driving pellets of rain. Kristy hoped the humidity wouldn't friz her hair.

Wearing jeans, sweater, denim jacket, and high-top Reeboks, she was told that everything she needed would be supplied by the studio. She hoped so, because she had no time to go home and change; besides, she'd promised she wouldn't go back to the apartment alone.

A dark car pulled up. Someone called her name. She lifted the umbrella and ran to the car. The door opened.

Halfway inside, Kristy hesitated.

"It's all right, Miss Van Raven. It appears I'm to be your chaperon this afternoon. Mrs. Nash had something of a crisis regarding her dog. Everyone is running behind. Hurry, you'll be soaked."

Kristy climbed in and closed the door.

"So how are you, my dear?"

"Fine, Your Honor."

"No need to be so formal. Today, Miss Van Raven, as far as you're concerned, I am neither a superior judge nor a contest judge. I am just a pageant official helping out in a pinch."

Suddenly, without knowing why, she sensed a pinprick of fear. "Sir, I forgot to call my mother to tell her where I'll be. I think I better do that first. It'll only take me a minute."

Matthew Corde pulled away. "Relax, child, you can call her from the studio."

Kristy watched the wipers on the old car sweep across the windshield. They made a sad, mewling sound.

She looked for the door handle. There was none.

She hugged herself and shivered.

7

Regina glanced at her watch as she pushed open the restaurant door. 12:06. She was always punctual, usually early, but the rain-slick streets had tied up traffic and caused at least two fender benders.

In her calico uniform, Sonya was leaning over an empty table just inside the door when Regina arrived.

"Hi, Sonya. Is Kristy in the back?"

"She had to leave, Regina. She told me to tell you she'd call you here."

"Where did she go?"

Sonya busied herself clearing a table.

"Sonya, where did she go?" Regina heard a rising hysteria in her voice.

"A photo session."

"What photo session? For the model search?"

Sonya nodded, looked away.

Regina clutched at her purse nervously. She whirled around, exasperated. "Why? Why would she do this after begged her not to?"

Sonya shrugged her shoulders, looking miserable.

"Where is she?"

"I don't know."

"Who called her?"

"One of the officials. She got the call about a half hour ago and ten minutes later she was gone."

"Her car's out there. Did Mrs. Nash pick her up?"

Sonya shrugged.

Regina went to the pay phone, found the number for the chaperon in her purse, deposited coins, and dialed. There was no answer.

Regina was returning to Sonya when she looked up to see the girl gesturing wildly at her from the cashier counter. She held up the phone receiver.

Regina hurried over

"It's for you, Regina," Sonya said. "He says it's urgent."

Regina grabbed the phone. Her pulse, sounding like ocean waves roaring in her ears, made it difficult for her to hear. "Hello? Hello?"

"I have your daughter. I will rape, torture, then kill her if you say a word to anyone. No police. Nobody. Do you understand?"

"Yes," she whispered, feeling faint. She cleared her throat repeated louder, "Yes, I understand."

"Go home. Wait for my call."

"I want to hear her voice."

The connection was broken.

8

Matthew Corde hung up the phone. He looked down at Amelia's pale body, the blood from his broken nose drying on her face and throat. He felt a renewed surge of rage. She was still beautiful even in death. She had beaten him. The fucking bitch had beaten him.

But the other one wouldn't.

He had to get the body out of his bed. Out of his house. There would be the other bodies to dispose of also, but he'd worry about that later.

He dressed Amelia in slacks, cashmere sweater, and the boots she had worn that morning. He omitted the bra be-

419

cause it was too difficult to put on. He doubted that anyone other than himself would know she would never be caught dead braless. He chuckled at the unintended pun. With an effort, he carried her dead weight down the stairs, through the large house, and out into the attached three-car garage. He propped her already stiffening form against the Mercedes. Then he went to a shelf containing cleaning, garden, and pool supplies. From the back he pulled out the plastic container of sulfuric acid, poured it into a mason jar, then cautiously carried the jar back to where his dead wife sat.

He wondered if the acid would react effectively on dead flesh. It had to if his plan was to work.

Standing now before her body, Corde positioned the head so the face would take a direct hit. He knelt.

"My only regret, my love, is that you're not alive to experience this," he said to the frozenlike head. "How you would have carried on to have your exquisite face destroyed."

He dashed the acid into her face, aiming directly at the milky eyes. The oily liquid made contact and began to run down her face. Nothing happened at first. Then her alabaster skin began to redden and change.

Never having seen the acid eat into flesh, Corde stared, fascinated. With the others he had heard the gasps, followed by the shrill disbelieving screams, but until now he could only imagine the horror that his elixir had created.

It was something he would like to see again — on living flesh.

Thirty

1

Regina had run out of the restaurant without a word to Sonya. Minutes later, at home, pacing the floor, her raincoat open and slapping at her legs, chewing her lower lip until it was raw and bleeding, she prayed for the phone to ring.

She longed to call John at police headquarters, but reconsidered. She dared not tie up the line in case Kristy's kidnapper called.

Kristy's kidnapper.

Judge Corde.

The voice—that rich, powerful, resonant voice that belied the man's odd, wimpish countenance—was unmistakably his. Twenty years ago that very voice had wrought repugnance in a seventeen-year-old beauty contestant. Now it wrought terror and images of pain and death.

In the event that she wouldn't have time to contact John, she scribbled out a note telling him that Corde had kidnapped Kristy and she had gone to meet him. She begged him not to contact the police.

Half an hour after receiving the call at the restaurant and ten minutes after entering her apartment, the phone rang. Regina answered.

"Regina," a male voice said. "I need to see you. Will you meet me somewhere?"

"Who is this?"

"Nolan."

In frustration she said, "I can't talk now—"

"Wait! You've heard already?"

"Heard what?"

"That she wants a separation. That—"

Even in her panicked state, Regina realized that Nolan was trying to make a last-ditch effort to win her over. He had been dumped by Donna and then Amelia. She would have laughed if she hadn't been so distraught. "You sonofabitch," Regina said, slamming down the receiver. The phone rang beneath her trembling fingers. She snatched it up.

"Go immediately to Fort Point. Alone. Inform no one or she dies. She'll be in a place where no one will find her until it's too late. And her death, I promise you, will be slow and quite agonizing. Twenty minutes. Do you have that?"

"I have to hear her voice."

Regina heard rustling on the line, then, "Mom?" The voice was squeaky, frightened.

"Kristy?! Are you all right?"

"I guess. I—"

"Nineteen minutes," the deep voice said.

Regina hung up.

To the note for John she added, "12:50 at Fort Point. Don't show yourself. He'll kill Kristy." She signed it, folded it in half, then ran out the door and down the stairs. At John's apartment she opened the door and rushed in. She pulled the rocker away from the wall, placed it directly in front of the door where John couldn't miss it and laid the note on the cane seat. In the doorway, as she turned to leave, she collided with her landlady.

The woman blocked her way. "Mrs. Van Raven—?"

"I can't talk now." Regina pushed past her. From the foyer she called out, "I've left a note for John. Please make sure he gets it."

She rushed out into the wind and rain.

2

Anna Szabo watched Regina Van Raven charge out the door into a torrential downpour. Her tenant seemed confused, upset, on the point of hysteria. Had she and Johnnie had another spat?

If they had quarreled, maybe things were not so good between them now? She hoped Johnnie was done with her. Ilona, a young woman of childbearing age, was certainly better suited for her nephew than a woman who had already planted a husband in the ground. And a career woman at that.

Ilona . . . such a sweet girl. She was in Anna's kitchen at that very moment, rolling out dough for the pinch noodles, having tea, and going through the worn family album.

When Johnnie returned home, Anna would insist he join them for dinner, then later, after glasses of sweet Tokay, she would run an errand, leaving the two alone.

She stepped inside John's apartment and lifted the folded piece of paper from the rocker, turning it over several times. She slipped the note into the pocket of her apron, patted it, sighed deeply, placed the rocker back against the wall, then left the apartment to return to Ilona, the noodle making, and her cabbage soup.

3

The rain came down hard against the side of her face. It stung in certain places, felt numb in others. She had to squint to keep the water from blinding her.

Corinne sat stiffly on the bench staring straight ahead. People scurried by, umbrellas tilting toward the driving wind and rain. Some of the passersby stared, but most were too preoccupied with the downpour to notice the hideously scarred woman on the bench, her black raincoat open to reveal a cheap shift, the hood like a bowl, filling with water.

She couldn't go home. Her father was dead and his body claimed. She had gone back to the house, had seen the emergency vehicles, and had continued on by.

She closed her eyes and thought of John. He hadn't changed, not really. He was still sweet and caring. And her feelings for him hadn't changed either. But he had Regina now. Regina, who probably never truly hungered for anything in her entire life, had John's love. Had Regina been born under a lucky star? Was she more deserving? She had been spared the hideous fate that had touched the others. Was she immune to disaster?

Corinne chewed at the inside of her mouth until it was ragged and tasted of copper. Hate and jealousy wound around her like barbed wire, cutting sharply into her. It wasn't fair that Regina had everything and she, Miss Classic 1970, had nothing. It wasn't fair . . .

Corinne had seen the assailant. She knew who he was.

The night before last she saw a man in black stealthily work his way along the hedge to the rear of John's building. Less than an hour later she watched him drop from Regina's window to the ground below and flee. Standing deep in the shadows, he had run right past her, and as he did he flung off the nylon stocking that covered his face.

Regina, damn her, had escaped once again.

A small child in bright yellow rain boots and a yellow slicker walked with her mother, the two sharing an umbrella. The little girl stared at Corinne with wide, frightened eyes, then turned and buried her face in the thick wool of her mother's coat.

It wasn't fair.

4

At 1:15, two hours after going to the police station to

meet Wilma, John was still waiting for Detective Lillard. He had reached the end of his patience. Regina had not returned and there was no answer at her apartment when he called. Wilma had ceased her pacing. She stood at a nearby desk, on the phone, trying to track down the detective.

John squeezed her fingers gently, leaned over and kissed her on the cheek. "Wilma, I can't wait any longer. I'm going to find Regina. If Lillard ever shows up, call me at my place. Okay?"

She smiled weakly, nodded.

John took a cab home.

He was about to enter his apartment when his aunt opened her door and called to him.

"Aunt Anna, have you seen Regina?" John asked.

She frowned. "Regina?"

"Mrs. Van Raven. Have you seen her in the past couple of hours?"

Ilona came up behind Anna Szabo. "Hi, Johnnie," she said.

"Ilona has come to help me with the day's supper. You must stay."

"Aunt Anna, Ilona, I can't, really. There's something very important I have to do."

"What could be so important?" His aunt took his hand and pulled at him.

He resisted.

"Johnnie, Johnnie, go do what it is you have to do and come back." Anna released his hand. "Time will only make the soup better."

It was useless to argue. John nodded. "Give me a few minutes," he said. He climbed the stairs two at a time to the second floor. He used the spare key, the one he'd taken from his aunt's place the night Regina had narrowly escaped being attacked, and let himself in.

After a quick search of the rooms revealed neither Regina nor a note, he checked her answering machine for messages. None. He suddenly realized she could be waiting for him in his apartment.

He hurried downstairs, entered his apartment, and called out to her, searching the rooms. He again looked for a note and, finding none, sank heavily in the wing-back chair to think.

She must still be with Kristy, he told himself. Instead of coming back to the apartment house, he should have gone to the restaurant where Kristy worked.

He rose, grabbed the phone book, looked up the number and dialed.

"Farm House," a woman said.

"Kristy Van Raven, please. It's important."

"She's not here, sir."

"Is Sonya Newman there?"

"That's me."

"Sonya, it's John Davie, Regina's friend. Did Kristy leave with her mother?"

"John, something freaky's going on here. Kristy gets a call and leaves. Then her mom comes in and she gets an urgent call from some guy and leaves too."

"How long ago?"

"An hour. Maybe an hour and a half."

"Any idea where Regina went?"

"No."

John hung up absently, a sense of dread knotting his gut. An urgent call from whom? Kristy? The police? The hospital? The man stalking her? How many people knew she was meeting Kristy at work?

He began to pace the living room. Corde was on to them. He was on to them and now he had them somewhere. No! Don't think like that.

On the coatrack in the entry he caught sight of the wool print scarf that had fallen from Regina's coat the night they'd made love on the fleece rug. He crossed the room, lifted the scarf off the hook, and, bunching it up, brought it to his face. He breathed in the rich, exotic aroma of her perfume. Images of her, soft and sensual in his arms, played across his mind's eye.

426

Christ, what the hell had he gotten himself into? After all these years of keeping a clear head about love and relationships, he had to go and get himself romantically involved. Both Corinne and Darlene had met with tragedy after he fell in love. And he'd walked into this one with his eyes wide open. Was he jinxed? Was it inevitable that suffering and death come to those he *loved?*

Regina, oh God, Regina, be safe.

"Call, damnit," he said harshly under his breath.

He wrapped the scarf around his neck and resumed his pacing.

5

He led her down the basement steps.

Outwardly he appeared kind and attentive, holding her arm loosely, telling her to watch her step. Despite his solicitous words and actions, Regina knew better than to relax her guard. She had seen the smoldering hatred glowing feverishly in his black eyes when he looked at her. He had no fear she would try to get away. He knew she would cooperate as long as Kristy was a hostage, that she would do whatever was asked of her in order to save her daughter.

They crossed the concrete floor to a wall of wine bottles. He reached into a pigeonhole in the wine rack. Regina heard a click, then another, and a portion of the wall, wine rack and all, began to move. It was a door. Beyond the doorway was a brightly lit room with bookshelves and expensive office furniture.

"Welcome to my sanctuary," Corde said, ushering her in.

Regina stepped across the threshold, her gaze searching frantically for her daughter. There was no one else in the room.

"Where is she?"

"You'll see her."

"I want to see her now."

"You're in no position to make demands."

427

"Where's Amelia?"

"They're together. Contemplating the error of their ways."

Amelia a prisoner as well? Regina wondered.

"Kristy's done nothing wrong. Let her go."

"Oh, but she has. Upstairs, when I gave her the opportunity to enhance her odds, she rejected me. Just as her mother did twenty years ago."

Regina's mind raced. What was he talking about?

He stared at Regina, a wily grin on his face. "I like to be near pretty women. I like to have them around me, tending to my needs." He slipped the strap of the handbag from his shoulder and dumped the contents onto the floor. With the toe of his shiny ox-blood shoe he stirred the items around, and seeing nothing that could help the prisoner, dismissed them. "I bet you never dreamed I have women catering to me. Lovely women like yourself and your daughter. Well, nor did I when I was young and without income.

"Rejection is not easy to accept," he said, reaching a coarse, hairy hand to her face, caressing. "Of course, you wouldn't know that, being the beautiful woman that you are. I lived with rejection all my young life. Women I wouldn't waste words on today cruelly spurned a young man's advances. I can pick and choose now. And if they choose not to desire me, then *they* are no longer desired. Cases in point: Corinne, Donna, and . . ." He paused. ". . . others."

Marilyn Keane, she thought, and Carmenita Flores. How many more? "You're doing this because I rejected you?" She fought the urge to slap his hand away from her face.

"You and the others."

"You learn that 'City Gallery' intends to do a show with all the finalists and this awakens your hatred toward us?"

He laughed without mirth. "It was *my* suggestion to air a show with the finalists. Fortunately for me, Nolan Lake jumped at the idea. You see, it was essential that the public be reminded of that tragic incident."

"Why?"

"You'll find out soon enough."

"Why bring me here? Why not just splash me like you did the others?"

"Patience." A hardness glinted in his bulging eyes.

He quickly reached down and cupped a breast. Regina instinctively pushed his hand away.

He eyed her shrewdly, then grinned, nodding his head. "Some never learn," he said.

Regina opened her mouth to speak. But no sound came out. She shook her head instead.

"I'll bring your daughter now. I trust you won't do anything foolish. There's no reason she should suffer . . . unnecessarily." He went to the door and inserted a straight, picklike object into a hole. The door opened and then he was gone, closing it behind him.

Regina quickly bent down and grabbed her container of mace from the scattered contents of her purse. The relief she'd felt when he'd overlooked the small blue leather case had been overwhelming. She unclipped the keys and dropped them back to the pile, then shoved the mace into her coat pocket. When he came back with Kristy, she would attempt to disable him with the burning chemical.

She stood in the middle of the room and looked around. There were no windows and only one door. It was like an office within a vault. Light radiated from fluorescent tubes in the ceiling. The desk top was bare. She quickly moved around the room, trying drawers and cabinets. All were locked with the exception of a bottom drawer in a file cabinet. There she found a Polaroid camera and a wooden box. The box was filled with photographs of nude women in countless compromising positions. Hastily she sorted through them until she found Wilma Greenwood among the bunch. A much younger, very striking, Wilma.

He had left this material out for her to see, Regina thought. To prove to her the power he'd had over these beautiful women. If they played the game, they had only to live with the degradation of that repulsive monster committing consensual rape, using their bodies whenever he wanted, any way he wanted. But if they didn't play . . .

She shuddered.

Where was Kristy? God, had he already—no . . . no, she guessed that wasn't his style. He would want her, the mother, to witness some horrific act as part of the punishment. Then what would he do? Disfigure her and Kristy? Perhaps. But she felt that was just a prelude to an ultimate goal. She and Kristy knew their attacker. Judge or no judge, he couldn't expect to get away with it. There was only one conclusion. . . .

Like Carmenita Flores and Pandora, they wouldn't live to tell anyone.

6

John slammed down the receiver, then pounded a fist against the wall. He had just spoken to Wilma. No word from Regina. Wilma would call the courthouse and check on Judge Corde. John prayed the judge was in trial.

As he waited for Wilma to call back, he resumed his pacing. He had to do something. He couldn't just hang around wearing down the carpet while the woman he loved had disappeared into thin air. *She was in danger.* He felt it in his gut. She would have called if she could.

The phone rang. He snatched it up.

"John, Corde's not at the courthouse," Wilma said.

"Christ."

"More bad news. The investigating police found a matchbook at the scene of the psychic's murder. The matches are from the Bull's Blood Lounge and there's a very clear fingerprint on it. John, it's yours."

"Aw shit," he groaned. "He's setting me up. Jesus, I should have seen it coming." He remembered the pistachio shell in the utility room of the gym. Somehow Corde knew his habits, likes, and dislikes. "You know I didn't do it. I

430

was with Regina at the time that woman was killed."

"I know that. And I'll vouch for you."

"Wilma, I've got to get out of here before they come or I'll be doing my explaining at headquarters and there's no time for that."

He hung up, started for the door, stopped. If he left and she managed to get to a phone, he'd miss her call.

"Goddamnit!" he banged the wall again.

"Johnnie?" His aunt Anna opened the door, poked her head inside tentatively. "Johnnie . . . ?"

"Aunt Anna, you've got to tell me. It's extremely important. Did you see Regina this afternoon?"

His aunt looked at him, her large brown eyes filled with concern for him. She reached into an apron pocket, pulled out a piece of paper, and handed it to him.

He read the note, his heart galloping wildly. The time at the bottom read 12:50. He glanced at his watch. 2:02. Well over an hour ago. Damnit, would she still be at Fort Point? He doubted it. More than likely he had taken her to his house in Pacific Heights.

He raked his fingers through his hair.

His aunt touched his arm. "Has something happened to Mrs. Van Raven? I didn't read it. I'm sorry if—"

He cut her off. "Aunt Anna, do something for me."

"Of course, Johnnie."

"Stay and listen for the phone. I want someone here if Regina calls. I'll check in later."

She nodded.

He called Wilma. "Corde has Regina. I'm going to his house now. Give me ten minutes, then send the police. Tell them it's a kidnap situation and to treat it as such. No sirens. The judge doesn't know he's a suspect."

"Godspeed. John, be careful."

He hung up and ran into his bedroom. "I'm taking your car, Aunt Anna," he called out as he rummaged through the nightstand drawer looking for his handgun.

The gun was gone.

"The fucking bastard," he cried in exasperation. Corde

431

must have taken his gun the night he broke into his apartment. There was nothing he could do about it now. He could only hope that the element of surprise would give him the edge he would need.

7

He located the leash hanging on a nail in the garage, not ten feet from the body of his dear deceased wife. Getting the leash had given him the opportunity to see the rotten bitch once more.

He stood in quiet contemplation over the sprawled form, his nerves deliciously keyed up, virtually humming with pleasure.

Amelia had believed in reincarnation, the afterlife, and out-of-body experiences. He hoped her spiritual self had managed to come out of the grotesque thing that sat crumbled on the concrete floor to view the ruins of the once-magnificent face.

Seeing Amelia again, being reminded of how he had been cheated of the prolonged torture that would have given him the ultimate satisfaction, renewed his fury at the woman in his basement room. He wouldn't be cheated this time.

He took the leash upstairs to his bedroom.

"Your mother is here," he said to the girl on the bed. "She wants to see you. Shall we get you ready for your visit?"

Above the silver duct tape across her mouth, Kristy stared at Corde with large, terrified eyes. Her gaze dropped to the chain leash in his hand.

"Oh, don't be frightened, sweet girl. I don't intend to whip you with this." He held the leash up. "I shall just put it around your neck so you won't be tempted to wander."

He tossed the leash on the bed, then went into Amelia's closet. There was no hesitation, he knew exactly what he wanted Kristy to wear. His body tingled with anticipation.

432

He returned to the room and laid the clothes on the bed. Then he leaned over and cut the pantyhose at Kristy's wrists and ankles and the one around her throat securing her to the headboard. The tape he pulled off slowly, reveling in the discomfort her eyes could not conceal.

"I trust you to cooperate," he said. "I'm sure you love your mother too much not to."

Kristy looked down, nodded.

"Put these on."

She stared at him, unmoving.

"I'm afraid you'll have to put up with my presence." His light tone turned harsh. "Do it now."

She undressed, turning away as best she could. Her modesty, and the brief snatches of nudity revealed to his eager eye, titillated him a hundred times more than if she had stood before him naked, desirous of his touch.

"The brassiere goes," he said.

The girl paused briefly, quickly removed her bra, then resumed pulling on clothes. When she was done, she turned slowly, head held high, refusing to look at him.

He scrutinized her carefully. Wonderful. So believable. He felt a stirring in his groin.

Kristy wore a pink taffeta dress with a pinafore of Swiss batiste, the sash tied in a bow at the back of her tiny waist, the ruffled hemline ending above her knees. She wore ankle socks and white Mary Jane shoes. She could undoubtedly pass for a prepubescent child.

"A pity you're so tall," he said. "Ah, well, such as it is. There on the bed, a satin ribbon. Use it to pull your hair up on the sides and tie it into a bow." He moved toward her. "Let me show you."

She jerked away. "I know what you mean." She stepped to the full-length mirror and arranged her long brown hair.

He handed her a jar of cold cream and a wad of tissues. "Off with the makeup and earrings."

While she did that, he went through Amelia's drawers and selected a pair of fishnet hose, a garter belt and a

433

demi-bra, all in black.

He turned back to Kristy, who stood waiting.

"Perfect."

Retrieving the leash from the bed, he approached her, looped it over her head, and pulled in the slack. When he tested the tightness, pinching her neck, she cried out and glared at him.

He gave her two smart swats on her behind, as an adult would swat a naughty child. "Behave yourself. I will not tolerate insolence," he scolded. "Come, child. Your mother is waiting."

He yanked at the leash, forcing her to follow.

8

John parked his aunt's Skylark two blocks down and ran for all he was worth to the Corde estate. Flashes of lightning lit up the sky to the north. He was thankful for the driving rain that, he hoped, wouldn't draw undo attention to a man in a hurry. His lungs felt about to burst, his breathing was labored. Once inside the Corde grounds, he ran, crouched low, staying well within the shadows of the three-story house, tall hedges, and walls. At the garage he slowed, wondering if he should go to the door in back—the one the housekeeper had allowed him to use—or try to find a way in through the garage? He opted for the garage. He would need some sort of weapon against an armed killer.

He didn' bother with the aluminum garage doors. They were automatic and would only open from the outside with a remote device. He found the access door on the far side. It had four small windows in the upper half. John bent, lifted a nearby watering can, and with the metal spout, was about to tap at the pane nearest the doorknob. The can went through the window sash. The pane was missing.

He didn't bother with the aluminum garage doors. They Glass, on a square carpet in front of the door, crunched under his shoes. Someone had broken out the glass before him. Had Regina come here instead of Fort Point, hoping to find and rescue Kristy before becoming a prisoner herself?

There were three cars in the garage. Nearest to him was the judge's Rolls-Royce. Next to that was a limited-edition sports car of some obscure make. The car closest to the interior door was Amelia's dark blue Mercedes. As he passed the Mercedes he tripped on something. He threw out an arm to catch himself and touched a soft mass that was unmistakably hair.

His heart seized.

Regina?

Please, no.

At that moment a flash of lightning illuminated the garage and the hideous thing at his feet. The shocking sight of it forced him to stumble back.

He was stunned, yet relieved. He'd seen enough to guess it was Amelia. John knew what Corde was capable of, yet he was totally unprepared for the atrocity at his feet.

He hurried on before another flash of lightning forced him to look again.

He was at the door when he heard a rustling sound, like someone moving. It came from behind him. He tasted bile. For a brief, insane moment he imagined it was the body making that sound—the woman, crazed, rising from the dead to seek her revenge, prepared to destroy those in her path as she sought her murderer.

He whirled, looked behind him. The dark outline leaning against the car hadn't moved.

In the dim light, he saw an assortment of tools hanging on a pegged wall. He reached for the largest and heaviest—the monkey wrench.

Then he slipped quietly into the laundry room.

Kristy's captor lifted the handgun from the dresser, flipped the safety lever, then shoved the gun into the waistband of his trousers.

They went down the stairs to the main floor. The choker chain pinched her neck when he pulled. She tried to hurry along so he wouldn't have reason to tug at it. As he led her through the house, Kristy thought of her mother waiting in another part. She knew her mother was in danger, the same as she, and she knew the judge would not hesitate to control them through threats directed at one or the other. It was all her fault. If she had listened she wouldn't be here now. She wished her mother didn't have to be involved, but God forgive her, she couldn't bear the thought of being alone with this creep. In her mind's eye, a scenario of the two of them somehow managing to overpower him and get away, fueled her spirit, giving her hope and strength.

Momma, I'll never disobey you again. Never.

The man pulling her along was a slimy, sexual pervert. She'd picked up that much upstairs. When he was tying her up in the bedroom his damp fingers had lingered a second longer than necessary on her legs and throat as his eyes raked over her body. He could have done anything he wanted once she was tied up, but she sensed he was restraining himself. Waiting.

She trembled. She and her mother were in a serious situation. How serious? A matter of life or death? The man was a superior judge. Would he rape them, burn them with acid — she shuddered visibly at the thought — and then allow them to go free? Not likely.

She remembered how she and Sonya had thought it was a kick when the bug-eyed official had made subtle passes at them during the preliminaries. They'd laughed behind his back, making jokes about his pop-eyes, bald head, and airy hands. It wasn't so funny now.

Why hadn't she told her mother about him? She knew why she hadn't. If she told her mother that a contest official, who was old enough to be her father, was looking at her like she was a double fudge ice cream sundae, her mother would have gone into a tizzy and might have forced her to drop out of the contest.

Oh, what a damn fool she was.

10

John heard the footsteps coming his way. He ran to a set of louvered doors. Inside were a washer and dryer. He jumped up on the washing machine and pulled the doors closed. Through the slats he saw a trail of muddy footprints leading to where he crouched. He held his breath, praying Corde wouldn't notice.

A pair of ox-blood shoes came into view ahead of a pair of shiny children's dress shoes. Both pairs of shoes stopped. John tightened his grip on the wrench. Moments later he heard soles descending wooden stairs.

The basement.

John slid back the door, carefully lowered himself to the floor, and hurried to the basement door. He opened it a crack.

The couple—he saw it was Corde and Kristy—moved across the basement to a wall-to-wall wine rack. The judge inserted his hand into a pigeonhole. A portion of the wine rack in front of him opened.

Christ, a secret door, John told himself. He debated trying to rush Corde before the man could disappear into the room and close the door, but he had waited too long. The couple were already moving inside and the door was closing.

John crept downs the steps. He hurried to the wine rack, located the pigeonhole where Corde had buried a hand, and reached in.

437

The hole was smooth terra cotta. There was nothing, as far as John could feel, in which to activate the door. He reached into several other holes. Smooth and cool. Nothing.

11

Regina had heard nothing until the soft click of the latch releasing alerted her that the door was about to open. She stood with her back to the wall, the mace canister clutched tightly in her hand, her breath locked in her lungs, waiting.

Kristy came through first, followed by the judge. But not enough room separated her daughter from Corde to afford Regina an accurate shot. At that moment Kristy looked to her left. The surprised expression on her face when she saw her mother pressed against the wall was enough to alert Corde to her presence. He tried to back up, but the door had closed behind him.

She raised the canister, but he yanked Kristy to one side, throwing her into Regina, blocking the direct opening Regina had counted on for a clear shot of mace into his face.

She pushed her daughter down and, with less than a positive position, blasted the spray blindly. She saw the mist filling the empty air. Corde was already well out of its path, under it, diving at Regina. He caught her around the hips and drove her brutally backward to crash into a metal file cabinet.

In a stunned fog, she heard Kristy scream. The back of her head felt as if it had been split in two, the air had been knocked out of her. She could only gasp for air.

Corde cursed and grabbed her around the throat. She tried to bring the mace canister up again for another shot, but the full weight of his body bore down on her arm; her fingers felt dead.

Regina forgot the pain. Her already starving lungs

ched with the unbearable pressure at her throat. His face pressed in on her, so close that she smelled his sour breath, felt the spray of spittle as he continued to call her foul names, saw the dried blood in one nostril. His eyes bulged maniacally and she could see the watery eyelids beneath the upper lashes. She blinked, looked up in time to see Kristy lunge at the madman choking her.

Kristy wrapped a hand across his face, fingers finding strongholds in eye sockets as she pulled hard, her other hand tangled in the sparse strands of hair that covered his bald pate.

Regina watched as Corde worked the pistol out of his waistband and brought it up to Kristy's face, and then she closed her eyes and prayed that she would die before she heard the explosion.

Thirty-one

Through nearly soundproof walls, John heard a muffled scream. He thrust his hand back into the first pigeonhole, his pulse racing out of control. *It has to be here,* a switch or lever to trigger the door opening device, *It has to be here!*

And then he felt something. A seam at the top of the cylinder. He pushed upward; then, with a fingernail he tried to pry it open. At last he discovered it was a sliding panel and he pushed it to one side. Inside he felt a switch. He flipped it.

A portion of the wine rack swung toward him. John squeezed the handle of the monkey wrench and charged through the door. What he saw made him both sick and furious. Regina was on the floor, Corde straddling her, his hand around her throat, her eyes wide and staring. Kristy had fallen on Corde, her hands around his face and in his hair, trying to pull the man off her mother.

John saw the gun come up and he wasted no more time. He hurled himself the few yards, his body glancing off Kristy, knocking her out of the way, to come down on Corde's back. But before he could bring the wrench up to swing at Corde, the gun exploded in his ear. White pain, like a cannonball through his brain, nearly blinded him.

His arms felt heavy, like lead appendages, and useless. All he could think about as he teetered on the edge of consciousness, was that he had failed her. He had again failed the woman he loved, and this time they would both die.

He sank to the floor on his knees. Corde jumped to his feet brandishing the pistol. He waved it toward Kristy and Regina, who were huddled together. Regina had a hand to her throat; she was purple and coughing, but alive.

Corde turned to John, the muzzle of the gun pointed at his face.

John steeled himself for the fatal round.

"You've a hard head, Mr. Davie. The next bullet will not bounce off your thick skull, I can guarantee that."

John reached up and touched his bleeding forehead. He felt ragged flesh just above his left brow—a two-inch furrow where the bullet had traveled briefly before angling off and away.

"Do you plan to kill yourself along with the three of us?" John was surprised by the echo quality of his own voice.

"Why would I do that?"

"Because the cops know all about you. A S.W.A.T team is upstairs now, surrounding the house."

"You're hallucinating, Davie. There is no reason for the police to suspect me. None whatsoever. It's you who are the suspect, then and now. Oh, the two of you thought you were so clever, coming here yesterday to steal something for your psychic friend. She saw my face, did she? Too bad she didn't see my razor." He chuckled dryly. "But I digress. You, Davie, came to my home to splash my wife. When she saw you, you had to kill her. Then you lured Mrs. Van Raven and her daughter to my home and killed them as well. Shot them with your own gun." He indicated the gun in his hand. "When you realized you couldn't get out alive, you turned the gun on yourself."

"What's my motive?" John asked, stalling for time.

"What difference does it make? Your motive shall remain yet another unsolved mystery. The world is filled with crazies. I ought to know, Davie. They come before me every day in the courtroom." He laughed out loud at that.

"Look outside," John said.

"Shut up," Corde snapped. "You interrupted something

441

vital between me and these two lovely ladies. I should like to get back to it before I call in the police. Now stand up."

John struggled to his feet.

Corde moved around to the side of John, positioning himself so he could see each person in the room. "Open your mouth, Mr. Davie. Let's make this clean and sure. I trust you wouldn't want me to slip, making you something less than human, dependent on others for your care."

"Fuck you," John said between clenched teeth.

"Well, then, in that case, *che sera sera.*" He lifted the muzzle to John's head.

Regina cried out and came to her feet, rushing into John's arms. He held her tight.

"How touching. I'm tempted to hold off on your execution, Davie, and let you watch this woman who obviously loves you tend to my needs." He kicked the black lacy undergarments to Regina. "But, unfortunately, I can't take a chance that you'll find a way to spoil my fun."

The gun came up again, its cold muzzle against John's temple.

The scream pierced his already throbbing head like a lightning bolt. Was that Regina screaming? He looked down at her. Though her eyes were open wide, her mouth was not. The shrill scream came from behind him. From the depths of his groggy brain, John realized there was a fifth presence in the room; its shriek froze the blood in his veins. He watched Corde turn sharply, the gun in his hand pulling away from John's head, faltering somewhat, before pointing toward the banshee that was flying through the doorway from the dark basement.

The gun fired.

The screaming thing flew backward, slammed against the door frame. Then it rebounded and something sparkled in its hands as it again came straight for Corde.

John watched, mesmerized, as the hands drew upward in a tossing motion, and a clear fluid sailed through the air in what seemed like slow motion. It arched, catching the light in a prism of color; then, before Corde could get off another round, the liquid dashed him squarely in the face.

Corde clawed at his face, stumbled about, the gun firing randomly. John grabbed his arm and tried to wrench the gun away, but Corde, swinging wildly, managed to pull back. He somehow found the door and, his moans rising to screams, fled into the dark interior.

Regina rushed back into his arms, clinging to him. John held her tight for an instant. "Are you okay?"

She ignored his question. "You've been shot."

"It's not serious."

Kristy joined them. The three stood hugging each other. Then, by unspoken agreement, John and Regina converged on the apparition in black, who at that moment was leaning against the desk, clutching a bloody midsection.

"Corinne," John said softly, "Oh, Jesus, Corinne." He gently folded her in his arms.

Another shot rang out upstairs.

John supported Corinne's body as it sank to the floor. He held her hand. Her hair was wet and plastered to her head. He could hear footsteps thundering down the stairs. "Hang on, Cory. Help is coming now."

Corinne smiled, turning the scarred side of her face away in what John sensed was a longtime habit.

She squeezed his hand, opened her mouth to say something, then closed it again. She smiled again and rolled her head, as though what she had to say was of little or no importance.

She died as the police and paramedics entered the room.

Epilogue

At the Meadowvale Inn, Regina and John sat close together in a booth in the Oak Room. Regina stared at the red mark on John's forehead made by the bullet. After two weeks, it was nearly healed, though still vivid. It would no doubt leave a dandy scar.

Her mind flashed back to that rainy afternoon in the Corde basement. Three people had died that day. All killed by the same hand. Amelia, Corinne, and the judge. With acid eating into his face and the police surrounding the house, Matthew Corde had put the gun to his eye and pulled the trigger.

Tammy Kowalski had been buried the day before, and ironically, the funeral for Corinne Odett took place the same day as the double service of Amelia and Matthew Corde. There was no service for Pandora Cudahay.

"I'm glad you don't have to go back to the city for the show tomorrow," John said.

"All done," Regina said. "That's the advantage of pre-recorded programs."

"Thought you preferred them live?"

She laughed. "That was when I didn't know what I was doing. Actually, it was Max's idea. Donna isn't crazy about live shows and as long as she's the star, we'll do it her way."

"Have you decided to be her cohost?"

Regina nodded. "She insists she won't go on unless I'm with her."

"When is she returning?"

"Anytime. Max wants her back on the air as soon as the doctor gives her the thumbs up."

"She turned out to be a pretty tough cookie."

Regina stared across the restaurant. "It's hard to believe that Donna and I are the only ones left. Five finalists, two survivors."

John squeezed her hand. "It's over, honey."

"Yes."

"Speaking of finalists, did Kristy have any regrets about dropping out of the model contest?"

Regina shook her head. "None. Especially since Sonya didn't make the last cut. They were a team, like Donna and me."

They ate in silence for several minutes.

"I saw Garrick last night," she said quietly. "He came to the apartment."

"Yes, I know."

"He left for Washington today. Back to his family." She stared at him, waiting for him to say something, but he only returned her gaze.

"How's the new book coming," she asked.

"Two chapters this week. I think I've finally broken through the writer's block. The galleys for *False Lead* came today. I'm going to be pretty busy for a while."

Regina looked into his eyes, then quickly looked away. She nodded, sipped her wine.

After dinner they returned to room 142, the same room they had shared before. The fire blazed and the love songs were soft, nostalgic. The champagne John had ordered sat chilling in a bucket on the table.

Regina stared solemnly into the orange-white flames. John came up behind her and handed her a glass of champagne. Déjà vu. She smiled, took it.

He lowered himself into the wing-back chair and gently pulled her down into his lap.

"This is nice," John said, his voice husky. "Did I mention that I love you?"

She swallowed, slowly shaking her head.

"I love you," he said softly.

Her eyes misted with tears, happy tears. Until he actually said them, she didn't realize how much she had wanted to hear those words.

"I've wanted to say that for . . . well—damnit, I was afraid to say it," he went on. "I thought if I said it out loud, you'd be taken from me."

"I'm tougher than you think."

"Too tough to love an amateur detective?"

"I owe that amateur detective my life. I love amateur detectives, I love authors, and I love part-time bartenders who wear leather bomber jackets and are hooked on pistachio nuts—the red dye . . . ," she kissed his stained fingers, then his lips, " . . . turns me on."

"What are you trying to say?" he coaxed.

"That . . . I love you, John."

He tightened his hold on her. She snuggled deeper into his arms, sighing.

"Everything in this room is exactly the same except for the rose petals."

"I suppose they're reserved for the bridal treatment," she said.

"Umm," he kissed her ear lobe. "I miss the rose petals."

"I miss them too."

The conversation was left unfinished, but the notion, like the heavy fragrance of the absent rose petals, filled the room.